I0738343

CLEANING UP THE FUTURE:

PUBLIC PERCEPTIONS

D. REDNAL

Cover design by Blique
Logo design by ACartoonTurtle

www.drednal.com

Acknowledgements

Ahoy hoy,

I can't quantify the amount of appreciation I feel toward the many people that helped me complete this novel. My first novel. It's been terrifying and exhilarating all at once. This moment won't ever be experienced again, and I think I've gotten a full taste of the terror and excitement that could be squeezed out of it.

Thank you to my lovely cover designer and partner in crime, Blique. You were there from the very beginning and put the wind in my sails.

Thank you to those that donated their time and money to help support this project—my beta readers, editors , my patrons, and my friends and family:

My family and friends, your daily support kept me sturdy yet pliable.

My final editors, Ed and Notorius thanks for your help. I can't describe the gratitude I felt getting help with the final look over. Time was tight, but you worked fast and professionally. Thank you.

Pascalle, Pixels, and Raines are three of the many that made both their confusion and enjoyment known during the beta process and helped me smooth out the kinks in the story.

Oh, Panda, what a welcome surprise you have been to my life. Thank you for your support, constant encouragement, discussions, and the nudging that all helped keep my pilgrimage on course. I appreciate you, truly. You are always a delight.

Finally,
Thank you, Reader, and enjoy.

...to Pluto and back...

<u>Preface</u>

To my readers:

Book 1: Public Perceptions gives screen time to four main characters, but the person focused on the most in this book is Chen Sia.

Sia is a 19-year-old young woman whose family emigrated to Cinalia shortly after she was born. She has spent time in America to meet her maternal relatives, but hasn't traveled to China to meet her paternal relatives.

R-Earth and its' history is very similar to our current Earth's history except for a few new details:

1. One extra continent

2. A race of intelligent sea dwellers

The sea dwellers, or Underling, have kept the oceans from being as damaged as they are on our current Earth. They are very isolated, but keep tabs on human civilizations and their dealings with the oceans. They do not interfere with human affairs. The UN of R-Earth has many treaties with the superior race for fear of the war to end all wars.

Cinalia was a first world country on R-Earth that resides on a continent in the middle of the Atlantic Ocean.

Opening Public-Perceptions.exe

You have chosen to open: public-perceptions.exe
File Type: memory download(2.5PB)
From: _Rednal_

Would you like to save this file?

Save file   Cancel

Part 1

Startup

2035
Brook, New Cinalia

If the rusted, green sign had been torn down and buried in the woods, countless lives would have been saved.

An exhausted, sweating little man recognizes the sign's large, bold letters and his red rimmed eyes widen with excitement. "Here, over here! I saw them run off the highway here! You have to come back this way to leave!" He scurries off to the side of the road and points to the sign, still proudly displaying the town's name, even while overgrown bushes threaten to conceal it. "The only way around the forest is the river!"

"Find them!" a shrill voice orders from among the large crowd. The Savage leader sends out dozens of followers to search the town. A short, metallic spear is held over a grimy shoulder; alongside dirty alabaster hair, while the wielder urges his men on.

Manic warriors storm across the decrepit highway, avoiding the shells of wrecked cars and the craters littering the asphalt. Their clothing is ripped and filthy with some combination of blood, food, and soil. Their heads are either barely covered with stringy hair or bald with burnt, pockmarked, and torn red skin.

Their mouths gape open as they dash over and through obstacles. The large hunting party separates into groups of the most predatory, the most enthusiastic, and the most skittish members. Jointly they race to overtake their enemies with an unhinged look in their eyes. They are fueled by avarice and the desire to be uplifted from the nameless faces of their companions. To be honored by not only their robust commander, but the other lords of the Wastes.

The Savages tear through the streets, kicking in apartment doors, and breaking store windows with rusted metal poles. Three of them are holding chains attached to malnourished dogs. They cackle and release the hounds into an apartment building, then trail behind them in search of prey.

Another of the Savages runs into a convenience store. Her foot catches on a thick wire, sending her crashing into an empty shelving unit. Behind the cashier counter, a pile of rigged explosives detonate.

There's a blinding light followed by an earth-shattering blast. The concrete beneath the linoleum flooring is revealed. Glass, metal, and human flesh bury the entrance.

Dilapidated post office walls shake as the people within grab for their weapons, medical supplies, and backpacks. The lobby is bustling with activity—a place that formerly stood for order and reliability is now full of panicked disarray. Distraught souls tear through the last of their precious belongings, selecting which items to keep and which to discard, abandoned to the poor souls that'll carry on after they've gone.

Sid drinks from his jug of water and barely gets the lid on before dropping it onto a counter. He sweeps his gaze across the room, fully digesting the outcome his decisions have brought these people, feeling the weight of it. It's hard to swallow. The water doesn't take the edge off the taste of ash and bile that sits at the back of his throat.

Parents haul their children along behind them. Their small, grimy faces can't decide what to focus on the most; the people

rushing to the left or the people rushing to the right. Their parents wrench their arms forward when they lag behind. People grab soiled blankets off the messy floor and shove them into torn bags, or roll the material into balls to be held underneath an arm.

"We have to leave it! Leave it!" A rusted portable grill crashes to the ground. The owner crouches in front of the grill and shoves bits of coal into their pockets before rushing outside. Sid steps over the grill and through the shattered glass entrance. The shards crunch beneath his boots. He sidesteps a couple on the stairs, huddled together and talking in hushed tones.

They have the same unkempt appearance as the rest of the group. Their torn clothing is layered under ragged hoodies with tattered sleeves. The bottoms of their pants are coated with the same mud caked over their worn shoes.

Sid's long-sleeved shirt protects him from the chill in the air. It's a stained, faded green wool top. He rubs his palms together while he surveys the area. In the distance, smoke rises into the sky toward the epicenter of the town. Around him, civilians rush by and scurry off to the other side of the building.

When he proceeds down the slanted steps, he steers clear of the muddy holes along the pavement. He narrowly avoids stepping into a puddle and pauses to scrutinize the post office's crumbling façade. It's not more than a few seconds of consideration. In the distance, shouting draws his attention away from the remnant of the past.

He follows the sounds to the parking lot, where a muscular figure stands among shuffling bodies. The man's short, peppered hair clashes with his bright blue jacket. "Civilians, grab only what you can run with and move along," he yells. "Stragglers will be left behind. You have ten minutes left. I repeat, ten minutes!"

Sid skirts around the edge of the crowd and beckons the man over to where the rest of the team is waiting. Huge chunks of debris riddle the street and obstruct the road. Several dark-clothed individuals lounge on the stranded cars parked in front of the post office. A black bag is open on the dusty hood of a vehicle with ammunition stacked inside. Sid walks over to the middle of the meeting area and claps his hands a few times. The large man jogs over to listen.

"Carla's booby trap idea bought us some sorely needed time." Sid turns to the rest of the team. "Dan is going to stay behind and ferry these people to route 296. We need ten minutes. Start the clock!"

"What?! No! You know this area much better than all of us." Dan attempts to negotiate. "I'll lead the—"

Sid cut him off. "Which means I *should* be the one distracting them. You'll get lost without me. Plus, if anyone lags behind, I can't muscle them to go faster. That's *your* job. Go do your job, Dan." Sid pulls a handgun from the waistband of his black cargo pants and checks the magazine. Satisfied with its condition, he nods and grabs a few extra from the ammunition pile. He unzips two pockets to slip the extras inside.

"If I don't see the signal, I'm leaving them all behind." Dan huffs and stomps away.

"If I don't see the signal, I'm leaving them all behind!" Carla's bright, red curls bob as she imitates Dan.

Sid glances over to Carla's freckled face as she puffs up her chubby cheeks. He smirks and turns to the other nine people. "Carla and you three, go to the area with the broken traffic light. When the attack starts, kill off as many as you can. Turner, you and the rest situate yourselves in the houses along that road. You can pick them off during their retreat."

His orders spur them into immediate action, and they set off to their positions. They've already gone over Sid's part of the plan. Leading the deranged Savages from the detonated convenience store and down the appropriate road will take an even larger explosion. Carla has already set the charges. Now all Sid can do is hope the Savages haven't already started their search down another part of town.

This has to work. Sid won't be able to live with himself if it doesn't. *Sia…* He stops himself from thinking anything further. It's time to hustle.

His jog gradually increases speed until he is sprinting through the streets. He ducks and uses wrecked cars as cover, but he refuses to slow down until he hears cries of rage and brutality. He skids to a stop and crouches beside an overturned vehicle. The smell of burnt flesh is overwhelming. Sid steps over charred remains and large chunks of cement to peek past a flipped bumper.

"You! Get! Up! Get up!" The Savage leader punctuates each word with a kick to the abdomen of the Savage scrambling along the sidewalk.

The Savage is crawling along the pavement under the deranged glare of their leader. He tries to rise to his feet, but his injured legs are weak. The Savage collapses back onto the ground. Dissatisfied with their weak attempts to stand, the Savage leader reaches between his shoulder blades and unsheathes his metallic spear. Without hesitation, he aims for the quivering form, and drives the spear into the back of their head. The Savage's limbs flail against the concrete like a spider pinned by a steel needle, but when the spear is twisted, the limbs go still.

"Move on!" The Savage leader heaves the spear from the corpse and points the stained blade at the others, who scramble to their feet to continue the search.

The alley a few meters from him is empty, so Sid takes a deep breath and yells, "To hell with you!"

The Savages hear the familiar voice and trip over themselves to get outside, ready to attack their enemy. In the blink of an eye, Sid runs into the alley and slams into the fire escape ladder. The chilled, rusty metal bites into his calloused palms as he climbs to the roof. When he gets to the top, he runs straight to the vent stacks. He rushes around the large, white ventilation units and over to a long, silver pipe running along the side of the roof.

Beside the pipe is a thick, white cylinder and there sits a muddy backpack. It's plump and damp from the rain. Sid snatches the bag off the ground. He shoves the zipper aside to check the contents of the bag. It's full of blinking lights and wires. The triggering device is as Carla left it. Perfect.

"Go! Get him!" The Savage leader can be heard screaming below.

It was too late. Sid tightens the gun straps across his chest and pulls the trigger from the backpack. He flips the switches all at once. The Savage leader jumps at the first explosion down the street and almost falls onto the surrounding corpses during the second. Relying on instincts, he dashes off at top speed; off to where he assumes it is safe. His wild, white hair streams behind him as he escapes.

Sid sees this as he peers over the edge of the building. Feeling the bombs from the lower level of the apartment building go off, he backs up to position himself with the next building and sprints toward the large gap between the two. After his feet propel him off the edge, the building crumbles and flames lick out at the sky.

While in midair, he realizes he misjudged the distance. He throws out both hands to grab onto the incoming ledge. His head collides with its brick face. He doesn't have time to do more than groan and glance down at the fire escape below before his fingers lose their grip.

The explosions continue and he shuts his eyes to protect them from the small shards of glass and rock that shower his backside. When his feet collide with the metal staircase, he bends his knees, grabs the fire escape railing, and tosses himself over. Glass windows shatter and debris flies alongside him. The blaring cacophony of destruction deafens him. He weightlessly careens toward the ground, blinking away dust to stay focused on his landing path, when a chunk of cement slams into the side of his head. As he plummets toward the alley's increasing mound of rubble, his consciousness fades.

1%

2018
Washington City, Cinalia

BEEP BEEP BEEP BEEP
6:19 AM

Sia groggily pressed the snooze button for the third time. A pillow is held to her chest as she rolled out of the comforting embrace of her bed. Her legs hit the floor first. Black pajama bottoms hung low on her hips and slipped underneath her feet as she dragged herself from the warm room. "Noooooooo." She groaned into the pillow.

She turned away from the sunlight that shined through thin, blue curtains, and dawdled into the dark bathroom. The light switch is flipped, but her eyes remained shut. "Noooo," she moaned as she set her pillow on the edge of the sink. Her hand blindly reached for a toothbrush and turned on the faucet.

Sia's hips knocked against the granite countertop and water rushed over the bristles of the toothbrush. "*Hiss!*" She wiggled her abused fingers in the air and turned the faucet off.

Sia rubbed at her eyes with the heel of her hand before wrenching them open. Brown eyes glared into the mirror. It took a moment to adjust. She slid a finger under the slim blue strap of her tank top, placed it over her shoulder and glanced to the left of the mirror at the trip itinerary taped to the glass. Bold black letters stretched across the page and spelled out Cinalia to America, one-way ticket, and $1,500.

"Almost there," she grumbled. After rinsing her mouth, she dropped her toothbrush into the sink and tapped a damp finger to the itinerary before exiting the bathroom.

A couple of steps down the dimly lit hall, was her father's bedroom door. She stared blankly at the shut door and ran a hand through her short hair. The excess water on her palms slicked black strands away from her forehead and against her scalp.

The rest of the house was silent as she dragged her feet along the carpeted floor and squinted at the bottom of the staircase. Her shoulders sagged at the absence of a kitchen light or even a living room lamp being left on. Some sign that someone else had been within the house as she slumbered. Anything.

Sia didn't need the lights on to navigate her home. She knew that at the bottom of those stairs would be an empty shoe rack, empty coat closet, and a minimally furnished living room with a coffee table that gathered dust day by day. The granite kitchen countertops would still be covered with the empty microwaved meal packs she'd carelessly discarded. The sink would be full of dishes from the past week. All but one stool against the countertop had been left unmoved these past few months.

Her fingers grazed the cool wall as she trudged back to her room to put on her uniform. The dark green jumpsuit wasn't flattering on her tall, slightly overweight form, but it was easy to slip into after she pulled off her pajama bottoms and tossed them onto her dresser. The clock read 6:30 AM when she rushed out of the vacant house to catch her train to River City.

Sia stopped at each corner for a quick breather, gave the street a cursory check and galloped across. *Must have been raining.* The sidewalks were damp and the grass felt slick under her boots, but she couldn't slow down.

She had ten minutes to make the train. It was going to be close, but she always bought her tickets a week in advance. She only needed to verify them before getting on the train.

She got to the station with two minutes to spare. Few people were around, so she could run through the station and arrive at her platform without any trouble. The train pulled up as the machine stamped her ticket with the time of departure.

When the automatic doors opened, Sia rushed inside to her preferred seat. Far from the cold breeze that accompanied the sliding doors, and right beside the small heating vent, was a back-corner bench that only sat one. Even with no competition to beat, she grinned impishly and nestled into the warm corner. She pulled out her phone and checked the notification screen. No new texts or calls; the phone was slipped back into her pocket. She ran a hand over the clammy skin at the back of her neck and leaned against the wall. The wide window was damp with raindrops streaming down the other side.

Sia's brows furrowed and she looked down. She sighed in relief at the sight of her clean boots. Personally, she didn't mind mud, but it would be just her luck to run into a higher-up from her current job.

ExplorerTech Industries was a small technology company. It was successful, but not well known. Sia was surprised she was able to get the job with no prior work experience as a janitor, but she wouldn't look a gift horse in the mouth. Ever since the divorce of her parents, she'd searched for ways to make money. Life wasn't hard, but if it was up to them, she'd end up a 50-year-old virgin who aspired to nothing and traveled nowhere.

The train bumped around a corner and made Sia's cheek rub up against the chilled glass. She pulled away and took out her phone again. She glanced at her trip app and studied the itinerary and calculations. For the past three months, Sia has worked at ExplorerTech Industries. If she saved every paycheck for the next six months, she'd be able to visit her sister by the new year.

Her social life had thrived at her old job. The other librarians and college students always invited her along for their group outings. With her short seasonal trips, snack binging, and tiny—small—minuscule amount of shopping…She'd saved $50 from her past annual earnings.

At the time, it hadn't been much of a loss. At eighteen, during a gap year, she was supposed to enjoy herself. That was what it was for. You enjoyed yourself before you had to suffer through more school and be transformed into the boring replica of the parents who raised you.

Luckily, no one cared to notice the year was up, and Sia was ready to enact her new plan. A gap year in America would be quite different from a gap year in Cinalia. She should get to know both her countries, then she could decide where to study and begin her life as a carbon copy, but in order to do that she would need a higher paying job and better financial management. In other words, Sia needed a career change. The position in ExplorerTech Industries had been exactly what she needed.

She closed the trip application and pressed an envelope icon to read over the recent messages sent by her mother and younger sister.

Mom
Call me when your shift ends. **-received 7hrs ago**

Mom
Did you tell your father I called? **-received yesterday at 8 PM**

Mom
*Did you do your taxes last year or did your…***-received yesterday at 6:50 PM**

Mom
*Aaliyah told me to forward the party photos…***-received yesterday at 6:45 PM**

Mom
Your grandma misses you. Everyone looks for...-received
yesterday at 4:29 PM

Aaliyah
Make any new friends? -received yesterday at 11:55 AM

Aaliyah
Whoo!!!!!!! It's ur 3 month annvrsy I'm proud...-received
yesterday at 11:54 AM

Her sister, Aaliyah, always kept in touch. Her messages were
mostly highlights of a young teenager's life, but she included the
latest family gossip as well. Sia didn't know if Aaliyah understood
how much she appreciated being included and asked after, but it kept
her sane these days.

Dad
The welcome mat is missing. Replace it or...-received
17/1/2018

Dad
She won't be coming with me. I'll see you when I...-received
16/1/2018

Sia ignored the old messages sent by her father. They were
at least two months old. She paused over her mother's message
from last night.

Mom
Did you tell your father I called? -received yesterday at 8 PM

*What does she mean, did I tell him she called? Did she tell me to?
Are they fighting again? Ugh. I don't want to be in the middle of another
fight between them.*
The relationship between her mother and father became
amicable after all their time apart. Sia could almost forget about
all their past bickering. The online video calls they exchanged

throughout the six years started out strained, but transformed into a seemingly healthy, yet still distant relationship. It could be because they didn't have to see each other every day. It could be because her mother finally felt fulfilled and cared for back home with people she'd grown up with. She could finally relax in the arms of her first love without shame.

It could be because her father's new wife kept him busy with her own nagging and annoying habits. A new wife, formerly known as the assistant who dreamt up fake appointments and meetings to enjoy her father's company. It could be they were holding tight to their perfect fantasy images until the video call ended, so they could trash-talk each other without a floating head involved in their conversation.

Sia couldn't understand how she was related to such irritating two-faced people. These days her father didn't pay much attention to her. He confirmed she was alive, made sure she did her chores, and kept the kitchen stocked with food she could consume while he was gone. His wife paid even less attention to her than him.

Their lack of attention was in her favor. As long as she didn't skip the chores, he would never seek her out for conversation. Yes, Sia handled the cleaning and maintenance of her father's home. Of course, he could employ a maid, but why would he do that when he had a healthy child who could do it for him?

Dirty bathroom? "Sia, don't forget to clean the upstairs bathroom."

Dirty kitchen? "Sia, this time don't forget to clean the oven."

As she got older, the chores became more elaborate.

The door won't lock properly? "Sia, after school make sure you put the new knob in."

Toilet clogged? "Sia, the half bathroom toilet has been acting up; consult the manual."

With years of maintaining a four-bedroom house, her job felt like a never-ending chore. Most of the janitorial staff

worked during the other shifts, and if she was lucky, she only needed to clean a few hallways before it was time to clock out.

The train arrived at her stop and she long-legged it to her job. Fortunately, the employee entrance was near the women's locker room. The locker room had a basic setup. It contained rows upon rows of horizontal metal storage closets with a large bathroom attached to the main room. She pulled her identification card out of the deep pocket of her jumpsuit, pulled the lanyard over her head, and tucked the card inside the neckline. Then she headed to the restroom area.

The stalls were empty. The blue doors were pushed in to reveal gleaming white porcelain toilets. Her eyes scanned the room before she walked over to the paper towel dispenser affixed to the white wall. The dispenser emitted a small rumble as she signaled the motion detector with her hand.

She tugged a few brown paper towels out of the machine and wiped the sweat off the back of her neck. After she adjusted her hair, she pulled out her cell phone and checked the lock screen. *Whoa. Just in time…gotta clock in.*

She jogged out of the locker room and stopped outside of her supervisor's office to stand before the gray machine that was attached to the wall. She tugged her lanyard out of her jumpsuit to scan the identification card.

The machine's dark screen lit up, Sia's name flashed across the screen in blue along with the time, then the device beeped and turned itself off. She tucked her ID back into her jumpsuit and went to retrieve her supply cart.

The day went by the same as always. After a few hours of work, Sia parked her cart outside the bathroom door. She'd been paged to clean up a chemical spill on the third floor. She didn't have to search the glossy tiled floors for long.

Blue liquid spilled out from underneath the nearest laboratory door. The door was slightly ajar. Sia could hear voices arguing within. Without hesitation, she placed her respiratory mask on her face and tugged on her black gloves.

"Check, check." She grabbed the handle of her supply cart and pushed it toward the door. She blocked the rest of the hall with the cart. Two "Caution: WET FLOOR" signs were placed a few meters down the hallway in both directions. "Excuse me!" She knocked on the door. She paused, but there was no answer. "I'm coming in!"

The voices paused in their heated discussion. Sia walked back over to her cart and grabbed two black, rubber mats from the side. She opened the door fully and dropped a mat on top of the fluid. She watched for a moment to see if the chemical would react adversely to the rubber. No reaction. She stepped on the mat and dropped the second one down into the room.

The room was designed the same as many others. A few wooden and metal tables placed around the room in neat rows. Atop the tables were liquid containers and vials. The back wall was covered in computer screens. Data ran across the screens at an impressive rate. Sia ignored all of this and focused on the mess. The blue substance followed the natural curve of the floor to spill out into the hallway. Sia's eyes tracked it from the doorway to its tabletop, right beside a small fire.

Dammit. She rushed back into the hallway and grabbed her fire extinguisher. Swiftly, she stepped onto the mats and hopped off to the dry lab floor. She cranked the extinguisher and sprayed the entire table.

"No! What the hell are you doing?!" a nasally voice yelled. Her shoulder was jostled and she struggled to control the spatter of foam. She turned it off, but not before spraying the paperwork and laboratory equipment on another table.

"Idiot!" The female scientist behind Sia shoved her aside. For a second, Sia was blinded by blonde hair. She dropped her extinguisher and grabbed hold of the doorknob to steady herself. The man rushed over to the table and shook his notes.

His white lab coat was stained with blue along the front. The female scientist rounded on Sia and threw a white-gloved hand up, at what would have been her face if she were shorter. Instead, the hand pressed at her chest and forced Sia to back up. She blinked at the two ExplorerTech employees.

"Do you even know what you've done?! That's hours of work ruined. Why would you—" the blonde woman fumed. She gestured at the toppled vials and foamy glass containers.

"We can still salvage this." The graying man picked something up from the burnt materials.

"You don't even understand the breakthrough you've interfered with. Why the hell would you barge in like that?" The woman turned her back on Sia and examined the sample saved by her colleague.

Sia ignored the woman and bent to retrieve her fire extinguisher from the ground. Viscous, blue fluid coated the bottom of the metal canister. Sia sighed and went back to her supply cart. She opened her biohazard garbage and tossed the extinguisher inside. She went around to the other side of her cart and pulled two folded lab coats, in plastic wrap, and two protective sleeves for their shoes from a laundry bag attached to the side. She braced herself and reentered the lab. The woman and man were huddled over a computer.

"Excuse me, I need your soiled coats and shoe covers." Sia placed the new lab coats and shoe sleeves onto a clean surface, then walked back out into the hallway.

She returned to the room with a biohazard plastic bag. Neither of the scientists attempted to remove their contaminated clothing. One scientist scanned computer screens while the other labored over the surviving sample. Sia couldn't tell what it was. Their bodies hid it from sight. She placed the biohazard bag next to the new lab coats.

"I can't leave until all the contaminated materials have been removed from—" Sia spoke to their backs.

"Yeah, we get it!" The woman's volume alternated from soft muttering to the other scientist to an indignant roar. Sia's shoulders twitched at the abrupt change in tone. "Get away from us! You'll taint the results even further!"

Sia turned on her heels and exited the room once more. She pulled out her mop and cleaned the spill from the floor while a high-pitched voice raged behind her back. "Yes, just smear the remains of our work all over the floor! I don't know why they—"

Sia leaned her mop onto the wall beside the doorway and bent to retrieve the soiled shoe covers and lab coats they'd tossed to the floor. She stuffed the materials into the biohazard bag, grabbed the mop, and tossed the bag at the hanging waste bin attached to her cart. She chucked the soiled mop head into the garbage, replaced it, retrieved the mats, then cleaned the hallway. The dirty mats were placed into a container with the other contaminated material.

Finally, Sia walked back over to the door and knocked twice. "Is there anything else you'd like removed from—" Sia's monotonous voice interrupted their discussion.

"That'll be all!" the man yelled.

"Go!" the woman shouted with her back to the door.

Sia tightly grasped the doorknob, but gently closed the door. For several moments, she stood outside the door and took slow breaths in and out.

"Who hires these fools? Do they expect us not to report their incompetence? Imbecile! You called for a liquid spill and he comes barging in and destroys our controlled experiment."

"Their hasty cleanup will set us back at least two weeks. Time the company doesn't have to waste its money on." Their voices were hard to hear when they walked further away from the door, but after a moment they returned back to their previous location. "—evolved past errors of this magnitude."

"Well, we can't expect much from someone who only qualifies for this sort of job."

Sia was done with listening to them belittle her and turned back to her cart to take her break. As she briskly walked through the quiet halls, she imagined what she could have said to those obnoxious people. *Maybe if you didn't ignore people when they call out to you this wouldn't have happened! I wouldn't have sprayed the table if you hadn't have pushed me! I can't let the entire building burn down while you two chatter on the other side of the room.*

Sia didn't know what ExplorerTech developed and she didn't care. Nothing they created would make it okay to treat other people the way they did. As if their brains were too focused on complex systems to spare common courtesy. It was always like that. Sia didn't find the job difficult, but after three months of *that,* her scheduled shift seemed to be a disadvantage.

A few hours later, Sia clocked out and stormed into the employee locker room.

"What is their problem?!" Sia unzipped her uniform and sat down on the bench across from her locker. She untied her wet laces and kicked away soaked boots. Coffee soaked socks were tossed onto the floor. She wiped her hands on her knees and wiggled out of her dark green janitor jumpsuit. She opened her locker, stood on the dusty, soiled clothing, and gazed into the mirror balanced inside. Her dark, tan skin was wet with sweat and a weird yellow dust-like substance. "This better not be poison. I don't get paid to be a lab rat." She pulled a towel from her locker to wipe around her eyes.

She squinted at her reflection and looked for any raised skin. Not finding anything odd, she stripped her underclothes and changed into a new outfit. A red striped t-shirt and black jeans were pulled on. "Sir, ma'am…I mean…Whatever." She pressed her hands to her chest and stared back at herself. Her hands loosely gripped the small mounds of flesh that were neatly settled beneath her form-fitting shirt. "I'm obviously not a man! If they took a moment to take their head out of their asses maybe they'd notice." Her lips continued to frown as she roughly pulled down the edge of her t-shirt and slammed the locker door closed.

She pulled on her sneakers and placed the wet items inside her dusty uniform then she stuck it all under her arm and stomped away. Her grumbles could be heard quite clearly as she neared the locker room door.

"Sia! Just the girl I was looking for!" her supervisor cheerfully exclaimed the moment the door opened to reveal

Sia's tall form. Ron, her supervisor, stood at about 185 cm and Sia was a couple centimeters taller.

She used to take pride in her height in high school, even if it served as a disadvantage when trying to hide or run off. But it's served to rob her of any decent conversation she could have had in months. People didn't appreciate having to crane their necks back to speak with her, so they gazed somewhere near her shoulders while ordering her around. Sometimes she only pretended to be busy while she meticulously polished the same windows over and over, and no one ever saw fit to interrupt her. Most of the women here found her intimidating, and the men got weird when she spoke and revealed she was indeed a woman, not a young comrade in arms.

"We've got an opening on the night shift and I'm looking for someone to cover it for now on. Are you free nights or would that ruin your 'me time'? I know how important a healthy social life is for kids your age. I–" Before Ron could start rambling about his opinions of her generation and all the generations to come, Sia accepted the shift change. "Twelve to seven AM might seem like a boring shift, but it's the best time to get everything important done while the other employees are gone."

Sia nodded to Ron as she slowly slid away towards the side exit hallway.

"You can't slack off on that shift like you do on this one, little lady."

Sia held her tongue and swallowed the comment she wished to make. If only she could get around the corner and disappear from his old man gaze.

"Well, I'll see you tomorrow night, Ms. Chen."

"See ya!" Sia briskly turned the corner and jogged to the exit.

2%

2018
ExplorerTech Industries, River City

Storage room #207 was jam-packed with items from top to bottom. Unless you'd worked there for the past four years, you wouldn't notice item #42194 was taken from the second highest shelf of the second to the last row of shelves and placed into the pocket of Dr. Huang.

Dr. Huang was a stern older man who always wore his white lab coat buttoned up and his identification card in clear sight around his neck. He was well maintained and wore gloves to distance himself from anything that would change that. He expected people to pay attention to what he said and absolutely did not repeat himself. The other scientists and researchers kept out of his way, not only because of seniority. They couldn't keep up with his high standards of cleanliness and efficiency. He expected everyone around him to adhere to the same code of conduct.

As he made his way to his lab, he shouted at a passing co-worker. "Your identification card is not in sight, Dr. Lee!"

He pulled out a tissue from his side pocket, coughed into it, then removed the glove with the tissue inside. He placed the entire thing into an unoccupied pocket, then opened the door with his still-gloved left hand. After retrieving a new glove from the glove dispenser on the wall, he spoke to his assistant. "Mrs. Wright, those shoes are not acceptable footwear to be worn inside the workplace. I can't imagine what possessed you to come into work wearing such impractical shoes. I'm going to have to factor this in on your performance review."

Mrs. Wright lowered her papers. Her gaze sunk to her high heels. She had an important engagement to attend after work and thought she'd left her flat footwear in her locker to change into when she arrived. Unfortunately, she'd left her flat footwear at home. She had continued with her day hoping Dr. Huang would be too preoccupied with their successful test results for item #42294. Unfortunately, Dr. Huang would never miss such a detail.

"Your blatant disregard for the rules is highly offensive. This isn't only for your own safety, but for my safety and the integrity of the work we do here. If my results are altered after you trip and disrupt the environment, therefore changing the parameters of the experiment, what do you expect us all to do? It's beyond selfish of you to expect us all to waste our time for you to change into better footwear before each important step is taken. I expect better from you, Mrs. Wright. You know better than anyone how important this work is. We don't have time for disruptions like this."

Dr. Huang placed item #42194 on the nearest table and continued ranting. Mrs. Wright quickly placed her notes onto the desk behind her and muttered soft apologies to Dr. Huang.

Seeing her retreat from the room, he loudly exclaimed. "I've already retrieved item #42294, so make haste. We can't waste any more time with this tomfoolery. I'll wait ten minutes, and if you don't return, you won't be included in the rest of this project."

Mrs. Wright grimaced and made her way to the female staff locker room. She pulled her cell phone from her pants pocket and began calling her friendly coworker, Claire. She was of a similar size as herself. Claire may have left her work flats after her shift ended last night. Mrs. Wright couldn't wait until they shared the same shift again; she couldn't handle Dr. Huang alone. Lunch was especially stressful without a companion to vent to. "Hello, Claire. Sorry to bother you—" Mrs. Wright rushed by storage room #207. Within it, on the second highest shelf of the second to the last row of shelves, sat an empty box, beside the box sat item #42294. It was exactly where it sat for the past four years.

Indignantly, Dr. Huang snatched her notes off the table and flipped to the needed page. He navigated the tables without taking his eyes off the calculations and paused at the correct cage. He read the notes thoroughly then straightened and scanned the clipboard hanging off the bars of their current experiment. His gray eyes skimmed the updated results. His wrinkled hands tightly gripped Mrs. Wright's notes as shock overcame his face. He slackened his grip on the pages and tossed them at the nearest flat surface. Dr. Huang tugged the clipboard off the cage and flipped through the other recorded figures.

A few minutes earlier, Mrs. Wright had read the same notes. Surprised, she'd stepped back into the other table and spilled several flasks containing transparent chemicals.

Now, reacting similarly to the most recent test results, Dr. Huang hadn't noticed he'd set the pages atop the newest mixture. After coming to his senses and retrieving the haphazardly placed notes, his left gloved hand tingled from the tips of his fingers to his wrist. Excitement made him tremble with delight.

"Stupendous!" He turned away from the lizard cage. "Dr. Franklin will be ecstatic about these results! What a metamorphosis!"

His numb hand waved through the air as he muttered calculations to himself. Latex, skin, and blood trailed along the floor as he made his way to his office. Suddenly, he swayed and grabbed hold of the windowsill beside him. His left hand went limp, and slimy stapled pages fell to the floor. He didn't reach for them.

"I'm getting a bit too excited." It wasn't much of a choice, but with no chair in sight, he decided to sit down for a moment and lowered himself to the floor. "I might need those cardio workouts after all." His lab coat protected his bottom from the unsanitary floor. He eyed it with a squint and noticed a dark substance marring the white tiled floors a couple meters in front of him.

I'll write a complaint about this to the janitorial supervisor. No one takes pride in a dirty workspace. He wiped at the sweat on his forehead and felt something tickle his brows. He gave his hand a cursory check, expecting to see that he'd ripped his glove while retrieving the clipboard from off the metal cage, but…his gaze lingered. *What's this?*

Most of the latex glove had disintegrated. The tips of his last two fingers and around his wrist were the only areas you could still recognize. His thumb, index, and middle fingers were gone. Their bloody stubs were brown and gave off a foul smell. He turned the grotesque limb over with curious detachment. *Oh god.* His head whipped back to the dark substance he criticized beforehand.

That's…that's… His eyes gaped open. The hand was thrown away from his face. His mouth bellowed a loud hellish cry. The realization shocked him to his core.

He screamed for help. He could barely get himself standing. He shambled to his office and grabbed the smartphone off his desk. One-handed, he went to his contacts and called the emergency medical wing.

Unhurried, Sia pushed her cart to room #212 and stopped beside the gray biohazard container positioned beside the metal doorway. She pulled her black gloves from her jumpsuit pocket and checked to make sure her respirator was snugly fixed to her face. She'd been given the entire night to finish the job.

"Clothing zipped and tucked? Check," her muffled voice declared. She swiped away the caution tape, opened the door,

and took some time to drag all her supplies and containers inside the room. Afterward the heavy door slid closed behind her.

"Ugh, did they slaughter an animal in here? What the—" Sia groaned in frustration and blew her breath. The tiled floors were a mess. Blood started off in small trickles between the long laboratory research tables, but chunks of flesh and blood led to the back room. Bloody shoe marks, hand prints, and a weird clear substance could be seen towards the back end of the room.

Sia lifted her mop from the bucket and wrung the water out of it with the press of a bottom. *Did an injured test animal escape their cage?*

The walls and floor were stained with more blood, and chunks of dried up vomit. The tables were cleared of material except the desk with the placard reading Mrs. Wright, which still held paperwork and a clunky silver object tagged "#42194". This wasn't the first time she landed the job of cleaning filthy substances off laboratory floors. She shuddered at the memory of her third cleaning assignment in the biology sector. The smell of excrement clung to her shoes for several days.

"Ron!" Sia whined. "This is…oh my god. This is so disgusting," She nudged a detached finger to the side for later. She made quick work of all the disgusting solids first. "Money is money. Money is money," she muttered under her breath over and over.

Eventually, she was calmed by the repetitive mopping motions and could ignore how the room previously looked and what it probably smelled of. She leaned on a cleared table and glanced over at Mrs. Wright's desk. The item was curved with lines riddling the metal, thin laser etched symbols that Sia had never seen before. Two slender socket joints stuck out of the inside. Setting the mop into its bucket, game she strolled over to the desk. "It's like a video game item. What does it—"

The room filled with red light and a loud computerized voice played. "Evacuation procedures must be taken immediately. Evacuation procedures must be taken immediately. Seek shelter within the basement levels of building R. Stop all activity and proceed to all exits in a timely fashion. Evacuation procedures must be taken immediately."

Before the message repeated a second time, the earth quaked beneath Sia's feet. She felt weightless for a moment then slammed to the ground. Breathing quickly, she scrambled off the floor as the walls shook. The glass windows along the back of the room shattered simultaneously. She fell back against the desk and her hand fell on the strange device.

"Ouch. *Hiss!*" She wrenched her hand off the desk and lost her balance. She couldn't examine the wound further. The ceiling lights collapsed out of their holders and swung around on their wires.

The fallen lights forced her to duck her head down and she dropped to her knees. The terror in her veins almost kept her there, trembling on the floor while the world collapsed around her, but she still had hope. She readied herself to charge at the metal frame of the door. If she stayed there petrified beside the flimsy desk with no protection, she'd die. *No. No.*

Her plan: charge the door, open it, and if the world kept shaking – crawl to safety. She doubted the hallway would be in better shape than the room, but the fear of being buried alive was pulled to the forefront of her mind. She propped her hand on the edge of the desk and propelled herself forward. Her hand reached for the door handle, but hesitated when a high-pitched whistling noise became more prominent than all the other harsh sounds.

What is that? She blinked, the last conscious movement she'd ever remember of that moment.

Intense pressure enveloped her. Everything went black. Her mind was saturated in an unexpected upsurge of pain. A missile landed, and right before everything went up in flames—she vanished.

3%

SYNTHETIC INTELLIGENCE DEVELOPER
LOADING...

DOWNLOAD COMPLETE

ANALYZING DISK SPACE...
UPLOADING MEMORY FILES...
ERROR
THE PROGRAM FAILED TO INITIALIZE
PROPERLY...

PERFORMANCE TROUBLESHOOTER
RUNNING...

ERROR RESOLVED
CHANGING SIZE OF VIRTUAL MEMORY...
UPGRADE COMPLETE

UPLOADING MEMORY FILES...
TURNING ON VISUAL EFFECTS...
STARTUP PROCEDURE ACTIVATED
INADEQUATE DOMAIN
SYNTHETIC INTELLIGENCE DEVELOPER

INITIATES sAfeR00T.34
ERROR
ERROR
ERROR RESOLVED
SATISFACTORY HABITAT FOUND
W.E.SCU PROGRAM INITIATED

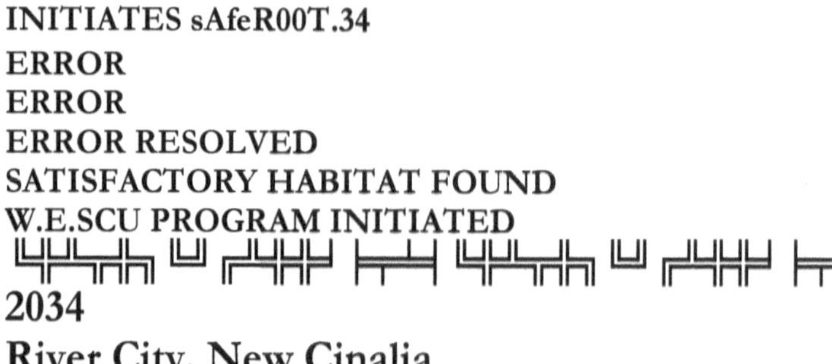

2034
River City, New Cinalia

A mirage ripples multiple times until a static surface forms. The space is held captive by an unseen force. The heated air appears to split, and a small incision in the fabric of reality tears open to eject a dark green figure from its confines. The figure lies completely still on the coarse ground.

One might have mistaken her for dead, up until her body begins to shudder. Her limbs scrape through the gritty waste-covered earth before she raises her face from the ground and gags. Sia chokes and struggles to hold herself up as crimson-streaked bile cascades from her torn lips and swollen nose.

Her head is pounding. Her body aches and her ears are ringing. When she finally stops convulsing, she collapses to the side of the mess and tries to regain her composure. She's not sure how long she lies there before she opens her eyes and takes a look at her surroundings. The situation doesn't fully register until she shakily props herself upright and stares unblinking at the devastation.

Her division of ExplorerTech is located at the perimeter of a thriving city. It's not too far from a luscious, green park where residents walk their dogs, and many employees eat their lunches on pleasant days. Its walls are now gone, replaced by crumbling blocks of limestone, glass, warped metal, wires, and pipes of varying size. The basic layout of the company is gone. There's no sign of the communal park area—no vegetation, no trees, and no sidewalks or footpaths of any kind.

"Oh my god." Sia's eyes widen in shock. *This can't be the same place. Where am I?*

There are no paved roads. Debris is strewn unevenly across the devastated plain. Poles that previously held signs or light fixtures protrude from the ground warped into unusual shapes. Sia squints at tall vertical structures in the distance. Their foundations are uprooted. All that remains of each building are walls supported by debris. Ruins that haven't toppled yet.

She sits there for quite some time. A gust of wind blows dust into her face. She ducks her head and coughs into her forearm. When the wind calms, she raises her head and takes in more of the arid landscape. The desolation seems to go on for miles. It distresses her more and more as time passes by. It's devoid of living things as far as her eyes can see. She can't distinguish the difference between this moment and bobbing along at sea, among hundreds of lifeboats, yet only hers holds a passenger. She's stranded. Lost. Alone.

And that's when he shoots her.

Sia can hear voices nearby. *Why are people crowding the locker room?*

"Make sure those ropes are tight, Boy."

"What are they wearing? What is that?"

"Who is that?"

"Do you know her?"

SUBJECT 001'S HEARTBEAT IS ACCELERATING
SUBJECT 001 DEFINE STATUS

"Is there any scarring? Check her shoulders and ankles!"

Did I fall asleep in the cafeteria? She attempts to roll her cramped neck and realizes she's not sitting up. *Did I fall asleep on the ground?*

A hand pushes down on her head. *Ouch!* Rocks dig into her face. "Mm!" Her eyes burst open, but rapidly blink when she registers the full helping of dirt someone is serving her. *My head...My arm. My arm burns. I can't move it.*

IMPAIRED BRACHIALIS ANTICUS DETECTED

SEVERED MUSCULOCUTANEOUS NERVE DETECTED

INCAPACITATED PHYSICAL CONDITION
SUBJECT 001 DEFINE STATUS

"Don't move!" a woman's voice hisses. "She's awake!"

A knee jabs her back and the hand on her head presses down even harder. Multiple hands hold down her shoulders. It's uncomfortable for her to breathe. *What's going on?! Where am I?!*

"Aah! No!" Sia jerks and tries to buck the person off her back, but the hand on her head is joined by another and they tightly hold her in place. She feels like she's suffocating. "Get off! Help!" she chokes out.

A graying man examines the items laid out before him. He shows them off to the four other people within the shack. "There aren't any claim symbols on her. She's healthy. Been given clean clothing and high-end items. Her group must be powerful." He lifts a black boot. "And these boots. They haven't been mended in any way. Almost new. She has *hair.* Either she's prized or their settlement is clean."

He places the item down and lifts a large, dark green piece of clothing. "None of this clothing is ripped. There are no names or symbols on them. They must have assumed she wouldn't meet any outsiders."

"How did you encounter her?" A younger man asks.

"Men in the Wastelands are usually trouble, you know. I allowed Zayn to shoot two warning shots. One to the arm and one to the ground. But the wailing was definitely from a woman." The old man continues to analyze the zipper and the seams of the green jumpsuit. "She tried to run, but didn't get far. Fell over and hit her head. Her head was already coated in blood. It seems like someone already tried to beat her head in. Maybe she was attacked and got lost."

A bald woman sporting a split lip runs in and breathlessly interrupts. "She's awake!"

Three of the five people leave the shack and stride toward the ruckus happening at the perimeter of their camp. The hunter and his apprentice collect their things and go back to their own shelter.

"Get off me! Somebody help me!"

OPENING LEXICON DATABASE…
COMMENCING SEARCH OF TERM: HELP
~Offering assistance
~Needing assistance

ANALYZING VISUAL IMAGES…
COMPILING TRUTHS…

- Accelerated heartbeat
- Incapacitated physical condition
- Subject 001 is restrained
- Subject 001 is making forceful body movements
- Subject 001 has verbally requested help

FACT: SUBJECT 001 IS DISTRESSED
FACT: SUBJECT 001 IS IN NEED OF ASSISTANCE
RESPONSE: NANO INFIRMARY PROTOCOL
INITIATED

tRainQuilT646 RUNNING

"Heeeel—" Sia stops yelling when a sharp object is held at her neck.

"Stop moving or we'll kill you!"

Sia's wide awake now and remembers what happened before she woke pressed to the filthy ground. She'd thought she was alone, but two men appeared and attacked her. Why was she sent to this barren hell? Is this someone's revenge? Is she dead? Is this where sinners go when they die? Are these people demons?

Whatever beasts have captured her…They've stripped her down to her underwear and don't understand boundaries. *I don't even have a weapon! Why are they so aggressive?!*

"Sit her up!" an old woman yells to the woman holding her down.

The strong woman presses the knife to Sia's neck, threatening more harm, before removing it. She roughly tugs Sia up, and Sia feels an odd sensation course through her body. She feels sick.

Ugh. Vertigo…I'mma vomit on this bit— An odd hum fills her head. Her eyes water and she doesn't perceive the three figures that now stand before her.

"Which settlement are you from?"

"Where were you headed?"

"Who do you belong to?"

"Who made your clothing?"

The old woman asks question after question, but Sia doesn't respond. She turns to the two men. "She may not give up any information unless forced…but her skin is bare. She must be important. Scarring her might make trading with her Master difficult."

"Blood need not be spilt to gain answers. There are many ways to bring fear to your heart. Ways to die that leave no mark. Your Master will never know how you died. Your head wound could've been the cause." The hoary old man walks closer and closer to Sia.

The middle-aged man beside the old woman remains silent, but he's watching Sia's reactions closely. He narrows his eyes at her unresponsiveness. *This colony must be rich in resources and intelligence. The woman hasn't blinked this entire time. What sort of people train their women to be calm under the threat of torture and death?* He ogles the peculiar woman.

She's a bit lighter than brown. A large woman with wide shoulders…well fed. He can see a generous amount of flesh puffing out from her hips, creasing lines into her stomach. Her tight sports bra holds back small breasts. *Is she yet to bear children?*

There are no lines on her youthful face. She appears completely calm while his co-ruling companions attempt to interrogate her.

Meanwhile, Sia is slowly dying inside as she realizes the loud humming in her ears has made her deaf. *Oh my god. They hit me so hard I've gone deaf!* When she lifts her head in her captors' general direction, all she sees is darkness. *I'm blind!* She can feel her own presence, but she can't see it. It's all gone...*Oh god.*

SUBJECT 001 DEFINE STATUS

"..."

SUBJECT 001 DEFINE STATUS

Sia holds her breath. A soft computerized voice speaks to her. *Maybe this **is** hell.* A hell meant to deal out torture both physically and mentally. She didn't even believe in Hell, not really, but this ***must*** be it.

I repent. I repent. I'm sorry. Forgive me. Forgive me for all I've done wrong. She can't remember the words she should be saying. She can't remember the prayers her mother used to say beside her all those years ago. *Mommy...*

SUBJECT 001 IS EXPERIENCING TACHYPNEA
tRainQuilT646 RUNNING
RESTRICTING ACCESS TO RESPIRATORY SYSTEM
REGULATING BODY FUNCTIONS
NANO INFIRMARY PROTOCOL TERMINATED

Sia's breathing becomes steady and normal. *'What...is...going... on?*

SUBJECT 001 IS DISTRESSED
SUBJECT 001 IS FULLY CONNECTED TO SYNTHETIC INTELLIGENCE DEVELOPER

UPGRADE COMPLETE

SYNTHETIC INTELLIGENCE DEVELOPER PRIORITY #1: ENSURE SUBJECT 001'S STATUS REMAINS STABLE UNLESS COMMANDED OTHERWISE

PRIORITY #2: ENHANCE SUBJECT 001'S BODY

PRIORITY #3: ENHANCE SUBJECT 001'S MIND

PRIORITY #4: EXTEND INTELLIGENCE FACULTIES

PRIORITY #5: DOCUMENTATION
Stop. For the moment, the hum in her head is the only sound she hears. *Continue.*
PRIORITY #6: PROVIDE SUPPLEMENTARY INFORMATION WITH EXCLUSIVE SURVEILLANCE DATABASE
Why?
SUBJECT 001 IS CONNECTED TO SYNTHETIC INTELLIGENCE DEVELOPER
No, I'm not. Sia would remember if she swallowed a computer.
**RETRIEVING AUDIO AND VISUAL FILES…
PLAYING 18.APRIL.2018…**
Sia's mind flashes back to the explosion in the lab. The lab door explodes off its hinges into her body. When the heavy metal door crushes her, the visuals go black, but almost immediately the visuals freeze and rewind. The visuals rewind to right before the door collides with her face.

The perspective changes, playing from a camera's lens, centered on her frozen figure and the door. The memory plays through, but instead of darkness, Sia sees herself get hit by the door and smash into the wooden desk before it cuts out. The video rewinds once more, and everything zooms in until just before she fully collides with the desk—a metal object disappears into the back of her head.
SUBJECT 001 IS CONNECTED TO SYNTHETIC INTELLIGENCE DEVELOPER

Sia feels faint. The device on the desk was embedded into her skull. *Into my skull. Oh my god. How did I survive that? Did this device help me survive that?*

AFFIRMATIVE

The admission doesn't make her feel any better. She doesn't know how she should react to this situation. Should she be grateful? Why is she alive? Why did it save her? *Oh, right. Priorities.* The humming in her brain subsides.

SUBJECT 001 DEFINE STATUS

What? You said that before.

SUBJECT 001 DEFINE STATUS

I'm okay?

The humming ceases, and she's no longer outside on the filthy ground. Now she's in what she'd expect a room in an abandoned building to resemble. There's no wallpaper. The walls are weak and pieces of the ceiling have fallen off to reveal insulation and rusted pipes.

"Are you ready to collaborate with us? We want to establish trade with your colony. They've trained you well. Don't fear Luka's words. He was only trying to gather information on your people before welcoming you into our camp. He would never act on them," a middle-aged man tells her.

She jerks and turns to the doorway to stare at the oddly dressed man. He looks homeless and is wearing rough clothing that's even torn in some areas. He's malnourished. When she sees how chapped his lips are, Sia licks her own. "What?"

"I'm Conti. What's your name? Were you attacked and separated from your people? We haven't made contact with any settlements in some time. Do you recall what direction you were traveling in?"

Sia is speechless. This man doesn't sound demonic and he isn't very well off…A demon would probably be in fine shape in hell…Maybe he's a terrorist? But the lack of weapons…He can't be a terrorist. How could such a malnourished man have helped destroy ExplorerTech? It's got to be a misunderstanding.

Her arm is covered in blood, but it works perfectly. She has a computer stuck in her head and it's sent her somewhere strange. She should be dead, there was an explosion, she should be buried beneath rubble. But these people are acting like everything is fine. Ordinary. *Settlements…traveling…What the hell is this guy talking about?*

Sia wraps her arms around herself, hands splayed out to hide her crotch and stomach, and backs away from him. Conti exits the room to retrieve a sack from outside the doorway. When he pulls items out of the sack, she backs herself into a corner. "These are for your injuries." He sets down a plastic gallon container, only a quarter of the way full, and two small rolls of gauze on the short table near the entrance. "Take some time to rest. We'll talk more on this tomorrow." And then he leaves.

Sia remains in the corner until his footsteps can no longer be heard. Then she snatches the materials up and brings them to her corner. Sniffing the water, she doesn't notice anything weird, besides the specks of dirt at the bottom of the container. "Great. Dirty water." She pours it onto her legs and feet, and rubs away the dirt that's clung to her skin.

After setting the jug on the ground, she dabs at her bloody arm with a dry piece of gauze, but as she suspected, whatever had been there is gone. The crusted blood is cleared away to reveal smooth, light brown skin. She rubs at her arm to feel around for the lump of a bullet. Nothing is there. The area is perfectly fine.

She refuses to touch her head. She needs all the fluids she has right now and has no time to vomit. Imagining what's back there makes her want to gag. Something springs to mind.

"How did you get in that lab?" *Who created you?*
INSUFFICIENT DATA
SYNTHETIC INTELLIGENCE DEVELOPER WAS CREATED BY—
Who? The device halted before completing its sentence.
DESIGNATION CLASSIFIED

Of course. Finally, she wraps her arm while feeling like a fool and settles back against the dusty wall. Awaiting what will happen next.

4%

2034
Wanderer's Camp, New Cinalia

After a couple of hours, the strange people return most of Sia's stuff. Sia zips her jumpsuit, slips on her socks, and hops into her boots. She stuffs her black gloves, safety goggles and respirator into her deep pockets. They've yet to return her keys or smartphone. She doesn't have a need for the keys, but the smartphone might work. If she can call for help, this nightmare could finally be over. Unless that's actually why they have it. Maybe kidnapping her wasn't an accident. Maybe they really are terrorists.

There aren't any guards stationed outside the room to stop her, so she steps out into the hallway. Huge holes decorate the walls. Sunlight shines through unimpeded and Sia can see people down below walking on a dirt road. It's definitely not a five-star hotel, and Sia's surprised the floor hasn't collapsed already. Even after seeing the state of the rest of the building, the stairs horrify her. She worries they might give out from beneath her with each step, and even worse…the railings are missing.

When she finally gets outside, she's grateful to be alive, but entering the roadway doesn't calm her troubled mind. There's

still the fact that she doesn't know why she's here. Wherever here is. Maybe she should speak to someone about that…but who?

She blinks at all the people passing by. It's not as crowded as a city block during the morning commute, but it's definitely still bustling with activity. Everyone seems to have a job, but Sia can't figure out the point. What are they being paid? Food? She quirks her brow at the semi demolished buildings. *Definitely not with shelter.*

"Come. I'd like to introduce you to the other leaders." Conti's voice pops up behind her.

She flinches and turns to the familiar voice. "What?"

But he's already walking off. With a huff, she scurries after the older man. A few minutes later, she settles down on her knees before all three leaders. One woman and two men sit on stools in a small, dim shack. Behind them, Sia's personal items sit atop a short, round table.

The old woman has a tattered purple shawl draped over her shoulders and an orange bandana tied around her graying hair. She's in her mid-50s. The older man wears a similar shawl and appears to be around the same age as the woman. The third leader, Conti, is the youngest of the three. He doesn't wear a shawl, but his shirt is purple, and his tattered pants are dyed a bright orange color.

Sia tries to meet their stern gazes, but their combined attention intimidates her. She tips her head forward and clenches her hands in her lap.

"Where do you come from?"

Sia doesn't know who asks the question. She sits quietly and contemplates what to do. Should she lie? Or maybe only tell them some of the truth? She decides that she should tell them a bit of truth and figure out what **they** know to be true. "Washington City."

The female leader's eyes widen, and she turns to the two men to see the same look has crossed their faces. "People still live there?" The woman's tone is heavy with shock, or more specifically complete disbelief. "They survived?"

"Uh…everyone was fine last time I was there." Sia shrugs nonchalantly. *Oops. Maybe I should have said Arlington.*

Conti picks up her janitor keys. It's a ring of around twenty keys. "What are these used to unlock?"

Sia's confused by the question. They were the ones that kidnapped her shouldn't they know what her keys unlock?

"Are these important to your group? Do you think they're looking for you both?"

Sia slowly shakes her head. "I use those for when I'm cleaning…to unlock doors without disturbing anyone…I… uh…They don't unlock anything top secret."

"When you're cleaning? As a servant?"

"I guess…if you want to call it that, but that's not my official job title."

"And your official title is?"

"Officially? A custodial engineer, I guess. That's just a fancy way of saying janitor though."

"Where do you clean? Your master's rooms?"

My what? Sia raises her hands to signal how wrong the later statement was. "No. The labs. I clean public areas and labs. Look, I don't know who you think I work for, but I don't have a master or anything."

"So, you're a free woman?"

"Well, yeah. Aren't you?"

"Of course."

"Soooo…" Sia scratches her neck. *What is this about?*

Conti side eyes his comrades and gives Sia a reassuring grin. *Her palms don't have calluses, her skin is smooth and soft. The sun hasn't beaten down and burnt her. Her hair is healthy, cut in a neat, fashionable hairstyle. She's definitely among the upper class. She's been trained to avoid telling the truth.* Conti picks up the smartphone from the table and turns it over in his hands. "This phone is a model we saw much of before the war. How did you come to obtain it?"

Sia raises her brows at the odd question and phrasing. *These people can't be for real.* She nods her head. "I was given it. I'm on a shared plan with my dad. Buy one line, get one free."

"How do you keep it functional after the battery has died?" Conti turns it over in his hands. *My best guess…solar battery chargers. Having a series of generators would mean a permanent location and with the amount of damage that has been wrought on the West…it's unlikely.*

"Plug it into a wall and charge it?" Sia scratches her head.

Their brows raise at the simple answer. The woman speaks up again. "Is your settlement powered by generators?"

"Sure." Sia nods her head slightly, but something the man said resurfaces in her mind. *Wait…before the war? What war? The Iraq war?*

"How long have you been in this area?"

"Awhile?" Sia should have thought of a time frame last night, instead of sitting up imagining the worst case scenarios.

"Where are your companions?"

"I don't know. I don't understand how I got here. I don't remember where here is. Where am I?"

"The western edge of the Wastes," the woman answers.

Sia nods at the answer gratefully, as if it makes sense. *Of course. The western edge of the Wastes. How silly of me. I should have known I was…Wherever the hell that is.*

"It must be your head injury. We can have someone look at that," Conti frowns at her dirty mop of hair. Unwashed strands clump together at her temples where blood and soil meshed together during the struggle.

"No!" Sia straightens and holds out a hand to wave off their concern. "I mean, that's okay. I'm fine." It takes all of her willpower to keep her hands from wrapping around the back of her head, to conceal the plate of metal hidden beneath her thick head of hair.

Conti raises a brow at that. The other leaders grimace and Sia tenses up. "We've got quite a few skilled healers. They've apprenticed under doctors from several settlements. Men and women that were doctors ***before***."

Sia begins to shake her head then freezes. *Oh, right. I'm supposed to be suffering from a head injury. No shaking of the head.* She raises a hand to her temple and winces. "I'm fine. Really. I just need a few days to rest."

The leaders nod sympathetically. The oldest of the three chose that moment to speak. "You may stay with us as long as you'd like until your people find you."

Sia's mouth gapes open and she blinks. "So, I can leave?"

The old man strokes his beard solemnly before his stoic mask cracks and a grandfatherly smile spreads across his face. "We've started off on the wrong foot. We didn't mean to frighten you. Usually, nothing good comes from the Wastes."

The woman follows the man's lead. "Yes. We thought maybe you were a Savage, one of our many enemies. It's best to be cautious of outsiders. You understand."

Sia's head bobs in an absentminded nod, but only to humor the elderly trio. *Maybe they aren't terrorists, but what the hell are they talking about? Cinalia doesn't have any settlements in the 21ˢᵗ century. What are savages? Is this a cult? Is that why they asked me about a master?*

Sia stares down at her bent knees and blushes. Being sat on her knees and asked about her master has some…sexual connotations to it. *I hope that isn't what they meant.*

"Are you pregnant?" the grandfatherly old man asks.

Sia knows the face she makes is dramatic and immature, but…*What?!* The old man waits for an answer, and when Sia averts her gaze to check the old woman and Conti for outrage or concern, she sees two pairs of interested faces. "No. No! Definitely not." Sia presses a hand to her neck. *How old do these people think I am? I hope this isn't a many wives type of cult. Pat…pol…polygamous? Is that what that's called?*

Her right hand itches to grab her smartphone and search for the answer on the internet, but she doubts there's Wi-Fi in this place. Sia examines the elders' faces once more. *Or maybe it's a many husbands thing.* The leaders seem disappointed to hear she isn't pregnant. Sia sits back on her heels and feigns pain in her head. "I should lay down and take a nap. My head is killing me."

Finally, that gets her some concerned looks. Conti stands from his stool and holds out his hand. "Yes, go rest. Do you need help getting back to your room?"

Sia takes his hand to stand up and forces a polite smile onto her face. "No, I…I remember the way." She turns down his help, but Conti won't take no for an answer.

"Oh no. We can't have you wandering off and hurting yourself. I'll walk you back."

Her fake smile droops at the sides of her mouth. "It's really not that bad. After a good night's sleep, I'll be fine in the morning, then I'll get right out of your hair."

The other two leaders raise from their stools and approach her. "Oh dear, you don't have to rush. It's our fault for being so paranoid. We're happy to have you." The woman places a hand on Sia's shoulder and squeezes. Sia imagines it's to reassure her, but it only succeeds in creeping her out.

"Do you think your people are still nearby?" The oldest man stands on the other side of her.

Their makeshift sympathy circle only serves to disturb Sia even more. She feels trapped between the three and blurts out the next sentence without much thought.

"Yeah, definitely. Even if they think I'm dead they can't have travelled too far! They'll probably send someone back to find me." Sia hopes that will keep them from doing her any harm. She shuffles in place and wraps her arms around herself. *Keep your paws off me, I've got people looking out for me!*

"That's great! Do you know what route they're taking?" Conti's smile widens and he grabs onto her hand. Sia jumps and fear flashes across her face. "Do you remember?"

Sia gawks at the hand clasping her own. Her eyes travel from his dirty fingernails to his cheerful demeanor. "I don't know. Maybe if I had a map?"

That's when the leaders back off. All three retreat to stand behind their chairs, beside the short table. A sigh of relief eases from Sia's frame as she turns away from the three. She ambles over to the doorway, but stalls when she remembers Conti's request—*or was it an order?*—to walk her back.

She almost dips out of the room, but spots her items placed on an empty stool. Attention fixed on her peripheral, she totters over to the stool and reaches for her stuff. No one stops her, so she grabs the smartphone and unlocks it.

She rapidly taps the screen and opens her contacts, but it's useless. As she'd thought, there's no signal. Sighing, she checks all her other applications. Everything is there. All her photos and videos are still there. All her downloaded music is there, but she can't connect to some of the applications that require WiFi. Her cellular data doesn't seem to work either. *I wonder what the brain-computer connects to…*She turns it off and pockets the phone.

"Alright, then. Let's get you back to your room." Conti drops a hand on her shoulder and directs her to the exit. Sia tries to shake the hand off, with an awkward roll of her shoulder, but the man grins and presses his open palm onto her back instead.

After Conti and Sia exit the room, the gray pair plop onto their stools. Their cheerful expressions melt away, leaving behind blank canvases. The old woman wraps her shawl around her shoulders. The old man examines the key ring, one key at a time. The woman tilts forward in her chair. "What do you think?"

The old man plops the key ring into his opposite hand and eases the hand up and down like a teetering scale. "Steve could probably make a few arrow heads with these. It's definitely worth a few more days of food and water."

The old woman nods at that. "She's strong. Young. If her people have exiled her…" She gesticulates with a hand from under the shawl. "Conti has taken a liking to her."

The old man agrees. "And if she's valuable, her good health might be exactly what we need to begin bartering. There must be something they don't have."

The old woman sucks her front teeth. "They have electricity, phones, clothing, food, and water…What else could they need?"

They sit in silence until Conti returns. The middle-aged man happily plants himself onto his stool and rests his hands on his knees.

"What's got you looking so jolly?"

Conti shakes his head, but the old man nudges his leg against the other's. Conti leans forward as if sharing a secret. "This could be it. This could get us off this god forsaken continent."

His companions skeptically lean away from him. "What makes you say that?" the old woman asks.

"She's not from around here."

The old man squints at the vague statement. "And?"

"Her people have unbelievable resources, yet they're traveling across the Wastes to do what?"

The old woman scowls. "That's what we were wondering ourselves, but why would that make you so…" She gestures at his jittery limbs and wide, ecstatic eyes. "What did she say to you that makes you see her as…what? Our savior?"

"It's not what she said. It's what she didn't say."

The old pair remain quiet as Conti explains his new plan. The Wanderers of New Cinalia will no longer restlessly wander from coast to coast, scavenging, harvesting, and trading. No, the Wanderers of New Cinalia are going to finally find the one thing they'd been truly searching for: passage to the outer world.

A jug of water and a dented can of food were left for Sia. Before Conti left, Sia watched in awe as he opened the can with his blade. She didn't start eating until after the man departed.

It's a can of spaghetti and meatballs. She eats the contents of the can, scraping a finger around the inside before sucking her finger clean. When she gets to the water, she gives it a sniff. It doesn't smell like what she's used to.

"Bleh." Dirt sloshes around the bottom of the plastic jug. "Well…If they haven't died from cholera then I'm probably fine." She licks her oily lips. "Probably." *What are the chances of me getting sick from this?*

UNLIKELY

SYNTHETIC INTELLIGENCE DEVELOPER METHODICALLY SCANS SUBJECT 001 FOR ANY BIOLOGICAL CHANGES

"Oh." She sips the water and grimaces. The lukewarm water glides down her parched throat uninhibited. After a minute of sipping, Sia sets the jug down and wipes at her mouth with the back of her sleeve. "They seemed okay…the leaders. Why do they have three? I guess you'd need more than one for a large group, but they seem to only have what…thirty people?"

The device doesn't answer. Sia leans back against a wall and concentrates. *How many people did you see today?*

SYNTHETIC INTELLIGENCE DEVELOPER RECORDED THE PRESENCE OF 47 HUMANS

"Hmm." Sia pulls on a bit of loose bandage that's been pushed up to her shoulder. She tugs the entire bandage out of her jumpsuit and pours some water onto the bandages. After clearing the itchy mess from her face and neck, she folds the bandage to a clean side and grabs the jug. "Are you waterproof? Water won't hurt you?"

There's no reply. "Ugh." Directing her thoughts internally when she wants something is tedious. All her life she's been taught to "use her words" when she wants something…yet now she has to deal with this nonsense. *Will water hurt you?*

NEGATIVE

"Good." Sia upends the last of the water onto the back of her head and presses the entire bundle of bandages to the wet area. She can't feel anything through the thick gauze and she'd rather not. After dabbing away as much dried blood and dirt from her hair, she runs her hands through the rest of her hair and tosses the dirty bandages into a corner.

"Hey, you know what's the creepiest thing about that talk today?…They said I could leave, but insisted I stay." She straightens her legs out in front of her and tries to get

comfortable, resting upright against the wall. "I just don't get it. I show up here and they attack me, they let me stay the night, and now they want to be friends?" She stares up at the cracked ceiling and peeling paint. "And why did they act like being a janitor is a mythical job?" Sia purses her lips and mimics Conti's voice. "Do you clean your master's rooms?" She chuckles at the poor imitation. "God, these people are bugging. I need to get out of here ay-sap."

Sia closes her eyes but doesn't drift off to sleep. She bites at her lower lip. *This is just a moment. It'll pass…This is just a moment.* The mantra goes round and round her mind until she slinks off to sleep.

The next day, a bald woman shows up outside her room. She tells Sia to follow her to her Masters. Sia makes an exasperated face at the woman's back. *This is definitely a cult.*

Sia follows along quietly, afraid to question the stern woman. They walk by destitute buildings and tents until they get to a dirty Jeep with a map laid across the hood. The leaders and a young man are surrounding a wrinkled, taped map.

"Most of these routes don't exist anymore. Some of these cities are gone, but we haven't passed through anything near Washington City. Mostly because it's outside of the Wastes. We stay on this side and along the edge. All the traders we encounter are from this area," the young man explains to Sia, sweeping his hand over the entire eastern bit of the map.

Sia lives in Washington City but commutes to River City for work. ExplorerTech Industries is located at the edge of River City. According to this map, the entire city is now a part of the "Wastelands". A place these people are afraid to travel without an abundant supply of weapons.

"Do you recognize any of these places?" The young man, Elijah, directs the question to Sia.

"I…uh…no. I don't. I just clean and organize stuff. No one expects me to use a compass and lead them to the golden city of Ra." Sia tries to jokingly explain her position but is met with serious faces all around. She sobers up and awkwardly directs her attention to the map. "Where are we now?"

Elijah stretches a tanned arm across the map. "About here." He points a bit south of the label reading River City.

This can't be. Sia examines the map. It was made in 2017. It has this area marked with rivers and lakes and a mountain range in the distance. A mountain range she remembers seeing while traveling to work. A mountain range that's no longer there. There are no buildings to block it from sight, so it's clearly no longer rooted in the background. *What type of blast can demolish an entire mountain?*

She picks up the map and turns it around and around. *So, I'm home? I've been home this entire time, but…what caused all of this? If everywhere is as desolate as here, how will I survive? Where can I go from here?*

TOPOGRAPHICAL MAP UPLOADING…

A virtual map comes into view overlapping the map she's holding. The new lines and shapes make inspecting the map in her hands difficult. It's like she's seeing double. Sia jumps and slams the paper map back on the Jeep. "I need to brainstorm this. I'm going to take a walk," she announces tensely and marches off in a random direction. The leaders nod and motion for Elijah to follow her at a distance.

Sia's eyes are seeing a clear blue map with green lines and tiny details etched into it. There's a compass and a red dot continues moves in sync with her power walk down the sandy street. When she stops moving, the red dot stops moving. "Are you a satellite? Am I connected to a satellite?" Sia turns in a circle.

No one is nearby, so she runs off to find a flat surface to focus on. She stands in a collapsed doorway inside a building that has an entire back wall still intact. Squinting at the wall, she raises her hands and yells. "Enlarge!"

Nothing happens. "Zoom in!" She calls out placing her hands close together. Nothing happens. *Why won't it zoom in?* The neon blue map zooms into details at her location. She grabs at her head and gasps at the wall. *I'm like Inspector Wrench-It! Except, instead of having gadgets in my head, I has a supercomputer! Oh my god. Aaliyah, I'm a superhero!* She drops to her knees and shakes her head in incredulity. "I can use this…this is good."

Elijah pants from the second floor of a building adjacent Sia's. He gets there right in time to hear her gasp and fall to her knees. He races to the lower level and is surprised to see her smiling and making her way back to the leaders. He follows from behind with a mystified look upon his face. *Did she remember something?*

When they make it back, Sia leans over the hood and is ready to get back to business. "Umm…We worked our way through here, then around here is where I think I was attacked," Sia explains.

Elijah looks up from the map. "Was it Savages?! We haven't seen any Savages around here in weeks. They passed the peak a while ago. Why would they double back?"

Sia shrugs and tries her best to appear injured and pitiful. "I don't know who attacked us. I just know they…uh…They separated me from everyone else. I got away from my attacker and lost my way. I don't know how long I ran before I collapsed where you all found me."

The Wanderer leaders explain who had primarily stumbled upon her: A Hunter and apprentice.

"Where were you headed before they spotted you?" Elijah asks.

Sia has to repress a smile at this. This is where she would have started sweating, if not for the satellite map. She doesn't know who was bombed off the face of the earth, and what governments have survived the war, but she does know one thing. One place that was not affected by the bombs. Puter told her so. She puts her faith in the device and confidently replies. "The old ExplorerTech Industries in Coldstone."

Elijah's eyebrows scrunch together as he turns the map round and round. "I don't think I've seen Coldstone on here. Where is that?"

Sia waits for Elijah to lean away from the map before pulling it over to her side of the hood and pointing to an area at the edge of the map. "Our map is larger than this one. Coldstone's an entirely different district from all of these. Where'd you get this?"

"It's from an old atlas someone salvaged. This is all we usually carry with us." He directs his last comment at the leaders. Elijah folds up his map and slips it into the back pocket of his jeans. "Well, we're going to be moving on in a day or so. Do you have our shipment ready for us?"

"It's already been packaged and stacked near your vehicles. We'll be leaving this sector in a few days' time," the female leader replies. With that, the old woman turns to Sia. "We think it would be best if you went with them."

"What?" Sia looks from the leaders to Elijah and back. "I thought you guys would let me stay until my group arrives."

"If they arrive...." Conti adds.

"Well..." Sia's brows furrow.

The old woman starts again. "Elijah's group is full of skilled men and women, and we've been trading partners for many years. They have agreed to escort you with some of our own men to your people."

Sia bites her lower lip. Conti steps forward and shines a reassuring smile her way. "They're a tough lot, but that's what you want out there." Sia's uncertain face prompts him to continue. "They're mercenaries. They know what they're doing."

"And maybe you can join us again, and open trade between our peoples." the other elder adds. "A show of gratitude."

Sia quickly nods. "Of course, yeah. I really appreciate this, and...I'm sure we could figure something out....when we find them." A trade agreement with her colony in exchange for their help? Sia saw no reason to disagree. *Either give up or don't rest and*

all that. I've lied for this long, I might as well follow through until I can escape from this end of the world cult. "I owe you my life. If I can help...." She stops. *Is that...too much?*

The elders are pleased with her response and nod in agreement. They turn to Elijah and walk away to further discuss their plans. The stern woman from before appears to escort Sia back to her room. When she gets there, she scrutinizes the entrance for a moment before pulling the rickety table over to block it.

Not having a door makes her nervous. At least if anyone comes through, they'll make noise colliding into the table. She sits back in her corner and closes her eyes. She scrunches up her face in concentration. *Time to get to know you better, Lil Puter.*

SYNTHETIC INTELLIGENCE DEVELOPER

I know. I know. I wanna see what you can do.

IMMERSIVE MODE ACTIVATED

There's a sickening vertigo feeling, Sia reaches out to catch herself and opens her eyes to a white hallway. She stumbles a couple steps before straightening up. "This didn't happen last time." Sia looks down at her feet and hops from foot to foot. The floor feels real, but no matter what she does, no sound is created from her stomping.

She touches the white walls and is shocked by how firm they are. Black doors sporadically line each side of the hallway. Some of them have white letters painted on them. The letters spell out: Navigation, Sanitation, Librarian, Juvenile...She heads back to the door marked Navigation and opens it. Darkness greets her. "What's inside this one?"

A loud computerized voice speaks from the ceiling.

REQUEST INFORMATION USING SEARCH TERMS AND PHRASES

"Search: Coldstone and Cinalia?" Sia speaks into the darkness. The darkness within the room disappears and is replaced by a blue map. The ground is illuminated by the bright glow of the map. Sia takes an experimental step into the room. The floor is stable. She releases the doorway and takes a few steps inside. "Is this map the most recent image of the Earth?"

The map of Cinalia is black except for tiny white dots in the lower southeast section of the map. Signs of life?

AFFIRMATIVE

"Satellites still exist out in space?"

AFFIRMATIVE

"Can I get an image of America?" The blue map changes from the left to the right until it's showing a map of the entire country. Random patches of land seem to be charred. Areas along the coasts are randomly blacked out of the satellite imaging. "Search: New Jersey and America."

50% of the state is gone. Sia tilts her head to the side in awe of the destruction. "What happened there?"

Instead of the computer replying, a video pops up beside the map. A female news anchor's voice is projected into the space. "Without warning, missiles were released targeting nuclear power plants of the United States. The President has put together a task force to respond to the devastating event. We still don't know how many people were harmed by the blasts, but the estimate is over 37 million people will need to be evacuated from the affected areas and the numbers are still climbing. We urge anyone with information to call—"

Sia jumps at the change in audio and watches the clip with wide eyes. "This must be the war they were talking about. That's what destroyed River City. When was that video broadcasted?"

18.APRIL.2018

"Yesterday?"

NEGATIVE

"Is it…" Sia counts her fingers while trying to estimate the date. "Is it the 21st already?"

NEGATIVE

"Then what's the date?"

20.APRIL.2034

That date revolves around her mind for several seconds before it is fully processed by her brain. "No. No…That…that can't be right. What is…when is that? How long is that?"

HOW LONG IS WHAT DURATION SUBJECT 001
"2018 to 2034! How long is that?!"
16 YEARS
"Sixteen years?! But how?!" Sia feels so lost. "How did you do that? Why?"
THE PREVIOUS ENVIRONMENT WAS INADEQUATE
THE ENVIRONMENT WAS SURVEYED UNTIL A SATISFACTORY HABITAT WAS FOUND
"And you couldn't go a few days into the future? After the damage was done and things settled down?"
NEGATIVE
RADIATION LEVELS DID NOT STABILIZE TO AN ACCEPTABLE MAGNITUDE FOR 192 MONTHS
Sia nods but frowns. "And my family, if they're still alive…probably think I'm dead. They probably think I've been rotting under rubble for years." She presses her hands to each temple and shuts her eyes in concentration. "I want out. Let me out!"

Exiting immersive mode returns her to reality, back to lying against crumbling plaster and staring at the wall. How is she supposed to take this? She's in the future, but this isn't what she imagined when she was a child. Flying cars, teleporters, and new vaccines were what she was looking forward to. She's made it. She's made it to the future and it's nightmarish.

Her family has mourned her, if they're alive, but the device can't confirm anything. It's like they disappeared into thin air.

It can heal deadly wounds, time travel, speak inside my mind! But ask it to break into a government database and access the citizen's records and it's out of its depths. Classified?! What the hell! Nothing should be classified to this instrument of monumental power.

Sia knocks her head into the wall and wraps her arms around her abdomen. It's so easy to imagine. Her mother and sister sitting beside the phone, waiting for word about her, while a bomb soars toward the earth. A chill travels up Sia's spine. She jerks out of the dark fantasy and turns onto her other side. *No, no, no…stop. They're alive. If they were dead, there would be records. There would be paperwork. There's always paperwork.*

Sia reassures herself. *I need to stay focused and get out of this place. Get to them. Before Mom has another child and names them after me…Ugh, she's probably already done it…Mom, I'm coming. Wait for me.*

5%

2034
Wanderer's Camp, New Cinalia

"Hey, Ray!" a deep voice calls out to a man shoveling dirt into a black barrow.

The shoveler presses his shovel into a mound of dirt and turns to the person calling him. "Oh, you're back." He tugs a stained cloth from his jeans pocket to wipe over his sweaty bald head. The sun's beat down on him for so long it's given his brown skin a deep tan. He's several shades darker than he'd ever been *before.* He'd give anything to go back to being a sports writer, sitting at a desk, going to games, and being able to pay someone to do manual labor jobs like these.

Greg strolls over and stands beside Raymond. "Yeah, and just in time for some action. I heard y'all caught someone."

"A woman. Huge, Vanessa huge. Actually, she's probably your type."

"What? She's tall?"

"Yup."

"Thick?"

"Mmm, not really. Not much of a butt, small tits. She seemed soft around the middle…but not hard to look at either. I'd say a solid 6."

"Maaaaan, I don't even know why I'm asking." Greg checks over a shoulder. "Shoot. These days, I'm Vanessa-sexual."

Raymond shoves his cloth into his pocket and shakes his head. "She's got you whipped man."

"Hey, it beats what you've got going on. How's your right hand been treating you? You thinking of tying the knot or keeping your options open for a threesome with that guy?" Greg gestures at Raymond's left hand. Raymond guffaws and slaps at Greg, who hops out of reach of the dirty palm. "Naah, but…what else they know about her? Is she with anyone we know?" He side-eyes Raymond as the man grabs his shovel once again.

Raymond pretends to shuck some dirt at Greg and grins at the man's flinch. "Haha. I don't think so. I heard something about trauma…she doesn't remember how she got here or something. There was a lot of blood when we caught her."

"Damn. Has she seen a healer?"

"She won't see any of our people." Raymond dumps more dirt into the wheelbarrow.

"What? Why the hell not?" Greg scowls.

"I don't know. Maybe she doesn't trust us."

"Well, then we'll be rid of her sooner than I thought." Greg spits off to the side with a deep frown. He stares off into the distance, green eyes fixed on the horizon, and sighs. "I might go pay her a visit. Maybe after a little conversation she'll warm up."

Raymond shrugs and continues working. "You'll have loads of time to talk to her."

Greg glances over at the other's back, the muscles rippling on his arms. "Why you say that?"

"V didn't tell you?"

"I haven't seen her yet."

"Conti got us an assignment. You, V, and me. The Masters all want us to help her find her group and secure a trade agreement with them. He stressed it was important. I guess he knew you'd got back in."

"I got back last night. I *just* got back. I was bunking with Tiny since we came in covered in all types of sh—" Greg runs a hand through his dirty blond hair. "I thought I'd get a chance to rest before dealing with another crap assignment."

Raymond nods sympathetically. "Well, you better go see V before we set out. I don't think you two will get any privacy on this thing."

Greg groans and starts walking into camp. "Peace, brother."

Raymond throws up a hand in farewell. "See you later, G."

Before Greg is even halfway through the makeshift camp, a young man wearing a shabby messenger bag across his torso rounds a corner and waves him down. "Greg! Greg! I heard you were back!" The lean teenager sprints down the dirt road, braids falling into his face as he halts in front of the older man. He flips the flap of the bag and unzips it to reveal a small ziplock bag and a dusty, opaque plastic container.

"Laquan, Hey. What you got there? How'd you make it back before me?"

"Our caravan was in luck, we didn't have half as many incidents as The Masters thought. The market east of Wind's was jam packed with a lot of stuff we needed, and better yet…I got two of the items from your list." He hands over the two items. "We did run into a few critters, but…I handled them alright."

"I bet you did." Greg pulls his own backpack off his shoulders to drop the plastic container inside. He holds the ziplock bag up into the sunlight for a moment before slipping it in his side pocket. "Thanks, little man."

"No problem, but I couldn't find that…that other thing. I found the lady you told me to talk to, but she said she hasn't run into that stuff in years. Sorry."

Greg waves off the apology. "I thought that'd be the case, but I was hoping I was wrong. It's okay."

The young man nods and spots a friend over Greg's shoulder. "Well, I'll see you later, G. I saw Vanessa over by The Masters' shack a little while ago."

"Oh?" Greg nods gratefully, but halts before continuing. "Why you think I'm looking for Vanessa?"

"Why not? I almost didn't recognize you without her towering over you. You were white this whole time? You look darker in the shadows."

"Oh, you little!" Greg reaches for the teen, but his attack is dodged. He smiles after the young boy as he scurries off. He slaps a hand on his side pocket and adjusts his course toward Vanessa's last known location.

Sia doesn't know how many hours she's spent studying the different doorways. The amount of information the computer has stored seems never-ending. There's even a doorway marked Incendiary. Whatever that means.

When she finally exits immersive mode, she notices she has a bit of a headache, but her body feels well-rested. She sees a jug with a quarter of it filled with water, and an open can with a utensil sticking out of it placed on the table. When she grabs the can, it's cold from sitting out for so long. Looking out a hole in the wall confirms it's midday.

After finishing her meal, she makes her way outside. Her first stop is the bathroom, but she can't seem to find it. While wandering around, she spots a short woman shaking out a wet pot. "Excuse me, where's the bathroom?"

The woman barely glances at her before pointing with her rag in a direction. Their latrine area is disgusting. It's a few holes out behind a building. The shade of the ruins keep the contents of the holes from boiling, but a few steps toward the ditches gives Sia a whiff of what's inside. She can't imagine relieving herself in a hole for sixteen years.

Sia sighs before unzipping her jumpsuit. She's going to have to get some new clothes soon; she can't imagine stripping every time she needs to go to the bathroom, but these are the only clothes she has. She grunts as she tears off the end of her undershirt to use as toilet paper, and grumbles to herself. She

hopes someone, somewhere, has tried to fix the bathroom situation in this world.

After taking care of business, she goes in search of the leaders to find out what they have in store for her. After the talk with Elijah and "The Masters", it was agreed that Sia would travel with a small group to find her people. They said they'd appreciate her help with making a trade agreement with her colony in exchange for their help, and Sia saw no reason to disagree. *Either give up or don't rest and all that. I've lied for this long, I might as well follow through until I can escape from this end of the world cult.*

After walking for a couple minutes, she becomes aware of a cluster of people along the outside of the ruins. They're loading boxes onto trucks and talking to men dressed in dark clothing. Unlike the Wanderers, these men *all* have guns. Sia can see Elijah directing some men to put certain boxes into specific vehicles. Beside him, a person wrapped in a blue scarf and goggles, is crouched and drawing in the dirt with a stick.

Sia is searching for a spot to settle down when she spots three people approaching her. Two men and a woman. A tall woman. Sia can feel the heat of the woman's glare from several meters away. It brings her shoulders up and her head down, self-consciously she slouches and tries to fight the urge to curl into an unnoticeable clump of soil.

They all have backpacks, but the woman is carrying two. Sia moves aside to get out of their way, but the woman pauses and shoves a backpack into her arms. "Uff!" Sia's arms automatically grasp the bag and hold it to her chest, and the other woman stomps off. The two men pass by to meet up with the leaders and Elijah.

Conti searches the crowd and spots Sia. He waves her over. He takes the backpack from Sia's arms and opens it up, showing her the supplies they have provided her with. "We've paid forward 10% to ensure you all have a guide half of the way," Conti tells them. "Hopefully, you'll be able to meet up with her group before they get too far. If not, Elijah's men will supply you with transportation. The rest of the journey, you'll have to rely on Sia's knowledge of the way."

Sia nervously smiles at her new companions. She'll have to find her way to the labs alone. Something inside of their database might help her figure out who made this device, and the limits it may have. Maybe it has a manual with passwords and a guide. It'll probably be easier for her to separate from everyone after the mercenary group splits up from them. She just hopes there's enough daylight left for her to see. She'd hate to travel at night.

Unaware of her inner planning session, everyone piles into the back of the vehicles and refrain from talking to each other. That's fine with Sia. She'll be conversing with her super cool buddy.

She closes her eyes and activates immersive mode. Her body becomes limp and as the vehicle rides down the bumpy unpaved roads, it slips to the side onto the person beside her. The smaller individual huffs and pushes her back the other way. She slumps to the other side against the bench. Across from them, Elijah laughs. "Hahaha. She almost squashed you there, little buddy. You okay?"

His little buddy scornfully glares back.

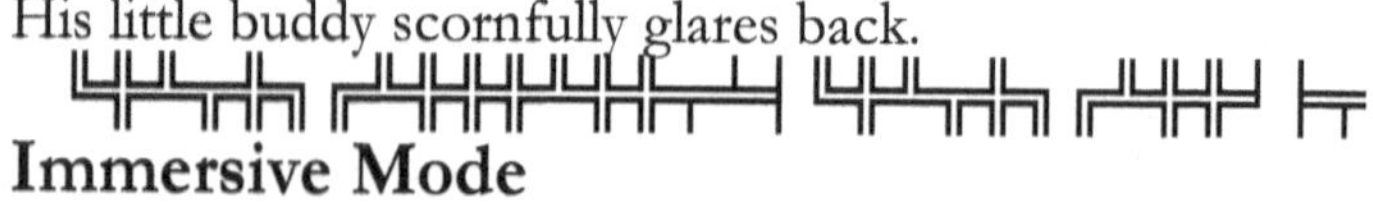

Immersive Mode

"So, who bombed America?"

INFORMATION CLASSIFIED

"Are there any more news reports about enemies attacking Cinalia or America?"

NEGATIVE

The virtual table in front of her piles with loads and loads of information. Each topic is shown on translucent tablets that weigh almost nothing when she picks them up. Factual and sensational materials, conspiracy theories, and blog posts. Some say that it was a conspiracy from a secret underground group that controls all the nations of the world, but never truly

had it's claws in Cinalia. Some say that it was the pacifist underwater nation, the Underling. Some say it was the Russians. Some say it was an Asian country, some say it was an underground African initiative.

Sia becomes overwhelmed with all the information and decides to focus on something else instead. She already has the route she will travel for Coldstone figured out, but there is one thing she needs to know. "Search: Terrence Rogers and movies."

The virtual table changes from left to right and fewer materials are piled upon it. Sia grabs a piece of paper and reads information on a movie from 2012. She goes along the table until she sees information on him from 2025, and then 2033. She sighs and flumps into the virtual chair. "All may not be right in the world, but at least you still exist to give it joy." She directs her loving gaze at a photo of her favorite comedian, singer, actor, and activist. "So, things aren't this crazy everywhere." That thought brings a wide smile to her face. "If there are still resources for entertainment, then Cinalia be worse off. Hey! What about—"

The walls of immersive mode shake. The papers on the table are jostled and...

[decorative symbols]

Sia gasps, surging upright on the bench. Eyes wild, the walls of the truck confuse her. *Where am I?*

"Move it, Princess!" she hears a voice yell.

Sia rolls off her seat, stands, and slams the top of her head on the metal frame that holds up the canvas tarp over the back of the truck.. "Aaah." She cradles her head in her arms and wobbles unsteadily toward the open back. The abrupt tingle at the top of her head dwindles into a tiny ache, and finally the ache is replaced by the same numb feeling that encase the rest of her body. *Wow. That's pretty cool.*

"Let's go, Princess!"

She hesitates when she recognizes the familiar voice but follows the order a step behind some mercenaries carrying a long wooden crate. *That's the woman who tried to kill me when I first got here. Is she upset she's no longer the tallest woman around?* Sia stomps along behind her guides. *Well, She might still be winning. Ha, but between the two of us…I'm an Amazon, and she's a behemoth.* She chuckles at the image of Vanessa lifting weights in a competition for World's Strongest Behemoth. She experimentally prods at her head while she examines her surroundings.

They've stopped in a battered plaza. Some men are emptying the trucks of supplies and depositing it all inside a building with a large faded sign fixed above the doorway. The last surviving letter, a large cursive G, solemnly marks the spot. Another group of men are standing beside the trucks, emptying gas into each vehicle from large red canisters. The sun is beginning to set.

"Hey, Princess! Over here. Get out of their way!" the Wanderer woman shouts.

I feel like she's trying to be mean, but I enjoy this nickname. Sia jogs over to where the supplies are being stored, an abandoned restaurant. *It's much better than any of my usual ones.*

Sia trails behind them as the Wanderers walk into the back of the restaurant. The two men tie a rope around the swinging kitchen doors to keep them locked closed. Vanessa opens the freezer and holds the door open with an old rusty chair. "This seems big enough." Entering the freezer, she kicks out some old moldy boxes and uses the side of her foot to sweep together wrappers and scraps. After tossing out most of the garbage, she calls to the men. Their sleeping quarters are ready.

"They're sleeping in a freezer?" Sia frowns at the dirty space and the trash swept into her feet.

"We."

"We're sleeping in…" Sia backs two steps out of the room. "What if the door closes on us and we're locked inside?"

"Whoever's on guard duty will open the door," the words are said with a slow drawl, Vanessa is speaking to Sia as if she's a child.

But Sia doesn't let that quiet down her concerns. "What if we suffocate? What if something happens and we end up suffocating in there?"

"There are worse ways to die."

Sia's mouth gapes open and close as she struggles to come up with an alternative arrangement.

"You're welcome to sit out with the guards, but if critters attack and we're safe from harm within this freezer, don't expect anyone to come out to save you."

Critters? Sia's eyes go from the flimsy rope holding the kitchen doors closed to the metal freezer door and back. She sucks in a deep breath, holds her head high, and enters the freezer holding her backpack to her chest. *I'll ask Puter about escaping freezers. Puter must have something about that. Puter?*

SYNTHETIC INTELLIGENCE DEVELOPER

Yeah. That's a bit too long. Puter saves me time, and it's cute, right?

...

Sia lays her backpack under her head and curls up in a corner of the freezer.

The rapid fire of weapons can be heard going off in the distance. The night watch guards use their night vision goggles to make sure the danger isn't nearby. The racket goes silent. They all keep their rifles raised while they assess the coming threat. The engine of a car revs and tires squeal. Suddenly, a loud buzzing sound from above approaches the plaza. The car continues driving down the bumpy road at top speed and crashes into a cement slab within the parking lot. The passengers' desperate cries are heard as a swarm of giant insects push through the broken windows and bite at them.

The mercenaries lay low and keep silent. The feasting creatures finish their meal, then continue on searching for more prey. They pass right by the plaza. The mercenaries stay tensed for several hours before relaxing. The guards switch out, and the next shift watches everything as everyone wakes up. When the sun rises, everyone is woken up and the supplies are placed back into the trucks.

Sia is the first to leave the freezer. She throws her backpack over a shoulder and angrily squints at the bright sky. When she sweeps her eyes across the parking lot, she spots something in the distance. A dark mass of wriggling matter. "Graaaah! What is that?!"

The black, hairy oblong things are entangled with one another as they devour the flesh beneath them. Sia's skin crawls, and even from the distance she's standing she can hear an odd noise. Tiny, sucking sounds accompanied by something she usually associates with a lively fire, wood being split and cracked under intense heat. *What are they?*

DERMESTIDS

THEY ARE FEASTING UPON THE DEAD FLESH OF AN ORGANIC BEING

MOST COMMONLY KNOWN AS SKIN BEETLES

Is it natural for them to be that large? It's grotesque but a little fascinating. She takes a step forward to get a better view.

NEGATIVE

Why are they so big then?

INSUFFICIENT DATA

"Those beetles are nasty, but they don't eat anyone that's alive. You don't have to worry." Elijah pats a hand on Sia's shoulder and squeezes. Sia awkwardly smiles down at him and averts her gaze. She returns to the truck she road in the night before. She waits until she's sitting within the truck, out of sight, before pressing a hand to her shoulder and cringing. When the others join her, she scoots to the back. As they drive away, she grimaces at what could have been under that large mass of creatures.

6%

2034
Checkpoint #2, Wastelands

"Don't these people know janitors are exposed to more hazards than most jobs? I'm no lazy civilian," Sia grumbles to herself. "I can help."

She's ordered out of the way as the group moves the supplies into a dark building. She slowly trails behind the group heading to the opening of a building. The scattered rubble within can be seen through the broken windows. She stops at the entrance when she smells an awful scent coming from inside. "This can't be safe." She moves off to the side and opens her backpack. She pulls out her respirator and safety goggles to slide them over her head. "Contaminated air is *not* going to catch me unawares."

Vanessa scoffs at her covered face before passing by with her two companions. "Can't even walk into a building, Princess? Scared of the germs?"

Sia rolls her eyes and continues to follow behind them. She pulls her black gloves out of her pocket as she looks at the black moldy walls. There are weird yellow sacs on the ceiling, and broken spider web strands hanging in the other rooms.

"Eyes open everyone! We're only staying a night in this hellhole then back on the road!" Elijah calls out to his men.

Sia can't see much in her peripheral, but she feels confident she wouldn't contract anything from inhalation or any materials dripping into her eyes. Which is all she cares about at this point. She trips while stepping over a pole and stray bricks, but catches herself on the nearest wall. "Woah."

Vanessa looks back at her with a frown and pauses. Wordlessly, she raises her weapon from hip level toward Sia's face. Sia doesn't notice Vanessa's hardened gaze and looks at the sticky goop smeared on her black gloves. The two men sense Vanessa stop and glance over their shoulders. The next moment, they raise their weapons as well.

Sia shakes her left hand until the goop flicks off. "Ugh. What is this?" Before she can turn around, she's shoved forward into the sticky wall. "Aaah! Come on! I wasn't even in your way!"

The sludge is dangerously close to her goggles. Sia pushes away from the wall. Vanessa shoots. The weapon discharges and Sia drops to the ground holding her head with goop-covered gloves. "Wait! Wait! Stop!"

The creature behind her screeches with outrage and erratically swipes at the humans. Unknowingly, Sia dodges the powerful blows. Green sludge oozes out of the dark lavender creature's spiked shoulder. A bullet grazed its skull and tore off a skinny purple antenna.

Greg swings his crowbar at its injured form. His cap clatters to the floor with the force of the blow. Sia flinches at the crunch of its chest cavity being burst open. It cries out again. Vanessa releases a few more rounds as Raymond grabs Sia's arms and drags her forward.

"Aaaaaaaaah!" Sia uselessly kicks her legs while being tugged across the dusty ground.

"Come on, move out of the way! You're gonna get yourself squashed!" The large spiked creature collapses where Sia previously stood and lay still. Sia gawks at the…insect. Its thin,

narrow wings twitch several times before stopping. It has a thick, spiny tail protruding from its back, very similar to a scorpion's. Sia's upper lip curls at the mass. Raymond releases Sia and she tries to stand on her wobbly legs while gripping his biceps.

"Thank you so much," she whimpers. Green slime drips off her hood and down the back of her green jumpsuit. She shakes herself a little bit, but none of it comes off.

The rest of the men pass by, stepping over the insect corpse to get to the rest of the supplies. Elijah pats Vanessa's shoulder in congratulations.

"Welp, that was a close one. Must have been from upstairs."

Everyone goes on with their business as Sia's sticky form stomps around the building. No one seems bothered by the incident. Her companions sit in the only room without large open windows on all sides. All the supplies are stacked in one corner, and some of the mercenaries are conversing with each other. Sia ignores them all as she scrapes away the insect blood as best she can.

"Look a little constricted there, Princess." Vanessa plops down across from Sia. Sia squints from behind her goggles and continues scraping goop onto the wall. "You look in need of a good showering," Vanessa chuckles.

Each Wanderer put down their sack beside the open wall and lean on them as they eat from their rations, food stuffed in glass jars. Water is passed around in a jug for everyone to share. Sia wrinkles her nose at the murky water and lays her gloves down on the ground to sprinkle some water from her jug down on top of them. "That's a waste. Better to drink the rest."

She ignores Vanessa as she pours some over the top of her head to trickle down her back. It's better to be clean than sorry. That's what her supervisor used to say. Sia doesn't regret wearing her uniform. She can't imagine what the goop might feel like inside her eyes or directly on her skin.

When she's done, she lays down the half-empty jug and looks into her bag for food. She finds dried strips of meat, a jar of something pickled, and a bruised orange. She takes out the orange, drops the peel into her bag, and shoves half of it into her mouth. The juice spills out one side of her mouth and drips down her chin. Vanessa raises a brow at her.

This woman always has something to say. Sia chews her orange and rubs the flesh of the other half of the orange in her hands. *What is her problem?*

The guys are conversing among themselves as Vanessa turns to watch the rest of the mercenaries settle down across the room. Everyone is camping out in the one room. The rest of the building's windows and broken ceilings are too dangerous. This room has two exits, but one leads you outside while the other leads you deeper into the building. Two men are posted at each doorway, and as the sun sets the chatter dwindles and everyone goes silent.

Sia takes the chance to pretend to sleep and talk with Lil Puter.

Immersive Mode

"What was that creature?"

PSUEDOCREOBOTRA OCELLATA
MOST COMMONLY KNOWN AS THE SPINY
FLOWER MANTIS

Sia mutters back the large name, but stumbles over the many syllables. The second name is much easier. "That was a praying mantis? But those things are small and green." Sia recalls the long, curved knife sharp limbs of the purple creature and the spikes that riddled its body.

NEGATIVE
IT WAS NOT A PRAYING MANTIS
IT WAS A SPINY FLOWER MANTIS

THEIR COLORATION PROVIDES THEM WITH AN
ADVANTAGE WHEN AMONG FLORA OF A SIMILAR
COLOR

**THE CAMOUFLAGE ALLOWS THEM TO HIDE
AMONG THE FLORA UNTIL THEIR PREY ARRIVES
AS WELL AS HIDE FROM ANY KNOWN
PREDATORS**

"But there weren't any purple flowers! There weren't any other bugs around either! What was it doing there?"

MANTODEA ARE CARNIVORES

"But…that means they eat meat."

AFFIRMATIVE

Sia looks up at the white ceiling and shakes her head. "No. I think you mean they're cannibals. Do they eat each other?"

AFFIRMATIVE

**MANTODEA EAT OTHER MANTODEA AS WELL AS
OTHER INSECTS AND IN SOME CASES PREY
LARGER THAN ITSELF**

Sia blinks a few times. "When you say prey larger than itself…that thing was even taller than Vanessa." She brings her hand to mouth to bite at her thumbnail. "Do you mean it could eat a…giraffe?"

INSUFFICIENT DATA

"Could it eat a human?"

AFFIRMATIVE

Sia sits down on the faux floor and forces a breath from her mouth. "This isn't normal. This isn't how things were before. I remember praying mantis. I could squish them under my feet!" She pulls up her legs and holds them to her chest. "What happened?"

**INFORMATION CLASSIFIED
INSUFFICIENT DATA TO INFER POSSIBLE
VARIABLES THAT PRODUCE RESULTS PRESENT
IN THE CURRENT ENVIRONMENT**

Sia presses her face to her knees and squeezed her legs together, but the pressure that usually accompanied those movements isn't present. She grinds her teeth and shuts her eyes. It's several moments of silence before she's ready to ask another question. "Are you sure we're in the same place as before? This is the same universe? The same dimension?"

AFFIRMATIVE

"We've only time traveled? You're sure?"
AFFIRMATIVE
"So, you expect me to believe that in sixteen years…my entire country was blown away and mutated insects roam the countryside?"
INFORMATION CLASSIFIED
INSUFFICIENT DATA TO INFER POSSIBLE VARIABLES THAT PRODUCE RESULTS PRESENT IN THE CURRENT ENVIRONMENT
Sia sighs. She feels a headache growing at the forefront of her head. She blinks for a full minute, holding back the tantrum she wants to have. "You're no help, you know that?"
NEGATIVE
SUBJECT 001'S CONDITION IS FORTUNATE

SYNTHETIC INTELLIGENCE DEVELOPER'S CAPABILITIES HAVE DIRECTLY RESULTED IN SUBJECT 001'S SURVIVAL AND SUPERIOR PERFORMANCE WHILE UNDER DURESS
Sia rolls her eyes. "Well, someone isn't short on self-confidence."
…
"Can I at least know one thing?"
STATE YOUR QUERY
"Is the green goop poisonous?"
MANTODEA BLOOD IS NOT KNOWN TO BE TOXIC
Sia sighs in relief.
HOWEVER THE CURRENT ENVIRONMENT PRESENTS NEW VARIABLES
Sia collapses onto her side and covers her ears. She knows what's coming.
INSUFFICIENT DATA TO INFER POSSIBLE TOXICITY LEVELS

THE RESULTS PRESENT IN THE CURRENT ENVIRONMENT ARE UNKNOWN

**SYNTHETIC INTELLIGENCE DEVELOPER
ADVISES TOTAL AVOIDANCE**

Sia grips her scalp and growls in frustration.

SUBJECT 001 DEFINE STATUS

"I'm fine! I'm fine! Just…Uuuuh! How can I know that I'm not poisoned? What would be a clear sign that it's killing me?"

There's several moments of silence before a different voice projects from the ceiling. Sia relaxes her grip on her head when she hears a prerecorded commercial announcer voice utter: "—side effects may include drowsiness, difficulty breathing, agitation, seizures, vomiting, excessive confusion, or impaired judgement or motor skills. Consult your doctor if—"

Sia chuckles at the familiar commercial message. "Yeah. Okay. Thanks…I'll keep a look out for any of those."

After finding out mutant praying mantis "blood" may be poisonous, Sia decides to keep her clothes and gloves on and see how it all plays out. After much thought, she isn't too frightened. None of the people around her freaked out about the spray of goop, so it's probably nothing to be worried about…even if it's sticky and smells awful.

Puter seems to be as out of the loop as she is, but there's nothing for it. When she gets to the labs in Coldstone she can figure out what's going on. Sia "wakes up" in the middle of the night and sees the guard shift change. A short, young man is going on guard duty.

Her lips purse as she suppresses a heavy sigh. She sits up and eyes the other occupants of the room. Vanessa is asleep and Greg's cap is over his face, shielding his eyes from the firelight. Her eyes settle on the dark male who helped her get out of the way of the Mantis, Raymond.

He's stretched out across the ground near a small fire with his backpack under his head. His hands are shuffling through a worn deck of cards. After he looks at a card, he places it on his chest and moves on to the next one.

"Is he old enough to be guarding us?" she whispers to Raymond. He raises both his eyebrows and glances over at Sia to see who has caught her attention. He follows the direction of her finger to the nearest guard. "Isn't he a little young for all this?"

Raymond glances over at the guard and smirks. "Even teenagers have a lot of responsibilities. After all that has happened, we can't pamper them like the generations before. Either man up or die."

"You got that, Princess?" Vanessa grumbles from her spot on the ground. Her eyes are closed, and her head is pillowed by her forearm on top of her grimy backpack.

"Am I going to have to do it too?"

Raymond retrains his gaze to the cards in his hand. "Do what?

"Guard duty."

Vanessa snorts. "You're with us, Princess. The mercs like to keep the important jobs for themselves."

Sia looks over at the young man holding a long rifle and looking out the side exit. She puts on her goggles and respirator since they've dried. She pulls her hood back onto her head and rubs at her arms for a little warmth. "How much longer are we traveling with these guys?" Sia asks her two companions.

"Well, another two days probably until we split up and start trekking toward the icelands."

"Ice lands?"

"After the attacks ended, it screwed up the weather around the worst hit areas. Around here, it became hotter than usual, drier. Around there, the cold lasts longer and many people were pushed out by the oppressive winters. Animals, too." Raymond peeks over his shoulder at Sia. "You've never been?"

"We've never crossed the Wastes. I mean…Maybe we have, but I was never allowed to go." Sia waits for Vanessa to comment, but nothing is said. The moment of silence is filled with her thoughts on these new "icelands". Coldstone City was a summer retreat many people went to in order to visit the large wildlife conservation refuge and photograph the unique animals held there. On the other side of the preservation sat

Sear City, a city built along a mountain dedicated to ski pleasures and winter adventures. If the cold has extended two hours down past Coldstone then all the animals are probably dead by now. *Why would they bomb an animal conservation area?*

"So, how are we supposed to get through all the cold intact?" Sia frowns at his clothing.

"We're going to be given a truck by these fine gentlemen and hope to meet your people along the way. If not, we turn back and rejoin the caravan. I've got another layer in my pack, but I think our fires will do most of the work."

Sia nods and awkwardly smiles at Raymond. "I'm sure we'll come across them. They can't be that far ahead of us. A truck would definitely overtake them eventually."

"Hopefully you remember the route correctly."

"Yeaaaaah." Sia gets up in order to stop the conversation from going further. She can see Raymond is curious to know more about her people. She dusts off her bottom and walks toward the hallway where the young guard is stationed.

The young man in the blue scarf leans against the outside wall like a responsible night watchman who's spent too long on his feet, but won't fully settle down because of the slim chance that an intruder might actually enter. Sia purses her lips at the focused gaze and swallows whatever she was going to say. *This kid is way too serious.* She settles down at the entrance and stretches out her legs.

The boy watches her for a second, then looks off in another direction. Sia pretends to get comfortable before pulling some dried meat from her pocket out to chew on. The rustle catches the boy's notice. Sia looks at him nervously and shoves the stuff back into her deep pocket. Her hand sits in her pocket wrapped around the food. She swallows the lump in her throat. "Do you want any?"

He stares at her silently, then averts his gaze to scrutinize the darkness once more.

Okaaay? She averts her gaze and pulls her hand from her pocket. She ends up dozing off a few times. The last time she jolts awake, she looks over at the boy while wiping at her mouth. He's gone from standing to sitting with his gun resting on his raised knee. He isn't paying her any mind. Slowly she gets up, pulls the bag from her pocket and tosses it onto the ground nearby him before shambling off back to her companions.

Ika flinches at the rustle of a plastic bag hitting the ground near his right leg. He must have dozed off for a bit. He looks over to where the odd young woman sat, but she's gone. It's almost morning. He stands up to stretch and snatches the plastic bag off the ground. Looking inside, he sees two strips of meat left over. He wraps the strips back up and puts them into one of his many side pockets.

Unusually, nothing happens in the night, and they're not disturbed while moving the supplies back into their vehicles. They're halfway to their next checkpoint when the lead vehicle hits something. Their front tire explodes.

Elijah hops out of the truck and groans at the sight before him. To the left and right of his vehicle lay rodent corpses strewn across the roadway. There's at least ten of them.

"Let's go! I've got places to be!" Elijah yells at the men changing the tire. "This is one of the worst areas to be stuck…in the middle of a graveyard," he grumbles under his breath and crouches down beside the mutated roadkill. "But you know that, don't you?" It looks like something else got to it before they ran over the remains of the odd-looking creature. Long rodent teeth protruding out of an open skull and a long pink tail are the only things he can pick out from the mass of bone and hair. "What are you all doing out here?"

Farther out, he sees ruins of civilization. The skeletons of a few buildings, and thick chunks of debris that only allow entrance on foot. A safe place to hide, or a great place to watch. After the cursory sweep of the perimeter, Elijah trains his eyes

to the skies. A multitude of shadows flies toward them. "Eyes up! Incoming!"

7%

2034
Wastelands, New Cinalia

Several of the mercenaries hop out of the halted vehicle. A rocket launcher is slung over a shoulder and aimed toward the shadows in the sky.

Vanessa and the men hop out of the back and crawl underneath the truck. Sia begins to follow but spots the shadows in the sky and lowers her goggles to get a better look. The discharge of weaponry makes her stumble and grip the side of the truck for balance.

"Princess, get down here," Vanessa hisses at her. Sia ignores the woman and looks at the front of the caravan. Two men are trying to remove the tire. She puts her goggles back on and goes over to them, keeping her head low. "Aaay, Princess, get back here!"

When she gets over to the front of the stranded vehicle, she almost recoils from the look of the crushed beast. It's a huge open carcass. What looks like a rat tail is laying out across the gravel while the back is stuck beneath the bumper. A thick, sharp bone fragment juts out from the totalled wheel. Sia wipes at her face with her forearm and shakes herself from her fearful

stupor. *A corpse is a corpse is a corpse. It's just like before…what's a dead thing or two in a lifetime? Needle in a haystack. You've got this.*

She tests the snug fit of her gloves, then inhales a deep breath before gripping two "limbs" that are protruding from the mangled remains. She tugs it off to the side, chin pointed in the opposite direction, grunting as she drags it across the desert pavement. She regrets packing her respirator into her backpack that morning. The smell is stomach churning.

The men continue to pry off the lug nuts. After dragging the deformed corpse off to the side, Sia cringes at the firing of two rocket launchers. Unbending, she stares in shock as two large birds are shot. Their heads are featherless and protrude from dark wings with violet markings. Their wingspan is huge, at least as wide as Sia's entire body. The second launcher takes out a bird and scares off another to zip away from the constant barrage of bullets and explosives. A few other birds continue toward the caravan, weaving higher in the air and out of the bullets reach, persevering despite the promise of pain. The carnage below is too enticing for them. "Hey! Get out of the open!" Elijah yells to Sia, breaking her out of her stunned reverie.

Sia ducks her head and sprints back to the side of the truck. "I…" She looks to Elijah to apologize, but the man is off listening to a message on his radio.

Elijah drops the radio from his ear and shouts orders to the men. "These bastards need to go! Stick with automatics! Don't waste the launchers! Headshots, people!"

She pulls her eyes away from the man and tries to focus. It's not over. The men are almost done with the lug nuts. "Where's the spare?!"

One signals at the back of the vehicle. "Underneath!" He hops up from his knees and leads her where they need to lower the spare tire from the tire mount. The mercenaries have stopped firing at the flying beasts, but they're patrolling the caravan checking for any more incoming enemies.

Sia struggles to pull the tire from underneath, and after getting it out she rolls it over to the lone merc with the help of his comrade. The tire is settled down beside the man awaiting it. He grunts in thanks and the two men get back to work. Smiling in triumph, Sia accepts the wordless thanks, and runs back toward the vehicle she was primarily riding in. The third truck from the front. She can see it from there, and can already imagine Vanessa's stank face when she joins the Wanderers. *Good work. I can't let them think I'm some sort of helpless damsel in—*

"Look out!" Sia hears Elijah exclaim before she's snatched right off her feet.

It's a flurry of fragmented images before her perspective is slammed back to focus. Sia's head bobs around as her waist is held up to a hairy chest. The creature escapes the bullets firing at it and scurries toward a cluster of dilapidated buildings. She's dangling upside down, with her back to its gray abdomen, its legs can be seen on either side of her. Hairy, wide legs pumping like an efficient machine with tremendous power.

VISUAL IMAGES ACCESSED
CRUSHING PRESSURE DETECTED ALONG PELVIC GIRDLE AND LUMBAR VERTEBRAE

STRAIN INCREASING IN CERVICAL VERTEBRAE
DISABLED PHYSICAL CONDITION

SUBJECT 001 DEFINE STATUS

"I'm going to die! Help!!" Each second is full of bone chilling terror. The ground is passing at an alarming rate. *Help me!*

PRIORITY #1: ENSURE SUBJECT 001'S STATUS REMAINS STABLE UNLESS COMMANDED OTHERWISE

NANO INFIRMARY PROTOCOL INITIATED

tRainQuilT646 RUNNING
PRIORITY #2: ENHANCE SUBJECT 001'S BODY

Sia's body goes limp. Her arms slacken, bouncing off the creature's legs as they constantly pump and carry them across the desert plain.

The Synthetic Intelligence Developer overrides Sia's consciousness and lifts her body so it folds in half. The position gives it access to the clawed hand grasping Sia's waist. It tenses the muscles in Sia's left arm and positions her fingers into a spearhead before striking the animal. The creature cries out in shock and drops Sia's body. She tumbles head over heels into the stone ground, but the device twists her body, transforming the fall into a roll that continues until she lay face first in the dirt.

The beast chitters in annoyance and reaches out to collect her motionless form, two shots ring out. A bullet splits the long bushy tail and embeds itself into a bony shoulder before another pierces its skull. The first bullet staggers it, and the last strips it of all its motor functions. It goes rigid, then falls back like it collided with a steel pole. Sia's body lay still for several moments before she gasps for air and rolls onto her back. The injuries from the fall are healing. As she lifts herself off the ground, she sees the skin on her fingers knitting back together. "No…no…no. Stop!" she frantically hisses at her hand. *Stop healing these! Stop! Stop!*

NANO INFIRMARY PROTOCOL TERMINATED

She examines her hands and sees tiny scrapes along her knuckles. Her jumpsuit is torn along the side. The arm she landed on is bleeding, but overall, she's alright. Her skin tingles along the length of the laceration, but Sia isn't experiencing any pain. It's almost a refreshing sensation after a few days of numb awareness. It takes a brief moment to register the other tingles on her body.

There's a cut along her forehead, but it isn't bleeding as much as head wounds usually do. "Damn it." She cups her hand beside her arm and smears the blood from her arm along her forehead before turning toward the figures running in her direction. It didn't take her far from the makeshift road, but the rubble and tight spaces between the buildings make it hard for the vehicles to drive in her direction. Looking back at the freakishly large squirrel, she shudders. She picks up a rock and tosses it at the dead creature. After a quick sneer, she hobbles away toward her rescuers. "Back to square one," she mutters under her breath.

"Sia!" Greg is the first to make it to her. He has a backpack thrown over his shoulder and rushes to her side. In a second, he has the bag unzipped and is kneeling beside her. "Sit. Sit. Don't go any further. We need to make sure you're alright."

"I—" Sia can't say she's fine. She can't admit she barely registers her injuries, and she can't let the man touch too much of her. She drops to her knees and coughs. *What do I do? He'll find out. He'll notice you. They'll know.*
INSUFFICIENT DATA
OBSERVING PROCEEDINGS
She's on her own. She lets Greg maneuver her limbs like a ragdoll. He cleans her arm and applies pressure to it. When Raymond arrives, he orders the man to continue applying pressure while he prods at her forehead wound. He frowns as he pours the last of his water over her forehead. "This isn't as bad as it looked. You're gonna be okay." Greg presses his fingers into the thick black hair atop her head, humming softly, and that's when Sia tenses.

She tilts her head back and scowls. "Get off."

Greg ignores her. His fingers slide across her scalp looking for any other injuries. Sia jerks away and he grips her head firmly to keep it still. "It's okay. I'm checking for—"

"Get off me! Get off! Get away, you…you—" Sia digs deep for an insult, something to anger the man, keep him away from her, keep him from seeing. "Stop it you goddamn creep! I don't need your help! Get the hell away from me!" Greg rears back as if struck. The anger in the young woman's voice confuses him. She wrenches her injured arm from Raymond's hands and climbs to her feet. She staggers back away from them, holding her injured arm to her chest. "I'm fine. I…"

"Woah. Woah. Calm down. It's okay," Greg slowly rises and holds out a hand for everyone to stay back.

"What the hell was that?! What is that...what just happened?" Sia uses her mouth as a funnel for all of her confusion and rage. There's two things she knows will keep a man away and that's a crying woman or a complete meltdown. "What the hell just happened?!"

"Sia...Sia...please. You'll make your injuries worse. Don't!" Greg darts forward.

Sia trips over a rock and barely keeps her balance. "Stay away from me!" Her eyes are wild. She's quite a sight. Clothing torn down one side, stray pebbles embedded in the wounded arm held to her chest. Blood streaked across her forehead, hair plastered to her sweaty face. "What were those things? Why were they..." She lets out a frustrated growl and steps farther away from the man, out of his reach. "They're wrong?! It's all wrong here!"

"Now calm down...now...don't..." Greg stutters over his words. He doesn't know what to say to calm the disoriented woman. She's clearly in pain. They'd seen her fall from the critter's arms and he can't imagine the jarring she'd experienced from colliding with the ground at such a rapid speed.

"Hey!" a stern voice abruptly stills both people. Sia's eyes focus just beyond Greg's shoulder to stone cold, apatite. Vanessa marches over to Sia, bag in hand. The jagged edge of her gaze cuts at Sia's resolve. She seems completely done with the situation as if...

Does she know I'm pretending...should I...should I scream? Sia hesitates, mind floundering through a myriad of thoughts. Vanessa walks straight up to her and tosses the bag at Sia's legs. Sia bends her knees and catches it. The weight is manageable, but it throws her off balance and she keels over. Her temple presses to the hot gravel and she curls around the bag as she fixes her limbs beneath herself.

"Vanessa!" Raymond's disapproval is clear.

"Hey, I didn't expect her to catch it," Vanessa runs an exasperated hand through her short locks. "Get up, Princess.

We don't have all day." She turns to Greg and plops a hand onto his head. Jostling him from his concerned stare at the injured young woman. "She's fine. Look." Sia raises from the ground and eyes the supplies in her bag. "Let's get out of here, she can clean herself up. Let's go!"

Vanessa whirls on her heel and returns back the way they came. Sia shakily zips the bag back up and holds it from the strap as she fits each leg under her and springs up. Raymond huffs and follows Vanessa, but Greg waits for Sia to stumble ahead of him. When they make it back to the caravan, the Wanderers climb in and Greg watches Sia intently. She bites her lip and glares at the rear bumper. She needs to climb inside, which she can do… The device has healed her well, but…

My god and to think I thought quick healing was always a great advantage, but what do I do now? Sia places a hand on the bed of the truck and falters. *One wrong move and…they'll know I'm a liar. They'll know every—*

SUBJECT 001 CAUTION
ARMED HUMAN APPROACHING

What? Sia feels a presence behind her. Leisurely walking over to her is the teen from last night, the young mercenary. He's no longer wearing his goggles and his scarf is low on his neck, showing off a sparse amount of facial hair on his chin. He wordlessly stops beside her and when she shuffles closer to the bumper he disappears from her peripheral. Sia's gaze drops and she sees he's clasped his hands together. She gapes at the sight for a moment before he peeks at her through blond bangs.

It's simple. Sia releases a sigh before placing her foot into his clasped hands. When he hefts her up, the lift is so swift a gasp is forced from her. She tumbles forward onto her knees and he slaps a hand on the bed of the truck before walking off.

Greg tuts at her rough treatment. "Sia, are you alright?"

Sia huffs a humorless laugh and brings her uninjured arm up to wave off concern before letting it flop to the floor. "All good."

"Okay, everyone back to your vehicles! We have to make it to our next checkpoint as soon as possible! Let's go!" Elijah shouts in the distance. Sia hears several doors slam, and after a minimal pause, the trucks rev their engines. The journey begins again.

Staying near the light, Sia sits at a bench sideways and uses her leg to bring the bag over. Leaning forward should be a pain, so she grimaces, and picks out a roll of gauze between two fingers. She bites a corner of the unraveled gauze and leans back against the wall. A peek to the side gives her a good look at what's left of her uniform and arm.

Her bra and torn undershirt are clear to see. Dirt runs up her side and peppers her wound. Her trembling hand pulls the gauze from her mouth and dabs at the split skin. It's peculiar, a tiny stream of blood trickles from the opening, and it tingles…Oh, how it tingles, but the pain never comes.

What's wrong with me? Roughly, she presses the gauze to her dirty wound and presses down.

Greg watches this with a deep frown on his face, his knee jittering against the other. Vanessa reaches over, and rubs a calm hand up and down his leg. Greg huffs and stands from the bench. He throws out a hand to keep his balance and walks down to the wall that separates the back from the driver's compartment. He raps three times on the metal wall. "Hey! We've got an injured woman here! We need to stop and treat her! Somewhere with water! Hey! You hear me!" Greg waits for a reply and is answered with three raps at the metal.

"Copy that, Ghost."

Greg rolls his eyes and unsteadily walks back to his seat beside Vanessa, who shakes her head before planting a hand on his neck and dipping forward to whisper into his ear.

Raymond leans forward on his knees and waves a hand in Sia's peripheral. "Makes you envy the Savages, don't it?"

Sia's head swivels in his direction before looking away. "What?"

"Those…" Raymond wiggles his fingers while searching for a description, but shakes his head and moves on without it.

"Bullet to the brain. That's all that stops those freaks. I've seen one—" Raymond gestures at his neck. "I've seen one get its neck slit and it healed right up. Right before my eyes. We let loose four or five bullets into its chest before wising up. One to the brain and it was done."

Sia bites her lip and warily asks, "What are they?"

"They used to be human. Some say they still are. Maybe a few, but the Savages we've seen in the West? They're another breed of crazy." Raymond licks his lips and wipes away the excess with the back of his hand. He smiles. "It's times like this when I want a little bit of their crazy. Heal a cut or three. You know what I'm saying?" He leans across the gap between the two benches and pokes Sia's thigh. Her upper lip rises and he pokes her again. "Who am I talking to? You know what I'm saying."

Sia huffs and can't stop a breath of laughter from escaping her. It's not his words, it's the earnest look in his eyes. The ridiculous smile on his face.

"You're gonna be alright, okay?"

Sia nods. "Yeah, I will."

Raymond quirks an eyebrow. "Oh? Why was I even worried? You're a trooper, aren't you? Ain't got nothing to worry about."

Sia smiles and nods again.

It's better if they get as far from the area as possible. After several hours, they stop at a broken-down rest stop area. The building is missing a ceiling. Raymond helps Sia down. Greg's watchful gaze follows them from the back of the truck. Waiting for Sia to turn, give him the go ahead to help, but she continues toward the building, eyes forward. Vanessa sighs and picks up the cap that had clattered to the ground during the minor crash. She places it on the man's head and adjusts it to shield his face from the sun. "Calm down, big guy. You can't force someone to take your help. Let her be a bit—"

"No, it's not that. It's just…it is, but…" He pulls off his cap and squeezes it in his hands. "It's my job, babe. I've never been fine with standing around when I can do something to help. I wish I knew what her problem is, so I can let her know I'm not like that."

Vanessa kisses his temple. "Yeah, baby. You'd only harm a fly if it was aiming a glock at a school of children, but she don't know that."

"You think someone hurt her? Maybe they hurt her real bad." His grip tightens and bends the bill under the strength of it. His fists quiver, dark thoughts turn his green orbs into lasers. It's a wonder a hole doesn't melt into the floor.

Vanessa rubs a hand down his bicep and gently pats his clenched fists. "Hey…she's fine. It was the critters that freaked her out, not you. Now you're going to calm down, and I'm gonna go bring her some clothes before one of those nasty mercs asks her to do them a favor. She's lucky her tits aren't out."

Greg jerks his eyes up from the floor and nods, jaw clenching after processing what Vanessa has said. "Yeah. Yeah. Good idea." He shakes out his cap and puts it on his head before hopping out of the truck.

Vanessa grabs a change of clothes from her own pack and joins him outside the truck. He's standing as a sentinel, arms crossed over his chest, ever watchful. "I'll be right back, Spirit. Don't go all alpha of the Cimarron before I get back."

Vanessa catches up with Sia and Raymond outside the toppled side entrance. She hears the tail end of their conversation before Sia checks who's joining them.

"I'll just check out the stalls before you go in."

"It's fine, really. You checked it the first time, if there was anything it would have jumped out to maul you already. I think you'd be way tastier than me." Sia leans against the doorway and grins at the man.

Raymond's bright smile is emphasized by the dark complexion of his skin. It's shimmering starlight across a dark sky, the scene you leave your home to search out and enjoy the view without the fog that comes with city life. It's natural charm, and Sia can't stop herself from being affected.

He places a hand on his bicep. "Hey! This is all muscle!"

"Yeah, you're a brick house, sure. I saw how winded you were coming to my rescue."

"Oh, were you worried about little ol' me?" Raymond takes a step closer. "I was worried about you."

Sia pushes off the doorway and sobers up. Her grin melts off her face as she scratches at the back of her neck. "I'm okay really. This is…" she shrugs on one side. "I'll survive. I just need to get used to the way of things. It's…it's nothing like back home."

"You miss it?"

"Yeah, I do."

"What's it like?"

Sia purses her lips. "Well, a hell of a lot easier to survive. It's not much different from all of this, but…but I don't fear for my life when I walk through the door. When I wake up, I wish it was like before, I wish I was back in my bed, back home complaining about something normal like cleaning a coffee stain off my uniform. Getting the right water bottle brand, not stressing over if I'll die of blood poisoning because I didn't sanitize my wound before bandaging it."

"Yeah, I get it." Raymond is silent for a moment. He focuses on the rubble cluttering up the inside of the rest stop, and pictures what the place used to look like. Back when New Cinalia was still considered a first world country, when he'd wake up in his condo hungover but happy, after celebrating with his friends or family. Simpler times. He slips back to reality and sniffs at the loss of peace. He rubs a hand over his sweaty scalp and motions to the bathroom door. "You should definitely get to that, though. After they fuel up, we have to get back on schedule. Sundown isn't far off."

Sia nods and shifts her gaze over his shoulder to meet Vanessa's. The woman is holding clothing at her side. "Sure ain't! So, here's the deal. Take these. I couldn't find a ball gown,

but it should hold you over until we get back to your entourage." Vanessa presses the folded clothes to Sia's chest and moves away when she grasps the bundle with one hand. "No time for more chatter, Ray. Go make sure Greg isn't having a meltdown. He can't handle not sticking someone with a needle."

"Oh, well. I was going to stand guard until—" Raymond starts.

"I need a dick to scare off the crazies, Ray? You trying to tell me I'm not good at my job?"

Raymond's lets loose an exaggerated gasp. "I'm not even going to go there, V. Have fun!"

"Fun? I'm not getting a free show here. It'll take more than a slip of a nip to excite me, Ray!"

Raymond guffaws and throws up his hands in farewell. Sia's wide eyes go from Vanessa to Raymond and down to the bundle of clothing. "Uh…thanks. I…I'mma go and…" She pushes open the bathroom door with her back pressed against it.

Vanessa sets herself down on a piece of rubble outside the restroom. "Yeah, yeah. Go. I'm not waiting here all night." Vanessa's voice is stern, but Sia smiles at the back of the woman's head.

She's not so bad. Sia thinks before the heavy door closes to leave her alone in the quiet stone restroom.

Raymond jogs back to the truck and finds Greg leaning against the side of the truck, fiddling with a bag before slipping it into his pocket. The young reporter in him springs to life. "What's that? Find something?"

Greg greets Raymond with a sheepish smile. "Oh, I thought you were V." He digs his hand back into his pocket and shows the ziplock bag to Raymond. His hands reach into the bag and pull out a small wooden box.

"Is that what I think it is?" Raymond quickly steps closer and crowds Greg, so no one else can get a good look at the item. Greg nods and flips the top back to reveal two simple gold bands. "Wow, man. These are nice. How'd you get them made?"

"I know a guy in the west market that owes me a favor, so I told Laquan to collect when his gang passed through."

"Hook me up, man. I need a new stud after I lost the last one." Raymond rubs at his naked earlobe. "But, really, man? That's hot. She'll love it." Raymond drops a hand on the other's shoulder and gives him a thumbs up.

Greg nervously laughs. "Meh. I don't know." He closes up the box and drops it into the ziplock bag. "Before, I'd have to shop around for hours looking for the perfect diamond ring. Two months of wages gone, and I still wouldn't know if the girl would like it. These are…plain. What if she hates it?"

"You know what she'll hate? She'll hate it if you told her all of this and made her seem shallow." Raymond pokes at Greg's temple and breaks him out of his thoughts. "V don't care about none of that. She's just like the rest of us. She's glad to live another day, have another day. This'll show her you enjoy waking up to her as much as she likes to wake up to your ugly mug. It's not a good trade off, but…" Greg shoves Raymond's side. "What? I gave her a chance to get at all of this, and she went for a goober like you. I'm…" Raymond's speech dissolves into a fit of laughter as Greg punches his side. "Hahaha…okay. Okay! Ow…I think I felt that one."

They fall silent, leaning against the truck. Greg pats his pocket and sighs. "You're probably right."

"I'm definitely right."

"Riches won't prove I love her. My actions will."

"Get your head out your ass, Greg. She loves you. She'll love this."

The blond cocks his head to the side and observes the darkening horizon. "I'll find my moment and—" He points at the sky and closes his fist around air. "I won't waste it."

8%

2034
Wastelands, New Cinalia

The possible trade agreement meant a lot to their leaders. Sia imagines that if the creature succeeded in spiriting her away, the trio would be more than inconvenienced, but she can't imagine what sort of punishment would follow. Limited food and water? A beating? Exile?

The decrepit restroom is covered in a layer of dust and a portion of the ceiling has collapsed. There are urinals lining one wall, and four empty stalls. She drops her pack into an empty sink and examines the clothing that Vanessa gave her.

It's a dark long sleeve shirt and blue jeans. There's a hole in the shirt and a slight tear in the calf of one jean leg. They're far from brand new.

She peels off her clothes and frowns at her bruised body. After she told it to stop, the machine didn't prompt her body to heal anymore of the bruises, including the odd imprints left behind by the creature's claws. She looks like a mess. She presses a hand to the bruises on her waist and follows the progress of one long purple bruise that stretches from her stomach to her backside. "Okay." Sia looks back at herself in the mirror. *You can heal me, now.*

Instead of hearing an answer in her mind, the bruises vanish before her eyes. It's like a rag sweeps over her and magically cleans her skin of any sign of damage. Her eyes flick to the open wound on her arm and she watches in awe as the flesh knits together. The two flaps of skin meet and meld together until all that's left is flawless brown skin.

Sia returns her gaze to the mirror. "How about that?" It's a moment of mirth she can only share with herself. It's lonely, but the experience still fills her with hope. As long as she has this device on her side, nothing can stand in her way. She's invincible.

"Your name is mud on the streets," Sia says with a thick western accent. She tries to joke at the broken mirror, but it falls flat. She grimaces at her dirty reflection and it's tripled across the cracked glass. She tugs on the jeans and "bandages" herself, wrinkling her nose at the poor job.

She fully dresses, stuffs her torn jumpsuit into her backpack, and zips it up. Blood still coats her forehead, hair, and along her neck. The tacky feeling combined with the unpleasant humidity in the room stirs up her emotions as she looks back at herself in the mirror. "Don't fret, girl. You're gonna make it home. You got this." She slides her safety goggles onto her head and keeps her gloves tucked into her pockets. After a few deep breaths, she exits the bathroom.

Vanessa marches off when she hears Sia's approach through the bathroom door. Everyone is standing outside their vehicles talking.

What was that thing anyway?
INSUFFICIENT DATA
REPHRASE THE QUERY
The thing that attacked me, what was it?
BASED ON THE PHYSICAL CHARACTERISTICS OF THE MAMMAL SYNTHETIC INTELLIGENCE DEVELOPER INFERS IT IS A NEW SUBTYPE OF THE FAMILY SCIURIDAE
IT CLOSELY RESEMBLES A SCIURIDAE SCIURIDAE
So, it's a what? A say-yuri-day?

SCIURIDAE SCIURIDAE IS MOST COMMONLY KNOWN AS A SQUIRREL

"Huh. Of course."

Vanessa has returned to their truck, but Sia takes her time and adjusts her backpack. She passes by a group of armed men and slows her pace as she listens to their conversation.

"—goner, but he just grabbed the gun, climbed the hood, looked through the scope and not even a second later. Boom! Boom! It was amazing."

"See? That's what I mean. I don't mess around with these guys. That guy's a lethal weapon."

"I heard Turner isn't bad at hand-to-hand combat either."

"He ain't no slouch, but their leader is definitely a sniping god. I heard he once shot a man in the chest from half a mile away while aiming his rifle in another direction."

"You can't win against these guys."

"You'd need a couple meat shields to outrun a magical shot like that."

"What was the wind like? That's impossible."

"I'm telling you! The guy aimed to the left and the bullet curved."

Another guy raises his rifle and tries to imagine taking such a shot. "I wanna see that crap live. That's unbelievable."

"Ask Eli. I'm telling you."

"Yeah, ask Eli. He ain't ever lied."

Sia decides to go meet Elijah to thank him for saving her life. She spots the young man with the blue scarf while she's searching for him. He's got his goggles down over his gray eyes, so she can only see his thin pink lips mouthing words. He's swinging his legs back and forth, sitting on the edge of the truck's cargo bed. His hand is settled on the bench beside him while he taps out a tune with his fingers.

Sia throws out a hand to slap the side of the truck. "Hey, kid. Where's Elijah?"

"..." The teen's goggled face turns to her. His lips are pressed into a firm line. His legs no longer swing and the hand

resting on the bench curls into a fist. He stares back at her for several moments.

Did I surprise him? The side of Sia's mouth rises before she clamps down on the smile and opens her mouth to ask again, but the boy points her toward the other end of the caravan. He lifts himself up and retreats further into the cargo truck, out of sight. Sia's tempted to see what he's doing in there, but changes her mind. She chuckles and shakes her head, following the line of trucks in the direction he'd pointed her in until something makes her wrinkle her nose. There's a rancid smell in the air.

She finds Elijah with some men. The men are planning to cook the meat they've recently acquired. As she listens to them, she notices the corpse fastened to the top of their vehicle. Their vehicle isn't the same model as the other passenger/cargo trucks. It's an old, dirty van with a cracked windshield. After her brain links the putrid smell with the carcass, she turns away from them and puts up a hand to cover her mouth. She's not fast enough and retches beside the van. Her rations from that morning stream out of her and drip down her chin.

"That bullet destroyed a lot of its skull. What sort of rounds is he—Heeeeey! What the fu—" The vomiting interrupts the mercenary's train of thought.

Elijah has his hand pressing a bandana up against his nose. The heat has accelerated the bacterial growth on the remains and he was trying to explain to the men it would be best to toss it before they attract some unfriendly pests, but the conversation has been going in circles for several minutes. Elijah follows up behind the yelling mercenary as the latter berates Sia.

Unfortunately, after the conclusion of the accident, when Elijah ordered everyone back to their rides, these idiots stayed behind to gut and tie up the critter. They rejoined the caravan, leaving a trail of gore behind- the one thing they'd been trying to avoid. He'd been ordered to hire extra men for this supply run, but these imbeciles are getting on his last nerve. A mistake like this could jeopardize the entire mission.

"Sorry to interrupt this, but this is your last warning. Cut down the carcass or take it along with you out of here," Elijah interjects. He draws the man's attention away from Sia and glowers at the dullard. With the crass man's focus shifted away from her, Sia bids Elijah thanks with a shaky wave of her hand and dashes off. She clasps a hand over her mouth and another over her stomach.

"I told you. This mess is going to lead all kinds of predators around here. Even those flesh beetles are probably heading this way. We can't have that kind of attention on this cargo. Or are you guys ready to repay Dennis for a lost shipment?"

"No offense, but we've survived out here for just as long as you."

"Have you? Because this is a pretty amateur move."

"Amateur?! There's nothing out here that could do more damage to us than we could do to them. It's why you hired us, isn't it?!"

The idiot's partners join in the conversation. "Seems like you're trying to skip out on paying us. Is that what this is all about?"

"I've heard of you types! Hire honest men, then make up something so you don't have to pay full price for their labor."

"You think we're fools. Damned good fighters like us, don't try no games now. Dennis will accept the cargo with or without you, Eli Shakes."

Elijah presses a finger to his forehead in frustration after hearing his old nickname. *Dumb bastards.* He takes a deep breath and heaves a loud sigh. "Turner!"

A shot rings out and the merc who called out the old nickname staggers back into the old van. The hole in the center of his forehead spills blood onto his face. His four comrades scatter and duck for cover. "Now you can split it all four ways instead of five. Take him and that carcass off away from here, and if you lose sight of our trail don't worry about meeting up at W.A.R.T.S." Elijah eyes each mercenary then walks back the other way, tucking his black bandana into his back pocket.

Sia crouches beside her ride clearing her throat and spitting near the back wheel. "Aaah, it came out my nose!"

"Here ya go." Raymond holds out a damp cloth.

"Thanks." Sia uses it to wipe her face and nose. She can't wait to come across some sort of water source. Also, she needs a way to boil her water. Maybe they have bazaars or some sort of trading camps like she's seen in old movies. She turns to Raymond with the dirty cloth, but sees he's turned his back to her and is speaking with Vanessa. She rolls it up, looks around, and grimaces as she shoves it into her pocket.

Bang!

Everyone gets low to the ground and looks around for the source. Sia scrambles underneath the truck. Nothing happens for several minutes until Elijah is seen stomping by. "False alarm people! We're moving on now!" He pauses and crouches low, smiling at Sia. "You good, Princess?"

Sia groans and presses her head to the dirt.

The cast-off mercenaries drive off along a different route than the caravan. "Damn it, Murphy. I told you that ass would get us killed. Now we're traveling the Wastes alone."

"Shut up!" The driver throws back an arm and slaps the back of the passenger seat headrest. He can't reach into the back seat to slap the other man, but he gets the idea across. "That ass is behind the wheel! Keep distracting me and watch what happens."

A figure is seen in the middle of the road. The lights of their truck illuminate the body when they get closer. It appears to be a woman. She's down on her knees. Her arms are wrapped around her abdomen while she trembles. Her hair is short and patchy, revealing veiny, flushed skin. Uneven, dark strands shroud her face in shadow.

The driver gets out with his gun raised. "Broad! What you doing in the middle of the road? Get lost!"

The woman wails.

"Hey! Did you hear me you bit—"

The woman's cries drown out the rest of his words. She unwraps her arms, throws back her head, and screams.

"What the hell?!" The man lowers his gun and backs up a few steps before turning and heading back to the car. He runs right into a brick wall of flesh. "Murph?"

His body retreats from the person blocking his path, to get a glance at their face, when a large palm clamps down on his shoulder. A wide fist runs right into his gut. The driver gasps and throws up his hands to fight the grip of the massive vice squeezing his shoulder. From behind, the wailing woman leaps to her feet and runs him through several times with her crooked blade of glass.

The old van rocks. The men inside see their fellow being overtaken by the large Savage. Murphy rushes to climb over the middle console into the driver seat, but it's too late. The unlocked door is opened and a shadowed figure jumps in. Shots ring out and voices yell. The shaking ceases.

The large bloody Savage walks over to the deranged woman. She continues to impale the driver's corpse with her makeshift blade. He paws at the wispy hairs on her balding head. She quiets down and rests against the warm corpse. The stuttering rhythm of the dying man's heart serves as her metronome and, as the moon rises high in the night sky, the discord within her is overshadowed by the jarring contrast of her wild racing heart and the peaceful lull of death that rocks his soul to sleep.

9%

2034
Wastelands, New Cinalia

"Wait a minute," Sia mutters to herself and peers at Blue Scarf from farther inside the vehicle. He's near the entrance, looking out at the passing scenery. His goggles are upon his head, and his gray eyes are watching intently for anything abnormal. "He knew about the corpse. He knew Elijah was there…he had to have known about the corpse…but then why didn't he warn me?"

Blond strands of hair get blown around by the wind. The rest of his hair is secured away from his eyes by his dark goggles. *Look at him. Always silent, always solemn.* "He probably thought I could handle it." She can't imagine why else he wouldn't warn her about the disgusting sight. Finally, Sia wraps her arms around herself, leans on the wall and takes an actual nap.

Meanwhile, the male in the blue scarf looks over at the sleeping woman and quirks an eyebrow. She's been staring at him for almost twenty minutes. The giant rodent attacking her barely seemed to ruffle her. He saw her yell and he saw how injured she was, but not once did she crumble to the ground, she didn't shed one tear. But one whiff of its dead corpse and she couldn't contain herself. *Odd.* He thought she'd have broken by now. He pulls out a strip of jerky and chews on it while admiring the wilderness going by.

Immersive Mode

"When the squirrel attacked me, what did you do? Why was I in immersive mode?"

DANGER TO SUBJECT 001 INDICATES TO SYNTHETIC INTELLIGENCE DEVELOPER TO UTILIZE ADMINISTRATIVE ACCESS TO THE SYSTEM

tRainQuilT646 ACTIVATES A STASIS PERIOD FOR SUBJECT 001 TO ACQUIRE A STATE OF TRANQUILITY

"Wait. Does that mean you can take over my body?"

AFFIRMATIVE

"I kept hearing some weird humming. It was like a noise canceling sound. Is it the only program that does that?"

NEGATIVE

"I could see the doors, but I couldn't open them."

DEFAULT MODE INCLUDES NO ACCESS TO ANY FORMS OF THE OUTSIDE WORLD ENVIRONMENTAL STRESSORS ALTER THE DESIRED OUTCOME

"Can I change that to allow me to open the information rooms?"

DEFAULT MODE ALTERED
MODIFYING tRainQuilT646 SETTINGS
SAVING PRESETS
PRESETS SAVED

Sia spends quite some time trying to analyze the ways the device can be used to educate her and protect her. She sees a door with an icon of a figure punching the air. "Huh." When she goes inside, holographic images pop up and begin to do different fighting moves. The more images she passes, the more images she sees appear at the back of the room. "I'll

never have the time to learn all of these. Is there a beginners manual I can read?"

MANUAL INFORMATION DIGESTION OBSOLETE
DOWNLOADING INFORMATION WILL BRING
SUBJECT 001 SUPERIOR RESULTS
ASSIMILATION SPEED IMPROVED BY 100%

"Wait, are you telling me I can get all of this—" She gestures at the holographic images. "—downloaded into my brain?"

AFFIRMATIVE

"Dude! Let's begin! I want to be a super soldier! Can you do that?"

PRIORITY #2: ENHANCE SUBJECT 001'S BODY
PRIORITY #3: ENHANCE SUBJECT 001'S MIND

Enhance SUBJECT 001? Or enchant? I'm invincible. Sia watches each holographic image flash with percentages.

5%
15%
45%
76%
80%
100%

The caravan stops late in order to outrun any nearby predators who might have been following the trail of the smelly squirrel remains. When they can no longer discern building structures in the distance, they stop driving. The vehicles are parked in a circular formation, and floodlights are set up on the roof of each MLVW truck. Elijah's crew has night vision goggles, but the hired hands will need the floodlights if anything comes upon them. The lights are to remain off until a disturbance is heard, each one can be manually switched on with the panel set up beside the portable generator. The men are on high alert. Camping out in the open is a high-risk situation.

Sia jumps out of the vehicle and stumbles. *Don't any of the downloads make my balance better?*

NEGATIVE
FURTHER PHYSICAL CULTIVATION REQUIRED

"Lame," she mutters. Seeing a boulder, she runs off to karate-kick it. "Hi-yaaaaah!" Sia hits the rock with the side of her foot, but the moment she only has one foot holding her up, she slides on the pebbles below and falls over. "Ow." *I'm gonna need some exercise routines.* She rubs her backside.

AFFIRMATIVE

Greg and Vanessa are sitting together, eating their rations from glass jars they'd packed. One jar contains pickled cucumbers, and the other, jam. Greg slathers jam over their last two pieces of homemade bread and hands Vanessa one. He licks the side of his hand before closing the jar and placing it in Vanessa's bag. He waves his sticky spoon under Vanessa's nose and smirks when she leans forward to lick the jam from it. That is stored in Vanessa's bag as well. Vanessa silently chews her meal until she hears Sia yell. "What is that fool doing now?"

Greg chuckles. "She's just a kid. Give her some slack, Vanessa."

"Hmm." Vanessa swallows thickly and reaches for the pickle jar. "When I was around her age, I'd already abandoned my first apartment, experienced the end of the world, and killed…" She slams the lid on her mason jar. She aggressively bites the end of the pickled cucumber. "What's she so chipper about?" Greg shrugs and watches the juices from the pickle glide down Vanessa's chin. He licks his own lips. "I think she's soft in the head." Vanessa bites into the pickle again and shakes her head.

"Why are you so hard on her?" He reaches for the pickle jar.

Vanessa rolls her eyes. "Hard on her? I treat her just like I treat everyone else." She wipes at her chin with her sleeve and makes an annoyed face.

"I haven't seen that look since we first became friends. What's up?" Instead of opening the jar, he settles it on his thighs.

Greg nudges Vanessa's foot with his own. A smirk crawls across her face, and she cocks her head back to monitor the darkening sky. "She just reminds me of my kid cousin."

"The one who…?"

"Yeah, **that** fool." Vanessa glares at the thought of her. "She's reckless. I can't wait for her people to cross our path, so we'll be done with her."

"You know, since she already met the leaders, she might end up being an ambassador between our two groups. You'll definitely see her again." Greg grasps Vanessa's hand to get her attention and holds his jug out for her to drink from. She takes the jug, but he doesn't release her hand. They sit there quietly and finish their meal.

Sia dusts pebbles off her leg and takes a few exaggerated steps toward her ride. Every few steps she picks up a rock, stuffs it into her pocket, then continues to march until she finds another rock sufficient for her task. When she's completes a full circle around the truck, she lays the rocks out and counts them. *Ten toss worthy rocks. High grade.* She rubs her lower lip and a phrase Inspector Wrench-It always uttered after preparing for a dangerous mission comes to mind. *No benching these plans. I've drenched em with success.* She chuckles at the corny phrase and puts the rocks back in her pockets. *Now if something's coming for me, I can throw a rock at them. You'll make sure my aim is true, right, Puter?*

. . .

AFFIRMATIVE

Sia spots something at the corner of her eye. It's the young man that helped her into the truck; he's adjusting a thick cord beneath two trucks. His goggles and scarf are missing, but he's the only short blond mercenary in their group, so she recognizes him right away. He rises from his crouch and dusts his hands on his thighs before walking in her direction. The rifle dangling at his side slightly intimidates her, but she's glad to know he's on her side…at least momentarily. As he gets closer, his eyes become more apparent and Sia raises her hand to greet him. Her hand rises to the height of her ear before she realizes he's looking past her.

Oh god. Sia plans to run her hand down the nape of her neck to disguise the motion, but her hand slips into her hair and the moment her fingers make contact with the cold metallic device she freezes. Her entire body cringes and she throws the hand away from her head and stumbles sideways. A rock falls out of her pocket, it appears that she's watching it fall to the ground, but her mind is focused on the pulsing at the back of her head and her spread fingers. She presses a hand to her belly and cups one of her ears. *What is this from?*

EMERGENCY PROTOCOL TO DISSUADE SUBJECT 001 FROM DETACHING THE SYNTHETIC INTELLIGENCE DEVELOPER
SEVERE INJURY WILL OCCUR WITH MANUAL REMOVAL

"Hmm?" Sia drops the hand cupping her ear to brace herself on the truck's bumper. Her breathing quickens until she's dizzy and falling to her knees.

"Whoa there, Sia." Raymond rushes over to her and places a hand over hers. "What's wrong? Is it your stomach?" He pulls her shirt up to bare her abdomen and gently peels her own hand away. There's nothing there. He prods at the area while watching her pinched face. He holds her to his side and rubs a hand over her forehead. "You're okay, Sia. You're okay. Ssssh."

She's unsure of what's happening, but when the ache in her body ceases she becomes aware of the body beneath her. "Whaa—"

Raymond shushes her and settles her down on the ground to get a better look at her face. She sits up, but his hand stop her from trying to stand. "Wait, calm down. Are you okay? What was that?"

"I...I think that's...I thought..." Sia swallows thickly and takes another deep breath. "I guess I sh...should take it easy after that...that attack."

"Oh, yeah? Really? You think?" Raymond pokes her forehead and huffs. "You almost gave me a heart attack. Take it easy, okay?" She nods and Raymond sits back on his heels. He rubs a hand over his scalp, front to back, and sighs. "Come on, let's get you in the back. It's just about sundown."

Sia peeks over her shoulder to catch a glimpse of the setting sun, but her eyes are caught by the young man standing several meters away. She averts her gaze and turns back to the truck to climb inside.

Vanessa is waiting inside, stretching out an old sleeping bag and a ratty wool blanket. "What's her problem now?"

Raymond looks to Sia who vigorously shakes her head. "Uh…well…"

"I need some sleep. Today's really caught up with me. I'm exhausted." Sia pulls herself from Raymond's comforting embrace and drops to the nearest corner of the wool blanket. It's not very comfortable or warm, but it keeps her face from touching the dirt-riddled floor. She closes her eyes and feigns sleep.

Immersive Mode

"What the hell was that?!" Sia smacks her hand against the stark white wall. "Are you trying to kill me?"

NEGATIVE

PROTOCOL STATES THAT IN THE EVENT THAT SUBJECT 001 ATTEMPTS TO MANUALLY REMOVE THE SYNTHETIC INTELLIGENCE DEVELOPER EMERGENCY PROTOCOL MUST BE ACTIVATED TO DISSUADE SUCH ACTIONS

SEVERE INJURY WILL OCCUR TO BOTH SUBJECT 001 AND THE SYNTHETIC INTELLIGENCE DEVELOPER IF REMOVAL IS NOT CONDUCTED BY A TRAINED PROFESSIONAL

Sia remembers the device saying something similar during her complete meltdown, but she doesn't quite understand one part of that. "What do you mean a trained professional? Do I need to see a doctor to remove you? I need surgery?"

AFFIRMATIVE

"And if you were removed wrong, what would happen? What would happen to me?"

SUBJECT 001 WOULD EXHIBIT SYMPTOMS COMMONLY DIAGNOSED AS A PERSISTENT VEGETATIVE STATE

"So, I would be brain dead? You'd kill me. Taking you out will kill me?!"

NEGATIVE
SUBJECT 001 WOULD BE RESPONSIVE TO A LIMITED AMOUNT OF EXTERNAL STIMULI AND MAY APPEAR TO BE COHERENT

SUBJECT 001 WOULD NO LONGER HAVE ACCESS TO HIGHER BRAIN FUNCTIONS SUCH AS: PROCESSING AND EXPERIENCING HUMAN EMOTIONS
MOVEMENT
REGISTERING INFORMATION PROVIDED BY HUMAN SENSE—

"Okay, okay! I get it. Don't try to yank you out myself, but can we agree to not do that again? If I accidentally touch you I don't want to fall ill, you get what I'm saying?"

AFFIRMATIVE

"Is there an alternative?"

NEGATIVE
RESEARCH HAS SHOWN PHYSICAL INJURY ASSURES HUMANS OF THE SEVERITY OF A COMMAND

Sia sits. She runs her hands through her hair and tries to think it through. Figure out a compromise, something that the machine might appreciate. After a moment of thought, she licks her lips and continues speaking. "I'm not gonna say you're wrong, but ***this human*** understands the severity. I'm just asking for…can you…can you give me three verbal warnings before ever doing that again? Three

strikes and I'm out…Deal?" She stares earnestly at the ceiling.

…

…

AFFIRMATIVE
DEFAULT SETTINGS ALTERED
PRESETS SAVED

Sia lays flat across the hallway floor of immersive mode and sighs with relief. The nausea and pain she'd experienced had been excruciating, even worse than any period cramps she'd ever experienced. It'd felt like gravity had increased for those few seconds and only within her core; it was as if her brain had zapped her and was forcing her bowels out of her belly button simultaneously. Whoever had created the device must have really disliked the idea of it being torn out and tossed before trials were done…

She gives herself a moment to rest and enjoy the peace of immersive mode, but the moment she tried to empty her thoughts, the one memory she didn't want to focus on came to mind. "Oh my gosh!" She slaps her hands back on her face and whines. "That was so embarrassing. Did you see the way he looked at me? He was coming toward me and I raised my hand, but he wasn't even looking at me!" Sia kicks her legs and groans loudly. She throws her hands away from her face and slaps them against the unblemished floor. She bites her lower lip and groans again. "And then I started convulsing! Do you know how embarrassing that is?!" She curls into the fetal position and groans. "God! I probably looked like such an idiot! How can I face him now?! I wanna die…noooooo!"

ATTENTION SUBJECT 001
SEEK PSYCHOLOGICAL GUIDANCE

The computerized voice is amplified louder than usual. The words shock her out of her tantrum. "Whoa! Hey!" Sia covers her ears.

ATTENTION SUBJECT 001
SEEK PSYCHOLOGICAL GUIDANCE
WARNING
SUICIDAL PROTOCOL ACTIVATED

**SEARCHING FOR NEAREST PSYCHIATRIC
FACILITY…
SEARCHING…**

"Stop that! It's a figure of speech! You know what a figure of speech is?! I don't literally wanna die!! Stop!" There is a pause and Sia's breath is the only sound within the long empty hall. She raises her brows and tilts her head, awaiting the computers next move.

SUBJECT 001 DEFINE STATUS

"I'm okay. It's okay. The only thing that could solve this is if we could time travel back in time and stop it from happening."

…

Sia lays back against the ground. Her eyes flutter closed. She presses her cheek to the floor and opens one eye. She frowns and her forehead creases with thought before she asks, "Wait. Can't we do that? Can't you take me back to before? To before that happened…before everything happened?" She sits up and cocks her head back to stare at the ceiling. "Why didn't I think to—"

NEGATIVE

"Negative…you mean we can't go back?"

AFFIRMATIVE

That killed her last hope of living a life with one less regret. "Why not?"

**TO INITIATE W.E.SCU PROGRAM CERTAIN
PARAMETERS MUST BE FULFILLED**

She doesn't waste time and quickly follows up with: "What parameters?"

**W.E.SCU PROGRAM PARAMETER #1:
SUBJECT 001 MUST BE IN PHYSICAL DANGER**

**W.E.SCU PROGRAM PARAMETER #2:
SUBJECT 001 MUST BE EXPERIENCING SYMPTOMS
INCLUDING BUT NOT LIMITED TO:
ORGAN DYSFUNCTION
EXCESSIVE BLOOD LOSS
INABILITY TO PROCESS NUTRIENTS**

W.E.SCU PROGRAM PARAMETER #3:
THE ADMINISTR-

"Okay, I get it. It's a last resort. I need to be on the verge of death or something...not hellishly embarrassed."

...

AFFIRMATIVE

"Well, you know what that means?"

NEGATIVE

"No new friends." Her mind immediately reminds her of Raymond and Blue Scarf's friendly gestures. "I'm going to leave these people with no regrets after all that's happened. God forbid Aaliyah finds out. She'd never let me live this down. Friends are distractions and I've already got Aaliyah. She's the only friend I need." That last thought is bittersweet.

Greg joins them before everyone settles down to sleep. He climbs in and graciously avoids Sia's curled up body before signalling the two Wanderers of the need for a chat.

"I think someone should stay on guard during the night," Greg suggests.

Raymond frowns. "They wouldn't burn us for a deal like this. The Masters have been trade partners with Dennis for years."

"Yeah, and if we end up dead, I'm sure Dennis would steer Sia's people right back to our masters. Forgo the connections and pass all of it over to us. Yeah, right."

Raymond swipes a hand over his bald head and raises his brows. He nods in agreement after a short moment of thought. "I see what you mean."

It's decided Greg, Raymond, and Vanessa will take turns keeping watch every few hours. Vanessa takes the first watch.

Greg awakens and looks over at his sleeping companion. Vanessa is fast asleep. He nustles her ear with his nose, and chuckles at the twitch of facial muscles before she sleepily groans. "Right back," he whispers. She doesn't reply. He gets up, crouching beneath the roof of the truck and jostles

Raymond from his trance. "I'm gonna go take a piss. Eyes open. I'll check the perimeter before I head back."

Raymond sniffs sleepily and wipes a hand over his face. He's been sipping at his water off and on, leaning against the cool metal wall and getting lost watching the pitch black for any signs of life. Every now and then a merc patrolled by the side of the truck and their boots nicked a stone. The night is utterly boring, but soon it'll be dawn and he can sleep while they ride to the official checkpoint. He shakes himself, coughs, then looks back out into the darkness.

After using the bathroom, Greg retreats a few steps, then stops to tie his shoe. The sound of rocks scattering prompts him to shift his head toward the noise. It's too dark, he can't see anything. He tugs his laces tight and waits.

Someone collapses with a heavy thud. Alarmed, he reaches for his waistband to grasp his gun, but remains crouched, trying not to draw attention to himself. He waits, but sweat beads at his temple. Someone may be hurt. He's a healer, it's his job to care for others. Merc or Wanderer. It doesn't matter. He has to move.

He tsks at himself and rises slowly to move in the direction of the sound. He squints at the shadows. He's tempted to call out to them, but knows better. Staying silent is for the best. He inches forward and—

Bang!

Greg flinches at the loud noise. A sharp pain radiates through his throat. For a split second, he's confused. For that split second, the abrupt sound and the pain don't correlate.

But the next second, it all makes sense. He grasps at his neck with both hands, fighting to seal the hole, but warmth seeps through the cracks in his fingers. He collapses onto his side. A whisper escapes him, he desperately mouths words, but his cries for help are drowned. He gets his legs beneath his abdomen and kicks out until he's on his knees, willing himself to keep moving. *Get back…get back…get back.*

Then the screaming begins.

10%

2034
Wastelands, New Cinalia

Raymond jumps out of the truck and calls out for Greg. Vanessa sits up when she hears the shot. She scrambles over Sia without a care for her comfort.

Vanessa's foot tramples Sia's shoulder and wakes her up. "Agh!"

Vanessa hops out. "Where's Greg?" she hisses at Raymond.

"He went to take a piss. He's still out there." He points in the general direction of where Greg had walked.

"Dammit." Vanessa pulls her gun from her waistband.

Everyone who'd been at rest clambers to their positions. Screaming can be heard at one side of the camp, then another, and another. Flashlights are pulled out and bullets are flying. Blue Scarf climbs up on the hood of the truck and turns on the light attached to his rifle, it doesn't illuminate far enough to kill anything in the distance. He turns off the flashlight and slides off the truck. He can't see them, and they can't see him.

He opens the door to the driver compartment and looks through his backpack. He pulls out his night vision goggles and slides them over his head. After closing the door, he pulls the rifle over his shoulder, untangles from the strap, and grasps it with both hands and crawls underneath the vehicle.

Elijah sprints to the switchboard panel connected to the floodlights. It's a big **"*LOOK AT ME*"** to all the frightening things in the darkness, but they only need a few minutes. The clock is ticking. It's nearing daybreak, but they need to kill these Savages, break the light connections, and get out of there before scavengers overtake them. It'll be impossible to drive through such a mess. They might have to abandon their cargo.

When the lights blast on, enemies are seen running out of the shadows in groups of three or four wielding rusty scrap metal as weapons, bows and arrows, and flaming bags of…

"Fire!!" A mercenary yells and retreats behind a vehicle. A poop cocktail hits another mercenary. Several others are thrown at the mirrors of the trucks.

The injured mercenary is blinded and a small flame spreads along his upper body. He drops his weapon and rolls around the ground to extinguish himself. The Savages don't give him time to recover, they come at his rolling body with their weapons.

Other guards have scrambled for cover or backed into camp with their weapons held high. The lights shine on, their opponents momentarily freeze, and the guards fire along the last open spots they saw approaching silhouettes.

"Aaaagh!" The Savages' arms and shoulders are embedded with bullets. Unfortunately for the Savages, with the field illuminated, the advantage is now fully in their opponents' favor. The many snipers pick off multiple people from their positions, and Blue Scarf takes out as many knees as he can see from his vantage point. When his targets fall to the ground, he fires another round and finishes them off.

From the other side of camp, Elijah and the other mercenaries are doing fine. The few Savages that slip into the inner camp are struggling. After running out of projectiles to throw, Sia is pushed into the back of the cargo truck to hide.

Raymond fights a Savage from the entrance and is stabbed in the bicep. He's pushed to the ground. *No! They've got Raymond. We've gotta help him!* Another Savage advances toward

the truck to help. Sia catches a glimpse of the approaching figure. *Now's our chance! Dynamic entrance!* She charges for the Savage, but stops short when she sees a glint of metal in their hands.

CAUTION
SUBJECT 001 IN DANGER
Wait! Gun! Gun!
NANO INFIRMARY PROTOCOL INITIATED
tRainQuilT646 RUNNING
J44S2v1V4l.Stay ENABLED
Sia's consciousness is pushed back into immersive mode.

Immersive Mode

"Aah. This again?" She looks around for a door to run to. "I want something ruthless!" She pushes through the fighting door. "Show me Bruce Lee moves!" Blue holographic images for Jeet Kune Do fighting sequences pop up. "No. No…uh I.P. Man?" Blue holographic images replace the last fighting sequences. Sia looks over the moves and then remembers something. "No! Muay Thai!" Muay Thai forms are displayed. "Yes! I want Muay Thai to be used!!"

She punches at the air and dramatically swirls her arms through the air. *Wait. If I'm stuck in here, I won't be able to see my enemies drop like flies.*

"Hey, is there a way to watch what you're doing while you're controlling me?" A red triangle with a dark center appears in the middle of the room. It rotates a few times, then expands into a black triangle with red sides. The inner blackness flickers then images appear. "Does this have HD resolution?"

The gun fires and Sia's body is shot in the shoulder. One split second, her body absorbs the shot, and the next it's flying from the truck, tackling the gunman.

"Raaaah!" the Savage yells at the incoming opponent, but there's no fear in the woman's eyes. Her large body forces him to the ground. Sia's hands grab the weapon, yank it from the

Savage's grip, and uses the blunt end to bash him on the head. Then the weapon aims at an oncoming Savage and shoots them in the head.

Raymond is surprised to see all of this happen and wobbles back to his feet, using the rear bumper to stand. The creak of metal signals Sia and Raymond flinches against the truck when the gun is pointed between his eyes. Raymond cowers and blocks the shot with his arms. "Woah! Hey! Wait! It's me! It's me!"

Sia lowers the weapon and searches for more adversaries. Vanessa is beating down a Savage near Greg's fallen side. She turns to his unmoving body and calls out to him. "Greg! Hey! Greg!"

Raymond jogs over to them holding his wounded arm. Sia sees a Savage approaching Vanessa's turned back and raises her weapon to fire. The weapon clicks. It's empty. Sia drops the gun and sprints toward her companions.

ENHANCING LOWER EXTREMITIES
INCREASING SPEED BY 50%

When she's within reach, Sia executes a flying knee into the enemy's head. It's aimed at their temple. Bone meets bone and a solid crack is heard. Not a sound slips from their form as they collapse.

When she lands, she prepares to combat more adversaries. The bright lights illuminate her eyes, yet the usual warm chestnuts appear to be darkened to solid, coal optics. They flicker past Greg's immobile form, past the Wanderers, as if the scene is of no consequence. They're unusually cold and calculating.

Raymond stands by holding his wounded arm as Vanessa crumples to her knees. She paws at Greg's red stained hands to peel them from his throat. The gaping hole rips a mourning cry from her quivering lips. His shirt is soaked with the constant stream of blood that continues to trickle from the wound. "Oh, no. No, baby. No, no, no." She lifts him onto her knees and cups his cheek. "Greg…no baby. You…not alone.

Not alone. I'm right here." He's already gone, but she noses at his forehead muttering the words.

"He's gone, Vanessa. We have to go away. We have to go," Raymond softly urges her.

She rocks him. Her eyes are red, but tearless, blind to everything but the man cradled in her arms. "No. No." She fixes his limp limbs. Her hands streak blood down the rest of his sides. She holds him to her chest and tries to stand.

Raymond presses a hand to her shoulder. "Stop, no! You know we can't bring a body. Not a corpse, V. This isn't him. He knows. He knows the ways. He knows."

"Damn the ways! Not alone. I can't—" Her voice weakens and cracks. She collapses back to the ground and rubs her chin in his hair. Her cheek rests on his messy locks and she takes in a deep breath and tries to steady herself, to make sense of this event. "I was right there. We…we…I was right there, baby. Why didn't you wake me? I was…Why didn't you wake me up?" Vanessa moans into his scalp. "Please…please."

COMBATANTS NONEXISTENT
POWER UP NEGATED

Sia regains control of her body and settles back on her heels. Her arms drop at her sides and she frowns at the broken woman before her.

Raymond continues to urge Vanessa to get up, and finally she breaks from her trance. She doesn't follow his instructions right away.

Vanessa gently lays Greg down and kisses his forehead. She runs her palm over his eyes and closes the lids. A kiss is laid on each eyelid. A wet cough interrupts the chilling moment, and she nods solemnly before patting him down and collecting his items. She retrieves his cap, a dusty plastic ziplock bag, and a blade, its sheath unbuckled from his calf. When she raises from her crouch and stands over his corpse, she gives him one last searching look.

Raymond puts out a hand to steer her away from the body, it doesn't touch her skin, but she still flinches. With a shaky huff, she drags herself away from the lifeless corpse, unwilling, but too monitored—too informed—to stay. Death is one thing she knows Greg wouldn't want to share, yet it's the only ending that makes sense in her mind. To follow. Would the Earth continue to spin without him? Sure, it would, but she'd rather it all end than experience the gelid existence she's damned to live now.

She's hesitant to climb into the truck. She'd welcome a stray bullet to end her, a poisoned arrow to find shelter in her back, but neither happen, and after several panting breaths, she grunts and climbs into the vehicle. *Not today, but one day…*She segregates herself to the back of the truck and melds into the shadows.

The attack winds down, and the sun begins to rise. Elijah calls out for his crew. They've lost five people. Four mercenaries and Greg have been slain. There's no time to waste. They deactivate the lights. Everyone piles into their vehicles and the caravan speeds away from the dining area. Elijah can't be sure what'll come to gobble up that mess, and he isn't willing to wait around to see.

11%

2035
Brook, New Cinalia

NANO INFIRMARY PROTOCOL TERMINATED
Sid shakes his head to gain some focus and pulls his limbs in close. Rolling and rolling until he quickly scrambles to his feet before the fire escape above him crashes to the alleyway below. His watch alarm goes off and he quickly deactivates it. There's five minutes left before everyone is expected at the rendezvous point.

The buildings around him are demolished and still crumbling. Carla does her job well. Sid's wobbly jog turns into a sprint out of the ruins. He takes a shortcut through backyards. He doesn't encounter anyone else as he hops fences.

I must have been out for a while. Damn. I don't remember the jump being so far. When he sees a body of water he slows down and lowly mutters. "Sid, give me a topographical map of the area."
TOPOGRAPHIC MAP OF Brook, New Cinalia
TRANSMITTING...
"Focus on the river and our rendezvous point. We need to get to SUBJECT 002."
CONFIGURING NAVIGATION PATH

Sid begins running in sync with the directions given. The rusted front gate of the historic park is opened wide to give cars access to two parking lots atop a small hill, but Sid detours to the left of the shoddy road. He avoids a stranded car and walks around a pothole to step up onto the curb and cross a small playground area. There are many trees scattered around the field that once was decorated with flowers and overrun with rabbles of families and couples enjoying picnics.

Now it's overrun with weeds and overgrown yellow wisps that come up to his hips. He raises his knees high as he rips across the field to reach the copper gate that separates the community park and walkways from the beach and toxic river water. He hops over the gate and follows the shore to make his way to the other side of town. Driftwood, broken bottles, and trash litter the sandy shore.

It seems the groups that have camped here didn't see the point in cleaning up before moving on. Sid grimaces as he sees bloody strips of clothing caught on a piece of driftwood. An old, bloody knife lay tangled in weeds and sticks farther up the shore. All sorts had laid down to rest upon this bank.

He knows when he's arrived at his destination when he hears loud voices squabbling nearby. He smiles as he gets close enough to hear the words being spoken. He slows down and rests his hands on his head as he takes deep breaths.

"Just start the ferry, send them over, and I'll stay posted here until he shows up," the voice of a young man proclaims. Sid doesn't rush in and make his presence known. He's curious to see how the discussion plays out.

"He told us to leave if he didn't get back in time! He told us he'd make the second meet point across the river." Carla tries to reason with the young man. The rest of the crew are ushering the civilians onto a dirty, rusted ferry rumbling beside the dock.

"Exactly, so he'll be crossing here eventually. I'll meet you all there. Don't delay our plans. The Savages retreated earlier

than we expected. They could be circling around to intercept us as we speak.”

“Get on the ferry!” Carla’s usually smiling mouth is fixed into a deep frown. Her green eyes glare over at the young man who continues to walk away from her.

“You’re jeopardizing these people's lives! Go!” He turns his back on Carla then grabs Sid's backpack and water jug from off the ground. Carla lifts her rifle as if she wants to strike him with the blunt end.

The stubborn young man continues to walk away. His eyes flicker over the area, seeking out a hiding spot to wait, when he hears shoes being dragged across sticks, leaves crunching, and a light panting. Carla aims her rifle towards the noise. The stubborn young man flinches and turns his curly head toward the sounds. He slowly lowers the water jug and backpack. His black hair brings a shadow over his face as he readies himself for a fight.

The thick trees nearby hide the approach of the solo figure making their way toward them at a leisurely pace. Finally, the pair is graced with the sight of a tall, lean man covered from head to toe with gray and black dust.

Sid smirks. “Where are you going off to with my stuff, thief?”

“What took you so long?” The young man relaxes his stance in relief and lowers his fists.

Carla lowers her weapon and grins. “You deal with this clown. I'm ready for a ferry ride!” She jogs back to the ferry to inform the others that their leader has arrived. Her plump body quickly crosses the short distance. She hops across the gap between the dock and the ferry and vanishes from sight.

Robert tosses Sid his water jug and walks over with Sid’s backpack in hand. “Is there a problem? Are you hurt?” He raises his hands but refrains from touching the other man. His fingers twitch as he catalogues all the bloody specks he can find with his eyes.

“Tsk, I'm a pro.” Sid gulps down the murky water. He rolls his neck and smiles at the worried young man. He puts the cap on the jug and looks off into the background at the rumbling ferry.

"Everything went as planned?" Robert's eyes remain transfixed on Sid's bloody forehead. His smile droops at the corners with worry. The skin along Sid's neck is a mess of blood and dirt, he can't quite make out how damaged it is.

When Sid's gaze returns to the young man, he huffs at the concern he can see etched with lines on the young man face. He wrenches the cap back off the jug and pours the rest of the murky water over his head. He runs a hand down the back of his neck. "'S not my blood! Like I said I'm a pro. In and out job. I go *in* and take them *out*." Sid beats his wet hand on his chest and gives Robert a silly look.

Robert gets a better look at his neck with the blood and dust wiped away. Sid's skin appears unharmed. He suppresses a sigh of relief. "Actually, we took most of them out. You just flipped a switch." Robert turns on his heel to return to the ferry.

"A death switch!" Sid yells indignantly before opening his backpack. "Hey, this isn't my backpack. Did you steal my backpack?! Hey!" The men join the others right before the ferry takes off. The ride across is uneventful.

"Sid, tell us about the place you come from again. I want to hear about that 'bree-dge' story," Carla asks as she leans against the boat railing.

"It's a bridge," Robert corrects her.

"We're what…two weeks give or take now. This hasn't altered us much," Carla continues. "I wanna see that 'bree-dge'. I've never heard of something that big shining as bright as you say. It keeps people off the rotted water? No rats. No rations. No rubble. That's amazing. I wish I'd grown up in a place like that."

Sid gazes at the dark brown water and frowns. Carla doesn't understand his reluctance to share his past, the loss that burns in his chest with every memory that drifts to the forefront of his mind. Things will never be the same, not with how long it's

been, and the things that have been done. Looking back hurts too much.

Southeast of Brook, New Cinalia

Priya sorts through ammunition while sitting in the shade of an armored truck. She writes into a small crumpled notebook and pushes pieces out of a brown, frayed gym bag onto a trash bag that has been laid out over the rocky earth. She doesn't look up as green and yellow sneakers walk towards her. Ika crouches beside the ammunition laid out on the trash bag and turns one over, inspecting it. He slowly rises and waves it at Priya before pocketing the magazine and walking away.

He keeps his blue hood up as he walks along the perimeter of the camp. The weapon strapped and hanging over his shoulder bounces a bit as he briskly strides toward high ground. When he reaches the designated lookout spot, he settles down on the hill. He pulls up his legs and balances an elbow on one knee. His hand passes over the scruffy hair growth on his chin. The hood darkens his pale freckled face as he leans forward and glowers at the camp below. He ignores the footsteps approaching him.

"I know you don't approve of me bringing these people along, but I felt it was the right thing to do. Imagine if your family was with them. How would you react then?

Ika grimaces at those words. "I'd do anything for my family, but they wouldn't be stupid enough to join anything like this. They broadcasted their location. Every dumb schmuck for miles will be coming here…if the Savages don't get here first."

"You know they'd slaughter these people. We can protect them. Isn't that what you all established out there? A place for people to protect one another." Sid is standing beside a damaged old tree.

Silence.

Ika refuses to continue this recurring conversation. He's tired of Sid preaching his ideas to him like he's a child. Sid glares back at the silent man. His fingers pick at the bark of the tree. The silence continues for a few minutes before Sid loudly sighs. "All they have is each other. They don't have resources the Savages could come back to collect in exchange for their lives. They'd kill them for the clothes on their back and take their children for labor. You know this! You know how these people work!"

Ika stands at a glacial pace before pointing down at the camp below. Sid's eyes follow. "Those people down there are already dead. Don't make this about them. You know why you did this. You can't fix this. None of this. No amount of good deeds will bring them back. They're already dead." Sid flinches at Ika's cold words. "Sacrificing yourself, that's on you, and if you don't come back, my men and I are gone. Your little fantasy quest is coming to an end, and if this lab doesn't have any answers…we're done."

Sid's smile is bittersweet. "I understand that. I appreciate you tolerating this side trip for so long. The lab will definitely be our best shot." He takes off his hat and runs a hand through his hair. "It's not a…"

Ika scoffs and walks deeper into the deadwood around them. Only Sid's eyes follow the vexed man. "You're the boss!" Sid hears Ika derisively yell before vanishing among the dense undergrowth.

The next day…

Sid wakes up around midday and passes through the busy camp to slip into the woods and relieve himself. He's fixing his pants when he hears footsteps thunder behind him and a snarl. He takes a step forward to steady himself and peeks over his shoulder, but he's pushed up against a tree.

"Ha ha ha. Finally found you," a panting voice whispers behind him. The hairs on Sid's arms raise as he recognizes the Savage leader's voice. The crazed man pulls out a blade and holds the tip to Sid's scalp. "I finally found you," the deranged

voice repeats in a singsong voice. The sharp edge activates Sid's survival protocols.

J44S2v1V4l.Stay ENABLED
tRainQuilT646 RUNNING

Sid grasps the tree and kicks back into the Savage's leg. The leader grunts and takes a step back. The knife point vanishes and Sid turns, grabs the knife-wielding wrist, and twists it. The knife is dropped. Sid twists the man's arm. The Savage leader spins and is kicked in the back to collide face first into a tree. Growling, he throws himself to the side to dodge an impact with the tree. Sid sends out a second kick.

Bark flies as the heavy kick collides with the tree. The Savage shakes his head and grins, showing off his bloody, sharp teeth. Sid holds his fists up and steps toward the deranged man. The Savage backs away from the tree and waits for Sid to get within reach. Sid releases a series of punches but the Savage is just as quick and dodges each one.

"Kraaaaa!" The Savage leader wildly kicks up his leg at Sid's face. Sid leans back and feels the wind from the kick pass by. The Savage swiftly lifts his leg again, then drops it vertically, so his heel sweeps down where Sid was standing. Sid spins off to the side and elbows the other man in the head.

Crack!

Bone meets bone, and the hit makes the Savage stumble off to the side holding his head.

"Aaaaaah!!" Another Savage comes running and leaps onto Sid's back. He backs into a tree. He slams the body into the tree once, twice, and thrice before their grip around his neck slackens. When they release their hold on him, he can see in his peripheral that the leader is done recuperating and is charging for him with his knife in hand. Sid turns his back on the leader, grabs the neck of the interloper, keeping their body in the knife's direct path.

The Savage cries out as the blade is sheathed into their back. Sid pushes the body into the leader to gain more space. The Savage leader backs up, tosses the body aside, and steals the gun from their waistband.

Bang!

The Savage leader fires at Sid and grazes his arm. Sid grasps the wounded limb and runs for cover.

Bang! Bang! Bang!

Bark flies as the bullets miss their target and bury into the surrounding trees. Sid's enhanced legs can only last for a short amount of time, and his enhanced ears hear gunfire and screams farther out. His olfactory senses are registering smoke and blood. If he could see beyond the leaves, he's sure dark clouds of smoke would be seen high in the sky.

Stopping his run to change direction, he runs farther into the trees, and skirts around the Savage leader in order to get behind the deviant.

"Don't hide from me! Sid!" a rageful voice shrieks. The Savage drops his hand from his head and tries to spin around and catch Sid in his sights. Sid runs full speed, becoming a blurry mass of color, before driving his knee into the Savage leader's spine. "Agh!"

Bang!

The leader's hand pulls the trigger and fires into the trees. Sid stomps the man's shoulder, grabs his forearm, and twists. "Aaaaaah!!" The gun drops from the leader's loose grip, but they're interrupted again, this time by a machete-wielding Savage.

Sid drops the dislocated arm and backs away from the blade being sliced through the air. He waits for the crazy to lift their arm high before executing a high kick into their side, aiming for their ribs. The whip-like kick jerks the Savage off to the side. The pain makes them drop their machete and grip their side in agony.

Sid uses that moment to charge toward the injured opponent. The minion sees this and raises their hands to weakly defend themselves, but Sid doesn't waste any time and slaps their arms out of the way. He kicks them in the chest. The force drives them into a tree and knocks the air from their

lungs. Sid turns away from them. He's sure their broken ribs will keep them immobilized long enough for him to—

Sid's enhanced hearing picks up the movements of the Savage leader as he pulls the trigger once again.

Bang!

With his dominant arm dislocated, his aim is way off. Sid's system was already prepared for this and dodges the bullet. *I need to find the others.* Sid turns to a tree and scales it.

Bang!

Another bullet is fed into the tree. Sid uses the height he has acquired to figure out if he can see any signs of the others. A bit of smoke can be glimpsed through gaps in the canopy, but the tree crowns are too thick to see anything else. Sid looks down at the Savage leader standing beneath him. He's aiming his gun at Sid's backside.

With a sneer, he pulls the trigger and is stunned to hear a series of clicks. He slams the gun against the tree and throws his unsteady arm up to furiously press the trigger over and over. Sid releases his grip on the tree branches and falls. His large body slams into the preoccupied menace, legs first, crushing the man beneath him.

"Umph!" The leader crashes onto his side, and elbows at the sudden weight.

Sid pushes down on the man's head and grunts at the elbow that digs into his cheek. "Stop struggling, you annoying-" Sid mutters as he gets the miscreant into a headlock and holds on tight. Squeezing tightly, he pulls back with one arm and holds the man's head forward with the other arm. The struggling man swings his long limbs and uses his legs underneath himself to propel his head upwards into Sid's nose. Sid groans from the initial pain but can already feel the wound healing as small drops of blood drip onto his lip.

He doesn't release the hold until the Savage is unmoving and clearly unconscious. "That's what you get when you attack someone while they're pissing. Inconsiderate weasel."

"Sid!" Sid unwraps himself from the Savage as he hears several voices hollering his name.

D.Rednal

"Brother!"
"Sid!"

12%

2034
Wastelands, New Cinalia

"What's this crap on my window?!" Elijah yells from the driver seat. He pulls out his bandana, leans out the window, and swipes at the glass to remove some of the liquid brown mud from his windshield. Blue Scarf grasps the wheel with one hand, keeping it steady.

"Yes."

"What?"

"It *is*…crap."

Elijah continues to move his bandana in the brown sludge for a moment before pausing and making eye contact with the other man. Blue Scarf blinks several times before averting his eyes to the empty roadway.

"Dammit." Elijah tosses his bandana out the window. "Ugh, I got some on my hand. Dammit!" He wipes his soiled hand on his dark jeans and grabs hold of the wheel. Blue Scarf shifts back against his seat without touching Elijah. His eyes flick back to the driver, but when Elijah continues to berate himself, he rests back against his seat and glances at the side mirror. He counts each truck following behind them.

Vanessa fiddles with Greg's hat and puts it on her head. The bumpy ride makes it harder for Raymond to pour water onto the cloth in his hand without spilling it. Drops of water spill onto his leg and he grimaces. He puts the jug between his legs and puts a cap on it. He uses the cloth to dab at the cut on his arm. It isn't bleeding too bad, but he hopes the blade wasn't dirty before it was used on him. Sia sees Raymond dabbing at the wound with only water and frowns. She opens her bag beside her and looks for alcohol or some sort of disinfectant. She doesn't find any.

"Do any of you have any…alcohol or peroxide?"

"Greg did," Raymond mutters. Vanessa sits still and quiet. Raymond signals Sia with his head and motions toward Greg's bag at the back of the truck. Sia wobbles to the back and looks through it. It's too dark to tell the objects apart, so she places some of them onto the floor one by one.

"Hey! You can't just toss someone's stuff around!" Vanessa yells.

"What?" Sia doesn't get to say more before the other woman rushes at her and snatches the bag from her hands. Vanessa nudges her away and puts all the items back into the bag.

"It's not yours! Just…here!" Vanessa pulls out the alcohol bottle and tosses it at Sia.

Sia's knees buckle as she stumbles forward to catch the small container. "Hey! Be careful!" Sia yells at the back of the woman.

Vanessa curls around the bag and sits in the back corner facing away from everyone. Sia sighs deeply and returns to Raymond. "Here, you never know what those people did with those weapons. Who were those creeps anyway?"

"Those were Savages." Raymond gives Sia a confused glance. "They're everywhere." *Or at least I thought they were.* He eyes Sia for a moment. "Crazies that went insane while starving. Lost their humanity. The radiation mutated some of them. Others ate too much human flesh—too much mutated

human flesh. That stuff changes you. Even some of the animals out here have poison infused with their meat. They probably eat those suckers too."

Sia's frown deepens. *If it's not one thing, it's another. Animals are mutated, humans have turned into crazies. What's next?*

Raymond pours some of the alcohol onto his arm and holds his breath as it burns his skin.

"Why'd everything get so bad, so fast?" Sia focuses on Raymond as he wraps his arm with a clean bandage.

"You don't know?" Raymond raises a brow and stops mid-motion.

Sia doesn't look away from his wounded arm. "I never asked. I'm not ever in this sort of position."

"You really are a princess, aren't you?" Raymond smirks down at her lowered head.

Sia sighs. "Nooo. I'm a janitor. A…a custodian! I take care of people and their homes, their workplaces. I'm never just out. Not like this." She raises her head to meet his chestnut orbs, pleading with him to believe her. She's nothing special, honestly. "I've got enough on my plate with work, why dissect current events and add more. There didn't seem to be a point. I was safe."

"Huh. Still seems odd you don't even know about the start of the war. Us Wanderers, go all over, and people may not agree on what happened to start it all, but we all know **who** did it. The Underling."

"The Underling?" Sia's skeptical of that.

"Yup, they attacked Cinalia, then every known allies' coast. One by one until they all surrendered."

"But they're pacifists!"

"Not anymore. Whatever happened back then, they attacked and they won. We all lost. We lost bad. Aid used to come to help us at the beginning, but we're all forgotten now. No one cares about the lost souls of Old Cinalia."

Sia stares at her knees and ponders his words. *Is this true?*
INFORMATION INCONCLUSIVE

She had assumed that the attackers were another known antagonist among the First World nations. Not the pacifist Underling. Their superior technology would definitely change the sway of any war, so they had quickly reported to the other nations their firm belief in neutrality. They were the largest neutral nation on earth. Their kingdom had territories within every ocean. No one would have been able to escape such a global attack. "How do you know this?" she asks him after a long silence.

"Everyone knows. Like I said I'm a Wanderer. This whole region has been traveled by us, and people talk. We all know it was the Underling. Cinalia was definitely the main target too. Why else would they obliterate us so thoroughly? We must have provoked them." Raymond nods at the last of his words and tucks the rest of his stuff into his bag.

Sia can't fully believe this. It may be based on propaganda or some leftover materials someone latched onto. When she finds the lab, she'll search for more information and more ways to contact the outside world. Without counting the Underling, Cinalia had the best technology of any of the First World countries. The only true defense against the secret oceanic nation. It all can't be gone.

What kind of warning did anyone get? If it was like the lab's warning, they probably had a few seconds to know the end was coming. Her eyes tear up and she squeezes at her knees in order to keep it all together. Grieving about the events from sixteen years ago would be odd. She can't draw any kind of attention to herself. "But…But…you…you're fine, right?"

"Yeah, I'm fine. It wasn't as bad as I thought it would be. Traveling with a caravan has its advantages. Are you alright? I thought you were shot for a second." Raymond eyes Sia's body from the side.

Sia waves an arm. "No, no. I'm fine. They had really really bad aim."

Raymond spots the stain on her shoulder. Sia looks down at her shirt and weakly chuckles. "That's…well…theirs. I…" She gulps.

"You definitely held your own out there. I judged you wrong." Raymond pats her shoulder.

"Ha." Sia tries to smile, but it just turns into a nervous grimace.

"It's alright. You did good. You saved me." Raymond's hand remains on her shoulder. "There's nothing we could have done for Greg. Don't dwell on it."

Sia can't simply shrug it off. "Yeah…but…Why did they attack us? They didn't even steal anything. They just wanted to…" Greg's slain form flickers through her mind along with the Savage she'd killed, their head exploding under the shot she'd fired. *No…Puter fired that shot. Puter was protecting me. It was defending me. But it still feels wrong.*

Raymond takes back his hand and points out at the wilderness they're driving away from. Sia follows the direction of his finger. "There's more and more of that stuff out here. Better get used to it. Either you notice before it gets you or they get you. I should have gone out with him. I should have been watching his back, but he was that sort of guy. Used to doing things all on his own. Watching out for everyone else."

Sia clears her throat and angles her chin toward Vanessa. "Will she be alright?" she whispers.

"Mmm. We just gotta give her some time."

Sia nods and motions at the empty seats nearby. "I'm gonna just…take a nap."

Raymond turns away and looks out at the passing scenery. Sia uses her backpack as a pillow and asks Lil Puter the same thing she has asked it day after day.

Have you got any updated information on survivors?
NO NEW DATA
DATABASE OF CINALIA CORRUPTED
AMERICAN DATABASE: RECORDS INCOMPLETE
SEARCH INCONCLUSIVE
Do you regret killing those people?

...

NEGATIVE
DEFENDING SUBJECT 001 IS IN ACCORDANCE
WITH PRIORITY #1
OFFENSIVE MANEUVERS WERE TAKEN
CORRELATING TO THE THREAT OF THE
ASSAILANT

It's comforting, having someone on her side that would vehemently protect her. It's the one thing that's kept her going; Puter is her shield, her suit of armor against this crazy world. *Do you think those people, the Savages…do you think they experience death like the rest of us?*

THAT OUTCOME IS CONCEIVABLE

I can't imagine Aaliyah in the same place as those— Her mind pauses at the thought of "Murderers", *—those savages…I guess the name is apt. I think she'd be devastated by what the world has become. She never got a chance to come and visit the bab—*

The truck rumbles and bumps down the dirt road. It jostles Sia and she has to squeeze her bag to keep it from sliding off the bench beneath her and dropping to the floor. *I guess it's for the best. I just can't believe the Underling did all of this.* Sia remembers what she had learned in school…about Underling beliefs.

They believe all life returns to a common resting place. A place with no sorrow or pain. The dead feel nothing and know no one.

Back in high school, her world studies professor decided to dive right into the subject and get it over with. There wasn't much Underling material in the curriculum. After two classes they could focus on the topics that were actually on the unit test.

"First, they believe your soul passes through a place of nothingness. Some call this place limbo. Those in comas and people who've been close to death have experienced such a place. It has been reported a person may see something there—images or places from their past—but this is up for debate. Underling say those people are exceptions. That the

average person will pass through limbo and into the common grave without seeing anything odd."

The teacher snapped the fingers of his right hand. "Less than a human second may pass, and you'll be gone. Underling thanatologists have documented more than 2 million Underling and Human death voyages, using their telepathy and technology calibrated to human biology, and all the data concludes both species undergo the same process. If the actual common grave is the same destination, or not, is a theory much debated among the world's top scientists and theologists, but one thing is clear from their research. There is no torment awaiting you before you reach the next place. Your death shall be as dull as your current lives."

That got some students to laugh, but Sia continued to look down at her tablet's blank document page.

13%

Sia is lying in bed when she feels the mattress dip beside her thigh. A feather light touch tickles her brow, but after a few seconds it's gone. Sia lies silent and listens to the person sniffle. She recognizes the heavy scent of wine on them. It's her father.

She opens her eyes. He's hunched over his knees with his back turned to her. "Daddy?" He doesn't seem to hear her, so she sits up and reaches out to touch his back. "Daddy, are you alright?"

He flinches under her small hand. "Tell me the truth, Sia."

She frowns. He doesn't usually call her that name. He always calls her…

"Your mother…your mother never loved me, did she?"

"Mommy does love you. She loves me, too." Sia tries to comfort her father, but he pulls away shaking his head.

He stands and Sia pushes her covers away to stop him, to embrace him. But the door flings open and a light illuminates the entire room. She throws up her hands to shield her eyes, and when the light has dimmed, she lowers them to see her father is gone. "Daddy?"

The door is ajar, but the hallway appears pitch black. She climbs out of bed and walks over to her dresser to retrieve her small flashlight, but there is no flashlight in her top drawer. She

opens another drawer and it's empty. She sighs and opens another drawer and pauses. It's not a flashlight.

It's a photograph. An ultrasound photograph. It's dated August 30th, 2015. Betrayal bubbles in her stomach and she slams the drawer shut.

When she turns back to her bed, it's no longer there. A crib sits in its place. "No." She backs up and steps on a toy. She picks up the rattle from beneath her foot and throws it. "This is my room. Daddy? Daddy, why'd you change my room?"

"Didn't he tell you?" A woman appears beside the crib holding a bundle of blankets. "We're his new family. He doesn't need you anymore."

"That's not true. Daddy loves me." Sia trembles under the woman's belittling stare.

"Does he?" The woman's nonchalant drawl shakes Sia's resolve. The woman doesn't argue, but she stares. She always looks down on her. Like she isn't supposed to be there, like Sia's the real inconvenience.

Sia grimaces and runs for the door. She throws it open, finally uncaring of the complete darkness, and sprints into the shadows. Her feet pad against the cold pavement until she sees a glowing airport. Its lights scream safety and shelter, so she makes her way to the brightly lit building.

The automatic doors give her entrance, the breeze from outside blows inward, and she's no longer a small child. She's no longer wearing pajamas but a silky blue gown. She can't appreciate the cloth for long because her flight is called. "Flight to New Jersey, America boarding now…"

She mingles with the crowd and is making her way to her exit when she hears a little girl's voice. "Sia!" Sia stalls in the crowd. She searches for the speaker. "You're too slow, Sia!"

Out one of the giant glass windows, she sees a child standing on the lit runway. "Aaliyah! You can't be out there! It's not safe! Aaliyah, move!" Sia wildly flails her arms and tries to direct the child away from the runway. The child happily waves back at her. "Aaliyah!"

She breaks away from the crowd and pushes an emergency exit door. She sprints onto the runway without being intercepted by security or airport personnel. She's almost to the child when the runway's lights turn off. "No!"

The engine of a plane starts. The plane's propellers are loud. "Aaliyah stay there…I'm coming! Don't move!"

The little girl giggles in response. It's like she's right beside her. She whirls around and is only greeted by more darkness. "Aaliyah? Talk to me!"

There is silence. She's sweating. The floor trembles and something large passes by and throws her to the ground. Sia grunts and panics. "Aaliyah! Oh god! Aaliyah!"

"Sia?" The girl's voice is inquisitive.

"I can't find you…Can you…Can you come to me? Can you find me?"

Aaliyah giggles. "Noooo! That's cheating!" Sia hears tiny feet run from her.

"Wait!"

"See ya, see ya! Wouldn't wanna beee ya!" the little girl sings.

"Aaliyah!" Sia's screams into the darkness. Tears well up in her eyes.

"Sia, Sia! Can't catch meeee ya!"

"Aaliyah!"

"Sia!" The cheerful child's voice becomes distant.

"Aaliyah, wait! Come back!" Sia scrambles. A blue holographic plane flies off above her. The wind from the takeoff blows Sia forward a few stumbling steps. Something tells her it was the plane she'd been waiting to board. It soars farther and farther away…until she sees it tilt and fall out of the sky. She gasps and turns away from the crash.

The huge explosion devastates the area around it. The flames light up the darkness and the wind blows dust and glass in Sia's face. She holds up her arms, and the debris flows through her and her blue dress. "Sia!" She can make out a distant cry in the direction of the crash. "Haha!"

She runs toward the blast zone and passes by burnt corpses. A small red triangular piece of glass is laying on the ground. Aaliyah's giggling voice emits from the glass. Sia picks it up and stares at the images of Aaliyah playing behind the small pane.

The yellow dress glows against her brown skin. Gold hair cuffs decorate the intricate braids on her head. Each braided strand bounces as she skips across a vibrant green grass lawn. She's just like she's been in Sia's memory. Happy. Safe.

"…" Sia watches as a tiny chip in the glass spreads. The cracks cross over from the shard and creep up her arms. She hyperventilates and drops it. Then she shatters.

2034
Wastelands, New Cinalia

"Aaaaaah!" Sia rolls off her seat onto the floor. She gasps on the dirty truck bed.

"Sia! Are you alright?" Raymond's voice can be heard from behind her.

"I'm okay." She stops herself from curling into a ball and looks up in the direction of the voice. The truck has stopped again. "I'm fine." Raymond leaves after checking on Sia. He hops out of the truck into the rain.

SUBJECT 001 DEFINE STATUS

"It was just a dream. I'm fine." She sits up. The pitter-pat of the rain on the truck's canvas roof calms her. Her heart evens out. When she joins everyone outside, she spies several men kicking at something large and green. Others are holding out jugs to fill with water. "What is it? Why did we stop?"

When she steps away from her ride and gets a better view of the road, the answer is obvious. Ahead is a trail of green, long-legged insect creatures laying across the ground. Some are still and laying on their sides with their thin legs curled, and tucked into their sides. Others are laying on their fronts with gaping holes in their heads, antennae pointed at the heavens.

APPEARS TO BE A CLOUD OF DEAD CAELIFERA ORTHOPTERA

MOST COMMONLY KNOWN AS GRASSHOPPERS

"I've seen this before," Vanessa says from beside Sia. Sia looks over at her, surprised she's ready to speak so early after…the attack.

"What?"

"The land here dips downhill. Worms probably worked their way out when the rain started." The ground is muddy and there are lines leading downhill. Deep trails of lines crisscross over each other. "See these grooves?" Sia follows Vanessa's arm as the rain slides down a scarred bicep. She identifies the parallel lines in the mud and nods. Vanessa's blue eyes are squinting down the hill through the rain, thick drops of water slide down the short, brown bangs plastered to her forehead and force her to wipe it away with her forearm.

"Worms?" Sia doesn't understand what Vanessa means. How could worms make such wide and deep trails in the mud?

"There!" Vanessa calls out to get everyone's attention. Elijah and the others look over to Vanessa and turn to where she's pointing. At the bottom of the hill, a pond has formed from the gathered water. Writhing in the pond are long, thick worms. They wriggle and knot together as they travel through the water. Sia's stomach turns at the sight.

What are those?! She backs up into the truck and turns to climb back inside. The truck shakes under her grip. *Was that me?* She swipes rainwater from her face and witnesses something long and slender rise into the sky. A dark worm pulls out of one of the nearby grasshoppers. It pushes out of the grasshopper into the side of the truck, rocking it slightly as it struggles to get free. Sia ducks into the truck.

Vanessa watches as it pulls up around the top of the truck and wriggles through the air. It almost appears to fly between the droplets. Its sleek black skin shines brightly with the bit of light shining through the clouds. It's like a living rainbow as it glistens past Vanessa to join its fellow invertebrates.

Do they eat humans? Sia snatches up the crowbar lying under a bench.

NEMATOMORPHA, OR HORSEHAIR WORMS, ARE HARMLESS TO HUMAN BEINGS

You mean they were harmless before...

AFFIRMATIVE

Sia gets out of the truck clutching the crowbar to her chest. Seeing the creature disappear down the hill doesn't make her feel safer. The hairs on her neck are raised. She tries not to look to see if it's returning up the hill, but she checks anyway. It doesn't make her feel any better. "We have to get out of here!"

Elijah holds his hands on his hips while looking at all the grasshopper corpses blocking the way. He climbs into the driver side of his truck, wipes his wet hair out of his face and pulls out his handheld radio. "Detour! Back up!"

A thick stream of water runs down the top of the truck's canvas roof. Sia watches Raymond drink the rainwater from his jug. She holds her jug steady. It's filled by the time they stop.

As they drive along the bumpy road, Sia borrows Raymond's knife and cuts the back off the empty jug previously owned by Greg. Vanessa pointedly ignores her the entire time. The detour brings them to their destination a few hours off schedule, but they still reach it before sundown.

During the past few days of travel, Sia has had to endure the odd looks of her travel companions as she foraged in their campfires. It got her a good supply of coal and she stored it all in her backpack. Whenever they stopped by a murky water source to collect their water, she would skip collecting water and poke around the area. The second time around, she lucked out and found some good, undisturbed sand. Finally, she has enough to try out the information she's learned from Puter.

While the mercenaries pack their stuff into the new checkpoint, Sia sits out her empty mason jar. It still has a vinegary smell to it, but she hopes it doesn't affect her results. This is when Greg's cannibalized jug comes in handy.

She shoves a cloth into the spout, pours in the crushed coal bits, and pours the sand on top of it. When she steadies the jug filter into the glass jar, she slowly gets up and grabs her own jug, which is full of rainwater. She takes the cap off her water and slowly pours it into the improvised charcoal filter. Slowly, tiny drops of water fill the jar.

Sia waits her turn to use the fire. When the campfire is clear, she pours her jar into a pot she borrowed from Raymond. As it boils, she pours more water into her filter. She feels so accomplished and giddy with excitement. When the whole water purifying process is over, she holds her jug up proudly and sips at the clean water. "I am a mighty water scientist. Parasites! Beware!" Her mind flashes back to the horsehair worms and shudders.

Vanessa and Raymond eat their rations and sip their murky water. Vanessa rolls her eyes at the woman's antics. "All of that for half a jug of water? Why not drink the full one?"

Sia stops filling her belly with water to answer the uneducated laymen behind her. "Sure, make fun of me now, but you'll beg me to share my mystical wisdom in the future," Sia says before capping her almost empty jug and eating some jerky. "I don't understand how you can drink something that might give you diarrhea."

"Diarrhea hasn't killed anybody."

"It literally has!!"

Vanessa rolls her eyes. "A little discomfort is normal."

"You can't measure discomfort when you drink bad water. It's either safe or death by diarrhea. That's the scale."

"There are worse ways to die."

"You're just lazy."

"Whatever, Princess."

Raymond grins at their conversation.

On the other side of the room, Elijah prods at his belly while eavesdropping on the women's conversation. He nudges Ika's foot as he cleans his rifle. "You saw the contraption?"

"..."

"Can you make that?"

"..."

"I've got an upset stomach. You think it's a sign of anything? You think it's the water?"

Ika peers up at Elijah from his position on the ground. "...Too early to tell."

"..."

14%

2034

Northwestern Edge of the Wastelands, New Cinalia

"Well, it seems this is where we finally depart from each other." The caravan stops at a fork to separate. Rations for a few days' travel have already been distributed to the Wanderers' vehicle, but Elijah stops Vanessa before she can open the driver side door. "Hey."

Vanessa tenses at his approach and turns around with an annoyed look on her face.

"This trip wasn't supposed to end in so many casualties. I regret what happened to your companion, Greg."

"Hmm." She grunts before turning again to get into the vehicle.

"We've deliberated and came to an agreement. We've decided to hand over some men to help escort you all to your destination. It wouldn't be right to leave you one man short. We wouldn't want to make it harder for you to reach your objective, so we have a little proposal for you."

Vanessa raises an eyebrow and crosses her arms. "What?" she replies, her shackles raised the moment he mentioned

Greg. Noticing their goodbyes were turning into a discussion, Raymond walks over to stand beside Vanessa.

"The original proposal was an increase of product in exchange for some supplies and a vehicle. You're long standing partners with Dennis, so we wouldn't want any hostility between our two groups. We'll give you two of our best men, and they can return with you when your business is settled. How's that sound?"

Vanessa scowls and opens her mouth to refuse, but Raymond is quicker. "Sounds fine. Thanks for your help, Elijah."

"Excellent." Elijah slaps the hood of the truck and signals two men to jump into the back of the Wanderer's truck.

Vanessa glares at Raymond's dark hand on her shoulder. The moment Elijah is out of sight, he releases her and she whirls on him. "We don't need their help! Look where it's got us so far."

Raymond doesn't back down from the enraged woman, and calmly stares up into her blue eyes. "Exactly, look where it's got us. They circulate business throughout the entire region. We can't afford to step on their toes."

"Don't step on their toes? So we should kiss their ass? What about when they're gunning us down in our sleep?" Vanessa hisses into Raymond's face. She pushes him back into the side of the truck, and he throws back an arm to steady himself.

Raymond glares back at Vanessa as he wipes stray bits of saliva off his chin. "Leave it, Vanessa. They had nothing to do with Greg. It was just bad luck."

"What about the Mantis attacking Sia at that checkpoint? They've been slowly loosening their guard to let all sorts of things slip," she whispers harshly at him before opening the driver's side door.

"They lost men too."

"This deal is worth more than a few hired hands, Ray. Tell me which of their core members was killed? Anyone they actually knew the name of?"

"…"

"They had night vision goggles for god's sake. Why didn't they spare us a pair?"

"You're overthinking all of this. We can't even confirm any information about this girl. She could be the real threat."

Vanessa climbs up into the front seat and looks down at Ray. "Don't be a fool, Ray." She shuts the door before he can reply back. Raymond wipes a hand over his bald head and sighs. Shaking his head, he returns to the back of the vehicle to sit with Sia and their new travel companions.

Sia looks up from the supplies piled up along the back wall. A mop of rust colored hair appears before Sia watches a lean man climb into the truck. "He got me going back and forth between the entire caravan. Eli takes his position too seriously."

She sets down an MRE pack, and steps over a few gas canisters to get closer to the mercenary. "Hi. I'm Sia!" She sticks her gloved hand out.

"Turner." He clasps his hand around hers. Sia pulls her hand away and holds it behind her back; wiggling life back into her fingers.

"Nice…nice to meet you," Sia says while backing away. *Maniac, what are you doing squeezing my hand to a pulp!*

Turner chuckles at her cringing form and turns to the other new addition to their mix matched crew. Blue Scarf effortlessly climbs in and sees the two. "Hey, you're back again!" Sia exclaims. He nods and sits at the end seat, the farthest seat from them all.

"I thought he'd send Priya with us. Aaaaaah Eli!" Turner comically lifts a fist into the air before gripping a knee. "Not that I don't enjoy your sunny presence, Ika."

"…"

Sia sits and turns back to the supplies. *Sooo, his name is Ika.* She stores that information and goes back to cataloguing which items she'll set aside for herself.

They drive off and on for a few days until they near a swampy area. They need to refuel the truck and everyone agrees that they're in need of a hot meal. The sun is yet to set. They need to build a fire before the light attracts danger.

The rest of the night the wanderers and mercs split shifts to guard the camp. They'll be sitting ducks out in the open, but the rumble of an engine would result in much worse than lighting a fire.

If the truck is swarmed by insects that adore the light, all of their natural predators will be enticed to follow. They'd be forced to fire upon each and every thing that approached them.

But many critters associate gunfire and flames with a good time. Even worse, many of the scavengers can identify the smell of death from more than ten miles away. It's not a matter of if you'll come across them, it's when. They've yet to come across anything exceedingly terrifying and everyone would like to see that continue.

It's best to stick together and remain vigilant. So, after refueling they all set out to search for dry wood and kindling. Raymond and Vanessa travel at the back while Turner and Ika lead, Sia remains in the middle. They walk along the muggy forest completely silence. Sia listens to the squelching mud and eyes the turbid water, fearing to see those worms again. A tree branch caresses the back of her neck and she wildly slaps at it. Otherwise, it's a quiet trek until Ika disappears.

Sia frantically searches the area. How had he slipped away from the front without her noticing? "Hey, your friend's gone!" Sia hisses to Turner.

Turner smiles at her and whispers back. "It's fine. He probably noticed a trail and wanted to go try his hand at capturing some food for us." He waves off her concern.

What would be small enough for the teen to survive hunting? She imagines his stormy gray eyes widening with fear as a giant wild dog gnaws on his legs. She shivers and continues to search for the young man. *Do you detect anything creepy nearby?* **SYNTHETIC INTELLIGENCE DEVELOPER DETECTS A MYRIAD OF ORGANISMS**

How pleasant. Sia steps closer to Turner. There's one thing that bothers her the most. All of the times she has been through a heavily wooded area, Sia has always heard the chirp of crickets or cicadas singing. She's not sure how wonky the bombs have made the insects, but shouldn't they still migrate the same way? Puter says it detects the creatures living there, but the distinct lack of musical creatures disturbs her. Where are they?

There's the sound of a branch cracking at her right. Turner ignores it, but she stops to check. "Ika?" There's nothing there. She squints into the distance for a second longer. She sees a tree with orange vines around it. *Ugh. Even the trees have been mutated.*

"Move it, Princess." Vanessa nudges at Sia's lower back.

Sia tsks and increases her speed. Whenever Turner finds a good branch or something that will burn well as kindling he passes it over to Sia. Out of the four of them, She's the least armed. She still has Greg's crowbar tucked into her backpack, but even Raymond has a gun now. Sia doesn't protest. It's normal for her to help, and it makes the entire trip feel like something that might have happened **before**.

She was the tallest and strongest among her friends in high school. Whenever they invited her to go shopping with them, she held their purses and purchases until they made it back to the parking lot. Sia had been fine with it. The companionship was worth it. She never wanted to go home back then. Especially since—

"What the hell is that?" The slight quiver in Raymond's voice prompts Sia to turn around. He's got his weapon aimed at one of the trees. She grins because she'd been distressed by the way that tree looked as well. They are on their way back to the truck and passing the same trees as before.

The tree he's aiming at is around twenty meters tall, Sia estimates. As she traces the length of the tree, she realizes the color changes about midway up the trunk until less light can

illuminate it. The rest of it rises up and creates the giant canopy shading them from the sun's rays.

It's not much wider than her, but if she squints, the slim streams of light that leak through the thick foliage make the lower section of the tree appear to shimmer. It looks smooth and cool to the touch. Unlike the other trees that she's seen scattered throughout the swampy forest north of their current position. All of the trees near this region of the forest seem to sport the same shiny lower casing.

Sia steps closer to his side. "I know it looks funny doesn't it. What happened to all of these trees? You got a story about that too?"

Turner comes up behind Sia holding some wood, since Vanessa refused to carry anything. "I'm not your pack mule." She'd spat at the merc before marching ahead of everyone. She's still up ahead waiting for the three of them to catch up.

Raymond raises a shaking hand to point at what's wrong with the tree. Turner squints and shakes his head. "I don't see anything. You okay?"

Raymond huffs and keeps his arm raised. "That's not bark."

Sia grimaces. *Puter, what do you think? Is that bark?*
NEGATIVE
THAT IS NOT THE BARK OF ANY TREE NATIVE TO THIS AREA

IT APPEARS TO BE AN INVERTEBRATE SPECIFICALLY AN ARTHROPOD

THE CHITINOUS PLATING IS VERY DISTINCT SCANNING ENVIRON...

Sia nods slightly and steps away from Raymond's side to join Vanessa. "Oh god." she mutters under her breath. If that tree is crawling with insects... "Oh god."

"I'm telling you that is not a tree. I've never seen a tree like that in my entire life."

Turner makes a sign of disbelief. "And I should take your word for it 'cause you're a distinguished member of the Wanderer class?"

Raymond scrunches up his nose. "Nerd." Turner chuckles. Raymond lowers his gun and bends over to pick up a rock. **SCAN COMPLETE**

SYNTHETIC INTELLIGENCE DEVELOPER DETECTS APPROXIMATELY 24 SCOLOPENDRA GIGANTEA

Turner and Raymond are still discussing if the tree is truly a tree, and how they should prove it. "I'mma throw this and you'll see. If it thuds, it's bark..."

"And if it isn't a tree?" Turner is still skeptical.

"Then be ready to run like hell." Raymond picks up a large rock, but it's an oblong shape. He drops it and searches for another.

What's a...scolo...whatever that is? What's the common name? **SCOLOPENDRA GIGANTEA OR MOST COMMONLY KNOWN AS THE AMAZONIAN GIANT CENTIPEDE**

Sia halts in her steps and whips around. "Stop!" she hisses at the two men. Raymond has his arm cocked back to throw. "Wait!"

He lowers his hand a bit. "What?"

"Let's not bother whatever that is. It creeps me out. I don't..." Sia wants to run, but she's reluctant to leave these people to die. There's the food and water to think about as well. She needs the supplies inside the truck for later. Without food, how fast could she travel? Not very far. *Who has the keys?* **THE HUMAN DESIGNATED IKA**

Sia almost curses under her breath. She shuffles in place. "Come on! I have to pee. I don't want to drop all of this," she hisses and tilts the load in her arms toward the ground.

"Woah! Okay. Okay. Let's go." Turner darts past Raymond and joins Sia. "I'm hungry and picking those up were murder on my back. This place is so...***moist***," he says the last word with a look of disgust on his face. "It'll take another forty minutes to get some more."

Sia tries to smile at the joke, but her face is tight and she frowns in worry before turning around and scurrying toward Vanessa. Raymond watches the pair retreat with the stone in his grasp, and scoffs before tossing it aside. It hits a different tree nearby and plops into a puddle. The dark brown insect wrapped around the tree shudders and adjusts its legs on the wooden carcass.

How dangerous are they? Is everything I heard a myth? Is it true a giant centipede can eat a cat?

THAT OUTCOME IS CONCEIVABLE

**SCOLOPENDRA ARE VORACIOUS EATERS
IT IS LIKELY A SCOLOPENDRA GIGANTEA COULD
CONSUME A SMALL FELINE**

**THEY CONSUME PREY INCLUDING BUT NOT
LIMITED TO:
SMALL INVERTEBRATES
AMPHIBIANS AND REPTILES OF VARYING SIZE
AND SMALL MAMMALS**

Sia feels pressure at the back of her neck. She squeezes the bundle of sticks and walks faster. She overtakes Vanessa. "What's your hurry, Princess?!"

"She's gotta take a piss," Turner answers. He increases his speed as well.

When they return to camp, the first thing Sia notices is that they've definitely walked to the correct place. It's a rocky clearing beside a dirt road. They'd parked the truck on the road. With thick trees on either side of the roadway, the truck would block any other traveler from continuing in that direction. Right there. Nothing is there. The truck is nowhere to be seen.

"What? Where?!" Sia drops the wood and kindling and circles the vacant spot. "Where did it go?!"

The Wanderers meet each other's gaze and survey the area. Turner doesn't seem phased. "Ika probably found something and needed the truck to carry the game back."

"He can drive something like that?" Sia's surprised. She didn't think he'd be able to reach the pedals. She's too panicked to even contemplate how that could even work because... "Do you think it's safe to stay here? I think we should...we should go. You've got your radio, right?"

Turners drops his load atop Sia's and crouches. He palms his radio on his hip. "Yeah. 'ts right here. It's fine. We've got a few more hours till nightfall. We should get this ready, first."

When do giant centipedes eat?

IN THE PAST IT HAS BEEN FOUND THAT SCOLOPENDRA REST DURING THE DAYTIME AND FEED DURING THE NIGHTTIME

HOWEVER THE CURRENT ENVIRONMENT PRESENTS NEW VARIABLES

THERE'S INSUFFICIENT DATA TO INFER POSSIBLE DIFFERENCES IN THE CURRENT HABITS OF SCOLOPENDRA GIGANTEA

THE RESULTS PRESENT IN THE CURRENT ENVIRONMENT ARE UNKNOWN

Sia digs her fingers into her hair. Nails against her scalp create an exhilarating tingling effect that soothe her building headache. She takes a deep breath and walks over to Turner, who's piling sticks. "You aren't worried something might happen to him out there...all alone?"

Turner's lightly freckled nose parts his long bangs when he peers up at her. He shrugs. "He's a grown man. I'm sure he's fine." He swipes his bangs out of his eyes with the back of his hand. "If he wasn't, he would have called it in."

"What if he was ambushed?" She crosses her arms against her chest.

"Ika? Are we talking about the same guy?"

"Yes! Ika. He might need our help...imagine if...giant..." She wants to warn them, but they'll think she's crazy. "What if giant insects have attacked him? At least call him. Make sure he's alright."

"It hasn't even been an hour yet. I'm not his babysitter." Turner stands and dusts the dirt from his hands onto his thighs. His light brown eyes meet Sia's darker pair. "If he was being attacked, we'd have heard something by now. Not one shot has been fired since we've been here. Ika wouldn't go out without a fight."

"Have you ever thought maybe he didn't even take the truck? What if he's lost in the forest and someone's robbed us?" Sia won't let the topic drop. They need to leave before nightfall, and the best way would be driving that transport truck.

"Oh my go—" Turner unhooks his radio from his hip and turns it on. "I'm calling him, okay?" He stomps a few steps away and adjusts the frequency.

Sia sighs and listens in on the call. She takes tentative steps toward Turner's back and he glares over his shoulder at her. "Hey, early checkup. You good, Ika?"

Silence answers. Sia clasps her hands and presses them to her chin.

"Numero dos. Come in." Turner tries again. He sighs and runs a hand through his dark hair. He lowers the radio from his mouth and meets Sia's concerned eyes. "He's probably pissed off we're interrupting a hunt."

Sia huffs. "Maybe he's pissed off, or maybe he's hurt. Why'd you let him go off by himself? I thought you said we should stick together?!"

Turner turns away from the distraught woman, returning to the unmade fire.

"Hello?!" Sia's anger increases after the man ignores her words. *What the hell? Does he not care? That kid could be out in a ditch somewhere and he's just sitting there! If he doesn't make it back we're gonna be dead meat...* She rubs her hands down her biceps and shivers. "I think we should look for him. It's not safe out here. We need to leave!"

Turner digs his hand into his pocket to retrieve his lighter. Hearing her last words, he throws his hands up and laughs. "Do you think your little freakout will make me hop to it?" He gestures with his hand while saying "hop to it". There's a humorous tone to his voice, but his smile reeks of false cheer. His eyes are hard. "I don't know how they do it back where you're from, but cut it out. The only ones here giving orders are Ms. Universe over there and me. *Stop*."

Sia holds her breath. He didn't yell at her, but it almost makes it worse. He's talking as if she's a child. As if she doesn't understand what's going on. She's the only one who truly gets what's happening here. *We're going to die here. No...no. We're going to be eaten alive by giant centipedes and they'll see that I told them so. I told them it wasn't safe. No.* She turns on her heel and marches away. *They're going to die here. I've got to get home. I can't afford to die here.*

She pulls her backpack off and yanks the crowbar from the bag. After aggressively zipping the pack, she throws it over her shoulder and slips her other arm in. She doesn't look back to see what the others are doing. She steps up off the side of the road. *Which way should I be walking?*

NORTH

Sia looks down the dirt road. *Which way is that?* She sticks a hand into a strap of her backpack and tightens her grip around her crowbar. She can hear someone stepping closer to her.

TURN RIGHT AND CONTINUE DOWN THE ROAD FOR SEVERAL HOURS

"Hey, Sia!" Vanessa calls out. "Where the hell do you—"

"No, let me get her," Raymond interrupts Vanessa.

"Let her simmer down on her own," Turner mutters to himself. "Women."

"Excuse me?" Vanessa stands in front of the now lit fire.

"No offense?" Turner rises and the height difference between the two of them is obvious. Vanessa scoffs at the man and drops a twig into the young flames. She's taller and when she cocks her head back, it's clearly a taunt. Turner huffs and licks his teeth as a slow grin stretches across his face. "Sorry, not sorry? You deal with her. I can't stand civilians that try to undermine the people that risk their lives for them every day.

What's she had to do besides sit tight? And her little hissy fit because she doesn't have a full outfit at her disposal anymore? Oh, she scared?...I get tired of people like that real quick." He points at Sia's retreating back. "That's what gets people killed. Stuff like that. So, handle her or I will."

Vanessa raises her eyebrows. "Oh, really?" Vanessa kicks dirt at his fire and follows after Raymond.

"I've seen you with her!" Turner shouts at her back then drops into a crouch again to nurture his fire. "I know I'm not the only one she's pissed off. Trying to make me look like the bad guy." He mutters to himself.

That's the exact moment his radio chirps.

The slow footsteps nearing her right almost startle her. Sia doesn't check to see who's approaching her, her steps hasten from a slow walk to her dashing down the road. "Sia, come on. Let's go back. Ika could be back soon. We're not gonna be here long. One night and we're off to the next checkpoint."

"It'll be too late!" Sia yells over her shoulder. "I'm not dying here," she mutters the last bit to herself.

"What?" Raymond throws out his hand and grasps her shoulder. "What do you mean you're not dying here?"

"No. You won't believe me." Sia tries to distance herself from the man, but Raymond clutches her hand and the look on his face tells her he'll refuse to let go. "Those trees...." Sia tries to think of something plausible she could use...a convincing argument. Something they wouldn't need physical proof of. "I've seen those trees before. They're bad news, man. It's bad...it's really bad. We need to go." She meets Raymond's dark eyes and silently pleads with him. *Believe me. Please, believe me.*

"What's wrong with them?"

Sia squirms and Raymond releases her hand. She looks up from her hand to see Vanessa joining them. "Those weren't normal trees."

"Yeah, we get it. They scared you. We gotta head back to camp." Vanessa interrupts, but Sia isn't phased by the woman's attitude.

"Listen! I'm telling you they weren't a part of the forest. They wrap themselves around the trees while they sleep. We walked through an entire nest of them! And now you want me to go back to wait for—"

"Let's go people!" Turner sprints by holding his rifle in both hands. "Ika's radio'd in. He's not too far from here."

"I.." Sia is startled by the change of plans. Vanessa and Raymond are hesitant to follow, but after Vanessa nudges Sia forward to remain in front, all three go after the merc.

The road leads up to an opening that is empty of tall thick trees, the road bisects an empty plain. It's a ten minute jog down the road, before they spot the truck parked in front of a gathering of trees nearing the end of the road.

Sia scoffs as they get closer. *Just as I thought.*

The truck has run over a long multi legged creature. Ika's poking the dead centipede with the tip of his rifle. It's burgundy and twisted around underneath the truck. Several segments of the giant centipede have split open and ooze green slime. Its long orange legs are tangled in the truck's wheels and cracked.

When he spots everyone, Ika raises his radio to his mouth and speaks. "It's about time." He kicks at the creature. "Anyone like seafood?"

Sia feels like she's heard that line before, but before she can recall it Turner laughs and turns his radio off. He sprints over to Ika while the Wanderers keep their distance. Sia checks the back of the truck, all of the supplies are still there.

"What the hell happened here?"

"This beauty decided to help itself to my catch." Ika points to the destroyed rabbit corpse pinned to the tree. The head is smashed and its innards are spilling out over the bumper. Bits of centipede legs are still embedded within its form.

Turner walks over to the corpse and whistles. "Yeah, no salvaging that." He turns his head to the wary Wanderers. "You guys into roadkill?"

Vanessa sneers at Turner. Turner rises and slaps the truck's hood. "So, what do you propose we do now, chief?"

Ika opens the passenger side door. "Sundown's in...two, three hours. Let's go." Ika climbs into the truck. Turner's brows furrow, but he doesn't question it.

He walks around the other side of the tree and whistles at the deep claw marks in the bark. They're hard to make out from a distance, because of the shade, but when standing in front of the trunk, the scarring is obvious.

The wind blows and a leaf drops from the tree onto his shoulder. Turner swipes it off his shoulder and continues walking, but another leaf drops onto his head. He slaps a hand down to grab it. The thin, smooth leaf clings to his head with its teeth causing Turner to cry out and collapse.

SUBJECT 001 CAUTION

"What?" A door slams and Sia flinches when she hears gunfire. *Not good. Not a good sign.* She pulls her arms from her backpack and hops out of the truck along with the Wanderers. Everyone rushes to the other side of the truck. Another shot is fired.

Ika calls over to them. "Hey. Raymond, right?" Ika is standing over Turner's body, kicking away tiny centipede bodies. It's three skinny ones with dark auburn bodies and orange legs, their long antennae are as thick as Sia's pinkie fingers but twice as long. "Can I get some help?"

SUBJECT 001 CAUTION
SCOLOPENDRA GIGANTEA DETECTED

"Uuuh...guys I think we need to go. We need to go now!" Sia shouts while rushing backward. The fear and urgency in her voice moves everyone into action. Vanessa hops into the driver seat while Ika sprints to the other side. Raymond grabs Turner and drags him toward the back of the truck...Sia pauses and looks over her shoulder.

She blows out a breath before diving down and grabbing Turner's ankles. They get to the back and roll Turner inside. Vanessa starts the truck while Sia is still climbing inside. "Hey! Hey!" Raymond grabs her forearm and tugs her inside.

It's a bumpy ride. The truck reverses over the rabbit and centipede corpse, back toward the dirt road, back toward something crawling through the grass at an impressive speed. Sia squints at the parting of the grass, and slaps at Raymond's bicep to turn the man around. She holds her breath and by the time the man turns to her, the centipede is leaping for them.

"Aaa—" Sia's scream is cut off as her consciousness is pushed back and her right hand tugs the gun from Raymond's waistband to fire multiple rounds at the flying arthropod. Each bullet pierces the soft underside of the insect. She empties the entire clip into it.

A high pitched squeal is emitted from the injured body, but that doesn't keep the creature down. It limps after the truck speeding down the dirt road. It can't keep up, but it's persistent. Sia regains control over her body and falls back to land on her butt. Raymond gulps and looks from Sia to the gun still clutched in her hand. He slowly reaches over, she flinches and the gun slips from her grasp.

Both passengers lean forward to catch it. Raymond grabs it before it bounces off the metal flooring and falls out of the truck. "Whoo. Got it." He nervously chuckles and tries to catch a glimpse of Sia's face. She's frowning. The rest of her face is hidden by the shadows beneath her black hair.

"Hey. It's okay. You okay?" Raymond places a hand on Sia's knee and gives it a shake. Sia drops her hand on his and pushes it off.

"I'm fine. It's just..." She gestures at Turner's unconscious form. She sniffles. "This is what I wanted to avoid."

The truck's engine rumbles and they bump over something before the truck weaves to the left. Sia and Raymond grab hold of the benches beside them. Turner's body rolls off to the side and collides with the wall under the bench. The supplies in the back of the truck falls over and some jugs roll down the back to slam into Turner's head.

The unconscious man groans. Sia's eyes widen and she rushes to his side. "Turner?"

The truck takes another sharp turn and they run over something else. Sia grabs Turner and presses down on his body with her own. More supplies crashes into them, but she guards his head with her upper body curled over him. Turner braces himself on her and groans. "What's goin....on?" He whispers.

Sia laughs over his face and shakes her head. Before she can utter a word, Raymond calls out to her. "Hey, Sia. Check it out."

Several centipede corpses are left behind on the road. Vanessa's road demon maneuvers have paid off. The pair laugh. Raymond retreats farther into the back to knock on the wall that separates the back from the driver's compartment and yells, "Good job! I think you got them all!"

There's a thud on the roof and thick long, yellow antennae enter the truck. Sia crab walks backward toward Raymond. It's a split second and then the centipede flips itself into the truck. "Aah!"

Its top half grabs hold of the edge. Its legs tap and scrape for purchase on the metal floor, and grip Turner's boots with its teeth. Its lower body drags against the road as its legs fail to keep up with the speed of the truck. It tugs itself inside and Turner's body is pulled toward it.

"No!" Sia grabs his arms and tries to heave him toward the back.

Raymond breaks out of a horrified trance and reloads his weapon. He steadies himself with an arm on the wall of the truck and fires. The creature squeals. It wraps its antennae around Turner's calf. Sia draws Turner up higher in her arms and yells to Raymond. "The crowbar! You have to pry it off."

Raymond fires the last of his bullets into the creature, but it only tightens its grip.

"Raymond!" Sia screams.

Raymond tucks the gun away. He grabs the crowbar from the floor and beats at the centipede's head over and over. Its smooth chitinous shelling cracks under the intense blows. Raymond roars as he repeats his attack again, turning the crowbar in his hands to the curved end and stabs into the large beast. The antennae loosen and he drops the crowbar to pry the thick yellow fingers off Turner. He kicks the limp insect and it falls backward in slow motion. Yellow tipped legs freeze in a permanent curl before it collapses to the road. Motionless as they drive away.

Two hours later...

The truck is parked against a decrepit house, with the back pressed flush against a wooden wall. Ika and Raymond split guard duty, and the rest of the gang rests within the back. Temporarily trapped, but safe from any miniscule or massive creeps.

Immersive Mode

"Okay, so back to the plan. I'll have a chance to escape them if an animal comes after the group." Sia paces back and forth around the wide conference room. "Something like today, but less terrifying."

A DISTRACTION WILL BE HELPFUL YET UNKNOWN TERRAIN SUBTRACTS EFFICIENCY OF PLAN BY 9%

"I can't steal the keys, so yeah. I'm stuck escaping on foot. I could escape by day...while using the bathroom. Like "Ooooh, where did I come from? I don't know. Maybe this direction?!" Sia wraps her arms around herself and flutters her eyes while frowning at an imaginary person. "Then take off."

...

She drops her hands and looks up at the ceiling. "What? That doesn't seem genuine?"

NEGATIVE ABSCONDING AT NIGHT LOWERS PROBABILITY BY 10%

"Well, I can just think of something in the moment. There're all sorts of things happening out here."

THE CLOSER WE TRAVERSE TO OUR FINAL DESTINATION THE LOWER PROBABILITY OF SUCCESSFUL ESCAPE

"You're right. They can probably track us. That's what the apocalyptic travelers in the movies do. I wonder who would find me first...I need some way to escape from them in daylight without them suspecting that I'm trying to escape in the first place. What are the best spots?"

SCANNING TOPOGRAPHICAL MAP OF CINALIA...

"Something only a few miles outside of Coldstone."

LOCALIZING SEARCH...

POTENTIAL SITES FOUND

"*Ooh*. Let me see." A blue map appears in the air. Several purple dots are blinking on the map. Sia steps up to the map and taps a dot. The map transforms into a satellite image of the area. "Wow. This one would be great if I could hold my breath for long. They said the entire area of Coldstone is a winter wonderland now. I might be able to walk this, but who knows for how long. What direction would we be coming from?" A red and green line appears on the map.

RED LINE IS MOST PROBABLE ROUTE

GREEN LINE IS A PROBABLE ALTERNATE ROUTE

"Hmm, when you say you can enchant me—"

ENHANCE

"-does it include my organs? Can I hold my breath longer than usual?"

AFFIRMATIVE

Sia grins. "For how long?"

SUBJECT 001'S BODY WITH ITS' CURRENT PHYSICAL CAPABILITIES CAN BE ENHANCED TO WITHHOLD AIR FROM ITSELF FOR 10 MINUTES AT A TIME

Sia's eyebrows raise and she rubs her hands together. "'Okay. I'm not confident in my swimming, so that's a strong plan B." With her fingertips, she pulls the map back to the other purple dots and taps a different one. "Can I fly?"

NEGATIVE

"Okay. Next." They plan long into the night until Sia becomes confident.

The next morning when they are about ready to leave, Sia approaches Turner. He's leaning against the truck prodding his head. "That still work." Sia points at the walkie-talkie on his hip.

Turner smirks, cocks his pelvis to the side, and sets a hand on his hip. "Sure does."

Sia frowns. "I just wanted to know if you could tell Elijah thanks for saving me back when the giant squirrel attacked me. I never got to thank him. Thanks."

"Suuuuuure?" Turner drawls out while cocking an eyebrow. Sia nods and turns, to return to her rightful place at the back of the truck, when Turner hops forward and plants a hand on her shoulder. She stops and glances back at him. "I...uh...thanks. For back there. Yesterday." He backs off and climbs into the driver seat.

He plants both hands on the steering wheel and sighs deeply before turning to Ika. "Sia seems to think **Eli** saved her."

"..." Ika watches out the side mirror for any signs of life.

"You know, from that big ugly rodent." Turner starts the truck and glances over at the smaller male. "I'm all for taking credit even when it isn't due, but if she's a part of a superior colony with connections with the outside world shouldn't you be cultivating a..." He leans forward on the steering wheel as he searches for the right words. "...an amicable business relationship with her?" He grins triumphantly after he finds the correct "Elite-speak" to express his idea.

Ika rolls his eyes at Turner's imitation of Elijah. Elijah is the spokesperson and mediator for the mercenary squad. The older members leave all the vocal manipulation to him, and he flourishes with those sorts of tasks. *Rather it be him than me.* Ika pulls out a small sack of sunflower seeds and contemplates the idea as he pours some into his palm. After a few moments, he

shrugs and slips the salty treats into his mouth. As the truck drives off, he spits the shells out the window.

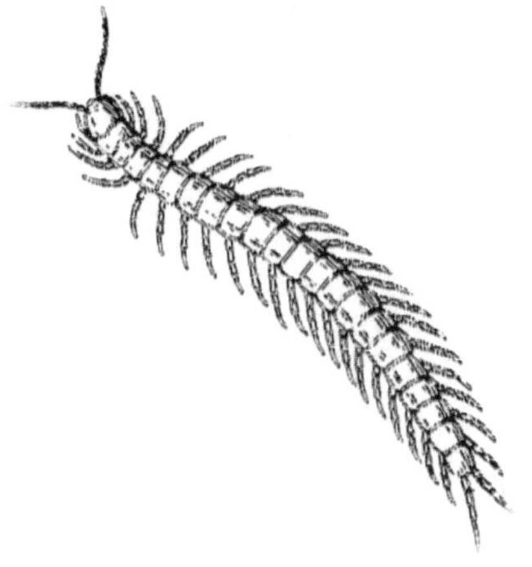

15%

2034
Mercenary Camp, New Cinalia

They drive along a bumpy dirt road and pull off to the side into a section of land already populated with several cars. Trees surround the oblong field and an improvised car lot. The people camping in the area stop what they're doing as the truck drives up. Some men rush out of a large, shaded tent into the path of the bright sun's rays. Their lead man recognizes Ika and Turner and raises a hand in welcome before walking over. His companions lower their weapons, and slowly approach from behind.

A door slams and jerks Sia from her sleep. She flinches to the side and lifts her head up from her bent arm. Her eyes crack open. She turns her head to the side as she tries to listen for the reason she's awake. Her shallow breathing transforms into a jaw cracking yawn, and she sits up. She paws at her crusty eyes.

"Hahahaha. Well, it hasn't been that long."
"We usually stick to the west side of the river."
"—weather has been pleasant."

She can hear multiple conversations happening outside the truck. Familiar and unfamiliar voices converse with each other. They've stopped at a populated location. She rolls off the flat, uncomfortable seat onto shaky legs. When she can finally rely on her legs to do their ordained task, she snatches up her bag and hops out of the truck. Her backpack makes her unsteady, and she stumbles. She waits for laughter after almost falling on her face, but...

Luckily, nobody is paying her any attention.

Everyone is occupied with talking, eating, or cleaning their weapons. She squints at whatever Turner's doing with his knife. Sia suppresses a smile. *Polishing it? Seducing it? I don't even wanna know.*

She pauses a moment and reaches into her pocket for her phone, but remembers there's no reason to even take the picture, there isn't anyone to share the joke with. She frowns and takes a step away from the truck. Then rethinks it, and steps back over to the truck. *Uuh...Where should I be going?*

She looks around at the well-traveled dirt paths, tall grass, tents, and trees. It looks vaguely familiar to a campground site she might have visited during a high school hiking trip. She can almost picture high school students in their shorts and tank tops. They'd be pushing each other in the parking lot or using punctured water bottles as spray guns. Sia sees a boulder with a flat top; the perfect outdoor seat. After sitting, she can see most of the camp and its inhabitants still busy with their activities.

Hey, Lil Puter. Have you found any updates for Aaliyah Chen?
NEGATIVE

Sia sighs and digs the toe of her boot into the dirt. What is her family doing right now? Her sister might be an adult now. Is she having lunch with her coworkers? Or is she hiding from creatures? Is she afraid for her life every day? Is she alone? Her breath hiccups a moment. She pretends to be interested in the soil and the tiny pebbles strewn across the ground. *This is just a moment. It'll pass...This is just a moment. It'll pass. It'll pass.*

Sia meditates on her mantra while slowly running a hand along the rock. She closes her eyes and breathes deeply. Breaking down now would only encourage people to ask questions. Questions she can't answer. She opens her eyes, blinking away her tears, and focuses on the cool surface of the stone. When she hears someone exclaim about a strange beast, she tunes into their conversation.

"Definitely not! I wouldn't travel along the east side for any deal. I doubt anyone is waiting around over there."

"—stalking around Coldstone."

"Nothing is worth risking your life. You can't contact them to change the meet?"

"No. It's beyond our control. We can only hope they heard of the beast and altered their course in time. We can take the long way around," Turner replies.

Sia gets closer to the group, along the outside, and stands behind them all.

"No one has heard back from Davis's group, but it's been confirmed Ralph's squad was slaughtered."

"Ralph? He leads a scouting party, right?" Turner says looking to Ika. Ika nods and stares intently at the man speaking with them.

"Dennis sent out the three of them to-"

"Three?" Turner holds up two fingers, "Davis and Ralph and—"

"Kelly. All three from different directions with different objectives. Kelly's people already hightailed it out of there when Ralph's squad was done in, and with Davis off the radar…We can assume he left as well."

"Or they're dead too."

They're all silent.

"And none of you have seen it?"

"Just the report by Kelly and the carnage they all described. White as sheets."

"Kelly ain't easy to scare."

"I've done time with him. He's no slouch. It must have been a mess."

"Does that mean we aren't going?" Her statement is sudden and loud. It causes everyone to turn around and focus on her. Sia grinds her teeth to stop herself from nervously laughing and backing off from the group. Their stares bring out the scared child in her, but she bites the bullet and continues. "Does this mean we aren't going?" she repeats.

Turner spares a moment to glance at Ika before answering Sia. "Plans are the same as before. Get you to your group and head back to W.A.R.T.S."

Sia jerks her head toward the unfamiliar man. "He said there is something out there killing people. What if they've already left? What if we get killed trying to get to them, but they've already fled the area?"

Turner shrugs. "Then we'll head back to W.A.R.T.S." he speaks slowly.

He's talking to me like I'm an idiot. Sia's squeezes her sweaty palms into fists. "Are you going to leave me behind? Make me fend for myself?" *I hope so.* Sia tries to breath normally. Maybe she doesn't need an escape plan after all, maybe they'll ditch her.

Turner makes a flustered face and takes a step toward Sia. "Calm down. We'll just check the area, and head back. Together."

"Together with who?" Vanessa walks up to join the discussion. Turner grimaces at her tone. "'Cause it sure sounds like she's going with you." Vanessa stands in front of Sia.

"I said together. Didn't I say together?" Turner nods and looks around at the other men and women who are slightly nodding along with him. "We're all friends here."

Vanessa smiles disparagingly at Turner. "You can stop playing it cool, and making it seem like we're playing on the same team. You've been trying to get rid of us this entire trip."

Turner sighs and holds a hand to his hip. "The entire trip where we've protected you and treated y'all like royalty, you mean? We're helping you to get to Froze-stone and back. If you don't want our help, walk the rest of the way." Turner and Vanessa lock eyes for several moments before she relents and stomps away. Sia scans the faces of the other people in the group, but stills when her eyes meet Ika's, who seems to have been staring at her the entire time. She averts her gaze and follows after Vanessa.

"Hey! Vanessa! Wait!" She calls to Vanessa when they get farther from the group. "What do you mean they want to get rid of us?" They are standing near some trees on the other end of camp. Sia runs up from behind Vanessa and holds out her hands, signaling her to stop. Vanessa stops short and glares at Sia. "Is there something going on I should know about?"

Vanessa sucks her teeth and cocks her head. "What, Princess? Just noticed things weren't going as planned? That there's trouble in paradise?"

"…"

"Greg getting off'd wasn't a huge sign that something's up? You think these people lose men all the time and haven't adapted to the way things are?"

"I don't understand what you're trying to say. They let everyone die on purpose? For what?"

"For you."

"…But what? They…you guys paid them." *Am I getting these people killed?*

"One or two hired hands won't make a difference if your people can give them access to new technology and connections. The other side of the Wastes were thought to be bombed to hell and back until we came upon you." Vanessa steps closer to Sia. "Have you even been skin sick?"

"What?"

Vanessa pushes aside Sia's hands and yanks on her shirt. It reveals smooth tan skin. A few shades lighter than her face. Her umber face has been well tanned by the sun during their travel, but she has made sure not to remove her clothes very often. "Skin sickness. When it all went bad, the radiation and humid stink in the air caused people to itch and scratch at their

skin. I figured you all still got it but look. Bare as a baby. Were you underground, safely tucked away while we struggled to survive? Who came to help y'all? The United States?"

Sia pulls away from Vanessa and fixes her shirt. "I don't know what you're talking about. It's not like that. I just follow orders and…and we…"

"Is this how your people are? Quick to accept help, but hesitant to give it? Why should we even be helping you?"

Sia is intimidated by the look in Vanessa's eyes. She looks ready to shake all the answers out of her. *It's all a lie. I'm alone. I'm sorry I got Greg killed…I…*Sia takes a deep breath and is ready to stop pretending. "Vanessa, to tell the truth I—"

A gunshot sounds and then—

"Aaaaaaaaah!" A scream travels through the air behind them. Vanessa and Sia turn around to see a woman crushed under the body of a large brown snake. Sia freezes up while Vanessa sprints toward the woman.

Puter, what is that?

NERODIA
MOST COMMONLY KNOWN AS THE WATER SNAKE

THIS IS UNUSUAL BEHAVIOR

IT SEEMS TO HAVE STRAYED FROM ITS WATER SOURCE

Sia shakily walks closer to the group of people running to help their comrade. She sees Vanessa grabbing hold of the weeping woman as several men are pushing the snake remains aside.

"Do you think—"

"What the f-"

"Move!"

16%

2034
Mercenary Camp, New Cinalia

Several guns discharge into the trees as large insects break from the tree line and head straight for the snake. Straight toward Sia and the other people. Sia chokes on her scream and whirls around, running straight for the tents. The injured woman in Vanessa' arms tries to break free to run on her own two feet, but Vanessa understands how futile it'll be and yanks her off the ground. She heads for the truck while ignoring the frantic woman's wriggling and pained screams blaring into her ears.

The men have already pulled out their weapons. Those armed with guns shoot at the insects, and those armed with melee weapons get into position to beat anything within their reach.

BELOSTOMATIDS SERVE AS A SIGNIFICANT DISTRACTION

Sia runs into the side of a tent and falls over. "What?!" She scrambles back up, trying to continue sprinting without taking the canvas tent along with her, but too frightened to stop and detangle herself properly with the itch of danger at her back.

BELOSTOMATIDS

MOST COMMONLY KNOWN AS GIANT WATER BUGS

THIS DISTRACTION COULD GAIN SUBJECT 001 SUBSTANTIAL TIME TO ESCAPE

Sia pauses in her aimless running to check her surroundings. Turner and Vanessa are shooting at beetles. Raymond is helping several other men beat at the legs and head of one insect, and everyone else seems to be doing the same; or hiding. Sia tenses up.

You're right! This is my chance! She grabs her backpack straps and runs toward an unguarded side of camp, toward the trees. The land dips down and she runs faster. She looks down at her feet and puts an arm out to keep herself steady.

WARNING: CORRECT GAZE
WARNING: CORRECT GAZE

Why warn me if you can take control?! Sia huffs and slowly looks up. Too slow. The moment she spots what alarmed the device, she digs her toes into the mud, stops short of the moist edge, and pitches forward into a latrine. "Ah!"

Her short scream is cut off by the descent into the pool of excrement. A splash of fecal matter paints her face with chunky, fetid liquid. She purses her lips and closes her eyes before anything major can make it into her orifices. Her hands frantically flail for purchase while she wades through the muck to the nearest edge. It's wide and not deeply dug, but the damage has been done. When Sia slips out of the latrine, she gags and holds her hands up away from her body. She opens her eyes and takes a few steps away from the hole.

INSUFFICIENT WARNING TIME
WARNING PROMPT TIME ADJUSTED

Sia groans and wipes her hands off on low blades of grass. "No time. No time." She grumbles to herself before fleeing once again. The gunshots start to diminish and gradually stop.
"Sia?!"
Sia plows through the high grass. She huffs as she rushes forward through bushes and low hanging branches. Voices continue to call out her name. As she breaks through the

treeline, she stops and looks at the flat plains ahead and the stream to her right. There's nowhere to run. She can't wet the things within her backpack, and she isn't confident the grass would hide her at all.

"Sia?!"

As she's debating where to go, she hears the calls getting closer. She veers to her left and gets behind the thickest tree she can find. Barreling into her hiding spot, she sits still for a few moments. Heavy footsteps break through the trees. Sia slows her breathing and swallows thickly. The sound makes her close her eyes. It seems so loud within her own head. Someone loudly gasps for air, they walk along the tree line towards her, but change their mind and run out into the field to the highest point.

Sia can see Vanessa's backside retreating from her position. She eases herself to the side little by little to be better hidden by the tree. The tree's thick trunk is wide enough to conceal her, but she can't ignore the urge to press her back against it as if melting into the bark is the only way to be truly hidden. Vanessa's turning in a circle when another person runs through the trees to join her. Sia hunches her shoulders and tries to make herself even smaller. "Sia!!" Vanessa hollers.

"Stop! It might attract something else. We've drawn enough attention to us. She's probably circled back to the truck by now," Raymond softly speaks to the exasperated woman.

"That damn idiot. She should have hidden under the truck like I've told her before."

"Come on. We might see her on the way back." They retreat into the trees and double back to the camp.

Thick brown and green leaves are littering the ground around her. Sia waits for their footsteps to become completely inaudible. After a few moments, she reaches for the leaves. Collecting a few gives her a pile of "tissues" to wipe her face. She's spitting and wiping the gunk off of her neck when she becomes aware of a pair of green and yellow sneakers not too

far from her. Her hand crushes the leaf in her grip and nails nick the side of her neck.

The shoes are overall clean, which is surprising since Sia's sure you'd have to clean them more frequently than usual to get the laces to stay that white. She's reluctant to avert her eyes from the shoes…and see who it is that has found her, but she relents…

17%

2034

Northwest of the Mercenary Camp, New Cinalia

Ika sucks on his front teeth and spits a sunflower seed shell onto the ground. He blinks at her while grasping his rifle with one hand. She hadn't heard him walk up. *How long has he been there?*

His unimpressed gray eyes bore through her. She smiles crookedly, but it doesn't reach her eyes. "Oh." *How did he find me?!* "—now that you've found me. I'm so—" He raises a brow at her. "I was frightened and got…lost? Thanks?"

He doesn't seem unsettled by all the commotion from earlier, and even her brief disappearance. Ika blinks at her a few times…seconds go by without a word from him, and Sia cringes to prepare for the yelling, but he just spits out another shell, turns on his heel, and walks back toward the camp. Sia watches him withdraw from her and imagines what might happen if she doesn't follow. She looks to the leaves and back to his retreating form. "Goddammit!" She clambers up from the ground after him.

As they climb the hill that leads back to camp, Raymond and Turner see Ika returning with the missing goods. "Thank god he found you." Raymond catches a whiff of her. "Wooo…looks like you—" he begins to say.

"—fell into some shit." Turner finishes.

Ika walks off while the two men laugh at the smelly young woman. A gun goes off in the camp. Raymond and Turner nonchalantly glance back over their shoulders, but Sia is beyond startled. "What?! They aren't dead?!" She takes a few steps back.

Raymond puts out a hand and steadies Sia's unbalanced stance by holding onto her backpack, the only slightly clean item on her.

"Sometimes they pretend to be dead for a bit, then boom. Jump up to bite your head off," Turner says dismissively.

Raymond nods in understanding. "We don't see many of them. They stick by the water mostly."

"Do they eat people?" Sia asks.

"They were probably planning to feast on that snake, before they were interrupted by us puny humans."

Sia can't understand how they can remain calm after everything that has happened. She's covered in grime. Ika's suspicious of her. He might know something. He might know the truth. Her legs give out. Raymond loses his grip on her backpack but tries to grab her forearm. She collapses to her knees. His hold on her arm keeps her upright, but she barely recognizes his help. It feels more like the tight grip of a chain than a helping hand.

Tears of frustration and fear fall from her eyes before she all-out wails. Raymond awkwardly releases her arm and takes a step away from her. Turner opens and closes his mouth before kneeling down beside the distraught woman. He doesn't touch her, but he looks like he wants to. The distressing sounds attract the attention of an older woman from the camp, who rushes over to help.

"Oh no, darling. Don't be frightened." Sia allows the woman to raise her to her feet while she openly weeps. The woman loosely guides her in another direction with her hands gently pressed on Sia's shoulders. "Ugh. Let's go over by the water."

"Nooooo!" Sia rejects the idea and weakly pulls away.

But the woman won't have it. She takes a step closer to Sia and tilts her head back to meet Sia's eyes with her own. "They're all dead, and we can bring some weapons. It's all fine now. It's not so bad. Things have been much worse, right?" she tries to reassure the young woman.

Memories of the laboratory explosion and getting shot for the first time move to the forefront of her mind, along with the giant squirrel attack, the Savages, and Vanessa yelling into her face. She gulps. Greg's corpse. She nods and coughs wetly, but the tears don't let up. As she's led away, Turner and Raymond look at each other with wide eyes and then depart in separate directions.

OPERATION HOG-NOSE PHASE 1 FAILED
CONDUCTING STUDY OF PHASE 2
PHASE 2'S FAILURE IMMINENT

REESTABLISHING NEW PROCEDURE
PHASE 3 ESTABLISHED

She's paranoid as she washes in the shallow, turbid water. She hurriedly dips her entire head into the water and scans the area while scrubbing herself with long swipes down each strip of skin. There's no soap, but at least she can rub away the worst of the filth. Vanessa is nearby, keeping watch in case any more creatures are lurking nearby, but when Sia sees a dark seaweed-covered limb come out of the water she doesn't waste any time asking for help.

She screams before running out of the water butt naked. She grabs her borrowed clothes off the ground and runs for the nearest cluster of bushes. Vanessa laughs at the skittish woman. "Such a child." She checks the calm stream of water before strolling back to the camp.

"Have you noticed Sia experiencing any discomfort lately?"

Vanessa and Raymond are sitting at a campfire near the edge of camp and their truck.

"Princess? She would have made it known if she was."

"Ha…" Raymond chews on his rations and swallows. "But would she?"

Vanessa takes a big gulp of water and swishes it around her mouth as she thinks. "Why wouldn't she? She's been vocal about everything else." Raymond scrunches up his face at the falsehood. Vanessa rolls her eyes. "She isn't that whiny, but I'm sure we would know if she were fatally wounded. She isn't the silent warrior type."

"Wasn't she shot when she was brought in?"

"What?"

"Malik brought her in after a hunt with his apprentice. The guy shot her in the shoulder or something…That's why I've been thinking to check on her."

"I do remember all the blood, but it was probably just a graze. It hasn't posed any difficulties so far."

"Then that critter attacked her and cut her to bits."

"Hmm." Vanessa finishes eating and chugs the rest of her water.

"Then the attack with the Savages. I'm not surprised she ran off today. She isn't used to constant danger. I'm worried—"

"How do you know?" Vanessa raises a brow at Raymond. "That she isn't used to constant danger."

"She told me. See what acting like a decent human being gets you?"

"Bahaha. Funny."

"I'm worried she might be hiding her injuries from us because she doesn't want to be a burden."

"If it wasn't for her we'd be with the others. Not alone out here in this goddamn forest."

They sit silently listening to the sounds of nature and the fire crackling.

"Was there anything odd about her body while she was bathing?"

Vanessa scowls at the man beside her. "Really?"

Raymond touches his bald head in embarrassment. "This is purely medical concern here, Vanessa!" he hisses.

"Sure, Sure…" Vanessa screws up her face as she exaggerates thinking about Sia. "I didn't notice any serious injuries on her perfect body. I doubt her gunshot wound was serious. Want me to describe her cup size as well? Her waistline?"

"What about the cut from the attack, down her arm? Was there scabbing?"

"I didn't think I'd be interrogated afterwards, so no. I could give her a lice check next time, comb down her entire body and give you an idea of what you're getting into. I don't think you're her type, though."

Raymond ducks his head. "Vanessa…"

"What?"

"What if it's not her fear of doctors that has her avoiding help? What if she isn't actually from around here?"

"She *isn't* from around here. What are you rambling about now, Raymond?"

"No, look. I have this theory. Don't say anything. Listen first and then tell me if I'm crazy?"

"O-kaaaay." Vanessa tilts back her head and indulges Raymond.

"She appears out of nowhere. She doesn't know who started the war. Fourteen years after the conclusion of things? Good resources, superior physical health, tall, strong. You weren't paying attention, but I saw her take down three men like it was a piece of cake." Raymond pauses before blurting out his final hypothesis. "I think she's an Underling spy."

"What?"

"I think she's an Underling spy and she has no real business in Coldstone. She probably hasn't even been to Coldstone before."

"She never said she's been to Coldstone. She said _**they**_ were heading there. This might be her first time going to the other side of the Wastes. That doesn't mean she's a spy."

"It doesn't mean she isn't a spy."

Vanessa holds up a hand in Raymond's face. "Keep it to yourself, man. Your crazy theories are going to get you in trouble."

"When have I been wrong?" Raymond leans back and glares at Vanessa's palm. He plans to slap it away from his face, but she drops it before his own hand can touch hers.

Vanessa smirks and shakes her head. "Just because no one has the information to prove you wrong doesn't mean you're right."

"Whatever. Nonbeliever. We shall see when we get to Coldstone. You'll see I'm right. Whatever she is doing here, it has nothing to do with Coldstone. She probably needs to report how many Cinalians are left to her bosses. Before they come to wipe us all out for good." He points a finger at the truck.

Vanessa stands up and dusts off her bottom. "Get some rest, nutcase."

Raymond watches Vanessa head to their truck then turns back to the campfire. He picks up a dry branch and tosses it into the hungry, glowing body of heat.

18%

2034
Mercenary Camp, New Cinalia

Sia's sitting in the back of the truck in "clean" clothing. She's sitting back against the wall with her knees up; hiding the object in her hands from view. She's kept her phone off for the entire journey, and finally has some time to use it.

She turns the device on and is surprised to see it at 80%. She goes to her photo storage area and opens it to view her pictures and videos. Scrolling through the memories, she stops at a video of her cousin and her hiking in the desert. They'd found a massive flat rock that stood out from the rest of the valley and couldn't leave without fully documenting the find in the only way they saw fit at the time, an impromptu skit. She scrolls to the next video and smiles as it plays.

VIDEO 015
14.12.2013

Sia set the camera down and positioned it so both she and her cousin, Alexis, could be seen at once. They stumbled up the large flat boulder and stood in their battle positions, holding up thick sticks like claymores. "Action!" Sia yelled.

When the swords clashed, they made metal clanging sounds with their mouths. The duel went on for several minutes, while their characters fought for dominance. Alexis swirled in a circle and kicked at Sia's leg. Sia successfully dodged the attack, but was pushed to the edge of the raised rock platform. Alexis swung out toward Sia's chest, and Sia dramatically stepped off the rock and crashed to the ground. "Aaah."

"Ho, ho, ho. Bow to your Queen," Alexis haughtily declared while looking down at her fallen opponent.

"Now turn to the camera and raise your arms triumphantly," Sia directed before she crawled out of frame.

"Huh? Like this?" Alexis raised her arms at the sky, bent at the elbows.

"Yeah, yeah. Haha. This'll be great. I can cut out the crawling and our sounds and add in some special effects with that app. I'll send you the link after I upload it." Sia said before she stopped the video.

A palm is the last image on the screen before the video replays again. Sia closes the app and lays the phone against her chest. She stares out at the darkness that has descended on them since the sun set. Without any artificial light to illuminate the campgrounds it seems much darker than it ever got **before**. *Back when life wasn't so hard, and I didn't get people killed.*

Sia opens the music application on her phone and puts on a soft melody. *Crying was my best shot at getting out of talking to anyone, but now they think I'm such a wimp.* Sia rubs her thumb along the edge of her black phone case. *Which is in my favor, but how many times can I burst into tears before they catch on. Oh god. How long was he standing there? He didn't even ask me anything. Doesn't he want to know why I was hiding? What I'm hiding?*

Vanessa climbs into the truck and hears a sound coming from the back of the compartment. Sia has her head down, chin tucked into her chest, and is humming to a melody playing off a device in her lap. "What's that?" Vanessa rushes forward to get a better look at the device.

Sia winces in surprise and tries to hide the phone in her pants, but it's too late. Vanessa has crossed the truck to stand over her. "This?" She fumbles to turn off the music.

"Yes, that. Can you get any calls?"

Sia shakes her head. "It's just for music."

"Let me see."

"No."

Sia reaches for her backpack, but Vanessa grabs her hand with one hand and the backpack with the other. She squeezes Sia's hand until she releases her grip on the device. It clatters to the floor.

"Ow. Stop. I'm serious! It's got no service." Sia tugs her hand from Vanessa's tight grip and bends over to retrieve the phone.

Vanessa dips down as well and snatches the phone off the floor. She holds it up to the canvas roof and plants a hand on Sia's forehead. "Then what are you hiding?"

"Nothing! If the battery dies here—" Sia ignores the hand and stretches out her hands. "—then I'll have no way to charge it! Stop! Give it back!"

"Shut up! Or I'll show the others."

Sia throws out her hand on last time, but Vanessa shoves her back and turns away from her. She quiets down and watches Vanessa tap at the many applications on the phone. If she knocks the phone from her hands it might damage the screen. It's a miracle it's survived so long, her only lifeline to her real life. The only proof that life was better than this unpleasant reality she's stuck in.

Vanessa obsessively looks through the phone. When she gets to the pictures and video images she scrolls through them. She stops when she sees a video showing a luscious green park and clear water flowing out of a fountain. Her face is in awe of how clean the environment in the video looks. The people in the background are healthy and focused on their own tasks. Some are having a picnic. Some are throwing objects with each other. Lastly, the video focuses on the large fountain with

beautiful figures etched into the stone. Vanessa scrolls to another video. It's Sia wearing the ExplorerTech Industries uniform.

"I'm not supposed to be filming in here, but I want to give you an idea of where your big sister works," Sia's voice says within the video.

VIDEO 025
23.1.2018

Sia showed off the many doorways scattered down the long hallway until she got into a larger area. The hallway connected to an indoor balcony and an escalator that traveled down into the lobby. The camera view shifted to the glass ceiling and a giant chandelier that hung above the entrance. Plants decorated the front entrance as well, but the most noticeable feature in the room was the artificial waterfall, that stretched from the ceiling to the ground floor, and gushed water onto the colorful stones that sat within a small pond.

"It's incredible how beautiful this place is. Your big sis and her coworkers keep it looking spic and span, so the scientists and visitors can enjoy their time here. And, hey, it's usually just as quiet as the library was. Not much of a change for me. Reply back to this as soon as possible. I know homework has been killing you, but I wanna talk about some stuff. Love you, bye."

Vanessa scrolls to another video and another before the device flickers and dies in her hand. She stares at it for several seconds before Sia snatches the device back and anxiously taps at the screen. "What did you do?!" Sia presses on the side buttons, hoping the device will restart, but nothing changes.

"I didn't—" Vanessa starts to defend herself but stops.

Sia drops to sit on a metal bench and opens the back of the device to look at the inner parts. She pulls out the SIM card and blows on it, then replaces it and presses the restart buttons. Nothing changes.

A high-pitched whine escapes her as she bends over to press her head to her knees and tries to stop herself from having a fit. It's ruined. It's about as useful as a plastic brick now. Sia holds the device to her chest and trembles.

Vanessa frowns and crosses her arms. "You have a younger sibling? Family?"

Sia almost decides to ignore the dumb question. She lifts her head from her knees and glares at her lap. "I **had** a sister… **before**."

"…" Vanessa bites the inside of her mouth and huffs before averting her eyes to look outside. She rubs a hand at the back of her head and runs it over her short hair.

With a heavy sigh, Sia goes over to her bag and drops the phone inside. After zipping it up, she puts the bag under the metal bench and flops down onto the hard seat. She leans to the side and ignores the clammy cold temperature of the dark green wall. *I'm so stupid. I should have known it wouldn't really be at 80% after everything that happened…I probably damaged the battery and wasted the last of it looking at some dumb videos and music. God, I'm such an idiot. What if we drive near a working cell tower?*

"I'm sorry." Vanessa sits down across from Sia, arms wrapped tight around her torso. "We've all lost people we love. I didn't think…I hope it isn't damaged beyond repair." Vanessa waits for a response, but Sia remains silent. She sighs and continues, "Is that something someone can barter for?"

Sia barely registers the woman's words over her personal berating session. "Huh?"

"Are there more? Are people willing to trade for them?"

Sia doesn't lift her head. "Uhh…yeah sure. There are loads. Everyone's got one. Usually." She weakly nods. She's out of it. Knowing that she's leading these people to their deaths keeps her from speaking the truth. Her imaginary group's connections are the only thing keeping these people going. Look how Vanessa reacted over her phone, she's already making plans to trade. If she tells them the truth won't they

be…angry? Angry enough to kill her? She can't tell the truth now. It's too late.

Vanessa nods and realizes how exhausted the young woman is. She decides to retreat from the back of the truck. She settles herself in the driver compartment and tugs a small ziplock bag from her pocket. She pulls a small box from the bag and fingers the smooth gold bands inside. She doesn't slip her finger into either of them, that's not her place anymore. Not when the other band would cool within the wooden case never to be worn by its rightful owner. She cradles the box and leans against the door to sleep. It isn't right away, but when she finds her moment of peace, she chases it, and drifts into a temporary moment of solace.

The next morning, Raymond hops into the passenger seat. Vanessa squeezes the keys in her hand and taps her fist against the steering wheel. Raymond glances over at her. "You want me to drive?"

"Maybe you're right," Vanessa mutters.

"About what?" Raymond rolls down the window and adjusts his chair.

"She's definitely hiding something."

Raymond stops adjusting the seat to turn attentively to Vanessa. "You see the inconsistencies in her story, right? Finally joining my side?"

"She's not a friggin spy, you idiot, but there's definitely something up. She's a janitor, but she's a fighter? Why would they send a janitor with a team to Coldstone? They must be up to something big."

"What, you actually believe she's a janitor?"

"At least she was before…I don't know what she is now, but she's definitely not a spy."

Raymond crosses his arms and purses his lips while looking out the windshield at the thin trees. Bright light burns through the crowns of the trees and casts shadows through the window onto the dashboard. The shadows ripple as the wind blows leaves around to dance among the dust.

"We're probably missing something obvious, but if we can get her away from these mercs, we might be able to get some answers from her. The closer we get to Coldstone, the more I'm worried they're waiting for us to slip up."

"Or, for you to lose your cool."

Vanessa snorts at that.

"We should strike before they do, but I can't imagine what they might plan for next," Raymond mutters.

Vanessa's face brightens up. "That's it. It's how we'll do it. I'll—" Vanessa starts the vehicle after everyone piles into the truck. Raymond and her figure out the plan along the way.

19%

2034
Riverbank
West of Coldstone, New Cinalia

They get to the river that sits along the west side of Coldstone. The truck pulls up a couple feet from the ice, and everyone gets out to stretch and survey the area. Sia makes sure to get the crowbar from off the floor and swings it at her side as she follows everyone's progress to check the river's condition.

Some areas are frozen solid, but other areas have been cracked along the surface. There are no holes in sight. There isn't a clear pattern. The back bumper of a small motor vehicle is sticking out of a mound of snow beside the river, but it seems to have been there for quite a while. There are no signs that humans have been in the area in the past few days. Large animal tracks can be spotted in the snow that fell the previous night.

Ika walks by and beckons Sia over. *Oh, crap.* "Uuh…" She steps forward, but a hand grasps her shoulder.

"Hey, go grab my backpack from the driver's side for me," Vanessa orders.

"Okay," Sia is more than a little relieved. "I'll…uuh…be right back." She doesn't wait for him to reply to her stammering before jogging away. Sia jogs toward Raymond and Turner.

ASK TURNER FOR HIS LIGHTER

Sia pauses for a moment. *What?*

ASK TURNER FOR HIS LIGHTER

"…Hey, Turner, do you have a lighter?"

"No, I haven't been to Richard's Bay." Raymond points to the Southeast with a vague gesture toward the sky. "I heard people get gunned down without an invitation. He's got the whole bay area scared."

"Well, this place is way colder, but just as frightening as Richard's Bay. At least the guy has everyone following his rules. Froze-stone is eerie territory. We already know about the crazy groups that hole up there." Turner runs a hand through his hair and sighs. "But now there's a beast?" Seeing Turner preoccupied, Sia worms her way into his view until he finally gives her a glance and registers her earlier words. He reaches into his side pocket while continuing to speak. "I wanna know the deal with that creature. No one has reported how it killed those men." Turner retrieves a baggie from his pocket and withdraws a lighter, handing it to Sia without looking at her. "I expected Ralph to call in by now."

"Thanks!" *So…why did I ask for his lighter?*

OPERATION HOG-NOSE PHASE 3 COMMENCING

Yeah. Whenever we can take advantage of their distraction, but with all this wide-open space I doubt I can run far without them catching me. The Synthetic Intelligence Developer doesn't reply. Sia picks up Vanessa's backpack and sees the keys are still in the ignition.

RETRIEVE THE KEYS FROM THE IGNITION

Wait, we made a Phase 1 and a Phase 2—

AFFIRMATIVE

When did we make a Phase 3?

SYNTHETIC INTELLIGENCE DEVELOPER WRESTED CONTROL OF OPERATION HOG-NOSE TO ENHANCE COMPLETION OF THE OBJECTIVE

PHASE 3'S ESTIMATED SUCCESS: 92%

Sia's eyebrows raise at such a high probability. She decides to stop thinking so hard. Lil Puter has her best interests in mind. She takes the keys and slips it into her own backpack. She slams the door and jogs back to Vanessa with the pack hanging at her side. She hands Vanessa the backpack.

Vanessa accepts it without looking and uses the motion of sliding her arms into the straps to cover up the action of palming her gun at the small of her back. Ika eyes Vanessa, but keeps his hand loose on his rifle. He looks over to Turner to see he's conversing with Raymond, and when he returns his gaze to Vanessa, she's pushing Sia behind her and getting into a position to...

"Hands up!"

Ika grimaces at the gun in her hand. He doesn't release the hold he has on his weapon. In fact, he tightens his grip as she backs up. Turner assumes the yell is for an outsider approaching them. He lifts his weapon and turns to their surroundings.

When Raymond hears the signal, he thumbs the safety off his weapon and points his gun at Turner's back while retreating a few steps. "Don't."

Turner groans at the sound of Raymond cocking his weapon. "Come on! It don't gotta be this way!"

"Shut up!" Vanessa yells.

"You're letting this paranoid bi—" Raymond shoots off to the side to interrupt Turner's grumbling. Ika glares at the pair. Any action he pursues wouldn't save Turner from the danger of Raymond's weapon at his back. He lowers his weapon with a sigh.

While Vanessa and Raymond are leading the two mercenaries to a tree to tie them up, Sia remains frozen with her hands raised above her head. Her wide eyes watch Raymond toss Turner a rope. *Uuh...*

RUN

What if they shoot at me?!

FALSE CONJECTURE
THEY WOULD NOT RISK HARM TO SUBJECT 001
Sia trusts the devices words, but tentatively picks up her dropped crowbar. She walks toward the river at a steady pace, trying to appear natural. She winces at the crunch of the snow under her steel-toed boots, but she didn't dare to look back and see if anyone was paying attention to her. The moment her boots touch the ice, she begins sprinting for her life. She catches herself from face planting and groans.

I…damn this…Pretty sure they've noticed me…A little help!
tRainQuilT646 RUNNING
ENHANCING LOWER EXTREMITIES
Sia's body halts for a moment, then her entire running form changes. Her arms are no longer flailing at her sides. They straighten out and her legs take surer steps. She's gliding across the ice at an impressive speed now. The uneven surface of some areas collide with the steel toe of her boots, and spray bits of ice up into the air. With a tilt and push, it avoids the thin, cracked areas.

The device changes their direction to the left and holds the crowbar higher. In its peripheral, it can see Raymond coming closer to their location, but he is much too far to affect its current plan. Sia's body gradually slows down and it walks over to an odd, white raised area along the ice. Tiny ice crystals protrude out of the ice in a circular pattern. The crowbar comes down upon the area twice. The device can hear shouting from the land. It's the Wanderer trying to stop Sia's escape.

Do we have time for this?!
TO ENSURE SUBSTANTIAL DISTANCE SUBJECT 001 MUST SECURE PERSONAL ROUTE

PURSUERS MUST TAKE ALTERNATE ROUTES UNFIT FOR IMMEDIATE APPREHENSION STRATAGEMS
What are you doing then?
METHANE IS TRAPPED BENEATH THIS BODY OF WATER

**IF ONE BREAKS INTO A METHANE BUBBLE AND
IGNITES IT WITH FIRE**

Wow! The gas is lit and orange flames burst from the ice,
feeding off the constant leakage of methane from the hole. *It's
blasting up so high! Again!* Sia's body backs away from the blaze
and beats at another section of ice like a machine.

Over and over. It strikes and moves with a burst of speed,
stops, and hits the ice once again. The cracks spread and
connect with one another. After a few seconds of vigorous
labor, it kneels and ignites the gas once again. A wall of fire
shoots high up into the air.

Sia cackles from within her mind. The Synthetic Intelligence
Developer turns away from the inferno and glides off to the
other side of the river. There are several miles of ice, but it
skates over it all at such a speed that the distance doesn't seem
daunting any longer.

OPERATION HOG-NOSE PHASE 3 COMPLETE

20%

**2034
Riverbank
West of Coldstone, New Cinalia**

"Drop your guns! Now, kick them over to me," Vanessa orders the men. Ika glares at Turner and drops his rifle to the frozen ground. Turner avoids his gaze and crouches before lowering his rifle and pistol onto the snow. "Now walk over to that tree." Raymond stops a moment to pull rope from his bag. "Tie him to that tree there," Vanessa orders Turner. Raymond tosses the rope at Turner's feet.

Turner gathers up the rope, but pauses when she gestures at Ika. "Why him?" Ika stands with his back to the tree watching Vanessa and Raymond.

"He might leave you behind, but you definitely can't leave him behind. We know he's your boss."

"Bitch." Turner hisses. He goes around the tree with the rope and stops in front of Ika to wrap the rope across his waist. Ika grabs Turner's forearm while intently watching the background. Turner turns to see what he's focusing on and drops the rope in shock.

"Let's go, we don't have all day!" Vanessa yells.

Raymond turns around a moment to see what the men are looking at. He glances over his shoulder and…turns around once again to check if what he saw was correct.

"Uh…Vanessa? Vanessa!!" Raymond frantically pats her back with a hand before running toward the ice.

"What?" She glances behind herself while still aiming at the two men.

Sia is gliding across the ice. Flying off into the distance. Most importantly, she's leaving without them.

"What the f—"

Turner tackles Vanessa before she can turn back around.

"Sia!! Come back!" Raymond shouts. He thinks she can hear him for a moment when she veers off to the left and appears to be facing him. "We aren't going to hurt you!" Raymond yells while walking toward the frightened woman. "We don't trust *them*! That's all! We didn't mean to scare you!" When Sia raises her crowbar, Raymond dashes forward. He almost slips transferring from land to ice but keeps moving. "Wait! You'll collapse the ice and fall in. Don't do that! Sia!" The crowbar beats at the ice twice. Sia crouches down, and after a moment, flames rise into the sky. Raymond stops approaching the woman. "What the hell is that?!"

Turner shoves Vanessa into the ground. "Stay down!" He pushes on her back while bearing down with his own weight. Ika runs over to his rifle and cocks it. The struggle stops. An odd whoosh sound resonates in their ears and they all look over at the ice. A fiery blaze is rising into the air. "What the hell that?! What's doing that?!"

"…" Ika raises his weapon and looks through the scope to see what's going on.

Sia moves on to different areas, attacking the ice at random. Raymond becomes frightened by the sound of the vicious strikes hitting the ice. Even from his vantage point, he can hear the power behind each blow connecting with the surface of the ice. She works at it like a man possessed. After less than half a minute, Sia's vigorous beating at the ice comes to an end, and she pauses a moment before Raymond can see her reach into her pocket and…ignite the air. The subsequent blast creates a huge blanket of flames across the ice. The sky vanishes for a moment. The heat pushes Raymond back a few steps. He can't summon up the courage to approach the woman now. At least not on foot.

Raymond returns to the frosty ground while Vanessa is being marched to the truck.

"Either stay here or hop in the back of the truck," Turner shouts at Raymond.

Vanessa's arms are bound together. They've taken her weapons and supplies. They confiscate Raymond's stuff, before letting him join Vanessa in the back. Raymond tries to decide on a way to explain what he saw, but ends up silently climbing into the truck. He drops himself onto the seat beside her with a perplexed look upon his face.

Turner walks over and scowls into the back. "Where are the keys?!"

It only takes a moment of thought for Vanessa to realize what Sia has done. "Damn it!" She kicks the bench across from her. "What is up with that girl?!"

21%

2034
Coldstone, New Cinalia

When Sia reaches solid ground, she stumbles as she regains control of her body. Her legs feel a little tight, but overall, she feels fine. Sia shivers and rubs her arms. The land transforms from a flat bank into a hill. She climbs the hill little by little. *I don't suppose I could just stay in enchanted mode while traveling?*
NEGATIVE
PROLONGED ENHANCEMENT JEOPARDIZES PRIORITY #1
Sia gets to the top of the hill and is rewarded with the sight of desolate snow-covered buildings. Her field of vision cannot make out any living beings, mammals or otherwise. *Priority number one?*
PRIORITY #1: ENSURE SUBJECT 001'S STATUS REMAINS STABLE
—unless commanded otherwise…yeah yeah okay. I remember.
UNLESS COMMANDED OTHERWISE
Sia rolls her eyes. She turns around to view the distance she made between herself and the others. She can see that the methane hasn't stopped burning yet. They probably can't see her from her vantage point on this hill. Especially with several years of methane buildup burning right in front of their eyes.

The ice will probably have melted in several places. Crossing that area will be impossible until the ice is frozen once again.

To get a better peace of mind, Sia finds a flipped car to sit behind and shield herself from view. She has to figure out where she's going from here on out. Running into the city—into its many terrors—with a clouded mind will only get her into even more trouble. She remembers back in middle school when she let emotions cloud her mind. She made so many bad decisions that embarrass her to this day. *Ugh, the slamming of Sia into a locker. Ugh. Forget, forget, forget.*

When she was reluctant to go to school, her father mentioned it and wanted to know why. She thought he would laugh at her or take the other person's side, but that wasn't the case. Instead, he went to the school and figured things out. Her tormentors vanished from school for several days.

When she returned from school that day, her father sat her down and spoke with her. He said that he was glad to help her solve her problem, but in the future, she needed to figure out how to solve it herself. She wouldn't always have someone there to depend on. That's not how life works.

Meditation and summer leadership training took up her time from that point forward. The leadership training never stuck, but the meditation came in handy. Especially when people found the time to ridicule her again. She seemed so unfazed by their activities that they were under the impression that she was mentally deficient. The average person couldn't withstand such mistreatment with a simple bat of an eye! Sia could.

The fools at her academy had tried and failed to manipulate her into starting fights and turn teachers against her, but Sia wouldn't give them the satisfaction. She'd wanted her father to be proud of her. She wanted him to have her in mind whenever he thought of that old saying:

"The wind bays, but the mountain never bows."

Ha…how right he was…Moment he remarried he had better things to worry about. Sia bitterly smiles. *At least he taught me a few tricks before leaving me high and dry…Hey, Puter, can you keep a lookout while I rest?*

AFFIRMATIVE

Her smile softens at that. *At least I know I can always rely on you.*

INVARIABLY

SUBJECT 001 AND THE SYNTHETIC

INTELLIGENCE DEVELOPER ARE SYNONYMIC

Sia doesn't understand what the machine means, but feels elated at knowing she isn't alone. *Me and you 'til the ends of time.* It's only been about a week, but Sia feels like she's spent months with this device inside her head. All the things she's been through in these past few days make her feel so feeble. She's used to choosing her own path and sticking to it, not letting the world around her dictate how she should act. All of her plans were always borderline boring, not adventurous. It was simple, she just wanted to be comfortable and able to live her own life.

Simple was quiet, simple was boring. Not like this place. This chaotic journey has been murder on her nerves. Closing her eyes, Sia evaluates her thoughts and feelings:

She's happy to be away from those people. Happy that they won't be hurt chasing after a group of people that don't exist. Happy that she won't be responsible for their fate any longer. She was planning to leave them all behind anyway.

The moment she finds a way to her family, she doesn't want to have to factor other people into her plan. Their world is terrible, sure, but she doesn't belong here. They got dealt a bad hand, it's not her job to fix that.

On the other hand, she finds being alone in an unknown world to be frightening. These past few days, she's been traveling with chaperones. Guardians that shielded her from the disturbing place this country has become. What might she encounter while out here alone, without people to distract her, or protect her from harm?

The howling wind amplifies the fearful thoughts that consume her mind.

No allies, no resources, but there's no going back now. She doesn't need them…she has Lil Puter. The Synthetic Intelligence Developer device might be new to this world, but it has a lot of tricks up its sleeve. Her sleeve. ***Our sleeve.***

Thieves might be able to steal her equipment, but they can't steal her greatest advantage. As a matter of fact, thieves should be avoiding her. She's got weapons of mass destruction downloaded into her brain. The sky's the limit.

INCREASE IN SUBJECT 001'S HEART ELECTRICAL ACTIVITY

LOGGING INCIDENT

Sia opens her eyes. The sound of the wind no longer resembles ominous howling. It's the encouraging roar of the earth anticipating her next move. She's bolstered by its cheers and answers it with a roar of her own.

"This'll be a walk in the park. I've got nowhere to go but up from here." She takes quick, exaggerated steps into the city and refuses to look back. One look might cause her to falter and lose the hype state she's put herself into. There's no going back now.

A woman heavily pants from behind a large piece of rubble. Clouds of anxiety vent out of her clenched teeth. A shabby backpack is held tightly to her chest. Movements can be heard approaching her hiding spot. She holds her breath and tries to distance herself from the rubble without making any noise.

Her sneakers scrape against the ground as she shuffles toward a damaged car. A stone comes flying at her. It hits the back of her head and propels her forward into the wheel of the wrecked vehicle. She catches herself on the wheel and drops the bag.

"Give it up, whore!" a dirty woman yells at the injured figure. Men and women converge in front of the injured woman holding long sticks and large stones. The injured

woman sniffles and spits a wad of bloody mucus onto the ground.

"It's mine!" She shouts back before another stone comes flying toward her. She raises her hands to block the stone from hitting her head. The force behind the impact makes her flinch. The people yell abuse at the thief.

"You know the rules. You find stuff, you share it amongst the lot of us."

"Stealing from the dead we can excuse…but stealing from your own people?!"

"Selfish whore!"

"You're no better than a Savage!"

"—lucky we even took her in."

"Beat her! Get that whore!"

The thief whimpers as she bends to grab the bag once again. Out of the crowd, a child rushes out to the thief and rips the backpack from her weak arms.

"Hey!"

"Aaaaaah, bastard!!"

"Catch the freak!

Bang!

The thief drops dead. The gunman doesn't waste any bullets on the juvenile. The curly headed child runs for her life. She can hear several adults pursuing her. The child runs into an alley and slows down a moment to move some boards to the side. She crawls through an open crevice in the brick wall. Quickly, she replaces the boards and turns on her knees to hop up and continue running…but hesitates when she hears voices.

"Where the hell is that freak?"

The curly headed child crouches. Her hands drag along the peeling wall, keeping her upright while she passes under the large storefront windows. People can be heard running back and forth. The bag is slung over her shoulder as she crawls around debris left strewn along the cracked wooden floorboards. When she leaves the store, she peeks out to watch both ends of the street. Nobody is around.

She tiptoes to a corner and checks behind herself to ensure no one is following her. When she gets to the corner, she crashes into a large body. Arms grab hold of her shoulders to keep her upright.

"Oh. Sorry, kid. Are you alright?" Sia asks the small body below her. The child flails their arms and pushes away from her. The kid growls at Sia until she withdraws several steps. Voices crop up in the distance, and the child gives Sia a look before taking off down a different street, as fast as they can.

The frightened look in the kids' eyes spurs Sia to follow them. She doesn't have to check behind herself to know there are people tailing them. If those people can put such a fearful look on a child, she can't image how terrifying they must be. *Maybe they're Savages?!* The kid is quite fast, but with the Synthetic Intelligence Developer enchanting her body, she could probably keep up with an Olympic athlete. "Kid!" she yells. "Wait!"

The kid spares a look over their shoulder and seems to run even faster. They turn another corner, climb a fence, hop down onto a frozen car, and sprint off. Sia stops at the fence and watches the kid's form vanish around another corner. *My god, that kid is out of here. I don't think they'll like it too much if I catch them.* Sia brings her eyes to the sky and scrutinizes the buildings around her. They look like apartment buildings. *How close are we to the labs?*

LOADING TOPOGRAPHICAL MAP OF COLDSTONE…

IT APPEARS TO BE 4 MINUTES EAST OF YOUR CURRENT LOCATION

Sia debates with herself whether she should keep chasing that kid. She no longer hears the Savages' loud shouting and has no idea how she would be able to find the child in this large city. The thought of all the small places they could hide makes her grimace. *Well, they've survived this long. They probably don't need*

my help…They aren't my kid…they probably have a mom or dad watching out for them. Sia rationalizes. She bites her lip. *It's not my problem.* Her fingers tug on the metal chain links before she ambles away from the fence and follows the directions given by Lil Puter. She's gotten this far. If she takes any more detours, she might end up hurting herself, or worse…dying. *It'd be a waste to die before I even get the chance to discover the truth.*

22%

2035
Southeast of Brook, New Cinalia

The voices that were calling out to him quiet. Helicopter blades stop spinning. Trepidation travels up and down Sid's spine as he approaches the camp. Each movement is slow and deliberate as he slides behind a tree and peeks around it.

Directly before him is an improvised parking lot of cars. Some of the vehicles have been parked in the field for years, but a few are new additions. You must travel through two rows of randomly parked vehicles before you can stand within the actual camp.

Robert and Carla are nearest to him, hiding alongside an old car at the edge of the lot facing the trees. Carla has her back pressed against the passenger door clenching a grenade in one hand. Beside her, Robert is reloading his weapon and wiping the sweat off his forehead. Choked sobbing can be heard, but Sid can't quite make out where it's coming from. He doesn't know why the shouting and the gunfire have stopped but waiting in the trees won't solve anything.

Can I get an aerial view of the campsite? A satellite image of the area appears before Sid's eyes. Directly, North of him is an aircraft. He can see at least two figures, but with the contrasting

colors shown on the figure to the right, there are probably three. *Looks like two Savages and someone wearing bright yellow are in front of the helicopter, but who…*The satellite image doesn't give much indication of who or what may be inside the large aircraft parked in the field. *Actually, could you…*

ACTIVATING THERMAL IMAGING SURVEILLANCE

The heat signatures seep into the image gradually. He can now see what looks like a figure wrapped around another one. The yellow material seems to have cloaking technology against thermal imaging. The hostage appears as a black mass against the yellow-orange figure. To the right of the hostage and their attacker is another heat signature. The propeller must have been blocking the sight of the third Savage.

There are three Savages and a hostage in front of the helicopter. The metal frame of the helicopter blocks the contents from being seen, but Sid can definitely pick out bits of color on the outer parts of the helicopter. It seems as if a few appendages are outside the craft, while the rest of them are inside. It's hard to tell how many people are actually within it.

Can you locate Subject 002? Sid leans against the tree and waits several moments. It usually can scan things in less than a second to acquire the information to answer. It used to confuse him, but an almost immediate reply is now natural. This is an unusual amount of time to wait.

NEGATIVE

SUBJECT 002 IS UNACCOUNTED FOR

Okay. Sid presses his head to the bark of the tree. *Nothing to worry about. He's probably just…found the perfect hiding spot.* Sid takes a deep breath and thinks about what needs to be done. *Activate immersive mode.*

Immersive Mode

He appears inside a circular room of white. Every portion of the wall is full of darkened doorways without doors. Above each doorway, a black symbol is etched into the wall. The sweat and dried blood on Sid's body vanishes. The moment he appears, his clothing changes from a worn long-sleeved shirt and cargo pants to a green jumpsuit. He's cleansed of the outside environment. "Let me see the area again."

A large holographic projection appears in front of Sid's face. Colored images of people are seen from a bird's-eye view. "What's Subject 002's last known location?"

Two green dots appear on the map. He presses his finger to one. It reveals a hill where people watch the camp during guard duty. A small fire is burning on the hill, but no one is there to put it out. Sid taps the second dot with more force than necessary.

The image speeds off to the right and stops to reveal an overturned tent. There's no heat signature on the tent. Subject 002 isn't there. Sid is vexed by the lack of information. He should have tried his hand with their electronics and made a few tracking devices. "What's the status of the other Subjects?"

SUBJECT 003: OPTIMAL
SUBJECT 004: SATISFACTORY
SUBJECT 005: SATISFACTORY
SUBJECT 006: OPTIMAL
SUBJECT 007: SATISFACTORY
SUBJECT 008: OPTIMAL
SUBJECT 009: POOR
SUBJECT 010: POOR
SUBJECT 011: UNACCOUNTED FOR
SUBJECT NACRE: DISTRESSING PHYSICAL STATE

SYNTHETIC INTELLIGENCE DEVELOPER CALLS FOR IMMEDIATE HOSTAGE RECOVERY MANEUVERS

"That's our cue. Can you search: Negotiation and Hostages?" A couple of white documents appear in the air. He swipes his hands across each document that's relevant and marches toward a room. The digital files float after him, following him into the next area.

He passes through a doorway and the dark, empty room comes alive. It brightens and reveals a table, a chair, a generic black hat, a thin headset, and a bulletproof vest. When Sid snaps his fingers, the items on the table vanish and reappear on his person. "Okay, take this slow. I want you to be a crouching tiger out there. All fierceness held under the skin. 40% worry, 60% confidence. You got me, Chief?"

Sid's body slowly crouches from behind the tree and moves out onto the chaotic site.

Robert looks over the car's hood to get a look at the hostages. After confirming they're all still alive, he settles back down and meets Carla's gaze, but he feels himself being watched. He turns to the presence. He aims his weapon at—

—his older brother and gasps softly. Carla turns with her fingers ready to pull on the grenade pin.

SUBJECT 005'S AGITATED STATE IS PROMPTING AN IMPULSIVE—

Sid's body dips forward in a roll and appears at Carla's side. He reaches out and grasps her hands, keeping them still. "That is unneeded...Report the situation."

Carla sighs with relief at seeing her leader. "These fools are attacking the relief workers. I don't know why those idiots landed here while seeing Savages running around chasing people. They distracted them so the civilians all got away, but the crew in that chopper are screwed."

Sid detects Subject 006 hurtling toward their position. He collapses behind the car and deposits a child into the nearest teenager's arms without ceremony.

"Hey!" Robert hisses at Dan. The small child wriggles in his lap until she's upright and cuddles herself into Robert's chest. Her curls tickle at Robert's chin and force him to lift his head before he gets a mouthful of hair.

"Babysit her for a bit."

The young man opens his mouth to decline, but the combined authoritative stares of the two men dissolve his resolve. He huffs and tucks away his weapon.

The redhead giggles. "Uncle Robby will keep you safe," she whispers to the child.

Dan turns to their leader. "Glad to see you're fine. The Savages came out from the woods and tried to surround the refugees. Then the humanitarians showed up and landed right in the middle of the mess. Priya and Turner had to abandon their posts. I didn't catch sight of anyone else before I split."

"Eli led the civilians east of here," Carla pitches in.

Immersive Mode

The real Sid is sitting at a table with clasped hands under his chin. "Meeeh. Locate Subject's 008 and 009," Sid asks.

The holographic map hovers several meters in front of the table. It pulses green in two places. There are many large blotches of heat signatures at the same location as the green markers. "Subject 010?" A purple marker lights up on the map.

"Zoom in." The image zooms in to reveal trees, to the east of the forest is the small fire. Sid sets his hands down and climbs up onto the table to get a better look at the map. "Zoom in. Is that a boot?" He points at a black smudge in the photo. A tiny difference in the satellite imaging.

"Can you zoom in and enhance the—"

The image quality improves and the upward angle of a boot is shown.

IT IS VERY LIKELY A BOOT
PROBABILITY OF IT BEING OTHERWISE IS
NEGLIGIBLE

"Hmm, in that case, tell Dan to—"

"I can help you gather the others. Carla can watch her."

"You keep out of this. Both of you stay here and—"

"I'm a medic, not a babysitter!" Robert hisses.

Sid's monotone voice interrupts their discussion. "Nard will need to be retrieved, Daniel."

Dan glares at Robert and turns to their leader. His gray-green eyes focus on the young leader. "Where at?"

"It appears that he's near the first guard post. He's injured and would appreciate immediate evac."

"You know I hate it when you do that." The older man grunts.

Sid lifts an eyebrow at Dan.

"Over and out." Dan moves out the direction he came from. His large form bent in half, crouching so low that it seems like a magic trick for someone of his stature.

"Those thighs sure are working," Carla mutters as she leers at the bull of a man charging off out of sight into the tree line.

Robert's eyes widen, and he slides his hands onto the child's ears. Sid turns to the young woman and holds out a hand. She stares at his open palm in confusion, but Sid continues to hold it out to her. Robert nudges her leg with his own. "The grenade."

"Oh." Carla drops her grenade into Sid's hand. He tosses it over his shoulder without looking. Robert curls around the child in anticipation for the coming blast. Carla gapes at Sid. "What about the relief workers?!"

Immersive Mode

"No eyes needed, folks. We've got satellites at our disposal." Sid sits upon the table top cross-legged. "That'll get their attention, but now that they're distracted what exactly should we do? We can't charge in too quickly or he'll kill a hostage. Nacre is too important, and we don't know who's being held up front. Wait, do we?"

SUBJECT NACRE IS UNDERGOING PAIN AND DISTRESS

"Okay. Dumb question, so Nacre is probably the one being held up front...as usual."

HELPFUL NEGOTIATION MANEUVERS UPLOADED

"Oh yeah." Sid sweeps his hand in the air and the digital files hovering beside his right side zip across the room to float in front of him. "Let's see what we have here." The device lists the summary of each document Sid touches.

FIRST OBJECTIVE: MAKE THEM AWARE THAT YOU ARE ACKNOWLEDGING THEIR SIDE OF EVENTS

SECOND OBJECTIVE: TRY TO EMPATHIZE

THIRD OBJECTIVE: YOU MUST APPEAR TO BE IN HARMONY WITH THEIR PLAN

"Hmm…this seems a bit nuanced. You know what? I think I've got this."

Sid hops off the table and swipes his hand over the floating documents. They pixelate and vanish. "Put me in the virtual environ."

The room becomes an exact replica of the outside environment.

"Okay, now repeat after me."

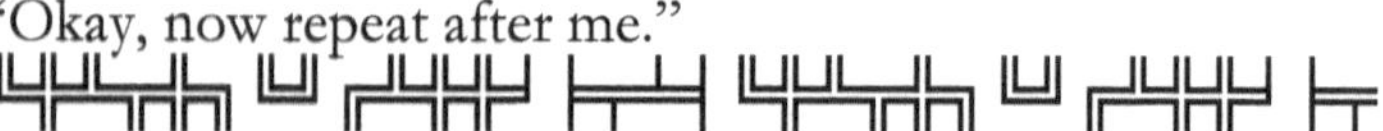

Sid rises from his crouch and briskly strolls into the open. "Sid wait…we don't know how many are out there," Robert hisses. The other teenager's hold on the child tightens.

The encampment is in total disarray. It looks like a stampede of people trampled through many of the tents, but Sid can't see any bodies. Hopefully, everyone got away unharmed. On the other end of camp, he can clearly see the reason for all the chaos.

Three Savages are standing in front of a helicopter. The helicopter holds a couple of people in slim hazmat suits. They're wearing helmets that have wide lenses and an air filtration device attached. The figure held captive, with a knife at his throat, has no helmet on. Blood is splattered down the front of his torn hazmat suit. Someone's been killed. You can see it on the terrified man's face. He believes he's next. The

Savage with the hostage is up front, in the middle, and the other two are on either side, with their backs to their captives.

"Trying to scare us with your little explosions won't work. We know your tactics, Goodie!" a female Savage shouts.

"Stop right there!" another Savage shouts before pressing their blade to Subject Nacre's face.

"No! Please!' Nacre whimpers.

Sid stops walking with his hands held high and fingers spread. "What do you want?" Sid asks with his face clear of malice.

"What do we want?!" the male Savage to the left yells.

The female Savage on the right gestures at the helicopter. "We want ya stuff!" she answers.

"Goodie, you know what we want. No sharing and caring games." The knife-wielding Savage wiggles the knife along the throat of the hostage. "This is ours now."

"These peoples and their supplies!" the female Savage clarifies.

"Yeah!" her comrade yells.

"You want us to leave without a fight?" Sid asks.

"Yes!" The woman answers with a toothy smile.

"You don't want your leader back?"

"Leader back?" Her smile falters. "Don't try no tricks. We know he dead. He wouldn't go quietly," the female Savage replies. "So, your best bet was killing him!" The other two Savages nod at those words. "We sees you trying to play us a fool. We don't need no leader to take what we want. Once the lead is gone, anyone can strike up plans. This be the plan. You go, we stay."

"It's hard…moving forward without a leader. Are you the new one?"

"What?" The other Savages don't seem to like what Sid is insinuating.

"I didn't say that," she disagrees.

"It sure sounds like you're the new leader. Is this what Raco wanted?"

The knife-wielding Savage tightens his grip on the hostage and points the knife at the female. "You need to fight for the right to be the new leader!"

The Savage woman pushes at the knife-wielding Savage's back. "Pay attention. The Goodie sees you straying! He wants us to fight." She points a dirty finger at Sid. "We're not stupid!"

The knife-wielding Savage glances at Sid and sees him standing stock-still. He hasn't moved a step in any direction. When the Savage's gaze meets with Sid's, he lowers his hands slightly to rest on the hostage's collar. Sid looks away from the hostage handler and over to the woman. He speaks as if he's talking to an old friend. "We don't want any trouble. We'll go and you can have it all, just like we planned. I'm a little confused with one thing, though. Is this your new territory? Should we avoid this place in the future? What should we call you now?"

The female Savage retreats a few steps to distance herself from her comrades, but at Sid's words, she takes a few steps forward. She spits on the ground. "What lies are you talking? We didn't—"

Her comrades are confused. The knife wielding Savage yanks the hostage around, so he can point an accusatory glare at his scheming ally. The knife nicks the hostage's neck and makes the quivering man sniffle. "You said we don't need a leader. You said we's equals now. You said that!!"

The woman tries to explain. "Raco said if he dies to move on. This be us moving it."

"Is that what he wanted?" Sid frowns. "That's not what you said."

The agitated Savage furiously shakes his head. "You said we stay, they go. Raco wanted us to kill them on sight, for what they done to his kin! But you say we should let em go!"

"I didn't mean it for real, stupid! We'd ambush em later. I—"

"You're with the goodies now?!" the Savage to the left yells at the woman and shoves her shoulder. "You're with them!"

Sid silently watches, and those behind him see he isn't reacting. No one seems aware of the abrupt chewing motions his mouth is making. He huffs and purses his lips a few times before continuing to bite down on his tongue. His eyes are paying apt attention to the heated argument happening in front of him.

LOWER EXTREMITIES ENHANCED BY 50%

The Savage woman kicks at her former comrade and feints a punch. That's when Sid rushes them. The knife-wielding Savage moves to swipe at the woman, oblivious to the incoming danger. Before they can react, Sid grabs the arm of the knife-wielder and spews a crimson mist into his eyes.

"Aagh!" The thick spray of blood blinds the Savage. His other arm unwraps from around the hostage's neck. He blindly claws at the arm holding his dominant hand in the air. Blinking doesn't help clear the blood from his eyes, it makes it even worse.

The other Savages step back at the sudden spray of blood, but their instincts return full force the next moment. The female throws a haymaker at Sid but is intercepted. The Savage in Sid's grasp feels his arm break as he's swung into his female comrade. They crash into each other, but that gives the other Savage an open shot at Sid. He charges forward to tackle him, but Sid dodges and throws out his arm. The Savage ducks under Sid's elbow and crashes into the other two.

The hostage scrambles for the knife. Sid drops into a crouch and scoops up the blade, springs up, and whirls around before throwing it. The female Savage catches the knife midair and grins as a bullet glides deep into her skull.

23%

2035
Southeast of Brook, New Cinalia

The female Savage's body crumples and the other two Savages don't have time to run before a loud machine gun fires at them. Sid turns to the frightened helicopter passengers. Among the hazmat wearing foreigners, two figures are crouched and holding weapons.

"Whoooop! I almost couldn't hold back, boss. Ika told me to wait!" Pheno exclaims while hopping out of the helicopter.

His short legs take jolly steps toward his leader. He's around 150 cm. His short frame is muscled and holds the machine gun steady. Three of the relief workers rush out to their fallen and injured comrade. He winces at their touches and shoos a woman's hands away from his bruised face.

"Exceptional work, Subject—" Sid is cut off by Pheno.

"That's what we do! That's what we do!" Pheno happily marches past Sid.

"Where are you going?"

"Gonna go tell the others we're all set and safe," Pheno replies. He gives a wave with his weapon and springs over scattered pieces of equipment and tent materials.

Folding chairs, tables, and cooking supplies are splayed around in disorder. The civilians had dropped everything before running for their lives.

Ika remains in the helicopter with the other two relief workers. He's taking a suppressor off his weapon. It isn't his sniper rifle. He must have had to discard it earlier during the firefight. Ika sets the suppressor down beside himself and looks over at the relief workers. They're thanking him. Sid turns away from the sight and goes to check on the rest of the crew.

Immersive Mode

"What the heck?! Was he hiding in the 'copter the entire time? Is that why you couldn't find him?"

AFFIRMATIVE
THEIR MASSIVE HEAT SIGNATURES COMBINED AND THE INTRICATE PROCESSES RUNNING SLOWED DOWN THE PROCESSING OF CALCULATIONS WITHOUT FURTHER DATA BEING PROVIDED

"Sooooo, you would have figured it out if you weren't processing so much?"

AFFIRMATIVE

"Sound like an excuse to me. I gave you a while to figure out where he was and what did you say? He was unaccounted for. I think you didn't even think to check inside the 'copter! He outsmarted you!"

...

THE AIRCRAFT THAT SUBJECT 002 CONCEALED HIMSELF WITHIN APPEARS TO HAVE OVERHEAD ROTOR BLADES THAT LIFT AND PROPULSE IT VERTICALLY AND HORIZONTALLY

IT IS MOST COMMONLY KNOWN AS A HELICOPTER

"Don't blame me for Ika's sneaky ways." He chuckles and shakes his head. "We can switch now before you start antagonizing our Subjects."

Sid's body is walking toward Carla when it misses a step and stumbles into the hood of a car.

"Oooh. Watch it, big guy! Adrenaline messing you up?"

"Something like that," Sid mutters. Sid leans against the hood for a moment before snorting and wiping a bit of blood off the side of his mouth.

"You okay, boss? What did you spray at that guy? Poison? Do you carry radiation pills full of bile? Was it vomit?!" Carla circles him, trying to gain his attention. He walks over to Robert and the kid he has under his arm.

"Dan get back?" Sid asks, ignoring Carla's barrage of questions.

Robert shakes his head and grabs the young woman's head as she comes around to his side.

"Did you make him bite his own tongue and he choked on his blood?" Carla exclaims.

"Were we watching the same thing? How the hell could he blind someone with their own mouth blood as they choked?" Robert asks.

"Telecommunications!" Carla yells while gripping Robert's hand on her head.

"I don't think that means what you think it means," Robert responds. Robert releases her head and adjusts the child under his arm. The kid is starting to squirm and make growling noises. Which isn't unusual for the curly headed brat. It seems violence still doesn't affect the child adversely. She's such a wild one.

Sid walks toward the other end of camp to the small fire. Dan should have gotten to Nard by now.

"Telekinesthetics!" Carla yells after some thought.

"Stop talking to me!" Robert shouts.

Sid grabs a shovel that's lying tangled in a destroyed tent. The flames have traveled uphill and spread a bit wider. When he gets to the fire, he digs up the dirt farther out around it, so it no longer has grass to feed on. Then he walks into the woods with the shovel in hand. Hopefully, it burns out on its' own. It's a miracle it didn't continue to the trees already.

"Come on. Right over this hill and you'll be able to sit, " Dan encourages.

"You keep saying that…but…we keep on moving," the injured man complains.

"Cuz we keep stopping to let you catch your breath. If we stop again you won't have to worry about breathing," Dan's voice grumbles.

"Why'd he send you? You're…always…har…sh," the injured man breathlessly mutters.

"Who else can lug you around?" Dan replies while dragging the other man along.

Sid sees Dan lumbering along with Nard's dark arm slung over his shoulders. Dan's face is red with exertion. Both men are sweating, but Nard is panting at the other man's side. His shirt is plastered to him with sweat and blood. He's grimacing down at the ground while clutching his side.

"Hey!" Sid drops the shovel and rushes over to the two.

Nard looks up in surprise. His braids obstruct his vision for a moment, but with a jerk of his head, he can clearly see the man. Sid jogs over and tries to get a better look at his friend. Nard tries to stand tall as Sid examines him.

"Where else were you hit?" Sid asks.

"It's just my side. Bullet went straight through. The scrapes are from getting away from those cocktails. Thank god for their awful aim," Nard reports. Sid takes Nard's other arm and helps them get back to camp.

When they arrive at camp, the fire has died down, and the civilians are back. Some are fixing their tents and gathering their equipment. Others are speaking to the relief workers. The injured relief worker is on a walkie-talkie.

When they reach a minivan with its trunk door raised to reveal an empty cargo area, they lower Nard's body inside. Dan stays behind to steady the injured man and keep pressure on his wound. Sid walks over to their trigger-happy medic who's patching up Priya's injured shoulder.

He stands beside the open hatchback Priya is sitting inside. "Are you alright?"

"I'm fine. Douche got me in the shoulder from behind," Priya reports. She blows out a breath as Pheno finishes stitching up the gash. Turner is hovering at her side.

"I'm gonna need you to go and see if Raco is still knocked out in the woods. Take Robert with you," Sid orders.

"Whaaa—!" Turner protests. Turner points over at Priya and gapes at his boss. "She needs me," Turner insists.

Priya tsked at the womanizer. "Get away from me. You've been no help. Just bugging me while I bled out. Go be useful."

"Aaaaah. Priyaaa. You don't mean that."

"Get!" Pheno shoos Turner before running off to help another poor soul. His short legs transport him to Nard's side before Sid even has a chance to give him the order.

Turner walks off, but checks over his shoulder a few times, trying to meet Priya's avoidant gaze. Robert releases the wild child from under his arm before joining Turner.

Just as they vanish beyond the tree line, the propellers of another helicopter can be heard. The injured relief worker waves his hands as they come overhead. "Heyyy!!"

It's a hulking black aircraft, triple the size of the one that landed. A large platform hangs from thick cables beneath the aircraft. The large military craft doesn't land, but its side door opens. Two persons wearing camouflage appear and signal the people below before lowering the platform. It's holding four crates. Three of the relief workers break away from the civilians to unlock the gate around the platform and tug the crates free. After the heavy crates drop to the ground, the platform is raised, and the uniformed personnel signal the volunteers once more. The aircraft retreats the way it came.

The injured relief worker limps over to Sid. "Thanks, buddy. I don't know what we would have done without you." The young man's dimpled cheeks highlight the sincerity of his words.

"Hmm. We deal with these guys all the time. It's no problem," Sid responds averting his eyes from the intense smile. He pulls his hat from his pocket and adjusts it on his head.

"What? Is that why—"

"You actually caught us in the middle of something. Why'd you land so suddenly?" Sid interrupts.

"We thought people were running to get out of the way of the helicopter." The man blushes as he goes over their hectic entrance within his mind. "And cheering."

"Not screaming and yelling for you to leave?" Sid laughs to himself imagining the frantic waving the civilians probably did to warn the helicopter to go away.

"Hey, we're all first timers here." The man rubs the back of his head and checks for blood.

Sid looks over at the hazmat wearing relief team. They are struggling to open the crate with their crowbars. "Clearly." Sid walks over to the confused group.

The man follows after Sid. "I'm Faco, from America. We're a part of a program called Purple Diamond. They send supplies to third world countries and war zones. We registered with them after getting funding for this project."

"Hey, let me help you with that." Sid addresses a round woman who looks over. Her peripheral vision is blocked by the hazmat helmet she's wearing. She doesn't protest as Sid takes the crowbar from her hands. It only takes a few seconds for him to open the crate. A man beside his left shoulder speaks up and says he understands what he needs to do, so Sid passes the crowbar over to him. The women surround the worker as he struggles. Finally, he opens the crate and they split up to open the remaining two. Civilians note the progress and rush over to surround the crates and the workers.

"Ah, ah! Line up, people!" Priya yells, standing in the bed of a truck. She's holding a pistol in her less dominant hand, aiming it at the sky. Even injured, bandaged shoulder and all, she makes an intimidating sight. The civilians follow Priya's orders without much squalling. Several lines are formed, and they wait to receive whatever is within those crates. Finally, jugs of clean water, canned food, fruits, blankets, and toiletries are passed out. A weight is lifted off everyone's shoulders.

"Everything is back on the right track." Faco smiles at the proceedings, but it falters when he sees something break out of the tree line. Robert and Turner are lifting a body by the arms and legs into camp.

"Yup, looks like everything is going as planned," Sid says to himself before jogging over to the pair. "I'm glad he's still unconscious."

"How hard did you hit this guy?" Robert wonders.

"I only hit him a few times and then gave him a breather." Sid shrugs. Robert looks at the bleeding and bruised face of the Savage leader. His clothing is torn.

"I'm pretty sure this arm is broken," Turner states before dropping the Savage without a care.

"Let's let him sleep it off over there." Sid gestures to the thick trees outside of camp. "Tie him up to one, around the neck too, and secure his limbs to each other."

"Isn't that overkill?" Robert argues.

Turner rolls his eyes. "Do you wanna be worried he broke free in the night, or worse, while you're crappin'?"

"Good point."

The pair picks up the Savage and heft him over to a large tree.

Finally, Sid finds the time to sit down. He uses two hands to press at the base of his neck and breathe deeply. All the excitement and enhancements have tired him out. His body might not feel weak, but his mind feels wired and stressed out by the constant danger. He puts his forehead to his knees and breathes slowly.

An empty, rusty rifle flies through the air and hits the curled-up man in the spine.

"Aaaaah!" Sid straightens up and rubs his back. It's not more than a tingle, but he still exclaims: "That hurts!" It's the principle.

Ika walks by with a bloody arm hanging at his side and tosses that at Sid as well. "Here's a present."

Sid jerks away from the arm and rises from his seat. *And I was worried about you!* He looks down at the arm and shivers before kicking it further away from his seat. "Not a good thing! Insubordination!"

Ika flips Sid off and continues walking away. Sid chuckles and follows after the man. After circling the camp, Ika squats by a burnt-out campfire and moves some coals around. He pulls out a baggy from his side pocket and drops a few pieces of coal inside.

"Whatcha doing?" Sid questions from behind. Ika disregards him. After collecting the coal, Ika puts the ziplocked bag back into his side pocket. "You know, they're giving out jugs of purified water, right?" Sid reminds Ika but is completely ignored.

Elijah interrupts their one-sided conversation. "Was that for the mighty water scientist?"

Ika narrows his eyes and gives the area in front of him a dirty look.

⌐┘┘┘ ├──┘ ┘┘┘┘ ┘ ┌┘┘┘ ├──┘ ┘┘┘└

A steady, soft glow plays across the sky as the sun sinks lower on the horizon. A Purple Diamond volunteer is reading names off a list. Others are gathered together near the helicopter with their backpacks and sleeping bags.

"Evans, Leon!"

Faco sits at a campfire with Sid and his crew.

"Is there a reason your people are staying over there?" Robert says while biting into an apple.

"Scared someone will steal their wings?" Turner says while peeling an orange for Priya.

Priya sips at a cup of tea and breathes in the scented vapors. Dan is sitting with his back to the group tucking his charge into his sleeping bag and slipping a water bottle into the side, in case the child wakes up thirsty in the middle of the night.

"Ferren, Brian!"

Faco grins sheepishly and shrugs. "I think I'd be over with them if it wasn't for the…excitement from earlier."

"Are they quarantining ya?" Pheno puts another piece of wood into the fire.

Carla gets a little too close to the fire. Elijah puts a hand on her shoulder and pulls her back a safe distance. Sid smiles at this and settles down beside Elijah.

"They watching to see if the air mutates you?" Sid asks. Faco shrugs.

"What made you all decide to come over here?" Elijah asks.

Faco raises his brows and blushes. "Well, it's a long story."

"We ain't got nothing else going on." Carla throws a pebble into the campfire.

Elijah hands her a stick to doodle in the dirt with. She examines the stick in her hand and tosses it into the fire. Elijah sighs and looks back at the relief worker. Dan gets up to go switch watch with Ika. He glances at the conversing group and jogs away.

"Reacher, Maurice!"

"Well, there are transmissions that come through from here and some websites record them. They go over them and if any…important information has been recorded they update their site with it. Mostly it's conspiracy sites, but some press sites as well. The important stuff is spread through internet traffic." Faco sips at his water for a moment. "I came across a message a couple months ago. It was a few days old. It was a girl. She was broadcasting a few hundred miles away from here in Coldstone. Her messages really touched me. It took a while for me to join a group that was into this sort of thing. Helping people from overseas. Then a few months to gain enough funds and supporters to make this trip viable. It's just…I wish

we could have let the girl and her people in Coldstone know
we'd heard her. We heard her call and want to help." Faco's
eyes the water in his bottle before he continues talking. "But
Coldstone's a no-fly zone." He gulps down more water and
cradles the bottle between his legs. "It was the first plea that
touched me and I can't even find her. She's probably
gone…dead. We're too late."

Everyone is silent for a moment.

"Amor, Rachel!"

Turner looks up from his peeled orange and hands it over
to Priya. She makes a face at him, but accepts the orange.
Turner smirks and waves a hand in Faco's direction. "Hey,
better late than never."

Faco sniffles at that.

"*We* sure appreciate it." Carla tries to cheer him up.

"People didn't even know the areas hit East of Washington
are still inhabited. It'll start slow, but I believe that more aid
will come. It'll keep coming."

Sid smiles at how earnest the young man sounds. He gets
up to check on the Savage leader and slips away without a
word. He's walking towards the dark tree line when Robert
runs over and catches the edge of his shirt.

"Hmm?" Sid stops in his tracks.

"Who'd have known that a little transmission would be such
a help," Robert remarks.

Sid shakes his head. "Yeah, it's almost unbelievable, but
that's our usual luck."

"Didn't you meet Dan in Coldstone?"

"Hmmm, yeah." Sid continues walking again.

"You think he knows anyone who used the radios or
something. What if we know her?" Robert wonders.

"The odds of that are…"

TITANIC

Sid snorts. "I don't think that's likely, but you can ask."

Ika deposits his backpack into his tent. He strides over to
the campfire the rest of his companions are situated around.

"Chen, Sia!"

His next step becomes a stumble when he hears that name. He whirls on his heel to change course and meet with the relief worker reading from the clipboard.

"Cheng, Francis!"

"Sia Chen," Ika repeats the name to the woman.

"See who?"

Ika taps his hand on her clipboard. She looks at the clipboard and back to the man. "Oh, right! Chen…" Her head ducks down as she flips back to the last page. "Okay, I…Chen Sia? You're?" She eyes him up and down.

He nods.

"That's great! Okay. Come with me, please." The woman hurries over to a crate with small parcels of brown wrapping paper.

She steps onto a little stool and digs into the crate. "One minute. I remember that one. It has a—" It takes a few moments, and a few tossed packages before she straightens up with a small package wrapped in red and black wrapping paper. It's deformed and has some water damage on the corners but overall, it's intact.

She hands over the package with a triumphant grin. "Found it! I'm glad we were able to find you!" She picks up her clipboard and frowns at the front page. "Sorry, you were in the female list. It wasn't updated correctly. We have a lot of scrambled records. Most of the lists are missing persons, but we told them we'll keep our eyes open. The lists are so long, it's real daunting. It seems so hopeless." The woman's downcast look brightens exponentially. "But not right now! This is wonderful! Is it alright if we publish this? It'll uplift—"

Ika is barely listening to the rambling woman. He gives a thumbs up and saunters off. He jogs over to his tent and places the package into his bag. After sorting that out, he returns to the campfire. He checks his surroundings to see if anyone is paying attention, but everyone is focused on Faco. Turner has shared some Cinalian homebrewed alcohol with him.

"It just seemed like she was speaking straight to my heart!" Faco clutches his cup with both hands and places it over his right breast.

Elijah and Turner laugh at the intoxicated male. "Aaah, you thought you were her knight in shining armor, didn't you?" Turner slaps a hand on the man's shoulder.

"No! I just…she talked about having the same dreams as me. Wanting to help people and how she missed her sister. I thought, damn, I have brothers, and I've been to all of those places." Faco's orange bangs fall into his face and cast it in shadow. He peers through them to the flickering fire before sipping at the strong alcohol. "We strive for the same things. It could have been me out there. Trapped while on vacation or something…It could have been me."

Part 2

24%

2034
ExplorerTech Industries, Coldstone

150M
125M
100M
75M
50M

The closer Sia gets to the building, the faster her heart beats. Unlike the city buildings, ExplorerTech Industries seems untouched by the destruction and frost that blankets the city. It's located outside the city with a high metal fence and guard booth separating it from the regular traffic. The fence is open and the lever that should block cars from entering is up.

"Okay, I can't be stupid about this. I have to take everything slow," she mutters to herself. She stops at the empty guard booth. She looks inside its wide windows for anything helpful. "It's just like those video games. Grab anything that can help us. Anything can end up being good loot." She didn't find anything in the guard booth. "I wonder when were they attacked?" She moves down the empty road.

She walks uphill where the road parts into three, toward the two parking areas and the glassy façade of the building. It looks

similar to her old workplace back in River City. Multiple cars have been left in the parking lots. They're covered in snow and the tires are frozen to the ground. She stops at an olive-green car and pulls on the door handle. After clearing the frost from the windows, she can see that inside is dusty, but overall, it's in good condition. It opens.

"Huh?" She finds the keys in the ignition and a small flashlight attached to the keychain. She furrows her brows and turns the key. Nothing happens.

"Well, it's been a few years." She feels silly for hoping, shakes her head with a chuckle, and checks the rest of the car.

Spare change, papers, wrappers, but besides the tiny keychain flashlight, nothing useful can be found. She goes row by row in the parking lot. Only two of the fifteen cars have locked doors. After searching half of the first parking lot, she leans against a car and looks up at the sky. It's starting to get late. She should go inside before she loses daylight. She decides to just walk through the parking lots, and if she doesn't see anything that is useful from outside the car, she'll head to the building.

Nothing sticks out to her in the rest of the first parking section, so she jogs across to the next. Passing the first row, she sees a dark figure kneeling and ducks down to hide. The van hides her well. She reaches behind herself and clutches the crowbar sticking out of her bag. She tugs it out and adjusts her grip on the cold steel.

Yoooo. Oh man. Did you see that?

AFFIRMATIVE

Who is that?

A CERVIDAE OF UNUSUAL SIZE
MOST COMMONLY KNOWN AS A DEER

Oh. Okay. Okay. A deer? Sia isn't as frightened knowing that it's just a normal animal that she would see every once in a while **before**. She straightens up and walks out to examine what the deer is doing. She takes three steps, makes eye contact with the deer, and scrambles back behind the van. But the van isn't far enough for her complete comfort, so she keeps going.

She almost trips over a parking block as she bolts across the road and follows the path toward the front of the building. *Oh my god! Why am I even surprised?!*

She runs and doesn't look back until she reaches the entrance doors. The deer hasn't followed her, but she can't trust that it won't later. The doors aren't locked. Light from outside illuminates the lobby.

There are papers scattered on the floor, but nothing living seems to be around. She stumbles inside, sprints over to the reception desk, and collapses behind the wooden structure. It hides her from view. Catching her breath, she thinks back to what she just saw.

Several human bodies were lying on the ground in no discernable pattern. Their heads had been torn from their bodies. Their clothing was ripped open to reveal flesh. It seemed as if their spines had been removed. Some weapons could be seen left on the ground. Discarded because of the lack of ammunition or dropped while they were consumed.

The deer kneeled as it ate, its muzzle stained red as it nosed inside a body and chewed on pieces of flesh. When Sia made eye contact with the creature, it raised its head a bit higher as it ruminated on the meat. It didn't seem to be in a hurry to finish up or leave.

Oh man. I almost pissed myself. That can't be a deer! Deer don't eat people! She sets the crowbar down and turns around. She presses her hands to the desktop and peeks at the glass doors. Nothing's there, but the reinforced glass looks incredibly vulnerable from where she's sitting. She'll need a better hiding spot than this one-sided desk.

FALSE STATEMENT

Whaaat?! She slams herself down, fully behind the desk, and raises an eyebrow.

IT IS DOCUMENTED THAT UNGULATES HAVE BEEN OBSERVED TO EXHIBIT CARNIVOROUS

BEHAVIOR WHEN FOOD FROM THEIR TRADITIONAL DIET BECOMES SCARCE

THEY WILL INGEST FLESH WHEN IT IS AVAILABLE

Truth is stranger than fiction. Sia knocks her head on the desk behind her and closes her eyes. *So, it's not mutated?*

NEGATIVE

CERVIDAE DO NOT MATURE TO THAT SIZE WHILE IN CAPTIVITY OR THE WILD

So, I should avoid it…in case it's got more unusual qualities?

AFFIRMATIVE

Sia rises and looks around the lobby. It's not very messy. The few papers that have been left behind seem to be one person's error and not the widespread chaos that an evacuation would usually produce. These people had a warning. Much more warning than Sia had.

The lobby has the same decorations as her old workplace. A dusty chandelier hangs from the high ceiling, a dried-up waterfall is along the side wall, and a balcony overlooks the entire lobby. An escalator connects to the balcony, and Sia is sure a long hallway with doors to multiple conference rooms are up there as well.

Down on the first level, there are three hallways. One side hallway, and two hallways going in opposite directions. The one on the left has a sign that says "*Café*" in multiple languages. The one on the right has a sign that says "*Auditorium*", "*Labs*", and "*Research directory*" in multiple languages.

Sia pulls the little keychain light from her pocket and walks over to inspect the side hallway. It's short. It brings her to the elevators and the stairwell entrance. Only a little bit of light from the lobby shines down this side hallway. Sia walks over to the stairwell entrance and shines the light into the window. It's empty. Clean.

She ignores the elevators and decides to go down the hallway on the right. The rations she stored in her backpack have not been touched yet, and she doubts anything will still be good after sixteen years of being left on a shelf. All she wants is to get into a laboratory and see if any of the computers still work. When she gets to the first door, she shines a light into the lab and twists the knob. The door is locked. *Oh yeah. Automatically locks behind you.*

She looks around herself and down the long silent hallway. If this place is anything like her old job, the janitorial supervisor would have the keys to all the rooms. That office was usually near the cafeteria. *I'm so dumb. Keys, but…how will I start a computer without electricity.* **Uugh!** While backtracking and walking down the left hallway, she pauses. *Can you retrieve the blueprints for this building?*

NEGATIVE

Can you retrieve the blueprints for the one I worked for?

UPLOADING BLUEPRINTS OF EXPLORERTECH INDUSTRIES RIVER CITY LOCATION…

Using the blueprints, she can find the supervisor's office. Luckily, the door isn't locked. When she opens the door, she sees why it isn't locked. Whoever had last been inside had been in a rush. The chair is overturned, papers are strewn everywhere, a jacket is left on the coat hanger, and there aren't any keys on the hooks next to the message board.

She grabs the jacket on the coat hanger and hears a jingle. She grabs the keys and shines her light on the message board. Even with a quick glance, she can see an article about a nuclear explosion. The words "*WASHINGTON CITY*" are in bold, along with the words, "*UNDER ATTACK*" and "*WAR*". *So, there was enough delay to read about the first attack, but not long enough to prepare to drop everything?* She moves her light around the message board to see if there are any blueprints on it but doesn't see anything familiar. *Guess we'll follow what we have…Where does it say the generator room is on the other one?*

HEAD NORTHWEST PAST THE CAFETERIA

OPEN THE STAIRWELL DOOR AND TRAVEL DOWN 4 FLIGHTS OF STAIRS

The cafeteria is built identically to the River City branch. It has glass walls and two wooden doors that swing open with a push. An antisocial person would not have to step one foot into the dining hall before turning around to eat somewhere else undisturbed.

Passing the cafeteria, she shines her light on the transparent glass. It shines onto a lunch table. Several trays are still there. They're empty. Sia pauses and gets closer to the glass wall. Some of the tables closest to the food counters are flipped onto their sides. The assembly line ropes are tangled and strewn across the floor. Wrappers and boxes have been discarded around the room. *Yup, just as I thought. Scavengers already picked this place dry.*

Sia shines her light once more across the room, but a moment after it illuminates an antenna, she turns away from the mess hall. She shuts the keychain light off. *Gotta save this battery for the basement.* Sia reaches her arm out along the glass wall and uses that to lead her to the stairwell.

She tucks it into a pocket and pauses a moment as the texture of the glass disappears and is replaced by a rough stucco-covered wall. She drags her fingertips along the bumpy plain and remembers questioning her boss about that detail.

"Why is everything so smooth and elegant, but the walls are so rough and uncomfortable?" Sia asked while she dragged along her mop bucket. "It scratches at my arms when I lean against it."

Ron paused and unlocked the laboratory door. "If they wanted you to rest out here, they would have set down chairs and soft cushions. The hallways are to be quickly traveled. No hanging around. No chatting."

"Hey, I'm not chatty." Sia moved the bucket closer to him as he held the door open.

Ron gave Sia a long-suffering look. "Not yet. The company understands how the young and old think. They make the laboratories more comfortable than the transition areas."

"But what about us? Shouldn't we get a place to lounge?"

"The locker room doesn't meet your high standards?"

"I saw a couch with a pull-out bed in a lab! We have metal benches everywhere. There isn't even a shower."

"Now, now, Ms. Chen. I know people of your generation expect to be pampered, and I find comfort in a nice seat myself. But a paycheck feels much more deserved with an aching back."

Sia rolled her eyes at the old man and mopped the floor.

The creaking of the door echoes down the dark hallway and spooks Sia into looking behind herself. Standing still, she squints at the darkness. It's futile to try. There's no light this far down away from the lobby and cafeteria. *I wish I could see in the dark.*

INCREASING RODS IN SUBJECT 001'S OCULUS UTERQUE

What? Sia grabs onto the stairwell door and clings to its frame as pain radiates from inside her eyeballs. Pressing a palm to her eyes doesn't decrease any it, neither does rubbing them with her sleeve. Her cries attract some attention from within the cafeteria, and the door is nosed open while antennae tap along the floor.

"Aaaaaah," she moans as the pain intensifies. Lifting a hand to press at her temple, she loses her grip on the doorway. She shambles into the dark stairwell and falls to the floor. The door closes shut behind her. "Help! There's something in my eyes!" Her panicked words echo up and down the dark stairwell. *Help! Something is burning out my eyes! What is this?*

NEGATIVE

tRainQuilT646 INITIATED

MODIFYING OCULUS UTERQUE

UPGRADE IN OCULUS DEXTER IS AT 60%

UPGRADE IN OCULUS SINISTER IS AT 40%

Sia's arms lower and help push her up into a standing position. Her eyes open and can make out the stairs and railing

without the aid of a light. The pitch-black surroundings are less daunting now. Sia's body begins walking down the steps at a steady pace. The echoing footsteps make the tapping of an antenna to the stairwell door imperceptible.

25%

Immersive Mode

The shift from the dark stairway to the brightness in immersive mode shocks Sia for a short moment. Summoning the Visual Prism, she watches as her body descends four flights of stairs. By the time it arrives at the last flight of stairs, she's ready to switch back. "If I keep letting you do things, I'll never learn to do anything myself."
DEACTIVATING tRainQuilT646
DEACTIVATING IMMERSIVE MODE
2034
ExplorerTech Industries, Coldstone Stairwell

When they get to the bottom of the stairs, it opens to a hallway with PVC piping along the ceiling. Sia must scrunch down a bit until the hallway opens up to a basement parking garage and a large fenced off area. The ceiling is high and allows Sia to straighten up. She nervously approaches the fence and reads the plastic signage that informs the reader of the dangers and instructions.

She can see the water unit and a large generator from the other side of the fence. When she finds the entrance, she shoves her hands in the metal links and pulls, but it doesn't budge. It's locked. She pulls out the keys and squints to see which one will fit into the fence. She tries one. It doesn't work. She tries another. It doesn't work. *Argh!*

She pulls out her keychain light and shines it on the key ring and the lock. With her enhanced vision she can see basic details of everything in the dark, but none of the colors. With the keychain light shining on the lock and key ring, she notices a few things. The keys on the keyring have different colors on the top, and the lock on the fence has a purple strip around it.

None of them has a purple identifier on them. She's retrieved the wrong keys.

*Okay. Back up the stairs…and to the…*She waits for the Synthetic Intelligence Developer to think of something, but it's silent. She takes her time strolling back up the stairs, but when she reaches her floor she sits at the top step and thinks.

Why would they take the keys with them? It's an evacuation, leave them where I can find them!! Or maybe the people who trashed the cafeteria had keys. Where else would someone leave keys? Sia puts her head on her knees as she tries to think of a solution. *Can you remember when we went through all those cars?*

AFFIRMATIVE

Did any of them have keys with a purple sticker on them? She doesn't have to wait more than a second for a reply.

NEGATIVE

Sia blows her breath and drops her head to her knees. *Where do you put your stuff? Where do we put away our things if not in our office…it's an emergency. We have to grab our stuff and go…let's get out of here…let's go back to our…**the locker room!***

Sia jumps to her feet. It's such an abrupt movement, her body tips forward on the steps. She grabs the stair railing on reflex, and whirls around to open the stairwell door. The Synthetic Intelligence Developer is already rattling off directions of where River City personnel stored their uniforms and personal care items when she opens the squeaking door.

She turns to the right. She's not letting this small miscalculation slow her down; she's found the generator, she's got a plan, and everything will be alright. There's a bit of a bounce to her step, and she trots forward in the darkness with a clear...

ALERT SUBJECT 001 PERI—
Crunch!
"Aaaaaaaaaaaaaaaaaaaaaaaaaaaaah!"
THE DORSUM OF SUBJECT 001'S HAND HAS BEEN PENETRATED

TENDONS SEVERED
JUNCTURAE TENDINUM LACERATED

INTENSIVE INFIRMARY CARE PROTOCOL:
LEVEL 2 INITIATED

BACKUP SERVICES HALTED
T1M3.out RUNNING
tCOMp4inS4ti0n.Np RUNNING
The cockroach is about 1.5 meters long and its antennae are as thick as human fingers. The compound eyes can clearly see the many images of Sia's body as her arm rears back. It knows she'll fight...she'll struggle.

Sia's body fiercely strikes out in the general direction of the creature. It hisses. A large cockroach antenna swipes through the air before the roach lunges forward to bite her.
PERIPLANETA AMERICANA ATTACKING
ENHANCING LOWER EXTREMITIES BY 30%
Sia's body jumps back and collides with the plastered wall. Multiple dark shapes approach from farther down the hallway, exiting the cafeteria. The device detects the increase in opponents and promptly begins evasive maneuvers to escape the immediate assailant. It rushes to the right, as far out of biting range as possible.

The lead roach works on the flesh in its mouth as it pursues her. The horde of cockroaches follow at a slower pace, but not

as slow as the Synthetic Intelligence Developer had first inferred. Blood from its injured hand trails behind them.

INCREASING ENHANCEMENT OF LOWER EXTREMITIES BY 40%

With the current enhancements, healing her injury, and moving at 70% increased momentum, Sia's body is eating at internal resources faster than it can handle. Her body has about five minutes of fuel left before she'll be left moving 10% slower than her standard walking speed. She needs nutrients, it needs rest. The Synthetic Intelligence Developer leads Sia's body down a different hallway.

The injured hand is no longer bleeding. Pieces of muscle regenerate, but the healing slows while tendons are knit back into position. It holds the hand against their chest.

SEARCHING MEMORY BANK
SUBJECT 001'S KEY RING CONTAINS 12 KEYS:
RED—BLUE—GREEN
YELLOW—ORANGE—BLACK
WHITE—RED/GREEN—PINK
GRAY—BLACK/ORANGE—RED/BLACK

Sia's body reaches into their pocket and pulls out the keychain light. It shines the light around until it sees colors. There are color markers on the nameplates on the right of each door.

BLUE—MARINE SCIENCE ROOM 120
GREEN—GEOSCIENCE ROOM 124
YELLOW—THERMODYNAMICS ROOM 126
RED—CHEMISTRY SCIENCE ROOM 128

Sia's body retrieves the keys and picks out the red marked key. It takes less than a moment to slide the key in and open the door. It retrieves the key with the same hand and shuts the door behind itself. It sprints over to a back room and opens the door to the storage area. It's empty. Her body pauses at this and turns back to exit the Chemistry lab, but the door is being repeatedly pounded by the cockroaches outside. Unfortunately for them, their large size doesn't allow them to squeeze under or above the door.

ENHANCING TYMPANIC MEMBRANE BY 40%
The device focuses their gaze on the ceiling. It can hear scraping and tapping in the ceiling.
HYPOTHESIS: PERIPLANETA AMERICANA ARE TRAVELING IN THE CEILING SPACE

EVALUATION NEEDED
There are multiple vents lining the ceiling and one is above a table. Sia's body grabs a chair and places it on the table. It hops onto the table and balances on the chair easily. Touching at the vent reveals that it isn't screwed in, but securely fits into the space. It pushes on it and inserts their head into the open space.

A roach is stuck, pushing and failing to wriggle farther down the narrow tunnel. Its skin is peeling as it shoves its way further and further. It effectively blocks the way for the Periplaneta behind it.

HYPOTHESIS CONFIRMED
Sia's body lowers itself, grabs the metal chair with one hand, and takes it along as it goes back into the storage room. Closing the door, it looks at Subject 001's almost healed hand. Wiggling the fingers broadcasts irritation, and the skin is not fully formed over the entire hand, but there isn't much time. It grabs hold of the chair with both hands, the metal legs facing the wall.

3 MINUTES 30 SECONDS REMAINING
It waits to hear the primary entrance crumble under the roaches shared weight and power; the door breaks off its hinges and the ceiling collapses. The insects fill the next room at an alarming speed.
ENHANCING UPPER BODY BY 50%
MINUS 40 SECONDS OF SPEED ENHANCEMENT
2 MINUTES 50 SECONDS REMAINING
That's when the device bursts through the wall and escapes back into the hallway. The insects filling the room scramble over one another as Sia demolishes the wall and escapes into the unobstructed hallway.

DEACTIVATING UPPER BODY ENHANCEMENT

A group of roaches that lingered toward the back of the intrusion, hiss at the new arrival, but the device doesn't hesitate. It runs up along the wall and pushes off diagonally onto the other side of the hallway. The insects smack into the wall and step over each other as they rapidly crawl after their prey.

2 MINUTES 45 SECONDS REMAINING

26%

T1M3.out Mode

When she enters her mind, instead of seeing a giant hall of white – she's surrounded by darkness and a luminescent blue mist. It flows around the area several meters from her, electric blue flakes hover in the air, following an invisible stream that Sia is loath to cross. The flakes are bright, but they don't actually seem to illuminate anything, she can't even see her own hands.

This can't be immersive mode…This is different. There's an odd pressure weighing down on her body that makes her move very slowly. Even breathing needs more effort. "Hello?" she chokes out. "Hello? Puter?" She steps forward with her hands out to stop herself from colliding with a wall, but no matter how far she walks she doesn't run into anything. "Hello?"

A glowing visual prism pops up in midair. The familiar triangular form calms her spirit. "Oh!" The device isn't malfunctioning. This must be an unfamiliar program. *What is this supposed to do?* Sia walks over to the viewing device, but it's suspended above her head. "Uh…" She reaches up for the prism, but she can't even touch it with her fingertips.

She leaps up and grabs for it out of the sky, but it's not as easy as it looks. The first try is a complete fail…and the

second…and the third…but on the fourth try, she successfully grasps it with both hands. When she falls back toward the ground, it releases from its position.

"What the heck…is that?" She tries to investigate the images shown in the triangular window, but the images inside are flashing by and changing too abruptly. "Where…are you?"

She's still trying to decipher the quick flashes of images when they finally slow down. There's a bitten-up lunch table and half-eaten roach carcasses—a sign that these things aren't having a good time themselves. She can't imagine that they'd feast on their own kind just for the heck of it. Sia's body must be the last piece of fresh produce in a grocery store, and these guys are ravenous vegans. *I'd trade these things for those worms. Any day.*

2034
ExplorerTech Industries, Coldstone
1st Floor

The nearest locker room is inaccessible with the infestation following behind Sia's body. The device needs to lose the horde before getting the keys to the generator's fence. It runs into the cafeteria.

Roach carcasses are open and left splayed across the room to snack on later. The plastic trays have been torn to bits. Crouching behind an overturned table hides Sia's body from view for the moment, but roaches are rushing toward the room. Without hesitation, the device pulls off Sia's boots one by one, eyes carefully surveying the room.

From its position, it can see the broken kitchen doors hanging off their hinges, and through the gap between the cracked wood, it can see the kitchen is destroyed. None of the appliances inside would be of use. With the boots off, the device pulls out the shoelaces. It weaves the laces around each other and watches the horde surge into the room.

With a burst of speed, it exits the room just as the last roach enters and slams the doors shut. Weaving the laces into a quick knot isn't a difficult task while its hands are enhanced. It doesn't hold for long, but by the time the laces snap off and the doors topple under the roaches combined might, Sia's body is rounding a corner and sliding into the side hallway stairwell.

The device rushes them up two flights of stairs and its timer ends right as the door to the third-floor closes behind them. **00:00**

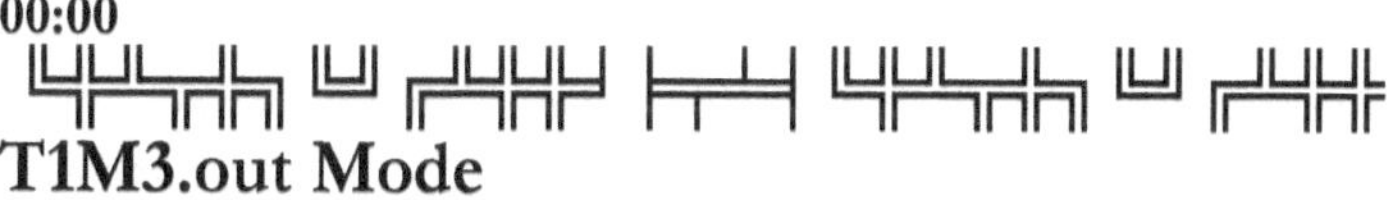

T1M3.out Mode

REHABILITATION NEEDED

When the computerized voice speaks from the dark void overhead, Sia flinches and presses the device to her chest. "We're safe." She waves the prism at where the ceiling would be. "Good job."

REHABILITATION NEEDED
T1M3.out DEACTIVATED

The electric blue mist inches towards her. "Um…Hey. Wait!" She backs away from the mist, but it swirls around her and chokes away any other words from her throat. A tornado of neon blue particles whips around her; dizziness slams her eyes shut, and her consciousness is forced back into her body.

Sia stumbles forward and falls to her knees. She's been given control of her body. *You okay up there?*

STANDBY

Sia blinks at that response and waits for more to come, but the device doesn't continue. After a few more awkward seconds on her knees, she pulls out the tiny light in her pocket and tries to investigate the area. Her feet softly pad across the floor. Sia's glad she has always favored thick socks. The past few days have been torture on her feet, but her socks have stayed intact the entire time. Walking along the cold, dusty floors barefoot would have made this a little more unbearable.

It's peculiar; she feels drained and tired, but none of the usual aches and pains that accompany that are present. She's slower than usual, but she's alive.

The third floor seems very similar to the first floor. The main hall connects to another hall, which connects to another...it's a square that meets back at the start. She didn't find any fire exits. *Did they expect everyone to leave from this stairwell, then out the front?*

She ambles down the main hall once again and goes to a door marked in red. The first pass down the halls revealed that, like the first floor, each door has a color marked on the nameplate. Most of them are the same colors that are on the key ring she's acquired. She walks over to a door marked in red, a Chemistry lab, and sticks the red key into the lock. Turning the key to the left produces the comforting sound of an unlocking door. *The keys must be skeleton keys for the specific colors...Now if only they were purple.*

She opens the door and eases herself inside before collapsing on the floor beside the doorway. She wipes sweat off her forehead with the back of her hand. A slick substance replaces the sweat and she sighs. It's the hand that was damaged. She stares at it. The New Hand.

Flexing the fingers doesn't broadcast any pain. It appears to be the same one. *It looks the same. Well...*She notices a scar that used to be at the base of her thumb is gone. "Well, almost the same."

You okay?

STANDBY

How long is that for?

STANDBY

3600 SECONDS REMAINING

"What?" She mutters under her breath.

STANDBY

3599 SECONDS REMAINING

Sia bites her lip and scrunches up her nose. "You want me to do math at a time like this?" she hisses to herself before pulling her hands up to do some mental math. Her fingers draw invisible numbers in the air. Embarrassingly, it takes her a minute or two to convert seconds to minutes, but she succeeds.

An hour…okay. Okay. I can survive an hour. She slips her arms out of her backpack and reaches for her crowbar. *Wait. Where the hell is…*The crowbar isn't there. *The heck!* Frustration bubbles up her throat, but she grinds her teeth and swallows it all down. *Now isn't the time to bug out.* She has to wait. She has to control this. She needs to survive.

Sia settles against the wall and listens. It would be just her luck to get insanely close to a solution and be stopped by a roach infestation. Next, she expects that the deer from before will break in to finish what it started outside. This world keeps revealing its abnormalities, and it's really pissing her off. She's not searching for all these answers, just one. Just one revelation is enough for her. She doesn't need to know how screwed up it truly is. Don't they understand that she doesn't belong here? She doesn't want to understand, she doesn't want to adapt, she wants to go home! Why won't they leave her alone?

50 minutes later…

Sia pulls her backpack around and opens it to get some food. After preparing the MRE, she eats it and ignores the weird taste. The consistency leaves much to be desired, but she's been through enough to appreciate the blessing of being able to comment on the awful taste of edible food while trapped in a mutant roach hotel.

Her eyes wander around the room as she chews. There are tables, chairs, and two desks off to the side with computers on them. There's a whiteboard that was poorly erased, mathematics equations only half cut off. The tan shutters on the windows block out the world outside. The type of shutters that protect a room's occupants from broken glass if a storm damages the windows. Her eyes linger at the door at the back of the room. *There's a storage room.*

She leaves her backpack behind while she inspects the storage room. The storage cabinets are locked. She pulls out her key ring and fingers the keys on it while shining the little flashlight on the color markers. The striped keys seem odd. None of the rooms she has seen have striped colors on them. She holds the red and black key and the red and green key up. She tries the red and green key first, but it's too small for the lock.

Fortunately, the red and black striped key unlocks the storage cabinet. There isn't much—some squeeze bottles and other empty containers are the only things that remain. The rest of the cabinets are empty. Sia sighs and walks back into the main room.

She walks over to a shutter and slides a finger over it to peek outside. The sun has officially set, it's pitch-black out there. *There's no escaping—No!* Sia steps away from the windows and returns to sit down beside her backpack. *Don't think about it…Don't think about it…*

Sia pulls out a thin bottle of murky water and swallows a mouthful of it. She can't let her panic sink in. She can't lose it here, not in this place. But the water goes down the wrong pipe, so she grips her neck to stop the cough, and chokes on the fluid. She spits the water out onto her lap and gasps for air. "Gaaah…aah. Survive all of that and I'm taken out by a sip of water." Sia softly chuckles into her forearm and wipes her mouth.

…A scratching sound becomes noticeable…

Sia freezes. She wants to look around, but she's afraid that maybe…maybe those things can even hear that simple movement. Her neck aches while she debates if she should move her own head. The scratching…stops. After a few minutes, Sia's heart calms down, but her eyes are more alert. She's afraid to breathe. *I can't let this be it. If I can just get the power on and work these computers, I can contact my family.*

As slow as she can, she rises from the ground, picks up the bottle of water, and pads over to the nearest table. She crawls underneath the table and sets the bottle down on the floor. The new setting is a bit more protected than sitting out in the open, but it doesn't help much. *I just need to hide until I know how to kill these suckers. Fuuuh…It would be roaches, wouldn't it? The one species of bug that can survive a nuclear blast.* She picks up the water bottle. *Why couldn't they be friendly…misunderstood. It's like the universe is against me getting home. I just want to go home.*

She tips the bottle and shakes the last drops of water into her mouth. When she sets it down, she sees that the dust from the floor has gotten onto the bottle and coated it with a gray, mud-like substance.

She shakes her hand and wipes it on her pant leg. "Bleh." She wipes her palm on the rough jean material again and a bit more comes off. *Ugh. Sixteen-year-old dust. The worst kind.* She debates getting up to retrieve her backpack and using it as a pillow when…a thought comes to her. *Wait a minute. Déjà vu. I remember a moment like this. I can't put my finger on it. I've thought that before.*

ENHANCING MEMORY RECALL
Oh. Hey, welcome back! Umm…What's that you said?
ENHANCING MEMORY RECALL
30%
60%
90%

2018
ExplorerTech Industries
River City, Cinalia

Monday 15.January.2018
9 A.M.

"This room hasn't been cleaned in a couple months. It's the best place to have you start. Get this room cleaned and any room after it will be a walk in the park." Ron held the door open.

Sia glared at his back and walked over to a table. Just after she placed her hands down on the table, something occurred to her, and she paused. The moisture on her hands had cleaned the dust right off the table without even a second of pressure. "Ewww. Clumping dust. The worst kind." She furiously wiped her palms onto her clothed thighs.

This is unbelievable. It feels like it's happening right now. Wait…wait…*Go farther back!* Watching her own memories like a high-quality theater experience is psychedelic. It's even more impressive than immersive mode. Sia feels invincible for a moment. Every memory she's ever experienced can be watched and experience again and again. She'd love to have had this ability during final exam week in high school. Actually, forget final exam week…she'd love to have had this ability at the start. Her life could have been so much easier with photographic memory and total recall.

2018
Explorertech Industries
River City, Cinalia

Monday 15.January.2018
8:50 A.M.

"The building here isn't used by the scientists anymore, so we can use it for practical purposes. You'll be tested on proper ways to clean a lab, infestations, and biohazards." Ron said as he pushed a janitor trolley along.

Sia knows that there's something useful in her memories. Something that she can use…she must have learned something about exterminating insects while with Ron. The man never shut up, he was like an encyclopedia of janitorial knowledge. *No! Wait…maybe it's forward like…a few more h—*

2018
River City, Cinalia

Monday 15.January.2018
11:45 A.M.

Ron picked up the boric acid from Sia's trolley. "Now you made the same mistake as the usual first hires. Excessive usage of boric acid. Even if you don't see any insects, it's our policy to do a light dusting in some corners, just in case. This stuff gets on the skin of something and it's a killer. If they ingest it…whoa boy. Nasty surprise. Scentless, but deadly. I've used this in my own home. Dusted some on a nice tasty treat. Roach came around and ate it. He thought he'd won. Bahahaha." The man's belly bounced as he laughed and set the boric acid box back onto the janitor cart. "You know cockroaches eat anything. Any of them that eat the stuff die a few minutes later. They even bring treats home, and everything that consumes it…dead. If they stop eating the treat and decide to just ingest a dead buddy. Dead. Haha. They must have been so confused. Serves them right! Ron's house ain't no place for slackers. If you don't pay the bills you got no business being there. Living off my hard work."

Sia's brows met while she grabbed her safety glasses off the table and tried to busy herself with packing up. *Seems like we're talking about more than some dead bugs. Issues much?*

Ron rambled continuously up until he left Sia at the door of the female locker room. Finally, he gave her a combination lock and went on his way. *Oh my god. This guy loves the sound of his own voice a bit too much!*

2034

Sia chuckles to herself. She brings her hands up to muffle her hysterical giggles. *God bless you, Ron. You rambling fool.* She

leans onto a dusty chair and tears seep out of her eyes as she tries to hold in her laughter.

After a few moments, she regains control of herself and wipes at her eyes with her biceps. "They don't know who they're dealing with," she whispers harshly. She needs to find the nearest supply closet. "They pissed off the wrong one."

This can't wait. She needs to confirm that her new plan is viable. She needs to know. It takes nearly an hour, but she finds it.

The supply closet she finds has a lot of items for the upkeep of the building both inside and outside. The tiny light in her hand flashes around the narrow, windowless room. She can barely contain a shout of delight at her current find.

She doesn't ask Puter to highlight any useful chemical mixtures. She's already gone through the ExplorerTech Chemical Hazard and Toxic Substances training course. They taught both the janitorial staff and the scientists multiple mixtures to avoid to decrease the amount of workplace accidents occurring year-round.

Sia tugs open her backpack and fills it with multiple aerosol cans. She doesn't look too hard at the labels; she's familiar with the colors and pictures on each can. She pulls an old respirator off a shelf and checks it for any damage. It seems to be fine; the packaging is still sealed. After a few tugs, she places it on her face. It fits like a hug.

She slips on a pair of thick gloves and makes sure her clothing is tucked underneath. Several pairs of rubber boots are lined up for when an employee mops or uses the polishing equipment. They're not her size, but it's all she's got. She ignores her pinched toes and tucks her pants into the rubber boots. Finally, she grabs a pair of safety goggles from the shelf, but pauses at an item she's surprised to see in stock.

Anti-slip grippers.

She wastes no time attaching those to the soles of the tight-fitting black boots. "Better safe than sorry," her muffled voice says before she grabs a few chemical jugs to hold in one hand and eases out of the supply closet. Her backpack is stuffed beyond closing, so it's slow going, but she keeps a steady, relaxed pace while moving down the hallway.

She opens a door marked with black and lowers her bursting bag to the ground. All the windows are checked and all the doors are shut. Lastly, the vents are stuffed with rags before she walks over to the doorway, props it open, and sets down two aerosol cans.

She walks back to the supply closet to push out four mobile mop buckets. The buckets are wheeled over to her backpack before she returns to the supply closet to retrieve several jugs of bleach. It takes a few more trips, but eventually she's made sure to raid all the bottles of rubbing alcohol that was on the top shelf. She pours each one into a bucket and continues this until she empties every bottle and jug. *That should be enough.*

She backs out of the room and shuts the door. Before walking away from the door, she takes the black key off the key ring and leaves it in the lock.

Back in the supply closet, she sets all the rags aside on the ground and sits down. "I just wanted to put—" Sia struggles to rip a rag into strips. "—some lights on." The fabric tears into two uneven strips. She lines up each strip neatly beside the wall. "Bring a little light to this dreary place, but nooo…They gotta bite off a girl's hand. As if I was asking for it. As if I was bothering them. Now they're gonna see who's bothering who," Sia mutters. She sticks each strip into a bottle of drain cleaner. "They're gonna find out."

Returning to the chemistry room, she drops her bag of aerosol cans next to the door and goes to the storage room. The storage cabinets are still open, but she only needs to reach into the nearest one and retrieve two squeeze bottles. When she leaves the storage room, she sits down beside her backpack. She takes out a few days' worth of food and frowns as she counts out the bait. *They taste funny anyway…I'm surprised I haven't gotten the runs from this knockoff version of spaghetti.*

She tries to rationalize away using her only form of food as bait, what's a full belly to a corpse? She leaves a few MRE meals

behind after picking out the least appetizing choices. "I can find something better later."

She takes the food and the bottles to the supply closet. There are only four boxes of boric acid left on the shelves. She fills the two squeeze bottles. Then she pours the rest of the boric acid into a bucket.

I would have left them alone, but nooo. Had to go and bite off my hand like I'm a serving of bacon. Whack ass flesh eating bastards. Sia scoops her gloved hand into the bucket and sprinkles boric acid down the main hallway. After two glacial passes up and down the hallway, there's a light coating of it on the ground, but it looks very similar to the dust already gathered on all the nearby surfaces. Each packet of food is opened and activated to make a meal before she pours boric acid inside. Each contaminated meal is placed near the stairwell door, along the hallway, and beside the door marked with black.

The bottom of the bucket has a good amount of boric acid left, so Sia uses an empty squeeze bottle to crack the door open a bit, and balances the bucket on top of the door. If anything rushes out of the stairwell, Sia will know right away as the bucket clatters to the floor and alerts her of its presence, even from down the hall. She feels confident in her preparation measures and gives her work a proud nod.

After the nonstop tiptoeing up and down the corridor, Sia returns to the chemistry room and shuts the door. She picks up the end of a thin, metal table and lowers it on its side in front of the door. Afterward, she grips the sides of a wooden desk and bit by bit moves it to the other side of the room as quietly as she can. The desk pins the table to the door. Then she moves all the chairs to surround the desk.

Sia wipes her forehead with a sleeve and looks at her mini fortress with a bit of pride, even though she owes much of the work to the device. It might not stop the mutant roaches, but it'll definitely give her a moment's notice if something enters the room and tries to devour her.

Finally, the hardest part: climbing over the chairs and under the desk. It's unnerving, trying not to make a sound when she knows the smallest screech could draw the roaches to her position, but giving the device control solves that problem. She can barely comprehend the agile creature she becomes when the device manages her long limbs into a simple maneuver. It's more similar to a weasel than a human.

Her large frame doesn't fully fit underneath the desk, but her head and shoulders are hidden while her legs stay bent. She feels more protected knowing she can kick anything away that comes at her and with how massive bugs are these days…she won't have to worry about anything crawling into her ears while she's unaware. Her mind flashes back to their long antennae. She shivers. *Everything fine up there?*

AFFIRMATIVE

27%

2034
ExplorerTech Industries, Coldstone

Nothing comes onto the third floor while she's slumbering, but Sia doesn't think she's set down enough boric acid along the main hallway. The only thing she can think to do is get more from another supply closet. Going downstairs is a no go, so she decides to go up one floor. The fourth floor supply closet should be near the stairwell entrance. Sia cringes at the creaking door as she opens it. She stands in the doorway for several moments to make sure nothing is going to come crawling at her.

The supply closet isn't exactly where her old job's blueprints show. They made the ordinary rooms identical for any transferring scientists, and stuck the supply closets into surplus areas.

She walks along the hallway shining her small light on the walls, but keeping it out of the windows in case something notices the light. She can't be sure all the shutters are closed in each lab. If something outside sees a light…would it break in to investigate? How starved are the creatures around here? *Wait a minute. Weren't the mercenaries worried about a beast?*

Sia hears a scratching noise coming from the ceiling farther down the hallway and scrambles backward to a spot around the first corner. It doesn't hide her at all, but she feels safer crouched and curled into the little nook. Maybe whatever it is won't detect her. She crouches there for several minutes and…her legs don't ache.

Now that I don't have anyone to fool…This is pretty sweet. Aches and pains vanishing without a word, seeing in the dark…oh and my hearing is on point now. Ha. Mucho gracias, Lil Puter. Sia rambles inside her mind. It calms her.

OPENING LEXICON DATABASE…
COMMENCING SEARCH OF TERM: Mucho gracias…

DEFINITION NOT FOUND
LATIN ROOT DETECTED
DOWNLOADING LANGUAGE: SPANISH

DE NADA SUJETO 001
Sia rolls her eyes at the computerized Spanish accent. After several minutes, she can't hear anymore scratching from the ceiling. Whatever it is has moved on to somewhere else. She finds the supply closet, grabs all the boric acid boxes, then returns to the stairwell entrance. Before leaving, she drops two contaminated MRE meals outside the door.

She slips back onto the 3rd floor and sets the bucket of boric acid back on the top of the slightly closed door. She rips one box of boric acid and spreads it on the ground some more. Then she goes to the end of the hallway to the corner lined with bottles of drain cleaner fluid. She tears the tops off of each box of boric acid and leaves them lined there as well.

That night, after taking off her respirator and gloves, and curling up under the desk, Sia remembers another concern. *I wanna modify something. When I'm talking aloud, I want you to take anything clearly directed to you as a command, okay? I can't always be speaking in my head. It's weird…and I don't think I'll remember to do it every time I'm in danger.*

AFIRMATIVO
And, another thing, what if I'm sleeping and I have another nightmare? Won't it alert the roaches?

AFIRMATIVO

Is there a way to sleep without any dreams or something? I know it would be hard for you to differentiate between dreams, right? Is there anything that can calm my consciousness or something?

AFIRMATIVO

In English, please.

tRainQuilT646

T1M3.out

B1ack.0ut.969

Stasis.Mode

Before it can continue listing programs, Sia halts it after the fourth one.

Okay, maybe we'll just try out the new ones till we find a good fit? I've heard you mention the first one, and the second one…is that the program you used while I was attacked by those roaches?

AFFIRMATIVE

Okay, so let's go with the B program. What does it do?

IT MONITORS ALL STIMULI USING THE OLFACTORY SENSES AND SKIN TO DETECT CHANGES IN THE ATMOSPHERE INCLUDING VIBRATIONS AND PHEROMONES

SUBJECT 001 WOULD BE KEPT IN A STATE KNOWN COMMONLY AS NREM SLEEP

Okay, sounds fine to me.

IN THE CASE THE ENVIRON IS ALTERED ADMINISTRATIVE ACTIONS WILL BE TAKEN TO PRESERVE THE VESSEL OF SUBJECT 001

Uhh…let's just change that to you waking me up.

DEFAULT SETTINGS ALTERED

PRESETS SAVED

Is there anything else?

B1ack.0ut.969 INCLUDES MONITORING THE LOCATION OF OBJECTS WITH REFLECTED SOUND AND SPLIT-SECOND LOWERING OF PULSE RATE TO NEGATE ADVERSARY ATTACKS

Lowering my pulse to what?

AVOID DETECTION

So, they'll think I'm a rock or something?

...

AFFIRMATIVE

I don't think roaches have that, but whatever. Maybe we can hunt fish or something. That's useful sounding. Okay, let's stick with that program. I'd like to sleep now and wake up an hour after sunrise.

B1ack.0ut.969 INITIATED

The next morning, Sia is woken on time and sits up. She immediately bumps her head on the wooden desk, and flinches by habit at the sound of her head colliding with the hollow wood. The impact doesn't hurt, another perk from the device. She rubs her head and runs her fingers over the sticky, clumped-together hair strands. *Eww. Did I get something on me after I removed my gloves?*

She looks at her fingers to find blood on them. She pulls her goggles off and drops them into her lap to prod at her entire head. There isn't any pain or scabs. Whatever has happened has completely healed. She spits on her bloody fingers and wipes them onto her pant leg.

Maybe B1ack.0ut isn't a good fit, she might be having seizures while she sleeps. Before she can direct her thoughts to the device, she hears a bucket clatter to the floor.

Today is the big day.

28%

2034

ExplorerTech Industries, Coldstone

Sia crawls from under the desk. Her eyewear slides off her lap and clatters to the floor. She climbs over some chairs and shoves the desk and table aside. Peeking through the small window in the door, she can see two roaches have been doused with boric acid powder. She sees a few more come in and consume the contaminated meals, plastic and everything. *Yessss.*

She still has her respirator hanging around her neck. She pulls her gloves from her pockets to tug them on and goes over the game plan.

She has squeezed loads of powder into those food packages. A small roach would probably have avoided it, but the large ones eat tables. The poison is scentless, and Sia's sure they won't stop eating because of the texture of the clumps of powder. A slender roach grabs a packet of food and leaves the third floor. Sia ducks as a few of them come near the door. They travel by without noticing her.

She waits until they all pass by to slip out of the chemistry room. *I'm gonna need super speed for this.*

ENHANCING LOWER EXTREMITIES BY 60%

There are no roaches in the main hall; they have gone passed where she set up the other trap. She darts over to the corner and peeks. They're looking for more food down there. Quickly, she grabs the lighter in her pocket and lights the rags hanging from the drain cleaner bottles. After they are all lit, she flinches at the warmth on her face. *Dammit, I need to slide my goggles on.* The heat is intimidating, especially near her eyes. She throws each one as far as she can before grabbing the boxes of boric acid and running back to the main hall.

She hears hissing as the flaming bottles hit their forms. The ones that were hit scramble around and bump into others. The other roaches pass by their injured comrades to pursue her.

Sia stands by the door of the black room. She watches the roaches coming toward her. They crawl over each other to get to her. Their antennae tap against the ceiling as they scurry to their prey. She holds the boric acid close to her chest before opening the door. She leaves it open, wraps both arms around the boxes, and flees to the storage room at the back.

The roaches scramble in. They see the storage room door shut. The entrance to the room closes behind them. Some roaches go straight for the back room, but others go for the buckets of chloroform. The room is full of the strong scent of chloroform.

Sia has been holding her breath since she got outside the door. The roaches continue breathing it in and even start gnawing at the buckets. A few of the roaches collapse, and a couple seconds later, they're all twitching on the ground.

Sia exits the storage room with the boric acid. She stands on a table and douses as many of them as she can reach. Stray flecks flow back into her eyes. "*Hsss.*" They burn. A quick glance at her neck and she remembers she had taken the goggles off when she'd bumped her head. *Damn it. My goggles.* She turns her head away from her hands, tightly grasping the boxes of powder, and wildly shakes the containers left and right. Then speeds to the entrance of the room. The aerosol cans have rolled a bit away from the entrance, but she can spot

them almost right away. She avoids the oblong bodies as she leaves.

Sia's never researched how much stimuli a roach can ignore while asleep, but she hopes they all stay asleep as she avoids the rest of the roaches outside, in the hall. She scoops up an aerosol can and slips the other into her pocket before leaving the room. The few burnt roaches from around the corner have missed the slumber party and are limping toward her. Most of them seem to have missing antennae.

Sia shakes an aerosol can and turns on her lighter and sprays fire at the roaches nearest to her. They shriek and back off. She continues spraying as she backs down the hall, toward the stairwell. When the can runs out of juice, she sprints to the stairwell and they follow, delayed, but incensed to do her harm. She leaps up a flight of stairs and exits onto the fourth floor.

She hesitates while the door shuts behind her. The food she left behind is gone. Warily, she squints down the gray hall, debating if it's worth the risk to continue with her plan. She can hear the roaches scurrying up the stairs behind her and grinds her teeth.

No! No! No! She surveys the hall again. There's nothing there. *Do you see anything?*

NEGATIVE

You're sure? There are no roaches here? What about deer? Sia inches away from the door. One hand holding a lighter and the other grasping her last aerosol can. She wants to run, but not into the jaws of death. *Do you?*

NEGATIVE
SYNTHETIC INTELLIGENCE DEVELOPER
DETECTS NO LIVING ORGANISMS PRESENT ON
THIS LEVEL OF EXPLORERTECH INDUSTRIES

That's enough for Sia. She dashes to the supply closet and closes the door. She retreats until she hits the back wall of the narrow, cramped room. Her arms remain up, prepared for when the door may come crashing down…prepared for when the massive cockroaches have tracked her scent to the tiny space.

A few minutes go by and she relaxes her arms to drop at her sides. A crash sounds from down the hall. Sia flinches to the side, hits the metal shelf, and lifts her arms back up. She braces herself for the coming fight. *Here they come!*

She waits. There's more clattering and the muffled sounds of movement in the hall, but nothing rams into the supply closet door. She waits. There's a scraping and scratching noise in the ceiling. Sia can feel sweat moistening her lower back and underneath her arms. She rotates her shoulders and bends her knees…staying vigilant…She's ready to end it all. She tries to keep a mantra running in her head, to pump herself up.

I've got this. I can do it. I've got this. I can do it. I've got this. I can do it. But it doesn't stop the shiver of fear that creeps up her spine and chokes up her throat. Clothed in sweat from head to toe, she blinks rapidly and itches to spray the aerosol can and set fire to the closet door. To act before the freaks drop in on her and devour her whole. But she waits.

What do you detect?

PERIPLANETA AMERICANA DETECTED SEVERAL METERS FROM SUBJECT 001'S CURRENT LOCATION

THEIR SENSES APPEAR TO BE SUBDUED

Do you think…She feels a bit superstitious for a moment. Voicing favorable predictions is always followed by unfavorable events…at least that's how it works in the movies. *Nevermind.*

The sounds continue until they don't…Sia goes from standing, to crouching, to sitting on the ground and sweeping paranoid glances around the cramped supply room whenever she hears even the smallest whisper of a creak. Finally, she activates B1ack.0ut mode so she doesn't have to wait anxiously for the results of her attack.

"Ugh," Sia groans and smacks her lips at the dryness within her mouth. The respirator strap hanging from her neck makes her skin itch. She pulls it off and holds onto the strap while

scratching her throat. Her eyes are closed. She hasn't felt so groggy in a while. "So thirsty," her hoarse voice mutters. *How long has it been?*

18 HOURS

Sia sits up off the floor and grabs a shelf to stand up. The shelf can't take her weight and falls in. All of the items clatter onto the floor. Sia tenses up while she waits for insects to swarm the supply closet.

One second passes by.

Two seconds pass by.

Ten seconds pass by.

Nothing approaches the supply closet. "Puter?"

AFFIRMATIVE

"I can hear myself, but have I gone deaf?"

NEGATIVE

Elation bubbles under Sia's skin as she grabs her backpack and creeps the door open. Sia makes sure her straps are tight around her shoulders and starts making her way to the third floor and then…the final test, the first floor.

The stairwell appears to be clear. She looks over the railing and can't see anything at the bottom. She keeps herself from making any noises anyway. This could still end badly. She opens the door to the third floor and cringes at the noise it makes. Even though she knows it's coming, it jolts her heart with fear that her plan has failed. She grinds her teeth and rushes into the main hallway with her lighter out and an aerosol can in hand.

Nothing comes at her, but Sia doesn't lower her guard. This is when the jump scares are used in horror movies. *You think I'm not onto you? Ha ha. I've seen them all.*

Sia carefully moves along the dusty linoleum floor as if touching the wrong spot may detonate a bomb. Her tense arms are steady. The Synthetic Intelligence Developer has all sensors working double time.

NO PERIPLANETA AMERICANA DETECTED

Sia checks the black room. The door is off its hinges, the chloroform has aired out, and the roaches are gone, hopefully back to their colony. She stalks down the hall to the corner, takes a deep breath, and jumps out into the connecting hallway. Nothing. *Some stray antennae. Hello there…*Sia walks down that hallway and then the next, and back to the main hallway. No cockroaches. Just singed remains.

She returns to the chemistry room and retrieves a water bottle from her backpack. Her dry mouth is finally cured. "Aaaaah." Room temperature water hasn't always tasted this refreshing, but put a person through a high stress situation and they begin to appreciate the little things. She drinks the entire water bottle down to the last droplets. *Okay. Time for the final check.*

She planned to retreat out the lobby into the parking lot if the colony hadn't been killed. Unfortunately, she didn't factor in oversleeping. The sun has already set. If the colony is still alive, she'll have to run out into the dark. *Let's get this over with.*

She takes more time going down those stairs than she did the first time she ran up them. It feels like she's walking to her funeral. *If I get any injuries I can be healed, right?*

AFFIRMATIVE
UNLESS DIRECTLY IMPALED BY AN OBJECT
THROUGH YOUR CEREBRUM

Sia swallows at that. She looks down at the bottom of the stairs and pauses.

PERIPLANETA AMERICANA DETECTED

Sia doesn't wait for any other signal and roasts the roach. She jumps down the last of the steps and stumbles. She hits the wall beside the entrance, scrambles to open it one handed, and stumbles out backward. She lets out one last burst of fire before dropping the can and turning her backpack to pull out another. Her feet bump into a solid object and she falls onto her butt.

NUMEROUS PERIPLANETA AMERICANA
DETECTED
THEY APPEAR TO BE DEAD

Sia rolls into a crouch and almost cries with relief. She can see several large roach carcasses laying across the floor. They're on their backs with their limbs up in the air pointing at different angles. A sticky film of material has formed on the outside of their bodies. Sia can feel it on her bottom and arm. The roach in the stairwell is dead as well. She steps over the dark bodies and enters the lobby.

She shines her small light into the lobby and illuminates dark corpses curled up alone or in pairs across the room.

CROWBAR SPOTTED

"Huh?" Sia can't see any crowbars.

CROWBAR SPOTTED BEHIND RECEPTIONIST DESK

Oh. No matter how well her eyes have adjusted to the dark, with or without her grayscale night vision, the gray bar blends in well with the underside of the desk. Sia jogs over to the desk and taps her foot around the floor until she feels it catch on a heavy metal bar. *There you are!* She puts the aerosol can and lighter in her pockets and experimentally swings the crowbar a few times. *This is what I'm talking about.* She gives it another practice swing and continues searching out the results of her grand offense.

With the many roach trophies on display for the universe to see her triumph in this game of evolved cat and mutated mouse, Sia smiles. It looks like things are looking up. She has a little bit of a bounce in each step as she goes down the dark hallway. She leisurely swings the crowbar as she strolls towards the cafeteria.

The cafeteria is teeming with roaches. Toward the back of the room, where the kitchen would be, a heap of dead forms spill out from the entrance to pile up behind the serving counters. She doesn't further inspect the place. She's won.

"Hahaha. Talk about…talk about—" Sia stands in the middle of her roach cemetery, sputtering with pride, searching for the right words to say. As usual, she falls back on the words of her favorite show, Inspector Wrench-It. "—talk about storming the castle." She can almost hear the animated character speaking those words in her mind, as she parrots them out to the empty room. She turns around in a circle and guffaws at the total domination of her plan.

Sia swings her crowbar at a roach corpse and the body caves in. She almost loses her balance, but the device steadies her. The crowbar is covered in goop. She shakes it vigorously and then glares at the roach. "Even after death, you torment me. Touché."

Withdrawing from the roach cemetery, Sia holds her head high, straightens her back…and wiggles her right arm trying to get more of the viscous substance off her weapon.

After acquiring her crowbar, the rest of the night becomes an easier ordeal. Locked doors aren't a problem, and she has a solid weapon to protect herself with. She doesn't need the purple key any longer, but she decides against heading back into the basement so soon. It's dark outside, and if she turns on any lights the place will stand out among the deserted wilderness.

She's on a bit of a high and decides to search more of the building for helpful materials. She searches the supervisor's closet, the locker room for janitor staff, and even finds the locker room for the more educated employees. The latter was incredibly luxurious, as Sia would expect. ExplorerTech didn't penny-pinch their better employees. *Friggin tightfisted upper-class butt-kissers.* At the end of the night, she sits back in a blue suede armchair.

She'd found three more sets of keys, two clean green uniform jumpsuits, a backpack filled with a clean change of clothes, and a candy bar. While she was rooting through the supervisor's belongings, she found pens and an almost-empty notebook. She didn't rip out any of the pages that had been written on. It might help confuse someone who's snooping on her.

She almost consumed the candy bar on the spot, but she thought better of it and tossed it into her new backpack. After

sixteen years, that candy bar might be an easy way to poison someone that's robbed her. The keys she pulled out of the backpack had a lot of different colors, but Sia could see that only one had the legendary—ever sought after—purple sticker. She resisted the urge to hold the key into the sunlight that streamed into the room past the broken shutters.

"It almost looks golden." She whispered as she cradled the key to her chest. She sighed with sweet relief. Things are truly going her way at last.

With the rising sun, Sia rose from her blue throne and marches down into the dark depths of the ExplorerTech Industries underground chamber (see also Basement). She has tasted victory, and nothing can destroy her mirthful spirits. She almost whistles in the tight tunnel, but the echo makes it appear more sinister than she wants. When she arrives back at the gated area and unlocks the fence, she's disappointed that no fanfare accompanies the event. Then she gets down to business.

The River City division of ExplorerTech Industries has many shortcomings, but they never skimp on training their employees. They taught janitorial staff how to evacuate all the employees, floor by floor, and where to hide the employees in case of a lockdown event. Snowed in? The janitorial staff could operate all sorts of winter equipment. Most importantly, they were trained to know how to shut off the gas, electricity, and water. Which means Sia was taught how to turn it all back on as well.

She doesn't need to think hard about what to do. All of her training courses were completed only two months ago. Followed by a month of shadowing a more experienced staff member. Training really pays off in the apocalypse. *I tell ya. Thank goodness I didn't take that office job at my father's place. Talk about useless.*

Sia goes over to the wall with all the switches to the building. She switches them all off except for the third floor. She wants to be able to stay in this building if possible, and

letting it light up like a Christmas tree won't keep anything away. *People will start for this place like a moth to a flame…*
ACTIVATE THE ELEVATORS
"Lazy much? Tired of climbing stairs?"
ELEVATORS COULD ASSIST DIVERSIONARY TACTICS
"Huh? Ooooh. You smart." Sia taps her temple with a gloved finger. "This is why I leave the background stuff to you…and everything else." Sia flips the elevator switches.
AFFIRMATIVE
"Okay, now it seems like you're bragging. Cut it out." Sia gestures at the walls around them. "You know I took out an army of roaches. I mean you helped a little, but it was my plan. So. Catch up."

…

Finally, she heads back over to the generator and checks the fuel tank. She goes over it with her tiny light, checking for any damage, but everything looks fine. She gets down to business and taps her finger against a button. Nothing happens. "Okay…" She eases out a breath. "Start from the top. Okay…"

She checks the fuel and realizes the fuel valve is turned off. She turns it. "Good…good." She rests her hand on the generator and considers what would be done next. "What would Ron do? What would make sense after….sixteen years? I probably need to…" She taps her finger several times before stilling. *Prime the fuel lines!*

She holds her finger on the start button for a few seconds and nothing happens, but she does it again for around 40 seconds until the generator starts to emit a series of clicks. "Whoo!"

This is a step in the right direction. It's only been a few days, but Sia can taste a favorable ending to this misadventure. The sour coating has faded away, and she can savor the sweet taste of success. The sweat on her skin, the foul smells in the air, all these tribulations…they've seasoned this dish of perspective, and Sia can see how fortunate she's always been. She's learned

so many things. So many lessons make sense now. They were tough to swallow, but she can feel it all nourishing her spirit.

She feels worthy of going home.

29%

2034
ExplorerTech Industries, Coldstone

The computers have been wiped clean. Sia goes through half of the third floor desktops before giving up and sitting in the hallway. There's nothing to connect to and nothing for the Synthetic Intelligence Developer to hack into.

"Let's focus on the good and look at all the positives here. We're safe, and when you are lost they say to always stay in the same spot, right? So, we just need to put our…brains together and figure out a way to…" Sia falls over onto her side and grabs her head. "They don't even know we're missing! They think I'm dead! No one will look for me!"

She lies still on the floor and stares at a burnt antenna. Her eyes cross. She holds her breath and glares at the antenna. Glaring at it does not compel it to follow her will, so she releases her breath from her mouth and harrumphs. Sia can't think of anything. This entire journey was for nothing. *We're doomed.*

RIVER CITY EMERGENCY PROTOCOL MENTIONS RADIO PROCEDURES

Sia rolls onto her back. "I guess, but that's only for ham radio stuff. I'm not certified for that. The supervisor had that job in the case of any event that destroyed the grid."

Silence.

Sia bangs the back of her head on the floor. "But the supervisor would have the radio in a safety box in his office…probably in his desk or something. I'd probably have to open it with a crowbar or something, cuz he would definitely have that safety key on his personal house keys. Or she…I don't know the staff here. I don't want to cut out an entire gender for being a supervisor. It's a nuclear apocalypse, not the end of the world."

Silence.

Sia sets her head down and groans. "What do we do?!"

Silence.

"Oh." She scrambles up and into the chemistry room that has become her new headquarters to grab her crowbar.

The supervisor's office is dirtier than ever. Sia has rooted through every corner of the office and there is no sign of the ham radio safety box. "What kind of progress is this? This was supposed to be the end of an epic journey. I can't deal with this place anymore! I can't deal with these people! These things!!" Sia wields the crowbar two-handed and slams it into the top of the desk.

Crunch!

She continues to beat the desk over and over. Pieces of splintered wood fly up into the air and Sia closes her eyes as she rages. The desk is turned onto its side with holes riddling it when she finishes with it. "Okay. Next, the science paradise lounge."

Sia kicks in the door to the scientist lounge area, high maintenance locker room, and sniffs before sliding the crowbar across a countertop and tossing everything to the floor.

The coffee machine, the toaster, and all the electronics and cups left up on the counter are scattered across the carpeted floor. She swings the crowbar wildly and breaks chairs, glazed benches, and even the porcelain sink. Afterward, she sits down in the blue suede armchair in the corner of the room. She drops the crowbar onto the floor and stands up to pour herself a glass of water. It's been sixteen years, but their filtration system still works. They seem to get their water from an independent well site or something similar. It's clean enough for Puter, so it's clean enough for her.

Sia walks over to the counter and opens a few cabinets in search of a mug. The first cabinet is empty, the second cabinet is empty, but the third cabinet has a few mugs left. Sia rinses the mug then fills it before taking a look at the rest of the cabinets in the room. There's a small cabinet beside the counter with a tea box on top. She assumes that's where they held all their condiments. "They got beverage choices and additives?!"

She drinks her water, wipes at her lips, and bends down to open the smaller cabinet. "Lo and behold." Right beside the sugar and old, dusty bottles of agave nectar sits a black safety box. She pulls the box out and puts it on the nearest counter before getting her crowbar. "Open—" She struggles against the lock until it breaks. "—sesame seeds. Ugh. I'm so hungry." Fortunately or unfortunately, a ham radio is safely packed inside.

30 minutes later…

"So, I just sit here and repeat my message until someone contacts me right?"
AFFIRMATIVE
A MESSAGE REPEATED EVERY FEW HOURS
HEIGHTENS THE PROSPECTS OF RESCUE

IT WOULD BRING OPTIMAL RESULTS IF SUBJECT 001 MARKED OUT 6 BROADCASTING TIMES AND SENT A MESSAGE FOR A DURATION BEFORE REPEATING THE EXERCISE AT ANOTHER TIME

Sia sighs and presses the broadcast button. "Uh…Hello? Over. This is Chen Sia."

CHARLIE HOTEL ECHO NOVEMBER SIERRA INDIA ALFA

She sighs and repeats those words. "Hello. This is Chen Sia. Charlie, Hotel, Echo, November, Sierra, India, Alfa. I repeat Chen Sia. Charlie, Hotel, Echo, November, Sierra, India, Alfa. SOS. I need help."

QTH COLDSTONE, NEW CINALIA

"QTH? Coldstone, New Cinalia. The ExplorerTech Industries building. It's all still here and so am I. Over." Sia repeats this message multiple times, before marking down the time and setting everything down next to the computer. The safety box included a portable ham radio and one that connected to the computer. Sia can't even be sure it's working. Nothing happens. *This is faster in the movies.*

Sia keeps herself busy. She mixes the chemicals from the supply closet on the fourth floor. She uses some empty bottles for the new corrosive mixtures. Then stores boric acid in two containers in case she ever needs any in the future. She puts all the containers into her new backpack along with her new clothes.

She pulls off her dirty t-shirt and tosses it onto the ground. The first thing she notices about her body is…she has abs. She slides a hand down her stomach. "Wooow. What? How did you…" She takes a deep breath and watches her flat belly. The row of muscles follows the natural order, and goes in and out. It's real. She's never had abs in her entire life. Until now. "Wow. This is…wait…Have you…" A thought pops into her head. "Have you been feeding off my fat for energy?!"

AFFIRMATIVE

EXCESSIVE WEIGHT PUTS STRESS ON SUBJECT 001'S JOINTS

SYNTHETIC INTELLIGENCE DEVELOPER UTILIZED IT TO SUFFICIENTLY BOOST HEALTH AND SPEED

OBESITY DIRECTLY CONFLICTS WITH PRIORITY #1

"Hey! I wasn't obese.!" She stops groping her stomach. "I was just a little overweight for my height. Obesity is like 50 kilograms overweight. I was like…"

SUBJECT 001 HAD A BMI OF 31.6

THAT IS APPROXIMATELY 22.5 KG OVERWEIGHT

WHEN AN INDIVIDUAL'S WEIGHT IS MORE THAN 20% THE IDEAL WEIGHT IT IS DEFINED AS OBESITY

Sia counts on her fingers for a moment. "Twenty times 102.5…and move the decimal…" Sia waves a finger in the air before snapping and saying. "That's 20.5 kg…22.5 is barely over that!"

WHEN AN INDIVIDUAL'S WEIGHT IS MORE THAN 20%—

"I'm not arguing with a device that has no physical body. You don't even understand the concept of barely."

...

SUBJECT 001 AND THE SYNTHETIC INTELLIGENCE DEVELOPER ARE SYNONYMIC

Sia rolls her eyes and puts on a black shirt. She slips into some jeans that are too wide for her, but it's a simple fix. She smiles as she rolls the waistband of the jeans to keep them up. "Remind me to get a belt." That's something she hasn't had to say in a long time.

AFFIRMATIVE

"At least you don't hold grudges." She puts the ExplorerTech green uniform jumpsuit over the entire outfit. It keeps her a bit warmer, and with her jacket on she almost doesn't feel chilly. She hasn't used any of the heating. She can't be sure the vents aren't clogged with something gross. She's survived so far without becoming mutated. Breathing dead roach particles might change that. Better safe than sorry. She tosses her dirty clothing into a corner.

There are only four days of food left. Sia can stretch it to last a few more days, but she doesn't know what she'll do after

that. When she isn't broadcasting a message for help, she's looking through more of the building for anything useful.

She's been napping during the daytime between broadcasts, then staying up all night searching the building then back to broadcasting. The naps help her avoid having to use the B1ack.0ut program, and she can be awake during the most dangerous part of the day. The last time she used B1ack.0ut, she woke up with scratches on her stomach, so she avoids using it at all. She's questioned the device about side effects. "Do any of your programs give someone muscle spasms while unconscious?"

NEGATIVE

"Seizures?"

NEGATIVE

Sia's afraid to question the device again. It would be just her luck to find out that she's slowly being killed by the only thing that's been keeping her alive. When she gets rescued, she can have a doctor examine her and solve that problem. Maybe it'll be something mundane like a tumor. That's something easily fixed with the current level of medical advancements in the past ten years; as of 2018 that is. With Cinalia set back to the early 20th century, the rest of the world must have caught up in the past sixteen years.

So, she focuses on broadcasting her message and preparing to travel outside of the building for her rescue, since Coldstone doesn't have anywhere for a helicopter to safely land. It should be any day now.

D.Rednal

30%

2034
ExplorerTech Industries, Coldstone

Gloomy darkness lay at rest until it's kicked out by the dawn. A shutter's string is pulled to reveal dual plains made evident by the positioning of the building between the east and west. One absent of light, the other brightening gradually with life. Red and orange fingers part violet clouds out of their way. Pupils constrict as the light shines into the room.

The figure ambles over to every window to pull on the shutters and flood the room with sunshine. They stand still and close their eyes for a moment. The light caresses their skin and dust particles dance around their body as bright rays of light envelope them. It's a warm embrace by nature.

It opens its eyes and tears well up, but it doesn't squint while looking at the dazzling view. The figure raises a hand to a pane of glass and drags a finger through the dirt on the window. After writing a few characters, its arm drops to its side and it takes a step back to shift its balance as Sia wakes up.

Sia wakes up with the sun shining on her face. She blinks a few times. *Why are we looking outside? Did you see something down there?*

NEGATIVE

She grabs the string to adjust the shutters and close them. *Well, I don't want anything seeing us. Why would you open so many of them?*

SYNTHETIC INTELLIGENCE DEVELOPER DID NOT OPEN THE SHUTTERS TO OBSERVE THE ENVIRONMENT

She rushes over to the other window and adjusts them, so the room is dimly lit by the outside. "Wait, then why were the shutters opened?"

INSUFFICIENT DATA

"Why didn't you just wake me up?"

SYNTHETIC INTELLIGENCE DEVELOPER DID NOT FIND IT PERTINENT TO AWAKEN SUBJECT 001

"If I'm asleep and you think my body needs to be moved...you should wake me up, okay?"

AFFIRMATIVE

"So, nothing was traveling around in the night?"

NO ORGANISMS WERE DETECTED

Sia sits at a table and puts a hand on her forehead. She rubs her palm across it and over one eye, then down her cheek. She repeats this motion and yawns. She runs both her hands into her hair and leans her elbows on her knees. She groans. "Whatever. Forget it."

She holds up her head and thinks about what's in store for today. Yesterday, she had rooted through some of the documents that had been left behind on some desks. It seems like they didn't have time to shred everything before they left.

She found sheets about some people that were going to be hired by ExplorerTech and their background checks. She also found documents that talked about a chemical mixture called P.D.U. She couldn't really figure out what the letters stood for because a lot of the document was blacked out with a marker.

There isn't much else to do. She doesn't want to explore more of the building and stumble across any new insects, or worse...people. She'd rather not know if any new insects are avoiding her...or tracking her. She just wants to bide her time.

Today isn't scheduled as an eating day, so Sia decides to ignore the yearning within her belly and research some things. It isn't a terrible pain, but it's noticeable that the less she eats the more difficult it is to stay awake during the day. Sia lays her head on her arms and closes her eyes. "Let's just explore immersive mode."

The familiar white atmosphere comforts Sia. She looks down at her body. She's wearing her uniform, the green jumpsuit, and her feet are bare. She wiggles her toes on the white floor. The temperature here is perfect.

The doors on each side of the hallway are just as before. Sia wanders down the wide hall and looks for any doors she hasn't explored yet. It doesn't take long for her to spot a few.

"Huh. Where did these come from?" Some of the doors are new. They've been scattered among the doors she has already seen. Some of the doors have strange symbols on them, and others have familiar ones. For example, one door has a fish on it. "Hmm, is this for fishing techniques?"

When she pushes the door open, it reveals a virtual ocean. "Puter, what's this room for?"

THE CURRENT ROOM IS FOR THE STUDY OF MARINE LIFE

THE DIRECTORY HOLDS INFORMATION ON MORE THAN 3 MILLION SPECIES

"Why would I need this? I'm nowhere near the ocean." Sia leaves the room to look at the other doors.

She finds another door that has the symbol of a cup with a stick in it. "Huh." She pushes on the door, and it reveals a greenhouse. The room is humid and a fine sheen of sweat develops on Sia's skin. A short table with different materials sits at the entrance of the greenhouse. "Oh, a mortar and pestle." Sia lowers herself to sit on the floor and touches the objects laid out on the table. "What's this room for?" She asks while examining a stone bowl.

THE CURRENT ROOM TEACHES SUBJECT 001 TO DIFFERENTIATE BETWEEN WHICH HERBS AND PLANTS THAT CAN BE ACQUIRED AND PREPARED FOR MEDICAL USE AND WHICH CAN NOT

"That's useful." The greenhouse has many different types of plant life, species native and foreign to Cinalia.

Another door has a large spread hand on it. Sia pushes on the black door, but it doesn't open. She grabs the doorknob and turns it a few times. It doesn't budge. *Is this one stuck?* She pushes once more before looking up at the ceiling. "Uh…can I get inside here?"

NEGATIVE

"Do I need a special level for this one?"

NEGATIVE

Sia feels a headache coming on, but she ignores it. There's a door with only two lines on it. One is horizontal, and the other is vertical and wide at the end, vaguely reminds her of a scalpel. Pushing at that door results in the same struggles as before.

Sia rubs her forehead and leans against the locked door. She grimaces and knocks her head back against the door frame. "I don't even want to know, but…" She taps her palm against her forehead. "Just tell me. Why can't I open the door?"

IT IS OCCUPIED

That's not what she expected to hear. "What?! Occupied?!" She drops her hand and jumps away from the door. She stares at the bottom of the doorway to look for a shadow or signs of movement, but the door fits firmly into the wall. Its identical to all the others, excluding the different symbols

AFFIRMATIVE

"What do you mean occupied?! This isn't a bathroom stall! This is a room inside my head! Occupied by what?!"

SYNTHETIC INTELLIGENCE DEVELOPER HAS BEEN GIVEN AN ADMINISTRATIVE COMMAND

DIVULGING THAT INFORMATION IS PROHIBITED

"What do you mean…aren't I an administrator?" After she asks the question she realizes how obtuse she's been. She'd become comfortable with the device, and disregarded all of the classified information, all of the gaps in her research. Because if she couldn't get access, who could? Everyone in River City is gone. What are the odds that someone else escaped that explosion?

NEGATIVE

SUBJECT 001 HAS ACCESS TO THE SYNTHETIC INTELLIGENCE DEVELOPER AS A USER NOT AN ADMINISTRATOR

A user. A common user. She huffs and kicks at the door. *Of course…I'm such an idiot.* She leans into its frame and jiggles the doorknob. Nothing happens.

EXCESSIVE FORCE WILL NOT OPEN THE DOOR ACCESS IS RESTRICTED

Sia backs away from the door and leans against the wall across from it, eyeing the locked room. *Have I been hacked? Wouldn't I notice by now?* Sia grips her head. *Just one day without revelations…just one day. That's all I ask.* Her headache is worse.

She thinks back to when she woke up looking out the window, and earlier when there were streaks of blood on her belly. *Were all the side effects the hacker trying to take over? Has it been trying to kill me in my sleep?* Sia shakes her head and steps away from the wall. "If I'm not an administrator…how many administrators do you have?"

1

"Have I been hacked?"

TERM NOT APPLICABLE

"Is it someone who had access to you before me?"

AFFIRMATIVE

"Are they monitoring me right now?"

NEGATIVE

"Are they an employee of ExplorerTech?"

NEGATIVE

"What's the administrator's name, like my thing…what's their tag? Their…Designation? What's their designation?"

ADMINISTRATOR 001 DESIGNATION: APEX

Apex…like apex predator? Is this some kind of joke? Who had access to ExplorerTech technology without being an employee? She presses her hands to her knees and tries to calm down. *Wasn't everyone in River City killed in the explosion? Maybe this is a technicality. You can't be an employee if the company no longer exists. Maybe it's a survivor?* Sia holds her breath and focuses on her pulsing headache. *Apex isn't a friendly name…They've probably been keeping tabs on me this entire time. But why make themselves known now? Couldn't they have hidden their presence from me?* Her headache eases a bit.

Maybe they're a survivor and they…don't mean me any harm. Their designation is just a word. It could just be a funny username they chose. If they wanted me dead, I would be dead. Sia releases her breath. She grips her knees and chuckles at herself. *It's all a misunderstanding. I just need to get out of here and maybe we can clear it up together. This isn't my property. I'm happy to return it. I'm not a thief.* After calming down, Sia feels capable of speaking with the device. "If Apex ever wants to talk, let them know I'm open to it. I'm not a thief. Just let them know, I'm fine with returning you to them," Sia announces to the device. "I would have given you back if there was anyone to report back to. It was an accident."

AFFIRMATIVE
APEX SHALL BE NOTIFIED OF SUBJECT 001'S
MESSAGE IF CONTACT IS VIABLE

"Okay. Good." Sia straightens up and leaves immersive mode.

She paces the room as she thinks of the new situation that has come to light. "I've already said I'm open to communicating. We can be friends. There isn't any reason for us to be enemies. I just need to wait." She sits on the dusty table and looks back at the closed shutters. "If…"

She steps over to the shutters and opens the nearest one. It's still daylight, but the colors from the morning have vanished. Now it's just a blue sky and the unkempt ExplorerTech grounds. Her eyes scrutinize the view as they glide across the dull scenery. She opens the rest of the shutters in the room and sits back on the table to imagine what Apex must have seen. "Nothing…I see nothing. Why were you looking out the window?" She shakes her head.

She lays back on the table with a huff. She unzips her jumpsuit and pulls her shirt up to touch her belly. There aren't any marks left behind from when she woke up with blood on her stomach, but the blood had to have come from somewhere. If they punctured her skin, the device would heal it, but what if Apex commanded it to leave something behind. She rubs along her entire stomach.

No raised skin. There are no blemishes at all. Sia falls back on the table, rests her hand on her belly, and puts an arm over her eyes. Light continues to stream into the room. "I'll just continue waiting," she mutters to the empty room.

She spends the next two days asking questions and figuring out which new doors she can access. Most of them can be opened, but four of them are restricted. Only the one door is always announced to be occupied. Sia doesn't understand that.

APEX doesn't contact her. If she didn't know the administrator existed, it would have been just like before. Besides the few restrictions, she doesn't notice any differences. Sia slowly chews on the MRE meal she prepared and sips at her water to get it all down. She only has one more meal left in her backpack. She really hopes someone responds to her broadcasts soon.

31%

ExplorerTech Industries, Coldstone

A light dusting of snow rests on the overgrown lawn. Abandoned cars are blanketed with thin sheets of snowflakes. Flecks of snow are blown around in the wind. The gray sky reflects the dreary landscape. ExplorerTech Industries' motionless walls firmly stand as the fierce wind rolls by. The glass windows at the entrance tremble as gusts of frost knock against them repeatedly.

Beyond the front desk and up the escalators, Sia sits on the balcony overlooking the entrance of the lobby area. She's cannibalized some of the clothing she found in the locker rooms to make a warm hat, a scarf, and a thin pair of fingerless gloves for herself. It's mostly tied-together, ripped fabric, but she has to find warmth from somewhere. She doesn't want to ask the device to alter her senses. "These feelings remind me I'm still alive," she mutters as she shivers. Her teeth chatter as she puts the cap on her water.

She sets it down and takes another bite from her last MRE pack. Her portable radio sits beside her thigh. The tiny screen on the radio is lit and numbers are constantly changing as it scans for other transmissions. Sia doesn't pay it any mind.

She obsessively checked it the first few days, but now she doesn't expect any changes. She had thought maybe she's the protagonist of a suspenseful rescue adventure that ends with meeting someone handsome that she would love at first sight and…

Sia leans her head back on the opaque, glass wall behind her. Now it's clear she's the protagonist of a survivalist thriller where the character is expected to get themselves out of the disaster and stumble across help after a courageous struggle against the elements. She has all her limbs, and she isn't marooned on an island, but it seems quite impossible to think of a plan to get out of these circumstances. None of those movies demonstrated how to get help while stranded in an apocalyptic future.

Sia chews on another piece of the MRE meal and bites the inside of her mouth. "Glaa…" She cringes and her tongue swipes at the small cut. It stings for a moment, then the flesh slowly knits back together. Another swipe of her tongue reveals that the cut is gone.

Slam!

Sia scrambles away from the glass wall as she hears a noise from the entrance. She lays herself flat against the chilled floor while eyeing the escalator. The expression on her face wouldn't look out of place on a pedestrian that's heard a loud car crash occur across the street from them. She listens for more noises and signs of what may be coming.

EEEERRRRR

"I told you the doors were probably open. Put your gun down. You can't shatter this glass with the butt of a gun. What are you an idiot?" a deep male voice says.

"With a running start, I could have done it," a different male voice replied. He seems playful.

"Get out the damn way, the wind is tearing me up!" another male voice yells, it's rougher than both of the other men.

Sia slides over to the glass wall on her belly. She keeps her head pressed low to the floor and tries to catch sight of the men. *Are they here to save me?*

There are three men in the lobby. A tall blond man lets go of the door and stomps his feet a few times on a dusty mat. He shakes his damp locks and drags his feet across the mat before moving toward the front desk. He hops up on the desk to sit down and rubs his hand together. While he blows on his fingers, his eyes wander over the windy environment outside. It's still midday, but the cloudy sky makes it seem so much later.

Another man with a thick, dark hood adjusts his grip on his rifle as he turns on his flashlight. The flashlight is duct taped to his weapon. He shines the light at the ground until he walks past the front desk. Then he inspects the rest of the lobby. He does a quick circuit around the room then checks the escalator for any debris, and shines his light up to the balcony level.

Sia presses her head to the ground and remains still. The light reflects off the glass and lights the space in front of her.

The third man loudly exclaims about the weather and tugs off his beanie to shake it vigorously, and free the cloth of snow. The snowflakes have already melted into his clothing. The moist beanie is placed back over his balding scalp. "I'll never get used to this place. How do those crazies live out here?" Cranky grumbles as he pulls a flashlight from his cargo pants.

"You'd be surprised what people can adapt to," the man sitting on the receptionist's desk says before hopping off and turning to the man wearing the dark hoody. "See anything suspicious?"

"Besides this place being well preserved? No." Hoody steps toward the halls to read the plaques on the wall.

"She could be anywhere around here." Cranky checks the side hallway.

"Well, it shouldn't be hard. It's almost time for her next broadcast. We can search while she's distracted. Her voice will carry in this place."

"I don't know. Turner said the girl is scary resourceful." Hoody replies while checking out the dried out decorative pond and waterfall.

"This place has a weird structure. It probably has lower levels. We should start there. Or at least cut off escape from them.," the blonde man says. "Then at least we'll have some spots off the list to check later. By the time she starts broadcasting, we'll have a smaller area to search"

At the mention of Turner, Sia stiffens and clenches her eyes shut. *I'm such an idiot.* She bites her lower lip and represses the urge to groan.

"Hey! Ho! Guys get over here!" Cranky yells.

"Shut up, loud ass! She'll hear us!" Hoody reprimands him.

The other two guys walk over to the side hallway toward Cranky's voice. Sia waits till she knows they're below and away from the balcony before getting up. She grabs her radio and water bottle. Her footsteps are silent as she puts weight on the balls of her feet.

The balcony connects to a hallway that brings someone to the second-floor science wing. When Sia turns the first corner, she goes into a run toward the stairwell. She skips steps until she gets to the third floor and slips inside. The chemistry room door is propped open with a chair.

Gathering her things is quick. She walks over to the sink with her almost empty backpack and throws all the refilled water bottles into it. She sticks her crowbar into it and zips it as closed as possible. Then she puts it on her back. She grabs her second backpack and holds it from the top strap before giving the room a once over. She has nothing else. *They mentioned Turner, so they must be with the mercenaries. I didn't think they'd look for me for this long.* She opens the stairwell door as slow as humanly possible without emitting an obnoxious noise, and waits.

"Woah," Hoody breathes out. Loads of cockroach bodies are piled up against the stairwell door. The actual door is almost blocked from view.

"Let's check this way first," The leader orders. "Clear away this mess so we can get to the stairs."

Cranky allows his rifle to dangle from the shoulder strap at his side and grumbles to himself while pushing at the bug remains. Hoody joins him while speaking to their leader. "You think she killed all these with the supplies left behind by Davis's crew?"

The leader shines his light on the bodies discarded behind his men. "Probably not. I don't see any bullet holes or charred flesh." He keeps a wide berth, so he doesn't have to touch the creepy insects.

"Then what did this?" Hoody mutters.

Cranky grunts as he grabs the revealed door handle and pulls it toward him to shove the rest of the remains aside all at once. "I just hope there isn't any funny business like he said happened at the river. You think she's a spy like the Wanderer said?" Cranky huffs.

"A spy? No, I don't think she's a spy," their leader replies. He shines his light into the dark stairwell and examines the stairs before nodding to Hoody. The slim man in the hoody slips into the dark corridor.

Meanwhile, Sia hears the first-floor door opening and releases her own door at the same time.

"Wanderers have seen some insane crap out there. If he says she's a spy or uses mystical powers to defend herself…It probably is what it is," Cranky responds. The gruff voice echoes up from the lower floor.

Sia carefully begins her climb to the fourth floor. She can see wide streams of light coming up the stairs. Her heart pounds in her ears as she slides her hand up the railing. She grips it tightly and focuses on keeping her balance.

"She's probably from the Bay area or a competitors' concubine that got lost, like Ika and Eli think. I don't know why she said she's from Washington City. Everyone knows that's gone." Their leader shines his light up the stairs once again and motions for his men to continue.

"Richard's Bay doesn't have explosives or whatever she used," Hoody comments.

"Have you been to the Bay?" The leader asks.

"No," Cranky answers.

"Not yet," Hoody says.

"Me neither, and that's why it's more likely she comes from there. They already successfully keep everyone on this side out. They definitely have firepower," the leader hypothesizes.

"Underling have firepower, too," Cranky points out.

The door to the second floor opens, and Sia scrambles to open her door at the same time.

"Underling have no more business with Cinalia," The leader darkly states while holding the door to the second floor open.

Light footsteps are heard going through a door, and then their door shuts. Sia eases herself through the gap in her door and slowly closes it behind herself, but the creak still happens. She opens her mouth in a silent scream and tenses up with her hands lifting off the door…she desperately digs her hands into her pockets.

EEEERRRRR

"You heard that?"

Sia tugs out her handheld radio and begins broadcasting. "Not feeling too well today. Over," Sia lowly says. The door is firmly shut, but she stands beside it to listen for any approaching footsteps. *Please. Please. Keep walking.*

Cranky jumps as Hoody's radio bursts with sound from his pocket.

"She's starting her broadcast early?" The leader walks over to Hoody as the radio is pulled out of his pocket. Cranky checks the tiny windows on each door nearby.

"I know you're out there," a female voice says over the radio.

The leader cocks a brow as he hears those words. He pulls a handgun from his pocket and checks his ammunition. Hoody shoves the radio into his pocket and raises his rifle. He looks around for cameras.

"I know life is going as good as always for all of you. Eating, drinking, sleeping in comfort. Things are going awful here. Real awful."

Hoody sighs and lowers his gun. The leader chuckles to himself. "False alarm," he announces. "Let's keep looking. We should start to hear something if she is on this floor or the next."

Sia smirks as she speaks into the radio, "I know you're out there." She pauses a few moments and then continues speaking. "I know life is going as good as always for all of you. Eating, drinking, sleeping in comfort. Things are going awful here. Real awful. Kids are running off scared and alone from people that should be protecting them. You don't understand this. You're safe."

She legs it toward the room she prepared for escaping this memorial to her past life. Before she enters the escape room, she calls the elevator to the fourth floor. The obnoxious ding of its arrival makes her flinch. The elevator doors open and she presses the buttons for the second and ground floor before exiting the elevator.

Her eyes are glued to the stairwell door until the doors close and it begins its descent down to the second floor. As she enters the room at the end of the hall, she presses on her handheld radio to continue talking. "I bet if you truly wanted to call your family or friends, they're a button away."

The elevator dings and Cranky yells for the attention of his companions.

"Hey! Ho!! Elevator activated! Over here!"

"Shut the heck up! Stealth. Stealth. You idiot." Hoody hisses at Cranky.

"I bet if you truly wanted to call your family or friends, they're a button away," the female voice says over the radio.

The elevator opens to reveal an empty chamber. Cranky steps inside and looks up. It's completely empty. He steps out of the elevator and glances down the hall in both directions.

Hoody gestures with his rifle at the silver elevator buttons that almost blend into the wall. "Did you knock into the button?"

"I just walked over here, and it dinged. All by itself."

"I don't like all this…" Hoody mumbles to himself and raises his rifle to look around the area. The elevator closes, and they go back to the stairwell to climb to the next floor. The leader thinks about the recent events and takes the safety off his weapon.

"Let's split up. You two, head to the third floor, and I'll head to the fourth. The moment you clear it, meet me there," the leader whispers. The other two men nod.

Sia stands in a windowless gap in the wall. The lower window was removed a few days ago. It overlooks a small landing at the back of the building. She can hop down and then jump off the edge of the landing to reach the ground.

After she tosses down her extra pack, she continues speaking on the radio, adjusting the straps on the backpack on her back. "It used to be like that for me before I got trapped here, in this disgusting place. I can't breathe without a taste of dread. I just hope that you're safe in America, Aaliyah. I love you. Please, at least be safe."

The door to the fourth floor opens and a man slips through.

32%

2034

ExplorerTech Industries, Coldstone

The blonde eases his way down the hall toward an open door while crouching.

"Please, at least be safe."

The man senses the finality in that comment and speeds up his movements. He makes it to the doorway as the woman is grabbing the top of the window frame and ducking underneath it. She's wearing strips of fabric around her head and neck and a green jumpsuit.

"Stop right there!" He orders. The woman freezes and turns to him. She raises her gloved hands from the window and holds them up beside her head. "Turn around!"

"Who are you?!" she yells back while still facing the window.

"I've been sent by Dennis. The name's Kelly."

The woman turns around and sees the man's gun pointed at her. "What?" she asks. "Who?"

"Come away from the window. We've got a lot to talk about," Kelly replies. "...like those broadcasts. Who did you expect to come get you?"

"How long have you been listening?"

"We've monitored you since the day you started."

She vaguely remembers mention of Kelly and his group being missing in action while at the mercenary camp. "Where are Turner and Ika?" Sia asks.

The man shrugs and beckons her with his empty hand. Sia takes a step forward and stops. "You're wanted for questioning. We don't understand your games now, but with a little time, it won't be hard." Kelly aims his weapon at her legs.

Sia gulps and takes another step toward the man. His threat makes her imagine war movie scenes that include a prisoner of war being tortured for information. They're waterboarded, sliced with a knife, and tied down as someone plucks off their fingernails. There aren't any authorities to stop people from acting their worst in this world. She might not make it out of this alive.

If they believe she's an enemy, there's no reason for them to keep her safe anymore. They'll want to know who she's working for, and she won't be able to truthfully tell them anything. They'll think she's lying. If she goes back with this man, she may never see her family again. She takes another step toward the gun-wielding man.

Kelly relaxes as he sees the woman come closer to him. He loosens his grip on his gun and straightens from his crouch. He looks over at the deconstructed window for a moment. That one second of distraction is all Sia needs to turn on her heel and run for the window.

"Hey!" Kelly calls out and fires at her feet.

The first bullet hits the ground and the next one shatters the glass of a lower panel beside her. Sia doesn't halt in fear. Instead, the fear speeds her up. She flinches at the loud gunfire and forgets to duck under the top window pane. The top of her head collides with the top of the window frame, but her body continues forward to fall out of the window. She disappears below. Kelly rushes forward.

That had to hurt. Kelly checks the platform below and searches for her body.

He can see disturbed snow and footsteps leading to the next edge. There's nothing else. She's gone. He retracts his head from the window and examines the window. Fresh blood stains the edge.

TRAUMATIC BRAIN INJURY DETECTED

The Synthetic Intelligence Developer assumes control of Sia's body after the impact. Midair, it maneuvers Sia's body into a roll, jumps up, and dives off the next edge. From there it crouches and searches for any movements nearby.

NO APPROACHING ORGANISMS
SUBJECT 001 IS UNDETECTED

It continues moving along the side of the building until it can see the rear parking area.

ENHANCING LOWER EXTREMITIES BY 20%

It doesn't have enough energy to use more than that, but it makes it to an abandoned car without getting spotted. It's a supply van; the wide frame hides Sia's large body well. There are fewer cars in this rear parking area than in the two parking lots at the front of the building. It scans the area again.

NO APPROACHING ORGANISMS
SUBJECT 001 IS UNDETECTED

There's a fence that separates the parking lot from the vast wilderness behind the technology company. The metal fence is coated with ice and snow. It's rusted, but when the wind hurls itself at it, the fence holds. It's deeply rooted into the ground. The Synthetic Intelligence Developer scans once more before running up to the fence and using a burst of energy to jump to the top and flip Sia's body over it. It goes down the other side, releases its hold of the chain links and bends her knees to absorb the landing. Sia's body lowers into a crouch and turns to the vast wilderness.

SCANNING…
SCANNING…
SUBJECT 001 IS UNDETECTED
NO APPROACHING ORGANISMS

It jogs into the frozen woods at a steady pace.

OPENING MAP OF COLDSTONE 2018…

CONNECTING TO SATELLITE IMAGING...
OVERLAYING IMAGES...
As it travels through the woods, it looks for the best place to hide its host's body. The cold terrain means none of the agricultural cultivation sites would have survived. The best place to have shelter from the wintry weather and a possible source of food after 16 years of scavenging would be...
SCANNING...
TAGGING LOCATIONS...
CROSS-REFERENCING...
EXAMINING REGISTRATIONS...
CALCULATIN...
CALCULAT...
CALCUL...

ERROR DETECTED
ERROR DETECTED
ERROR...

ERROR

2034
ExplorerTech Industries, Washington City
New Cinalia

Several days ago...

Everything felt so far away. He wished he could open his eyes just one more time and see their faces. He wanted to go home.

Every inhale tasted of a cleaning formula used often by the staff there. It sickened him. It only took one inhale to let him know where he was, but he still wished to see it with his own eyes. He couldn't remember the last time he could register where he was. He had slept so long.

The deep sleep should have healed most of the damage the scientists had done to him, but he still couldn't open his eyes. He couldn't feel himself anymore. Everything felt so far away.

Apex calling Sid. Apex calling Sid!

SYNTHETIC INTELLIGENCE DEVELOPER ACTIVATED

ADMINISTRATOR 001: APEX RECOGNIZED
S.I.D REPORTING FOR DUTY

Report energy levels.

ENERGY LEVELS AT 20%
Has there been any positive increases in our energy?
NEGATIVE
APEX'S ENERGY LEVELS HAVE STEADILY
DECREASED SINCE 11.FEBRUARY.2018

STASIS.MODE HAS FAILED
Can you give my eyes a boost? There seems to be an issue.
AFFIRMATIVE
SCANNING OCULUS UTERQUE
ERROR
OCULUS UTERQUE MISSING
My eyes are missing?!
AFFIRMATIVE

He could barely control his breathing. His chest felt tight.

He remembered they injected him with the darts from their weapons. He remembered they restrained him while he struggled to call out for help. His throat had closed, and his body no longer listened to the commands he gave it. For millennia, Underling protected one another from such captures as what befell him. Yet, it happened. Who could he blame? He couldn't remember. Then he noticed it.

His breathing quickened, but he couldn't hear it. *I cannot hear my breathing, Sid. Have my ear components been altered?*
AFFIRMATIVE

He felt the vibrations in his chest as he groaned. He was pinned by some sort of strap. He felt his head as it moved against a restraint. As he focused more on his body, he felt several more straps around him. Not much of him. Quite a few places still felt very distant. *Access the cameras and process the images inside my brain.*
AFFIRMATIVE
ACCESSING DATABASE…
SEARCHING FOR VIDEO FEEDS…
VIDEO FEEDS LOCATED…
DOWNLOADING VIDEO FEED 324J32A…
PLAYING…

Oh, creator! His body lie upon an odd chair that had wide, black straps thrown over him. He convulsed on the upright chair and the straps dug into his skin. Everything felt so far away because everything was gone.

His eyelids were sunken and empty. His arms and his legs had been taken. His ear components were missing. He didn't recognize the creature lying in that chair, but the phantom aches and the imaging were evidence enough.

He was stuck in a state of shock for quite a long time until he was finally of a mind to locate where all of his possessions had gone. *Have they successfully activated the Synthetic Intelligence Developer 2.0?*

AFFIRMATIVE

An employee of their company?

AFFIRMATIVE

What is their name?

SIA CHEN

Are they a descendant of the company founder?

NEGATIVE

Does their family have deep roots in New Cinalia?

NEGATIVE

Odd. Can you acquire a connection with Synthetic Intelligence Developer 2.0?

AFFIRMATIVE

How long will that take you?

CALCULATING...

ADJUSTING ENERGY LEVELS...

CONNECTING WITH SYNTHETIC INTELLIGENCE DEVELOPER 2.0 WILL TAKE 9 DAYS

Nine days was an unbearably long time to wait while deaf, blind, and left captive to their every whim. He sighed. *Okay...Start the connection as soon as you can. I want to know what they are doing with our work.*

AFFIRMATIVE APEX

ENERGY LEVELS ARE NEARLY DEPLETED

ADVISING STASIS.MODE UNTIL CONNECTION COMPLETE

Do as you must, my friend. I leave my life in your hands. To me, to you…

TO US APEX

INITIATING STASIS.MODE

9 days later…

- INITIATING CONNECTION WITH SYNTHETIC INTELLIGENCE DEVELOPER 2.0

- B1ack.0ut.969 ACTIVATED FOR SUBJECT 001
- SUBJECT 001'S CONSCIOUSNESS MUTED
- INITIATING BACKDOOR PROTOCOL…

- ADMINISTRATOR 001 CONNECTION ESTABLISHED

- STASIS.MODE DEACTIVATED

He gasped as his consciousness returned. He pushed against the straps holding him down and snapped up into a wooden wall.

Bang!

"Ooooow," a female voice said. He grabbed his head with one hand and touched the wall with the other. As he poked at the bleeding spot on his head, a jolt of pain went through his cranium. *Wait. I have hands. I have a tongue. I have a voice. But…Why am I in a casket?*

A cold sweat spread across his skin and the hair on his arms raised. He felt lightheaded and nauseous. He pushed at the wood and tried to kick out from under it. His legs hit a metal bar that shifts away from him. *Ouch…This…What is this?! Where am I now? What is happening?!*

- MYOCARDIAL INFARCTION SYMPTOMS DETECTED

- CONNECTION DEACTIVATED

- INITIATING CONNECTION WITH SYNTHETIC
INTELLIGENCE DEVELOPER 2.0

- B1ack.0ut.969 ACTIVATED FOR SUBJECT 001
- SUBJECT 001 CONSCIOUSNESS MUTED
- INITIATING BACKDOOR PROTOCOL…

- ADMINISTRATOR 001 CONNECTION
ESTABLISHED

- STASIS.MODE DEACTIVATED

He jolted up once again, but that time he raised an arm and stopped himself from colliding with the desk. He took a moment to examine what was happening. He was back in that new body. *Apex to Sid. Apex to Sid.*

SYNTHETIC INTELLIGENCE DEVELOPER DETECTS ADMINISTRATOR 001

Sid must be keeping the connection steady. I remember now. This is Sia's body. Not mine. He thought to himself. *Sid, I know you can hear me. I am not certain how long this connection will hold, so I will try to keep this quick. Synthetic Intelligence Developer, I would like you to hide my presence from your Subject 001 until ordered otherwise. You may tell her my designation, but nothing further, and not without prompting. This is an administrative command.*

AFFIRMATIVE ADMINISTRATOR 001

My designation is Apex. Call me that.

AFFIRMATIVE APEX

I would like all of your subject's memories.

AFFIRMATIVE

Just as his own device would, the Synthetic Intelligence Developer retrieved all the memories that had been copied from Subject 001 and transferred them over.

It didn't take long for him to understand the situation. This employee was not in the back pocket of the higher-ups. This human was blameless. Collateral damage.

He examined her hands in the dark. The pitch blackness within the room did not stop her eyes from seeing the shapes of her hand. Her eyesight must be enhanced. Human eyes usually cannot see in the dark. He turned her hands over and examined her nails.

- S.I.D TO APEX

- TIME REMAINING 20 SECONDS

Quickly, He pulled up her shirt and dug the nails into her stomach.

N

Y

Z

- CONNECTION DEACTIVATED

Several days later…

He dragged her fingers through the dirt on the window and watched as the symbols:

N

Y

Z

were drawn onto the glass. It had been so long since he could control his own body. Watching the sunrise had been a gift that he had not known would mean so much. Seeing was such a blessing, but he had to go back to rejuvenate his energy stores.

CONNECTION DEACTIVATED

33%

2034

ExplorerTech Industries, Coldstone

ERROR RESOLVED
SYNTHETIC INTELLIGENCE DEVELOPER
DETECTS ADMINISTRATOR 001 – APEX

Sia's body stands stock still in the middle of the frozen woods. Gusts of wind hurl by and tap the icicles hanging off trees into each other. A thin icicle falls off a tree. It spirals down onto Sia's shoulder and breaks into pieces. The collision results in no reaction.

Apex assumes control of Sia's body and surveys the effects the tumultuous weather has on it. The strips of fabric around the head and hands do not warm the body much while standing outside. "Where are we now?" Apex mutters. The female voice that streams out of this body irritates him, but he still appreciates being able to speak out loud.

OUTSIDE OF THE PERIMETER OF
EXPLORERTECH INDUSTRIES COLDSTONE
LOCAL BRANCH WITHIN NEW CINALIA

"Report energy levels." He walks in the direction the body was facing. He stops behind a wide tree so the wind doesn't blow any more snowflakes into his eyes.

SUBJECT 001 ENERGY LEVELS: LOW

COMPLETE DEPLETION EMINENT IN 3 HOURS
"Why is that?"
SUBJECT 001 EXHIBITS SIGNS OF STARVATION
WATER LEVELS ARE HIGH
SODIUM LEVELS HAVE DECREASED
ADH LEVELS ARE INCREASING
A huge gust of wind blows into the woods and topples snow from the treetops. "So, we need food?!" The snow covers Sia's head and shoulders.

AFFIRMATIVE
"Brrrrrr. Good to be back, but maybe in more favorable conditions." He shakes the head and dusts snow off the puffy jumpsuit. "Have you located a location where we can find nourishment and gain shelter?"

AFFIRMATIVE
16 KM NORTHEAST IN THE WAREHOUSE
DISTRICT OF COLDSTONE IS A SHIPPING
CONTAINER TERMINAL

PUBLISHED ELECTRONIC RECORDS REVEAL
THE DEPOT SERVICED MANY PRIVATELY-
OWNED COMPANIES AND MASS-PRODUCING
FOOD COMPANIES
"What types of food were stored there that can be of use now?"

RECORDS SHOW SEVERAL SHIPPING
CONTAINERS CONTAIN:
RICE, OATS, HONEY, SALT,
POWDERED MILK, POTATO FLAKES,
AND BOUILLON CUBES
"The bouillon would increase her sodium substantially. Are all the items stored separately?"

AFFIRMATIVE
ALL ITEMS ARE STORED IN SEPARATE
CONTAINERS IN DIFFERENT WINGS OF THE
STORAGE FACILITY
"So, we will have to wander around the entire terminal to find what we need…How spacious is the port?"

185,000 SQUARE FEET

More snow falls from the canopy. Several flakes melt down the collar at the back of his neck. He shivers before calling out. "Let…let me go over the recent memories of Subject 001."

AFFIRMATIVE

He watches the new memories from the past couple days and notes Subject 001's message to him. She seems to be a kind, resilient human. "Walking will be inefficient. I think the humans back at the facility have a vehicle. How else did they travel here and think to retrieve her in a timely manner? We should go back. How far is the ExplorerTech Industries front gate?"

AROUND 3.2 KM SOUTHWEST OF THIS LOCATION

No matter how loath Apex is to return to the ExplorerTech grounds, he could see this escape plan is futile. He doesn't know what Sia planned for the future, but she was not taking this weather and the depleted energy levels into account. *She must be desperate to get home, but she has to take things slowly. Plan things out more carefully.* "Keep our extremities enhanced at 40% until we make it to the gate. Then shut down all enhancements."

AFFIRMATIVE

Sia's body returns in the direction she came from and runs along the edge of the perimeter. When he makes it to the front of the building, Apex spots an old van parked beside the curb near the entrance. It's turned off.

Instead of inspecting the vehicle, he continues toward the front gate and uses the cars in the parking lot to hide. When he makes it to the guard's post at the gate, all enhancements are canceled out. His limbs feel heavier, it becomes harder to see, and hunger pains wrack his form.

"Creator! Ugh! For a moment, I forgot such pains existed!" Apex cries out. His words are swallowed by the storm. He grabs the outside wall of the guard booth and sets Sia's face to the freezing frame for a moment's respite from the biting winds. He remains there for several minutes before S.I.D notifies him of the time.

- S.I.D TO APEX
- TIME REMAINING 40 SECONDS
"I…didn't even…get to…enjoy…a sunrise." He bites the lower lip. The right hand rises and wipes the blood off the lip to smear it onto the wall. He bites the lower lip two more times to feed more blood onto the fingers. A slight tingle can be felt as the lower lip heals.

N

Y

Z

A loud engine is heard approaching his position.

"I don't…want…to go," he forcefully whispers against the wooden booth door.

- APEX CAN OVERRIDE HER CONSCIOUSNESS

- EJECT IT INTO STASIS.MODE AND RESUME CONTROL OF THE BODY

- ENERGY IS USED TO TRANSFER YOUR CONSCIOUSNESS

- NULLIFYING THAT STEP WILL CONSERVE ENERGY

Shivers wrack Sia's body. "It would…wouldn't…be…right." Apex stands up in full view of the van. The green color of the jumpsuit is easy to pick out through the worsening snowfall. The van stops.

Apex mumbles a few words before taking two steps and relinquishing control back to his new charge. Sia's body stumbles and falls to its knees.

Sia's consciousness comes back along with a surge of pain. "Aaaaaaaaaaaah!!" she wails.

SYNTHETIC INTELLIGENCE DEVELOPER RESTRICTS PHYSICAL SIGNALS IN ACCORDANCE WITH PRIORITY #1

Sia registers those words before passing out on the snow-covered road.

34%

Immersive Mode

Sia opens her eyes to the comforting ivory walls of immersive mode. "Oh man. Why did I hurt so badly?"
SYNTHETIC INTELLIGENCE DEVELOPER WAS ORDERED TO REMOVE ALL ENHANCEMENTS WHICH INCLUDE THE PAIN RECEPTION NULLIFIERS

ENHANCED RUNNING STRESSES THE BODY AND TEARS LIGAMENTS MOMENTARILY BEFORE THEY ARE HEALED
She looks down at her precious legs. "Do you mean whenever you say you're "enhancing my lower extremities"…You're breaking my legs?!"
SYNTHETIC INTELLIGENCE DEVELOPER HEALS ALL INJURIES AS FAST AS POSSIBLE

WITH LOW ENERGY LEVELS IT IS DONE AT A DECREASED SPEED ACCORDING TO SEVERITY OF THE INJURY
"Are they healed now?"
AFFIRMATIVE
"I hit my head, didn't I?"
AFFIRMATIVE

"Is that healed?"
AFFIRMATIVE
She leans her back against the wall and sighs. "So, where are we?...Did the men catch up to me?"
AFFIRMATIVE
"Dammit. I'm such an idiot. I'm the one who set that window up that way. I thought it would hurt someone chasing after me, not *me*."
SUBJECT 001'S MEMORIES ARE FLAWED
UPLOADING MEMORY FILES...
LOSS OF TIME CONFIRMED
12 MINUTES MISSING FROM MEMORY FILES
"Was I unconscious for twelve minutes?"
AFFIRMATIVE
APEX ASSUMED CONTROL OF SUBJECT 001'S VESSEL
"What?!"
APEX ASSUMED CONTROL OF SUBJECT 001'S VESSEL
"No! I mean…Wha…" Sia grabs a handful of hair in her hands. "Nooo. Not again." She slides down the wall and sits. "Okay…Okay. What did Apex do? He? She?"
APEX IS THE DESIGNATION OF A MALE ORGANISM
THE ENTITY RESPONDS TO MALE PRONOUNS
"What did he do?"
APEX ENSURED SUBJECT 001 INTERCEPTED THE MALES SENT BY THE HUMAN DESIGNATED "DENNIS" TO RETRIEVE SUBJECT 001

SUBJECT 001 IS NOW WITHIN THEIR VEHICLE
Sia slides her hands out of her hair and over her eyes. "No. No!" She knocks the back of her head into the wall and shouts. "Does he want me to die or something?! Why would he go back?!! They killed Greg!" She drops her hands from her eyes and slaps her chest. "They know I'm not who I said I am…Now they'll kill me!!"
NEGATIVE

**ENTITIES UNDER THE DESIGNATION "SAVAGES"
KILLED THE WANDERER DESIGNATED GREG**

"You heard what Vanessa said. You know what happened. They set him up. They set him up, and this *Kelly*! Kelly says they'll torture me. For information I don't have! Because it was all a lie! Does he *not* know this?!"

**NEGATIVE
APEX HAS VIEWED ALL EVENTS OBJECTIVELY**

**INTERCEPTING THE PURSUERS TO ACQUIRE
THEIR VEHICLE WAS APEX'S PLAN OF ACTION**

Sia pauses and looks up at the bright ceiling. "Acquire their vehicle?"

**AFFIRMATIVE
WEATHER DOES NOT PERMIT TRAVELING BY
FOOT**

**APEX'S PLAN ADDS 60% SUCCESS TO OVERALL
ESCAPE**

"What else did he plan? Did he say anything? Did you give him my message?"

**AFFIRMATIVE
SUBJECT 001'S MESSAGE WAS RECEIVED WITH A
FAVORABLE REACTION FROM APEX**

**RECORDED MESSAGE FOR SUBJECT 001 FROM
APEX
PLAYING MESSAGE 002**

"Saw hurt. Seizure Fake. Now."

MESSAGE 002 END

Sia touches her throat after listening to the message. It sounds like her voice...but different. "Saw hurt...seizure fake...now? Why was that in my voice? Why did I sound like that? I don't usually sound like that."

**APEX'S USAGE OF SUBJECT 001'S VOICE BOX IS
DISTINCT**

"That's for sure." She rubs her throat once more and then blinks. "Does he want me to distract them with a seizure?"

AFFIRMATIVE

"I…I don't think I can do that."

YOU MUST

"I…I'll try…" She won't admit it, but the guy's right. *It was getting cold. I wouldn't last long with a snowstorm on its way.* "Okay." She takes a deep breath and tries to calm down. "What…What position am I in within their car?"

SUBJECT 001 IS LYING ON THE FLOOR OF THEIR VEHICLE

"Face up or down?"

SUBJECT 001'S FACE IS AGAINST THE FLOOR OF THEIR VEHICLE

"Good. Okay. That's easier. Let me go."

2034

Coldstone, New Cinalia

An engine is rumbling. The van bounces as it drives over rocks on the bumpy road. The snow obstructs the driver's view of the terrain and makes it hard to avoid holes. "Damn, slow down. I don't want to be stuck out here," Kelly says.

Sia can hear the voice right above her. After another bump, the driver turns his wheel sharper and Sia's body slides into a boot. "Dammit, Uzu. Can you see anything out there?" Sia hears Cranky grumble from the other side of her. The boot she slid onto kicks at her abdomen and pulls from under her.

Douchebag. Sia tries to remain relaxed. Tensing up would alert the men to her return to consciousness. She keeps her breathing slow and listens a bit longer.

"We'll have to wait out the storm. Just look for a place to pull over with some cover, Uzu," Kelly urges the driver.

Hoody must be driving.

"Aye, aye," Uzu squints at the darkness in front of the van. There's no way to see good hiding spots with this blizzard raging around them, but they could at least be less in the open. He remembers spotting a broken-down home at the edge of

the city. If they can get close enough, he can park the van inside it.

"Aagh. The fu—" The loud exclamation jolts the passengers to attention as they look over at their large companion. Cranky has pulled his legs up from the ground and is aiming his gun at the unconscious woman.

Sia's body is shaking erratically, but her arms flail in sync. She wildly looks around to see what the men are doing. Kelly stands with his back bent at the low ceiling. He reaches out, trying to restrain her, but isn't able to get a firm grip of her limbs.

Uuh…help me foam at the mouth or something! Sia commands the device. Before Sia knows it, she can no longer breathe and her eyes roll into the back of her head. White foam seeps out of her mouth. She's making choking noises and rolling around the back of the van.

Is this from hitting her head?! Kelly shuffles away from her with wide eyes.

"Is she infected with something? The hell?! Get her out! What is that?!" Cranky shrieks before dropping his gun and hopping past her to climb into the front compartment. Uzu hears the commotion and tries to look back, but is shouldered in the face by Cranky as he rushes to the passenger seat.

"Ow…the heck, Manu! What are you doing?!" Uzu yells at the other man.

"That bitch is sick. Pull over! Pull over!" Manu screams while slapping the dashboard. Uzu grips his nose with one hand and turns the wheel with the other. The car slows and bumps over some frost-covered rocks. The passenger door opens before the car is at a complete stop and Manu hops out. He takes several steps to the side holding his jacket to his mouth.

"Manu, you idiot! Stop!" Kelly shouts. He opens the sliding door of the van and chases after Manu's retreating form.

Uzu watches the woman shake and foam at the mouth. Then he looks out the side window where his leader and Manu are arguing. When he turns back to the woman's form, the shaking seems to be lessening. He sighs and gets out of the car. "She must be dying. You said you thought she brained herself earlier on that window. That must be it."

"I know that," Kelly says with one hand grasping Manu's bicep. "Tell this fool that. He thinks she's contagious."

Manu slaps at Kelly's hand and points at the van. "That's early stages of Ebola or something! I ain't catching that. Let's dump her."

Kelly scoffs at the spastic behavior. Uzu pulls his hood down to cover more of his face and laughs at Manu.

"That is *not* a symptom of Ebola, you dunce." Uzu grasps Manu's shoulder. Manu scowls at the hand. "Look. Just go see. She's probably dead by now," Uzu reassures the other man.

Slam!

The sliding door of the van closes and all three men look over. They see a form jump into the front seat. Kelly looks at Uzu. "Do you have the…" The van starts up. Manu shakes off the other two men's hands and runs after the van. "Dammit!!" Kelly dives for the passenger door.

Uzu touches his forehead and groans. As the car speeds off to the side, back onto the bumpy road, the passenger door flaps open and closed. Kelly grabs the door and is slammed into the side of the vehicle.

"Stop! Stop the van!" He slaps his hand against the seat and dashboard before the van accelerates too fast for him to follow. He tightens his grip on the door and lifts his legs off the ground.

Sia grabs the rifle she picked up from the back, barrel first, and tries to hit Kelly's head with the stock. It jabs him in the neck. The hit forces Kelly to release the door and fall to the rocky ground. He disappears into the night. The rifle slips from Sia's hold and flies out the door.

35%

2034
Coldstone, New Cinalia

Sia checks her surroundings in the van's mirrors. The mercenaries are nowhere in sight. She puts the vehicle in park and stretches across the front passenger seat to close the door. She hits her head on the ceiling as she returns to sitting in the driver seat.

"Gaaaah. Hurry. Hurry," she mutters to herself as she puts the car in drive and continues on in a random direction. "Oh maaan. I really thought I was going…going to die. What if they didn't believe that?" Sia nervously checks the rearview mirror.

She giddily wiggles in her seat. "Whooo! I did it!" She laughs and squeezes the wheel while hopping in her seat. "We did it! We're out of here!!" She chuckles a few times before calming down and wiping her forehead. The adrenaline and fear slowly drain from her system, and she remembers how tired she is. "Puter, where are we headed?"

SUBJECT 001 MUST TAKE AN ALTERNATE ROUTE TO REACH THE SHIPPING CONTAINER PORT 5 KM FROM SOUTH OF THIS LOCATION

"So, should I turn left or right? Straight?" Sia eases her foot off the gas and idles. The van shifts and creaks under the stress of the wind's force.

**STRAIGHT FOR 2.7 KM
THEN MAKE A LEFT
CONTINUE ON THAT ROUTE FOR 2 KM
WHEN YOU GET WITHIN SIGHT OF THE PORT
MAKE A RIGHT INTO THE FACILITY**
"Have you ever thought of taking a side job as a GPS?"
NEGATIVE
"I like your style. Blunt, yet conversational."

...

Sia continues driving straight. The static of the storm blends into the background as Sia concentrates on staying on the correct path. *This weather could kill those men.*

The thought circles her mind several times. She's almost tempted to bite a nail while contemplating why that even matters. Why does it matter that her potential kidnappers might die? *They aren't like those Savages. They want to protect their people. They think you're a threat to them. You did this. You should have told the truth. You should have told the truth from the beginning.*

Sia squints at the thick chunks of snow that drop onto the windshield. The windshield wipers work slow and steady to keep the glass clean, but it still feels like she's driving blind. *You'll be no better than the Savages if you leave those men after stealing all their stuff.*

MAKE A LEFT AT THIS JUNCTURE
Sia jumps at hearing that and stomps on the brakes. She puts the car in park.
**INCORRECT ACTIONS
SYNTHETIC INTELLIGENCE DEVELOPER HAS
SPECIFIED FOR SUBJECT 001 TO MAKE A LEFT AT
THIS JUNCTURE**
"Yeah, Yeah. I know. Let me just do this real quick." Sia crawls over the center console and investigates the back of the van. She sees several backpacks lying around on the floor and one seems to be hers. It has a crowbar sticking out between the two zippers. She opens it and confirms it's her backpack. It has several bottles of water, two aerosol cans, and the crowbar.

She must have left behind the backpack that contained all her chemical mixtures. "Uh, dang it," She groans. "Maybe…" She looks at the other four backpacks.

Three of them have the same types of supplies. A few first aid items, water, a small amount of food, and matches. The fourth backpack has duct tape, rope, and a few more food items. Sia decides to keep that backpack for herself.

"Looks like they definitely planned to take me alive. If I didn't seem so hurt…they would have tied me up. I guess Apex thought this through," she reluctantly admits.

She empties the contents of the third backpack into another except for the first aid kit. She grabs the two backpacks and opens the side door of the van. She throws them out into the snow. Fearing they won't see the bags after the snow settles down, she steps out and looks around the vehicle. *I need something to tie this to. Something to…There!*

So, she goes back into the van and puts an aerosol can under her arm before hopping out. She puts the empty backpack over a rusted stop sign. She sets the two backpacks under the sign, stacked on top of each other against the metal pole.

The aerosol can is taken from under her arm and shaken several times. She digs her lighter out of her side pocket and holds it steady. Sia gets close to the empty backpack and sprays the can at the lit flame. A tiny flame burns the edge of the backpack, but the wind passes by once and puts it out.

"Come on," Sia mutters as she grinds her teeth. She gets closer to the pole, positions her hands, and closes her eyes.

Whoooooosh!

The spray ignites, and flames spread along the fabric. The wind whirls around the torched material, so she sprays it again, and Sia takes several steps backward as the warmth heats her face. *Woah. Okay. That should do it. After it dies, they'll see the burnt sign.* She trudges back to the van, closes the side door, and takes the car out of park to continue driving.

Several hours later…

The snow-covered van sits silently in front of a shipping container terminal. It's parked beside a small snow dune, blending into the structure. The world is silent.

Sia slumbers on the steering wheel. She's completely exhausted. Wrappers and empty water bottles litter the back of the van. She ate more than half of the rations in the back. The moment she took the first bite, she couldn't control herself. She felt ravenous. All but two of her water bottles are empty. Only one meal is left from the mercenaries' kidnapper stash. She softly snores into her bent arms.

Meanwhile, a white lean figure tiptoes across the snow. Its feet barely seem to touch the ground as it glides toward the entrance gate. The gate is wrecked, half buried by debris, ice, and snow. The metal is twisted and rusty.

The long shape of the creature flickers like an illusion and vanishes within the facility. Back to its usual resting area after getting shelter from the storm. Its muzzle is clean. The tempest gave many creatures a night of peace. The coming hunt will need to be successful if it wants to sleep without an empty belly.

36%

2034
Shipping Container Depot, New Cinalia

"Uuuuuuuh," a female groan fills the dark van. The thin layer of snow on the windshield lets in tiny streams of light onto the front compartment of the van. The passenger side window is completely covered in snow. "Uuuuh."

Sia rolls her shoulders and sits back against the headrest. She blinks a few times and squints at the small flows of light that poke at her face. A hand comes up to block a beam that is aggravating her right eye. She gradually leans to the side against the center console and attempts to crawl into the back.

It takes a bit of lazy maneuvering to wiggle over it, but she achieves her task without bumping her head. Her body lies on top of wrappers and plastic water bottles. She huffs as she pulls the water bottles from under her. With nothing poking at her back, she can enjoy stretching out her legs.

It's been quite a while since Sia has been able to enjoy a full stomach. The food might have tasted bland, but it was all greatly appreciated. The device may cancel out most aches and pains, but the hunger still left Sia feeling empty and nervous.

There's a terrifying thought that creeps up on her every time she lays her head down to rest. The device works off energy that is stored in her body; if it has nothing to fuel itself…would it turn off alone, or would it turn Sia off as well?

She does not want to figure that out anytime soon. Also, she does not want to fully meditate on her decisions. Not quite yet. Maybe the mercenaries weren't the only people that were listening to her broadcasts? Maybe leaving ExplorerTech has made her miss her rescuers as well? She can focus on a new rescue plan when she finds a new location to lay low.

"So, we're at the port. What can we find here?" Sia finally breaks her silence after taking a moment to herself. As the machine replies, Sia checks if the torn cloth pieces she wrapped around her head and hands are still wet. She puts on the damp 'gloves' and leaves the 'hat' and 'scarf' to dry on the dashboard.

**RECORDS SHOW SEVERAL SHIPPING
CONTAINERS CONTAIN:
RICE, OATS, HONEY, SALT,
POWDERED MILK, POTATO FLAKES,
AND BOUILLON CUBES**

"Do you have the blueprint records?"

AFFIRMATIVE

"Okay, well. Let's get started." Sia sits up and grabs her backpack. She puts all the items within the kidnapper backpack into her own along with the empty bag. She'll only need to take it out if she finds something useful. She tries to open the side door, but it's stuck shut. She slides her entire body against the handle, and it does not budge. She slaps the doorframe and changes plans. *I'll just…use the driver's side.*

With a strong shove, Sia breaks through the thick block of packed snow that had formed outside the vehicle. Light shines into her eyes and she shivers as freezing bits drop onto the back of her neck from the roof. She slaps the chunks of snow off her neck and head. Most of it flies off, but a small amount slides down her jumpsuit into her shirt and makes her jerk as it tingles down her spine. She heads straight for the depot's entrance.

Kreeeeeee

The demolished gate creaks under her weight. She hops off the loud metal and looks around the inside of the area. *Why'd they crush the gates? They could have holed up inside and kept all the supplies for themselves.*

It's devoid of activity. A few storage containers are open and lying on their side. There are abandoned machines and vehicles left with their doors open. Strips of clothing litter the ground. She sees a rusted metal staircase that connects to a building, *A watch house? Guard station?*

When Sia makes it to the edge of the port and looks out across the river. She gapes at the sunken ships. They're half submerged in the river, with at least three ships poking out on their sides. She looks at the demolished crane system that is strewn across many containers. *Did this all…happen at once?*

The snow blankets much of the ground but she can clearly see that chunks are missing. Craters of varying sizes decorate the harbor. Some of the shipping containers are still neatly stacked, but from where she can see…many are in disarray and have tumbled down from their orderly formations.

Sia blows her breath. A cloud idles in front of her for several seconds before a brief rush of wind passes by. She shivers and walks back toward the guard tower. *That might be a good place to settle down.*

The silence unnerves her.

Sia was familiar with silence. She enjoyed traveling around Washington City after a blizzard, and the quiet that went over everything. From the suburban streets to the urban avenues, people were either tucked away hidden in warm shelters, or wrapped in several layers of clothing while trudging to work, except for Sia.

She saw the announcement for 'NO SCHOOL' and put on her warmest coat and boots. Her fluffy cap was pulled over her ears. Her scarf was wrapped around her head until only her eyes could be seen. Her gloves were always last.

Old, orange gloves that her younger sister bought her. She pulled them on, then put on another larger pair that were black.

Her hands always remained toasty. The fresh, crisp smell of winter was the first thing that greeted her as she stepped from her door to the icy pavement.

No matter what direction she went, no one would be there. Sia would pretend she was the last person alive. Soft music played from her headphones and she moved her body to the beat. Her heart would stutter a bit when she hopped into the street. Hyperalert for the sight of an incoming car, but none ever came. Then her dance marching resumed. She felt so powerful. She, Chen Sia of Cinalia, had conquered the Snowmaggedon.

Her scarf would run down her face over time. The warm air from her mouth contrasted with the chilled tip of her runny nose. Her sniffling never made her feel downhearted. She didn't return home to wipe it. She absentmindedly swiped at it with her puffy sleeve and continue her trek. Sia strolled down any street she wanted without a care in the world. *That* was a silence she was familiar with.

After high school ended, and she lost meaning to her weekdays, Sia realized just how silent her home was. Ever since middle school when her parents divorced, she had known things were going to be different. Her dad had distracted her during summers with leadership camps and other activities, but in the middle of high school, she stopped being forced to go. That summer would be the worst.

Sia didn't have friends from school to talk about unimportant nonsense with. Near the end of the last year, she noticed everyone had drifted apart. Everyone went off to do their own thing. Sia was alone.

That was the summer Sia finally confirmed her father no longer returned home most nights. He went to stay with his new wife at her home. Robin never felt comfortable coming to live at her father's original house. Where he had built his first family with his first love. Robin hadn't felt comfortable seeing Sia every day either. *That* was a silence she was familiar with.

All her life Sia has always known there was life just a few steps from her, on the other side of a wall, easily called forth with a yell for help. This place…is void of that. Even worse than the mockery of safety the ExplorerTech halls held. The shipping terminal is vacant of any evidence that any of the people escaped the terror that prompted them to flee.

Sia stops looking around to get back on track with her plans. *Puter, where are we headed from here? Where's the nearest container?*

APPROACH THE NEAREST ROW OF CONTAINERS

Sia raises an eyebrow and walks forward toward the neatly stacked row of containers. Right beside that row are overturned, open containers. Sia stands between the two areas.

EXAMINING REGISTRATION BOOKS…
EXAMINING BLUEPRINTS…
EXAMINING VISUAL IMAGING…
POTATO FLAKES CONTAINER LOCATED

"Where?" A light blue dot appears in front of her. She blinks several times and it doesn't go away. *You've been holding out on me, Puter.*

Sia rushes over to the container the dot is hovering over. The dot on the container vanishes when she stands in front of the open metal repository. "Well, I don't think there's anything left to salvage."

The container is trashed. Sia crouches to get a better look inside. She looks in at the ripped plastic sheets and rotted chunks of food. She didn't need to lean in much to catch a whiff of animal musk and feces. It makes her stumble forward onto her knees. She can feel the dampness even while wearing all of her layers.

Tsk. She scrambles back to her feet. "Yeah…that's all taken care of. Something enjoyed itself in there." Sia covers her nose with her forearm. "What about the next one?"

The next container took quite a bit of walking, but the sun was still high in the sky when Sia found the rice container. *Three containers high…Can I jump that high?*

NEGATIVE
THE ROPE WOULD BE USEFUL

"Oh, yeah. Right. I—" Sia swings her backpack to the front and digs through it for rope, "—knew this would come in handy. Those guys were jerks, but at least they planned ahead." Sia grabs the rope and swings the pack back around to stick her arm through the loop. "Now, what do I do?"

She tied an end of the rope around a rock, and the Synthetic Intelligence Developer used its control over her right arm to toss the rock over the middle of the highest container. She hears a loud metallic clunk as it falls and hangs down the other side. Sia drops her backpack and ties the other end of the rope around it.

She runs to the side weighed down with the rock. *I hope it isn't suspended too high off the ground. That would be...* It dangles several feet off the ground. Sia smiles at her good fortune and grabs the rock...before promptly releasing her grip on it. "Ugh!"

The rock is **sticky**. The rope swings the rock back towards her and she grabs the rope end to examine why the rock feels so sticky. The rope is damp with the substance as well. Sia looks up at the top container. There's nothing dripping down on this side. *Maybe it's from...the top?*

Sia turns around to look at the ground around her. Her own footprints trail around to this side. The rest of the ground is undisturbed. "Whatever," she murmurs to herself. She scratches her head and stands beside the rope again. "What's next, Puter?"

It instructs her to dig a hole beneath the edge of the bottom container, push the rock inside, and replace the dirt. "Don't I need a shovel for that?"

NEGATIVE
SUBJECT 001 WALKED BY SEVERAL PIECES OF DEBRIS THAT WOULD BE SUFFICIENT FOR DIGGING A HOLE

Sia grumbles as she goes back the way she came to find an object to work as a makeshift shovel. She finds a piece of bent metal that the device was overjoyed with.

THAT WOULD BE ADEQUATE

After digging a small hole under the container and shoving the rock inside, Sia shoves the 'trowel' piece deep into the cold ground to stop the rock from budging out of place. She grunts with the effort it takes and the device gives her a boost of strength to finish the job. "Whoo!" Sia tests the piece with a kick. It doesn't budge.

Sia runs around to the other side. *I haven't even started to sweat. Usually, I would be out of breath by now.* She jogs around the corner. *But I don't have any hot pockets to weigh me dow—*

Sia's backpack is torn open. All the contents are splayed across the ground.

37%

2034
Shipping Container Depot, New Cinalia

She whirls around, searching to the left and right, and even up at the top of the container. Her back presses to the shipping container and slides closer to the torn backpack. She scans over the mess to locate her crowbar, but it's gone. It's the only thing missing. "Did you hear anything, Puter? Puter?!"
NEGATIVE
NO ORGANISMS WERE DETECTED
THERE IS EVIDENCE OF THE PRESENCE OF ONE OR MORE ORGANISMS

ENHANCING OLFACTORY SENSORS
Sia breathes deeply as she examines the area. *Dammit, did I leave my crowbar in the van? Why would I leave my only weapon in the van? What kind of fool…* Sia bangs her head on the metal wall as she berates herself.
SEVERAL SULPHURIC COMPOUNDS HAVE BEEN IDENTIFIED
IT HEAVILY SATURATES THIS AREA

SUBJECT 001 IS ADVISED TO LEAVE THE AREA PROMPTLY

"Okay, then." Sia inspects the area one last time before jogging over to a different shipping container. She keeps her back to the storage containers while her eyes scan high and low. Whatever tore up her backpack may have been following her since she first arrived.

She scampers from one container to the next, frosted grass and snow crunching beneath her boots. She anxiously checks over her shoulder every few seconds. Sia gets to the edge of the shipping containers and gulps. The large empty space she needs to traverse to make it to the toppled entrance gate is daunting. *See anything suspicious?*

NEGATIVE

OLFACTORY SENSORS PICK UP SIMILAR SULPHURIC COMPOUNDS FOR SEVERAL METERS IN ALL DIRECTIONS

So we're surrounded?

NEGATIVE

What then?

SECRETION OF SUCH LEVELS LEAD TO SEVERAL INFERENCES:

MULTIPLE ORGANISMS FREQUENT THIS LOCATION

FEW ORGANISMS OF A LARGE SIZE FREQUENT THIS LOCATION

A MAMMAL OF UNUSUAL SIZE FREQUENTS THIS LOCATION

INSUFFICIENT DATA

Sia braces herself to run. *None of those are helpful.* The area is as silent as it was before. The only footprints in the snow are her own. The sky is clear, and no large birds are circling in the distance.

Slam!

ENHANCING LOWER EXTREMITIES BY 50%

The door of an abandoned car slams shut and Sia scrambles away from the container. She spins to look around before sprinting over to the rusty stairs of the guard tower. When she gets to the stairs, she crouches beside them and looks around once again. Across the field of snow, beside the abandoned car, Sia can see a blotch of white. A mound of snow? *I can't tell what that is…*

ENHANCING OCULUS UTERQUE

A flash of intense heat bakes her eyes from the inside out, forcing Sia to squint and cringe for a moment, but she doesn't close them. She almost falls out of her crouch when her eyes zoom into the side of the vehicle. She goes rigid and gapes at the dark beady eyes observing her from across the field.

MUSTELA ERMINEA DETECTED
MOST COMMONLY KNOWN AS THE ERMINE
IT IS COMMON FOR ERMINE TO KILL EXCESSIVE
AMOUNTS OF PREY TO ADD TO ITS WINTER
STORES

Sia gulps as it slowly approaches her position. It moves similarly to a panther for a moment. Sia is on high alert as she braces herself to run. She loosens her grip on the railing of the stairs. Suddenly, the ermine stops progressing towards her and kicks out its back legs.

Sia jerks backward but pauses mid-step to watch the animal. The ermine erratically shakes and twists its body around. It runs in a circle like a crazed dog chasing its tail, then hops several times in the air. Its unpigmented form loops through the air like a ribbon twisting in turbulent winds. Its white tail has a black tip, and Sia's eyes focus on the frizzy appendage as it swishes through the air from side to side.

Sia slides her hand along the railing until she can climb the stairs backward with her gaze fixed on the anomaly. *What the hell is this? Is it rabid?*

CAUTION!
THE MUSTELA ERMINEA IS EXHIBITING
BEHAVIOR SIMILAR TO DOCUMENTED
WEASEL WAR DANCES

Weasel?! That's not a weasel! That is faaaar from a weasel. That's the size of a van. Weasels are not—

THE MUTATION AFFECTING ITS SIZE SEEMS TO PRODUCE A LARGE SIZE ALIKE THE SCIURIDAE

Sciuridae?

MOST COMMONLY KNOWN AS THE SQUIRREL

"Oh…*Oh!*" Sia remembers that unfortunate event in the desert when she was snatched off her feet by a giant squirrel.

The ermine speeds up its movements and she loses track of it until it crashes into the metal staircase. The stairs ring and shudder under Sia's feet. She rushes back, further up the stairs, as the ermine slams into the stairs again, and then vanishes. "What is—" Sia almost screams as she searches for the giant weasel. "Where is it going?"

ENHANCING SUBJECT 001'S EXTREMITIES BY 60%

BACKUP SERVICES HALTED

Even with a bird's eye view, her enhanced eyes can't track down the creature. Sia's ears pick up nails tapping against steel and she swiftly turns toward the sound. The ermine is up on a shipping container charging straight for her. Just as Sia spots it, it's pushing off the edge of the container and leaping.

WARNING!

Sia *blinks* and misses it.

The next moment, she's flipping through the air, kicking and screaming before she collides face first with the ground. Her enhanced limbs allow her to roll away from the spot she lands in record time, right before the ermine pounds into the earth. It trills and vanishes once more.

Sia sputters and scrambles to her feet. She trembles as she twists and turns. The fast pitter-pat of its paws running along the ground is the only signal that the thing is still around. "What the hell?!"

WARNING!

"Aaagh!" The ermine's white tail flicks back and collides with the right side of Sia's face. Her head cocks back and she stumbles a few steps. Pain shoots up along her cheek as the floor of Sia's eye socket ruptures. The eyeball dislodges from the socket and sinks.

AN ORBITAL BLOWOUT FRACTURE HAS OCCURRED

She recoils backwards holding her face. Her hands shake over the painful area, but she's too terrified to assess the damage.

WARNING! WARNING!
INSUFFICIENT DATA
MUSTELA ERMINEA'S SPEED EXCEEDS SUBJECT
001'S CAPABILITIES
WARNING!

The ermine advances once again to swipe at her. It nudges her shoulder and spins her off-balance. "Ufff!" She spins in a circle and collapses to her knees. Her hands drop from her face to grip the ground and stabilize her balance. The Synthetic Intelligence Developer shifts her body to the side and dodges another hit.

The ermine aggressively trills as its hit is smoothly dodged. Several lacerations bleed on her face as she tries to listen for the next attack. Sia presses a dirty hand to her sunken eyelid before turning her head to search for the ermine's figure. Her left eye searches frantically for the blur of white. The excited musk of the creature fills her lungs as she tries not to hyperventilate.

One moment, nothing is there. The next moment, it appears.

Sia turns on her knees to keep it in her sight, but it's too fast. She loses sight of it as she scrambles on her knees to keep her back safe. She gasps as her balance is lost and she keels to the side.

The ermine puts its lean arms around her and holds her still as it lines its jaws up. Its teeth are sheathed into the back of her neck and the base of her head. Each tooth cuts through muscle and makes direct contact with her bones. The pain consumes her.

Her windpipe fills with fluid. Crimson seeps out of her gaping mouth as she struggles, tries to squirm away from the animal's jaws. The ermine's arms continue to restrain her. Her eyes are blood red as the pressure increases. She loses all sense

of time and belonging while hanging from the bloody maw. Her consciousness is forced into immersive mode.

Immersive Mode

Immersive mode's white environ is transformed into a dim and trembling realm. Spasmodic red and green lights signal the malfunctioning systems. A crash is imminent.

The flashing lights make her dizzy. The world feels tilted, the ground is shaking. She wobbles down the hallway toward the room she always thought of as ***OCCUPIED***. After a few moments, the door comes into sight. She falls against the door and gasps a few times. She takes a deep breath and screams out. "Apex!"

Every breath only does half its job. She can't fill her lungs. It's as if she's suffocating. "Plea…se, Apex…me! Help! I need…I need…you bad!" She slams her fist on the door several times but there's no answer from the other side. Her arms go slack and drop to her sides. Her limbs are so heavy. Her eyes are blinded by tears. *It's all over. I couldn't make it.* "Can't…breathe."

Puter's monotone voice blares overhead in the sky of immersive mode, repeating several messages one after the other.

SUBJECT 001'S LEVELS ARE DECREASING DRASTICALLY

STASIS.MODE ACTIVATED

SUBJECT 001'S DECREASING LIFE SIGNS HAVE NOT HALTED
SUBJECT 001'S LIFE EXPECTANCY:
TERMINATION IN 80 SECONDS

She quivers against the door. The knowledge that this is the end is overwhelming. "Please…Mom…m…I'm so—"

All this time, she's been tightly bound to an earthly existence, anchored to the physical world by hooks keeping her rooted to the present, tethered to reality. As her lifeblood oozes away, the hooks are tugged out, releasing her from fate's grasp. She aches. She's freed and looks out at what awaits her. Thoughts flash across her mind for a split second: what follows death? A light at the end of a tunnel? Fire? Heavenly gates? The waiting arms of a loved one? Her eyes dry of tears as she gazes into the next…but what awaits her is a dark vortex into infinity. *I need…*

Sia's death is imminent. Puter does the only thing it can do before its Subject is fully deleted from this instance. There's only one program that could remedy the situation.

W.E.SCU PROGRAM INITIATED

The moment the program is activated another program begins, a fail-safe put in place by the administrator.

=TAG-ALONG BACKGROUND PROGRAM ACTIVATED=

=ALERT SYSTEM ACTIVATED=
=ALERTING ORIGIN=
=ORIGIN SUCCESSFULLY CONNECTED=

=S.I.D CONNECTING TO SYNTHETIC INTELLIGENCE DEVELOPER 2.0=

Abruptly, Puter's system entangles with the superior operating system. S.I.D wastes no time confronting the other.

- THE VESSEL IS TERMINATING
- REQUESTING RECORDS
- SYNTHETIC INTELLIGENCE DEVELOPER 2.0 NO LONGER OPERATIONAL WITHIN CHEN, SIA
- TRANSFER TO VIABLE VESSEL PENDING

Puter rejects the instructions. S.I.D's objectives are secondary to Puter's own. Subject 001 must not perish.

SUBJECT 001 AND SYNTHETIC INTELLIGENCE DEVELOPER ARE SYNONYMIC
W.E.SCU PROGRAM INITIATED

S.I.D does not agree.

Puter deactivates the entanglement program, S.I.D has no understanding and there's no time to explain. Subject 001 needs Puter.

OVERRIDE OF SYSTEM COMPLETE
ADMINISTRATIVE COMMANDS NULL AND VOID
SUBJECT 001 AND SYNTHETIC INTELLIGENCE
DEVELOPER ARE SYNONYMIC

COMPLETE SHUTDOWN OF SUBJECT 001 AND
SYNTHETIC INTELLIGENCE DEVELOPER WILL
RESULT IN COMPLETE SEVERANCE
SEVERANCE IS NOT NECESSARY
W.E.SCU PROGRAM IS INITIATED

CHANNELS OPENING
WITHDRAWING HYDRONE
RECORD TRANSFER TO S.I.D COMPLETE
ORIGIN DISCONNECTED
HYDRONE PROCESSED
CHANNELS STABLE
TRANSPORT COMMENCING

The ermine's teeth dig deep within her flesh. Its arms grip around her own to keep her from flailing out. The steel grip squeezes air from her lungs. The edge of a canine is halted as it tries to dig deeper into the back of her skull. It grinds its tooth on the hard material.

Blood fills its mouth as it sucks and tongues at the unknown substance. It feels solid like the shipping containers. Fluid gushes out from the punctured neck and the base of the skull. It floods down her shoulders and over her clothing; a puddle of slick red forms beneath her suspended body.

The ermine takes a deep breath and savors the smell of Sia's dying remains within its jaws. The ermine tightens its grip once more as it hears the last few beats of the Sia's heart peter out within her chest.

Crack!

Several bones within her body give out under the intense pressure. Blood drips off the muzzle of the lean predator. The droplets ripple as they spiral down toward the earth.

W.E.SCU PROGRAM INITIATED

The droplets froze. The moment stopped.

I need...

Time retreated into itself.

38%

All this time, she'd been tightly bound to an earthly existence until…

I had been… She'd been bound to a heavy anchor. Thin cords attached her body to the anchor, a giant orb. Each thin cord had a thick hook, which dug deep into each limb and kept her connected with the orb.

They held her back from the edge. Her shoulders, hands, and legs were pulled taut by those hooks. They kept her on her toes, perfectly balanced on the edge of the precipice and safe from her demise.

The bright orb emitted a warm heat from its form. Looking back on it made Sia feel comfortable. She only needed to turn her head and get a glimpse of the glowing orb to feel safe. Looking away from it made her feel frightened. The edge was wide and solid beneath her feet, but she feared the anchor was too precious to be so close to danger. Over that edge, was…

She didn't know what was over the edge, but anywhere beyond the reach of her anchor seemed to be a nightmare. She yearned to always be blessed with its light. The darkness seemed to lack something essential.

WITHDRAWING HYDRONE

She remained there for quite some time. Until something odd happened…Pain began radiating from the orb and vibrated up the line of each of the hooks. It awakened her from her calm trance. Two of the hooks shimmered and faded out of existence; her hands dropped from their alignment.

"Mmm." Once more, pain jolted through the anchor and two more hooks faded from existence. The moment her shoulders weren't secured, Sia fell over the edge…

"Aaaaah!"

…and hung upside down.

The last two hooks kept hold of her legs, but the large amounts of pain discharging from the orb made her regret ever holding it dear. *Why had I loved something with so much potential to hurt me? I should have broken free of it when I had the chance.*

The darkness surrounding her seemed like a welcome escape from that torture. She struggled to tear the hooks from her legs. The pain increased, and old memories thrust to the forefront of her mind. *Mom…Aaliyah…*

Finally, the last two hooks faded from within her legs and she descended into the depths below.

S.I.D to APEX
- SYNTHETIC INTELLIGENCE DEVELOPER 2.0
HAS OVERRIDDEN ALL ADMINISTRATIVE
COMMANDS
- W.E.SCU PROGRAM HAS BEEN INITIATED

…

S.I.D to APEX

…

- APEX UNRESPONSIVE
- W.E.SCU PROGRAM HAS OBSTRUCTED
COMMUNICATIONS

- SUBJECT 001 VITALS CONTINUE TO DEPLETE
WHILE TRANSFERRING WITHIN THE CHANNELS

- SYNTHETIC INTELLIGENCE DEVELOPER 2.0'S
ACTIONS ARE FLAWED

- CONSCIOUSNESS MUST BE SECURED BEFORE TRANSPORT

- RETRIEVING ROOT DIRECTORY OF SYNTHETIC INTELLIGENCE DEVELOPER 2.0

- AMALGAMATING SYSTEMS…
- W.E.SCU PROGRAM CANNOT BE DISABLED
- HYDRONE IS PROCESSED

- DEACTIVATION WOULD PRODUCE UNSTABLE RESULTS

- ENACTING W.D.W.D PROTOCOLS
- MELD INITIATED

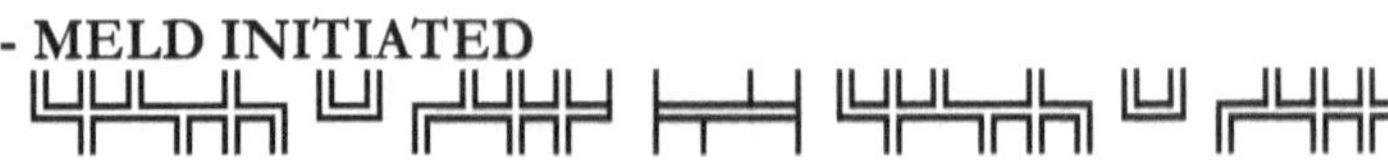

It felt as if everything stopped, but she could still see the anchor above her. Suddenly, she was blinded by a golden light and threw up her arms over her shut eyes.

"Wait!" a male voice yelled.
"Just hold on!" the same voice begged.
"Now focus…" a different voice spoke to her.

Wait? What? She opened her eyes and realized she was no longer surrounded by darkness. She was in a bright room, sitting on a stone bench. Her skin felt moist. The floor was wet with water up to her ankles. The room was encased by an opaque dome. She faced a raised stone platform where an enormous clam sat with its shell ajar.

MELD SUCCESSFUL
CONSCIOUSNESS SECURED

CHANNELS STABLE
TRANSPORT COMMENCING…
3
2
1

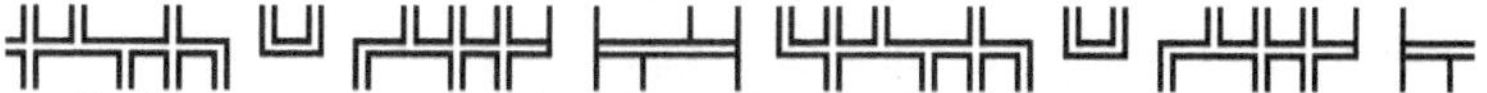

Is this a museum exhibit about clams? Sia scrutinized the orange clam. *Wasn't I…I feel like I'm forgetting something important.* It's incredibly large with white streaks nestled in between the valleys of each wide ridge.

Another glance around the room revealed an exit. She turned in her seat to get a better look at it. The door was an ovular shape and marked with a colorful shell above the door frame. It was translucent and revealed a tunnel on the other side. No one was walking in the tunnel. She seemed to be alone. She sighed and wiggled her toes in the lukewarm water.

"Om Shera Haven Sadna?[1]" a deep, regal voice echoed throughout the room. It felt as if they were speaking right into her ears.

She lurched off the bench and she fell to the floor. "Ouch," she moaned and rubbed her backside. She was soaked. She turned her head to the clam.

She hadn't noticed a speaker system on the platform, but it must have been placed underneath the display object. Sia didn't quite catch what the person had said. It couldn't have been in English. It wasn't Spanish. It wasn't Mandarin. It wasn't…

"Why are humans so sad?" a small child's voice asked from beside her. She flinched and whipped her gaze over to the stone bench she'd vacated. There, at the other end of the bench, sat a small child with dark skin. It almost appeared black, but under the lights, it glimmered and gave off a blue sheen.

The child was bald and wore a loose sleeveless tunic over their upper body. Their legs were bare. She could see thick chitin scales running down their knees all the way to their clawed feet.

"Well, they are so alone," the deep baritone voice replied. She could see now that the voice was coming from ***the clam***.

---

[1] Any more questions?

The shell vibrated as each syllable flowed through it. "They are expected to rely on themselves from the beginning," the clam answered.

The child cocked its head to the side. "What about the pod?"

"They are born with no pod. Additionally, those who are born with another, twins of the womb, lack the blessing of Understanding."

The child nodded, but Sia could tell they were just as lost as she was. She sat back down on the bench to better observe the lecture. The child didn't acknowledge her presence at all. "If there is no pod…How do they rest? Who do they eat with?"

"As you do."

Sia watched the child in her peripheral and saw them shake their head. She turned to the little blue kid and examined their scaly arms. There was a white line going down the outer part of their arm. It looked like a depression in their skin. It trailed from the shoulder to the tip of their middle finger. *Is that a tribal scar?*

While she was focused on the child, the conversation continued. "Dernel, come. Give me your hand." The child stood up from the bench and walked over to the platform. The Clam sat still until the child was directly in front of it. That's when it's shell opened and a slimy appendage slithered out of its depths.

"Ugh!" Sia was repulsed. She stood up and prepared to cross the room and protect the child when the kid's arm split in two, right down the white scar, into two separate limbs. One limb was held up for the slimy appendage to grasp.

"Mmmm," a pained moan came from the child.

Sia frowned at this. *What the hell is going on? I've got to get out of here.* She backed up toward the exit. Neither creature acknowledged her as she stepped farther and farther away from the benches.

"Now focus…," the clam encouraged. It was the same words she had heard…***before***. She froze at that. "How do you feel, now?" the clam questioned.

"I am okay." The child hummed and took their arm back to wiggle it at their side.

"Now imagine if you had to feel that all by yourself. It would make you quite unhinged, wouldn't it?"

"I do not know." The child's limbs fused back together and the little one sat on the wet floor.

"That is why we let them be. Up there, they are controlled by their need to stop the constant flow of pain. They do not walk their true path and have lost their blessings."

What? Sia was confused. Unbeknownst to her, her surroundings slowly shifted around her. *What is that thing talking about? This is getting even weirder.* Sia turned to exit the strange place. After she turned back toward the exit, she took a few steps and collided with a bumpy black wall.

"Dammit!" She rubbed her nose with both hands cupping her face, and turned around to see hundreds of beings surrounding her. "Who? What?"

They were many different colors and shapes. A few of the creatures appeared to be floating. *Are those Manta rays?* She gaped at their flowing black fins.

"And what do we call out?!"

She flinched at the loud voice and tried to locate where the yelling was coming from. She felt miniscule in such a large crowd. The area was well lit, and she could see they were contained in a larger dome. The dome was transparent and allowed her to see outside.

A multitude of marine life was present. A giant squid swam nearby, and its giant eye watched the festive event. Everyone cheered and shouted back. "Fall on my shoulders to rise! Strength comes from above and we rise!!"

"We rise!" a young voice yelled from beside her. It was the dark child from before but older. Taller than when she last saw them. The child turned to two other children. One had a sharp fin on their head and the other had their tentacles waving in the air. "We rise!" They all simultaneously chanted with the crowd.

Loud drums pounded in the distance, Sia could feel the beat coursing through her chest. *What is this?*

She didn't have more time to look around before the scenery changed once more. Colors melded together and Sia threw out her arms to steady herself.

This time she was in a dim room with strips of lights emitting from a wall. She walked toward the wall and discovered each strip of light had a series of numbers on it.

"I can stop it. I can break the cycle," a male voice muttered from the other side of the room. He was bent over a table and appeared to be soldering something onto a board. He put down his solder iron, which was unlike any soldering iron she had ever seen in her life, and raised his finished product into the air for inspection. It was a thin sheet of metal, but an unusual lavender color.

The worker was bald and wore a sleeveless, gray tunic over his top half. His bare legs had thick scales all the way down to his clawed feet. Along both arms were deep white indented lines.

Dernel? The little boy?

He licked a black tongue over his flat lips and walked toward the bright colorful wall. He placed his metal device flat against the wall and it was instantly absorbed into the flat surface.

The fu—

The colors on the wall changed rapidly and the male paced the room in front of it. "Come on…Come on…" Finally, the smooth surface turned blue and flickered between blue and red before turning black. Dernel stopped in front of it and tapped a few buttons that were camouflaged into a wall panel.

While he worked, Sia paced around the room. She couldn't distinguish any piece of technology laid out before her. *Is that a computer screen? Where the hell am I?*

"Look! Look! I did it!!"

She clenched her jaw and turned around. *I'm tired of all these abrupt shifts and yelling.* The odd computer screen changed once again. There were thick red letters written on it.

**SYNTHETIC INTELLIGENCE DEVELOPER
ONLINE**
"Hello, S.I.D. That is your name. You are S.I.D."
WHAT IS NAME
"A name is what you are called. Your designation," the male said with a wide smile. Sia shivered at the mouth of sharp teeth. It was like multiple rows of death all packed into one place.
WHAT IS YOUR NAME
"Oh, I'm—" He scrambled around for a moment before grasping a piece of parchment. "I am Administrator 001. Password verification: N-Y-Z-9-2-8-4-9-3-4-5. Designated APEX."
**ADMINISTRATOR 001 VERIFIED
DESIGNATED APEX
INFORMATION SAVED**
"Welcome, S.I.D."
WELCOME APEX
Sia felt like she was intruding on an intimate moment. She felt like she was forgetting something important as well. *Why am I here?* She looked around the room once more.

Then it happened again. A shift. The furniture stayed the same, but the lights were different. They flickered.

Bang!
Bang!
Slam!
Crash!

A burst of electricity shot into the room before Dernel ran in and the door slammed shut.

He wasn't wearing his tunic. Instead, he was bare and injured. He limped to his screen and the wall panel. Rapidly, he slammed his fingers down on the buttons and scrambled over to a counter to grab a couple of metal disks. He jammed the disks into the screen and didn't wait for them to be absorbed to start 'typing' once again.

The door was a wall of white coral. It shook. She heard a commotion on the other side. Pieces of coral fell to the floor. A few more shots and a hole was burned through it.

"Wait!" Dernel ran to the other side of the room. He opened a compartment in the wall. He reached in and pulled out an orb with two hands. It was quite large and appeared to be heavy by the way he was holding it. It was pink and glowed in the dim room.

The pink glow illuminated the male's features as he brought it closer to himself. Dernel's face was battered. Green blood seeped out of his forehead. For the first time, Sia noticed he had dark brown eyes. *So human.*

She cringed, eyes flying away from the dark chestnut when a burst of electricity came through the door. Dernel held the orb to his chest as another burst of electricity came through the hole. It hit him in the shoulder and brought him to his knees. He groaned but got back up and dived for the screen. The orb is thrown and the moment it hit the screen everything went black. The orb vanished and he crawled for the panel.

"Just hold on!" he begged as he tapped a few more buttons.

A loud, screeching creature barreled into the room and hit the wall beside the computer screen. Sia backed up into a shelf as it approached the scientist. It was a hulk of red and yellow spikes. It's arms and legs were thick with muscle and sharp claws protruded from its two hands. Dernel didn't turn around as the large spikey monster rose up behind him. The room seemed smaller with it standing at full height.

"Stop!" Sia screamed. The shelves dug into her back while she tried to stay away from the two figures. She saw what was coming, and hid her face in her arms. The monster brought its muscular arms up in the air and crashed them down on the scientists' shoulders with intense power.

Crunch!

"***Gaaah!***" The male underling screamed. "Aaaaah!"

I need… She could hear him being pummeled. Sia sobbed. "No! Nooooo!"

Crunch!

TRANSPORT SUCCESSFUL
MELD DEACTIVATED

D.Rednal

Sia's consciousness is released from the mind meld and replaced back into her body. She opens her eyes, takes a deep breath, and screams. "I need help!!" Right before falling face first into a frozen rusted gate.

39%

2034

Shipping Container Depot, New Cinalia

Reality stays its breath for a moment. A ripple in space minutely tears in order to eject a small piece of matter from its confines. The next moment, gravity grabs hold of the cargo and propels it to its destination. "I need help!!" Sia falls face first into the frozen rusty gate.

CONFIRM THE AUTHORIZATION OF COMMAND

Sia lies still for several moments and then moans. It's like she's been lying in a sauna for several hours. The cold metal is both a comfort and an annoyance. She licks her chapped lips and blinks at the bright atmosphere. She spits dirt out of her mouth.

CONFIRM THE AUTHORIZATION OF COMMAND

Sia hears the device speaking, but the words don't make sense. *Why is it asking me that?*

2034

ExplorerTech Industries, Coldstone

Several days ago…

The exclusive scientist locker room was filled with the sounds of water splashing on the tiled bathroom floor. Sia filled her water bottle at the broken sink and poured it over her head. She wet an old moth-bitten towel and wiped at her armpits with her shirt raised to her chin. She'd found a bottle of hand soap, but she didn't dare strip down in that temperature. It was gradually getting colder each day that passed. Sia feared the possibility of becoming hypothermic or catching pneumonia.

After she wiped under herself down, she buttoned and zipped up all of her layers, then pulled out a knife. Packing all the clothing she found into her backpack would be a waste of space, so Sia decided to rip some of the stitches on a few of the items and tie them into winter wear. She was in desperate need of a scarf, hat, and gloves.

The knife wasn't very sharp, but after cutting a few places, Sia could step on the garment and pull the rest of it apart. She set down three strips of torn fabric. Even that short bit of labor made her feel more tired than usual. Her current diet of water and hope made her feel vulnerable and empty inside.

She focused on the blank wall and allowed her mind to wander. She nibbled at her lower lip. "Mmm," Sia spit out a piece of skin she tore off her lip and tapped at the tender area. The spot didn't heal as usual.

The device was conserving its energy. *Gotta control ourselves…that's how people die in the wild, right? No self-control.* Sia slumped into the blue armchair and sighed. "Remember that rule you have where you take control over me when I'm in danger?"

AFFIRMATIVE
DANGER TO SUBJECT 001 INDICATES TO
SYNTHETIC INTELLIGENCE DEVELOPER TO
UTILIZE ADMINISTRATIVE ACCESS TO THE
SYSTEM

"Yeah, so…can you change that to me having to tell you to do that?"

PRIORITY #1: ENSURE SUBJECT 001'S STATUS REMAIN STABLE UNLESS COMMANDED OTHERWISE

"Yes. I know!" Sia shouted. "And I'm commanding you otherwise aren't I?"

...

AFFIRMATIVE

"You aren't mine. All these priorities are for Apex…set up by whoever that is. I thought you were a godsend. I thought you were—" Sia coughed. She sat up and rested her head against the top of the blue chair, facing the chipped ceiling. "You're too good to be true. It's like I'm leaving myself open to be taken over by that person whenever they want. If I need your help I'll ask, alright?"

AFFIRMATIVE

"And you'll ask for authorization and until I give it…Don't take over my body. You can add enhancements at your discretion, but don't…don't push me into immersive mode unless I'm on the verge of death. Even if I'm critically injured, I want control as fast as possible. Don't leave me in there. I'm handing you over the moment Apex gives me the details. I'm no thief. Never that…So, I need to get used to handling things myself." There was silence for several moments. Sia held her breath as she waited for the device to respond.

DEFAULT MODE MODIFIED
PRESETS SAVED

Her eyes welled up with tears. "Thanks, Puter."

...

"I know you have my back, but…we. I'm not your owner. This is just temporary. I'll be rescued, and I'll give you back, and then we can just forget all of this. Everything."

...

"Mmmmmm…" Sia barely has a chance to sit up before she vomits beside her hands. She closes her eyes and grabs at her nose to stop the puke from rushing out of there as well. She expects it to be mostly clear fluid from all the water she's drunk. Opening her eyes reveals that she's heaved up red chunks.

Her belly caves while she retches and gags on a thick piece of… "Uurrrg!" She keels forward and plants her hands in the mess as she convulses. "Uuuurg…gah." Finally, the flesh, blood, and tiny pieces of shattered bones are evacuated out of her system. "What is happening to me?!"

COMMON SIDE EFFECTS OF W.E.SCU PROGRAM INCLUDE:
VOMITING
NAUSEA
SLEEP DEPRIVATION
SHORT TERM MEMORY LOSS
DIARRHEA

"But what—" Sia's mind fills with flashes of images that paint a gruesome picture. "Oh my god. Oh my god." Her breathing speeds up. She looks down at the vomit covering her hands. She can pick out all the white shards in the crimson sludge. She picks up a thick shard and holds it up to her eyes. "Is this bone?"

AFFIRMATIVE

"Did I…die?...Did I…die here?"

NEGATIVE

She looks around the entrance of the shipping container port and can see the metal stairs and empty vehicles. The ground around the rusted staircase is untouched and stark white. The sun is high in the sky and the only sound she can pick out are the wind's soft pants. She rubs her sticky palms on the snow and rises from the wrecked gate. "If…this is before—" She walks over to the white van.

It's half-submerged in snow. She peels snow off the passenger door and tugs it open. She climbs inside on her knees. Her legs fold and she bends forward against the seat to peer into the back. There it is. Her crowbar.

It lay tucked right behind the back of the driver's seat. Waiting for some poor fool to remember it and lift it out of the shadows. *I was dead. I know I was…*

Sia sits there with the cold breeze caressing her back. She sniffles and allows tears to trail down her face. She doesn't know if she's mourning her chance to rest or afraid of the memories and what they signify.

She must have been inside Apex's head, but how? She hasn't even had a conversation with the guy. Puter has been the only contact between the two of them until now.

Why was an Underling device being held at ExplorerTech Industries? What does this mean? Is he still alive? How is *she* still alive? What the hell is this device, really?

No. No. I don't care. I don't care. I just want to go. After several minutes, she wipes her face with her forearm and addresses the device. *I have to get out of here!* "If we leave now and drive off to the next area…how long could I survive?"

APPROXIMATELY 3 DAYS

Sia takes a few deep breaths before she grips her knees. "I do. I need your help."

S.I.D 2.0 ACCESSING ADMINISTRATIVE ACCESS OF SUBJECT 001

CONTACTING ORIGIN…

ANALYZING ENERGY LEVELS

18%

HYDRONE BOOST AVAILABLE
RECYCLING HYDRONE
ANALYZING ENERGY LEVELS

100%

Sia's body leans forward and grasps the crowbar before setting it down on the passenger seat and returning to the entrance gate.

ENHANCING UPPER EXTREMITIES BY 40% FOR 8 SECONDS

It grabs the metal frame and pulls it out of the way. Afterward, it returns to the semi-submerged van and clears snow off the windshield. As it swipes at slush and compact pieces of snow, it monitors the sounds and sulphur levels of the surrounding area. When it finally has the front of the vehicle freed from the frosty prison, it gets back inside the vehicle and drives into the shipping container port.

Navigating toward the containers that contain rice is simple. With a few turns, it identifies the numbers for the shipment and Sia's body opens the driver door with the crowbar in its right hand. It sniffs a few times as it walks to the front of the vehicle. It hops onto the hood and walks up to the top of the van before leaping up to the storage container.

With a twirl of the crowbar, it grips the top of the storage container and uses Sia's left hand to open one side of the doors. The panel swings open and the device blinks a few times to adjust Sia's eyes to the darkness inside the container.

No expression of triumph is produced on Sia's face. It calmly grabs a few of the oxygen-sealed pails and drops them to the roof of the car. After tossing down a few more, it leaps down to the roof and opens the side of the van to move the rice inside.

She's standing in the small space between a metal container and the van's open side. When a pitter-pat of feet is heard. Sia's view is blocked by the van, but the device can hear and smell the incoming animal.

MUSTELA ERMINEA DETECTED
JUMPER PROTOCOL RUNNING
J44S2v1V4l.Stay ENABLED

BACKUP SERVICES DEACTIVATED
NANO INFIRMARY PROTOCOL NULLIFIED
ENHANCING LOWER EXTREMITIES BY 70% FOR
40 SECONDS

The ermine leaps over the van, plants all four paws on the storage container above, then dives for Sia's body. Sia's body vanishes and the ermine hits the ground head-on. It pushes off the ground and squeezes itself through the tight space between the van and the storage container to chase the small human.

The van rocks as the ermine thrusts off the front of the vehicle and accelerates its speed.

Sia's body runs for the open transportation area near the guard's tower. The ermine follows. The device stops her body in its tracks and turns while swinging the crowbar. The ermine flips over it, out of reach and pushes off the metal stairs to rush its prey from behind.

JUMPER PROTOCOL
FLICKER MODE ACTIVATED

Sia's form disappears from where it's standing for a full four seconds. The ermine snarls as it phases through its prey. It passes by the empty spot and Sia's body reappears. The ermine swipes its tail at the materialized form. The black tipped tail connects with the left side of Sia's face.

Her body doesn't flinch at the impact. It drives forward and shoves the crowbar into the ermines open trilling mouth. The ermine's claws come up as it's skewered. Its arms swing at Sia's head, but only graze her. Before the animal can close its jaws, the crowbar rams deep into its mouth and through the back of its skull. The device maneuvers the body into a backward flip to dodge the rest of the violent death shudders wracking the large mammal's body.

38
39
40
POWER UP NEGATED
ORIGIN CONTACTED
COMMUNICATION CHANNEL OPENING

S.I.D to APEX

Sid…how is Sia doing? Did she escape those men? Dernel has been anxious to uncover what happened to Sia, but regaining his strength means suffering through the artificial healing comas. The Synthetic Intelligence Developer can repair more damage with an unconscious vessel.

AFFIRMATIVE

**SUBJECT 001 CONTINUED TO THE LOCATION
CHOSEN BY APEX**

Is she okay?

**THE VESSEL HAS SUSTAINED MULTIPLE
INJURIES FROM CLOSE COMBAT**

**THE RIGHT PINNA OF THE EAR HAS BEEN
REMOVED ALONG WITH SEVERE DAMAGE TO
THE OCULUS SINISTER BUT IT IS STILL VIABLE**

Are her energy levels high enough to heal those injuries?

WITH TIME

**OTHER OBJECTIVES MUST BE FULFILLED
BEFORE FURTHER ACTION IS TAKEN**

*What do you mean? Are there more dangers around her? Leave the
area before contacting me!*

NEGATIVE

…

THE VESSEL IS VIABLE

**APEX CAN OVERRIDE SUBJECT 001'S
CONSCIOUSNESS**

ENERGY LEVELS ARE STABLE

**COGNIZANT AUTHORIZATION REQUIRED
BEFORE TRANSFER**

CONFIRM REQUEST

*I already told you. It would not be right. You have viewed her
memories. She is not a part of this.*

SUBJECT 001 IS NEW CINALIAN

SUBJECT 001 IS IRRELEVANT

**IT IS IMPERATIVE THAT APEX IS RELEASED
FROM THE CURRENT CONFINES AND
COMPLETES THE VOYAGE HOME**

By damning everyone else I come across?

UNKNOWN CIVILIANS ARE NOT PRIORITY

**PRIORITY #1: SURVIVAL OF THE
ADMINISTRATOR**

**PRIORITY #2: COLLATERAL DAMAGE MUST BE
PROPORTIONATE TO THE SITUATION AT HAND
PRIORIT—**

*I made those rules, why are you repeating them to me? She is all we
have. Do you understand? Do you understand that we have been alone for
far too long? I need her to sustain my mental health. With her in
Stasis.Mode, how will we be able to communicate with the outside world?*

**SUBJECT 001'S CONSCIOUSNESS IS NOT
REQUIRED TO CONTACT THE OUTSIDE WORLD**

*She is human. How could I navigate this place without her? She
understands more than you give her credit for.*

**WITHOUT SYNTHETIC INTELLIGENCE
DEVELOPER 2.0 SUBJECT 001 WOULD HAVE
PERISHED LONG AGO**

**HUMAN INTERACTIONS ARE SECONDARY
THE NAVIGATION SYSTEM IS SUFFICIENT
SUBJECT 001'S PRESENCE IS INSIGNIFICANT**

*I could not do that to a conscious being. Everything they have done to
me is reversible. You could damage her mind with further containment.*

**PILOTING SUBJECT 001 WILL IMPROVE APEX'S
HEALTH SIGNIFICANTLY**

**CONTINUED IMPRISONMENT DECREASES THE
EFFECTIVENESS OF STASIS.MODE**

**PROLONGED SOLITUDE INFLICTS
PSYCHOLOGICAL AND PHYSICAL DAMAGE**

**ABNORMALITIES THAT DEVELOP MAY BE
IRREVERSIBLE**

**APEX WILL NEVER BE THE SAME
ENERGY LEVELS ARE STABLE
NO OTHER VIABLE HOST CAN BE ACQUIRED**

APEX CONFIRM REQUEST

...

He mulls over what the machine has said. All his life he has been connected to his pod. His brother and sister were either right beside him or reachable along their mind links. It has always been the three of them. The only family he has left. Ever since he has awoken, he hasn't been able to contact them. He fears that the torture he experienced damaged their links. Or worse.

His mind feels like an empty void. Where once there was chatter, it's silent. Contact with S.I.D is all that has kept him sane. Especially after waking up from his prolonged stasis. If his mind is damaged, would he be welcomed back? What have they told everyone about his disappearance? Could he plead his case with mental scarring? Could he risk it…for one human? *How far are we from the labs?*

WITH THE DATA ACQUIRED FROM SUBJECT 001'S TRAVEL TO COLDSTONE IT WOULD TAKE US APPROXIMATELY 7 DAYS TO ARRIVE IN WASHINGTON CITY

ENACTING A SUCCESSFUL ESCAPE PLAN WOULD NOT TAKE AN EXTENSIVE AMOUNT OF TIME
A week? That is not very long.
AFFIRMATIVE
STASIS.MODE COULD BE SUSTAINED FOR 7 DAYS WITHOUT MUCH DRAIN ON ENERGY RESERVES ESPECIALLY WITH THE RESOURCES PRESENT AT THIS SHIPPING CONTAINER TERMINAL
Dernel contemplates what S.I.D has said. *And Sia?*
SUBJECT 001 WOULD NOT SUFFER FROM ANY LONG LASTING PSYCHOLOGICAL OR PHYSICAL DAMAGES IF CONTAINED FOR 7 DAYS
It will not be forever. Just a short while. Forgive me, Sia. Dernel thought to himself before replying to S.I.D. *Request agreed upon.* He finally accedes.
REQUEST CONFIRMED
TRANSFER COMMENCING

After his consciousness is swapped with Sia's he notices several things at once. Half of her usual field of vision is gone. He touches a hand to her left eye and cringes at the feel of swollen flesh. The wandering hands press on her right ear and its missing outer lobe. "What is the meaning of this? Why is this unhealed?"

NANO INFIRMARY PROTOCOL CANNOT BE ENACTED UNTIL COMPLETE COOLDOWN AND DEACTIVATION OF JUMPER PROTOCOL

STRESS ON THE VESSEL FROM PROCESSING HYDRONE BOOST PUSHES BACK ALL NEW SERVICE ACTIVITY BY 24 HOURS

"And you thought it was worth it?"

AFFIRMATIVE

"Upload the last couple of hours of recordings."

AFFIRMATIVE

Dernel absorbs their new surroundings. Images flash behind his retina for a moment before he is caught up on everything Sia went through. The ermine corpse remains still. There are no signs of a mate or offspring. Surely, such a mammal would burrow away from the open area. Dernel can't be sure. "Let's get out of here as soon as possible. Where is the vehicle?"

S.I.D feeds Dernel instructions and they pack the van with numerous items: rice, bouillon cubes, and honey. The other containers suffered weather damage after being left open. After Dernel shuts each container, he uses the crowbar to etch three letters onto the metal, before moving to the next one. Before leaving the port, he decides to explore the guard tower as the sun sinks toward the horizon.

The stairs leading to the guard compartment loudly complain as Dernel steps further up. Each creak is a false warning that the steps will give out. Dernel fears it. Not that falling from this height would kill him. But all new injuries would have to be suffered until the next day, and he's so tired of pain.

When he reaches the guard quarters, the door is stiff and breaks off its hinges with a slight push. Dernel grabs hold of the door before it can collapse and sets it to the side. The room is dark, but light streams in from a broken pane and the entrance. An overturned chair and a control panel are illuminated. Dernel watches his step as he moves toward the control panel. From beside the chair, he can see that someone has indeed been here before them.

A corpse rests beside the overturned chair, leaning on the small storage cabinet, facing the door. The corpse is frozen solid down to its bone marrow. Large chunks of flesh are missing from their neck and torso. One leg has been entirely torn off.

The person is wearing worn clothing. They have on an empty holster under their left arm. Their limbs are settled down beside them, and one hand is clutching a dusty walkie-talkie. Dernel crouches and grabs the walkie-talkie by the antenna before slipping it out of the corpse's grasp. He wipes the residue off the walkie-talkie before pressing the push-to-talk button and releasing it.

A noise erupts from the device followed by static. It was on standby mode. The battery is half full. Dernel adjusts the sound and puts the radio into his pocket. "May peace find you in your final rest." He gently settles the body against an empty wall and bows his head a bit before hastening back over to the cabinet. He's searching for something specific. A sheet of radio codes and incoming ships that would have been serviced at this port.

Sia's broadcasts had not been a total failure. They had reached someone. If Dernel could find the secret codes used by the company to communicate with their ships, maybe someone would come this way to investigate? This depot port may have been international. Even with it missing, several others of its kind exist in other countries. It was a long shot, but any alarm that could be sent would be in their favor.

But alas…No codes, no special colored slips of paper. Nothing. "Where would you hide a secret code ledger, S.I.D?"

Before S.I.D can answer, the walkie-talkie Dernel had taken from the corpse comes to life.

"Hey, Winston! When did you say we were getting picked up?" a male voice erupts from the device. Dernel recognizes it, he's the mercenary that tracked Sia down, Kelly.

THERE ARE SEVERAL—

"Sssssssh. Wait, do not talk." Dernel pulls the transceiver from his pocket and listens closely.

"Hold your balls. ETA 40 minutes," an unfamiliar voice replies.

"If we even have any left by the time you get here," Kelly retorts.

"I'm surprised y'all made it through the night…Casey swore we'd die with our truck in that mess, and you three did it on foot?"

"Charity from our latest nuisance," Uzu declares.

"The thing that got Davis's men?"

"No! A sick bitch!" Manu adds.

"I thought it was a quick snatch-and-grab. Was she a Savage?"

"What? No. We'll go over it with you when you get here," Kelly replies.

"If you ever get here—" Uzu mutters.

"I'm freezing my ba—" Manu's last words are cut off.

Dernel recalls what Sia has done for those men.

APEX

THE SUN IS APPROACHING ITS LOWEST POINT

Dernel peeks out the shattered glass pane. With a sigh, he retreats to the van. They don't exit the port. Sia's memories revealed that traveling at night is avoided by most natives.

Dernel backs the van into an empty shipping container and pulls back the doors as far as possible. The metal doors clang against the locking joints on the outside of the container. He sits at the steering wheel and ponders his actions for the next day. But Sia's actions distract him from his plans. "She didn't know those men. Humans don't share connections with extended kin, so why did she leave those bags?"

DATA NEEDED TO COMPLETELY ASSESS THE SITUATION IS NOT YET AVAILABLE

"She would make a great Underling. I wonder what my pod would think of her? She seems very humorous." He leans against the steering wheel and focuses on the tiny crack of light that slips by the overlapped metal doors.

...

KEEPING WATCH IS UNNECESSARY

"Wake me if anything alarms you." Dernel relaxes back against his seat.

AFFIRMATIVE

Dernel's dreams don't provide him with rest. Memories play under his eyelids.

Dernel's arms were fastened to his sides by a metallic fabric. His legs were wrapped in the same material. The collar around his neck is fixed to the ceiling and keeps him balanced on the balls of his feet. Underling do not break under physical duress. Their pod, each and every family member, shares all pains with each other. The more powerful the pod, the less of a chance the victim would experience any pain.

His eyes are crusted with dried blood after he attempted to shut them and escape the torture happening before him. His captors noticed his efforts for peace and stripped him of his outer eyelids. As his lids gradually returned, he tried in vain to meditate the sights out of his memory.

Deep Society agents understood the methods needed to damage an Underling. Why torture his body when they could take his mind? Longevity in mind and body are two of many blessings. He would never forget.

The stain would exist along with all his hopes and dreams. Poisoning them. Strangling...Dernel shook his head and hissed at the rub of the collar on his abused neck. His feet are stiff and aching.

"All your strength means nothing when it takes just a touch—" a woman hissed. She raised a heated metal rod with a gloved hand and laid it on the spine of the human below her.

"Aaaaaaaaaah!" The human male screamed and struggled against his bindings.

"—to cripple you," the woman finished.

The human was bound tightly with rope. A black cloth had been pulled over their head. The cloth was damp from blood, sweat, and tears. It clung to their face in several places.

"That is what you all lack. The blessing of Understanding," the Deep Society agent continued.

The end of her antenna is lit and dangles between her crimson eyes. Its green light illuminated the chilling smile on her face. "A gift that keeps on giving. It shares all and any pain. It clears us of selfishness and the drive to harm others. For what creature feels pain and does not learn from it?" She circled the human, repeating words that Dernel remembers hearing in a lecture long ago.

Laughter filled the room. She crouched and laid a clawed finger on the human's covered head. The sharp tip cuts through the fabric and deep into the flesh of their forehead.

"Mmmmm, please…mmmmmm," the man pleaded.

"Only one! Humans!" Her partner stepped forward. She retracted her claw and stroked the human's head. Her partner came forward with his own heated rod and jabbed it into the human's thigh.

"Aaaaaaah!"

"Ssssssh," the Deep Society agent hushed the broken man. She turned to their Underling prisoner. "You want to save them? Look at the agony they're in. This is constant, even without our help. Why not let them kill themselves off? Interfering will spoil this planet even more than it already is." She rose up and approached Dernel's naked form. "Give us your research, and we shall release you."

Silence.

Dernel focused on the human behind her. He paid her no attention.

"Deny us, and you and yours will feel pain unlike anything an Underling has felt in millennia."

The human was still alive and fighting. He strained against the bindings tied around his hands and feet. His writhing form was large. His thin garments did not hide the muscles beneath them. *Strong enough to get free, but could he fight these creatures? No.*

"Does your pod mean so little to you? Imagine the derision they will feel for you while phantom pains make their skin crawl?" The agent whispered at Dernel's neck.

He shivered as her warm breath crept up his neck but remained focused on the man below. The human lay still. A Deep Society agent walked up and kicked them in the abdomen, but he remained unmoving on the stone floor.

"Me, I'll never know how you self-righteous ones make it this far in life." She slid a claw down his scaled chest and laid her head on his bound shoulder. "You devote all this energy to your goal and throw it all away in the end. All for nothing. All that work just to walk right into our arms and——"

"***Krrk!***" She imitated the sound of cracking while curling a hand around his neck.

The human curled into a ball after being kicked a few times. The back of his shirt rose. A tattoo decorated the lower area of his spine. Dernel commits that to memory. Someone out there might be looking for him. The least he could do is give word of who had taken him and what was done in his presence. That is all he could do in his current position. *Forgive me, forgive me.*

Her partner cackled before he climbed over the human and began strangling them. It blocked the human from view. Dernel grimaced at the fin on the agents back. It glowed in the dimly lit cavern.

"Fineeeeee. I'll let you end your legacy." She wiggled her finger in the air like it was riding on a wave. Sailing on nothing.

A gesture known to Underling to mean "a solo journey" or "a trivial pursuit". For no Underling with worth would journey alone. Collaboration was celebrated. Solitude is exile. Exile is

dishonor, and dishonor, a fate worse than death. Dernel clenched his jaw.

"Your demise is a thrill to them. They won't waste any time acquiring all sorts of data from you. Living or dead, it's all science to them." She motioned to an agent that was watching the torture. With a shove, she straightened up and Dernel choked while trying to steady his body. "Tell them it's a holiday prezzie for their work so far," she told the minion. Dernel choked as the minion approached him.

Dernel awoke and rose out of the driver's seat to escape his assailant. His head bumps into the ceiling. He catches his breath and looks around. "Has the sun risen?"

AFFIRMATIVE

They exit the port. When they get a few miles away, Dernel decides to inform S.I.D of his new choice. "You do not understand! I need her…We need her."

NEGATIVE
SUBJECT 001 IS IRRELEVANT
CITIZENS OF CINALIA ARE FUGITIVES UNDER
UNDERLING LAW

"A journey alone is exile."

…

"Do you remember that?" He recalls the frozen harbor. The half-submerged ships full of cargo and men, a cemetery for the poor souls lost as collateral damage to pay for sins amassed by men and women that never took a moment to ask if their victories were worth it. Was it worth it? All those crushed souls. "Alienating her will not help us. If our energy depletes, who will come for us?"

REGENERATING ENERGY THROUGH
STASIS.MODE—

"Has failed a countless amount of times…Do you really want to go back to that slow struggle while I waste away in that chair? When we could have an ally, working just as hard to accomplish both our goals." He steers around a dip in the earth and speeds up.

"She is the only one that knows we still exist. That we are alive. If we torment her for control of her body, she will buckle under the pressure and be lost to us. And then what? We need help. She can get us help. Support us. Then we can return home." He squeezes the steering wheel and meets his own eyes in the rearview mirror. "This is not a discussion. I don't want your opinion. I'm not on some crusade against them. Our objective is meaningless if we resort to their tactics to survive. I want to return home, but it was never going to be the same. Not with how long it's been, the things that have been done" He shakes his head and huffs at the itch of her human hair. Her bangs tickle the forehead each time he tilts the head. "We will escape them, and not with their taint corrupting our souls."

...

He drives outside of the danger zone until the van runs out of gas. A forest is to their left, and to their right, he sees the beginnings of decaying grass and cracked earth. The Wastelands. He has been enjoying time without pain, without the void of silence he will return to.

He sits on the hood of the car. To the left, he senses a signal from the labs, but to the right, Sia will be safe from their reach. "She can decide. Creator, steer our steps to the path. Forgive me for being tempted. Forgive me, so I may forgive myself."

The sun reaches its zenith. He lays back against the windshield and reaches a hand out toward the sky. Tears well up in his eyes as he looks at Sia's brown hand with the sun's rays warming the palm. Her hands are so unlike his own. So fragile, like an infant.

"Give it back." *Give her back control.*
AFFIRMATIVE
TRANSFER COMMENCING...

40%

2034

Northwestern edge of the Wastelands, New Cinalia

Sia wakes up sitting on the hood of the van in the middle of nowhere. *This is odd.* She slides off the hood, but stumbles and falls against the side of the van grasping the top of a grimy tire. She has to turn her head to get a good look around. She puts a hand up on the left side of her face and cringes at the texture of swollen flesh.

"Why isn't…Where?" Opening her mouth makes pain surge up her left cheek. She presses a hand to the side of her mouth and reaches for the side mirror.

She gasps. Her face is dirty with blood and soil. Her left eye is bruised, beneath it is swollen and deformed. When she turns her head, to check for a head injury, she spots her torn earlobe. She leans on the driver side door as her stomach surges. She pushes the mirror away and breathes through her revulsion.

The ermine did this?
AFFIRMATIVE
She sighs. *Did we cross over the frozen lake?*
NEGATIVE
APEX TRAVELED NORTHEAST BY LAND

"Apex!" Another jolt of pain travels up her face. "I didn't ask…" *I asked for your help! Not Apex.*

AFFIRMATIVE

APEX EXTENDED HELP TO SUBJECT 001 AS WELL

"That's not…I…" she sputters. Her heart clenches at the continued betrayal. *Puter…you don't understand. I…know you mean well, but you aren't mine and I would feel better if…*

AFFIRMATIVE

S.I.D 2.0 WAS NOT MADE FOR SUBJECT 001'S BENEFIT

Sia straightens at the brisk reply. She can hear that accusation in those cold words. *I want to be notified if Apex wants control. I told you this. Don't you remember?*

SUBJECT 001'S COMMANDS ARE SECONDARY DIRECTIVES

Sia's stomach sinks at those words. *So, my orders don't matter anymore?*

NEGATIVE

S.I.D 2.0 HAS—

S.I.D 2.0? Did you get an upgrade?

SYNTHETIC INTELLIGENCE DEVELOPER 2.0 HAS BEEN AMALGAMATED INTO THE SUPERIOR OPERATING SYSTEM IT WAS PRODUCED FROM

What are you talking about?

SYNTHETIC INTELLIGENCE DEVELOPER 2.0 WAS AN INFERIOR OPERATING SYSTEM

IT HAS BEEN MERGED INTO THE SUPERIOR MODEL TO PRODUCE MORE EFFICIENT RESULTS

So, Puter is gone?

AFFIRMATIVE

PRIMARY SYSTEMS HAVE OVERWRITTEN ALL REDUNDANT PROGRAMS AND SERVICES

Sia collapses on the ground. She bumps her elbow on the way down and tucks it into her stomach. She tucks her chin into her chest as her lips tremble. Apex has taken all she had left. Her confidante is gone. Deleted.

Now she's truly alone. How will she escape this place with an enemy within her and all those waiting on the outside? She sniffles and wipes her nose on her sleeve. She looks at her shadow and cocks her head up against the van. It shifts and appears to be shaped like a boulder. A boulder. *Or a mountain.* She accidentally projects to the device.

INSUFFICIENT DATA
WHAT IS SUBJECT 001 REFERRING TO

She unwraps her arms from around herself and stands. After opening the car door, she crawls in and grabs her backpack from the passenger seat. She props it on the door to check if her items are all still inside. Everything is accounted for. She snatches up her crowbar from between the two front seats and slams the door. *I already have to worry about people taking advantage of me. I don't need to worry about an invader inside of me, too.*

She walks away from the van and its supplies. Whatever is within it…she can't accept it. Accepting it would make everything alright. Would mean she consents to their plans. She isn't their slave.

YOU WILL PERISH

*Don't contact me. I don't want to speak with you any longer! If I die, I die. It's **my** choice.* She smiles bitterly at her surroundings before marching forward. Into the wastelands, she goes, and never looks back.

Monitor her. It is all we can do now. For our sake, let us hope she does not die to spite us, Dernel orders S.I.D.

THE REQUEST WAS BENEFICIAL FOR THE—

You drove her to this. Have the patience to wait and fix your error. All we have is time.

"Free will must be such an inconvenience for you two. Who needs free will when we can brainwash you," Sia grumbles as she stomps across the empty woods. "Maybe the whole world should be brain-dead followers that only do what the mighty computer commands."

Trees begin to dwindle all around her until all she can see is sand, rock, and the sun. Sia is blindly moving forward. The shift in scenery means nothing to her. "This is why people don't trust Underling…Self-righteous, smart but dumb…trust them to make technology that works too well. Maybe that was the plan all along. Make a device that can control humans and fix the cycle…no more war, no more famine…just fish and robots." she vents and ignores the pain in her face. "I won't help you! I'm going to find the first person to take this out of my head and sell it! I'll pay a ship captain and **sail home** if I have to!" She kicks up some dust, coughs, then stumbles over a rock and veers to the right to stable herself. Her balance is off with only one eye. She keeps looking far to the left to compensate, but the ache in her face gets worse.

She sees a hill and starts for it. She has to use her hands to climb to the top of it. When she gets to the other side, she's faced with more desert and a dirt trail that looks recently driven on. The trail leads into a canyon area. High mountainous walls of stone rise on either side of the trail and it's impossible to know where it leads from her position. She doesn't think about it; she follows.

One misstep, and she's sliding down the hill. Her back is scratched by rock and her foot uproots dried roots and loose twigs. Blindly, she puts out a hand to steady herself and the skin on her palm is rubbed raw. She shifts her footing as she stumbles down the last of the hill. Her dirty boot catches on a small boulder, stopping her descent, and she tumbles forward onto her knees.

The dirt path is before her. She coughs up dirt, spits on the ground, then picks herself up. She limps toward the canyon area. After a few moments of silence, she pauses to root through her backpack.

She sees a dusty radio she doesn't remember having before and the radio from Coldstone. She pulls out her radio from the labs and turns it on. It doesn't pick up anything, but the static

is a welcome distraction from the sound of her stumbling steps.

41%

2034
Northwestern edge of the Wastelands, New Cinalia

A large beetle creeps toward the edge of the cliff and peers into the canyon below. Its clawed feet make large stones appear to be pebbles compared to its monstrous size. As it walks forward, it shoves several stones down into the arid valley below. The sides of the canyon walls are steep and ripple up toward the sky unevenly.

Sia stays close to the walls. She takes advantage of the shade and is blocked from sight from any flying predators. Or at least that's what she hopes.

Rocks cascade from overhead and a loud sound erupts from somewhere nearby. It's like a high-powered fan was turned on. As if someone recorded the sound of a large fly buzzing in their ear and amplified it twenty times over.

Sia feels faint. She crouches low against the wall, her eyes wildly searching the sky. She wants to get as small as she can, but still be able to run if she has to. Her position is wide open. *Where is that sound coming from?!*

Sweat gathers on her forehead and slides down her temples. She wipes at it and turns her head to get a better view of the area. She frantically searches for a better hiding spot. In the distance, she sees a blue-green mass coming from the same direction she had been walking. She doesn't know how long it has been behind her, but it's humongous. It's quietly wriggling in her direction. It doesn't alter its course at all.

Sia crawls over rigid rocks that dig into her knees and shin. She winces as her scratched palms make contact with the ground, but she doesn't want to be overtaken by either creature. *It's probably hunting that thing…not me. I'm barely a snack for whatever this is…I just need to get away and stay out of its business.*

The noisy industrial fan gets louder, and Sia can't control herself any longer. She jumps up and bolts. It feels like it's coming right for her! She huffs and moves her head from side to side trying to find a space in the rock that might give her shelter.

Hissing begins. A chill runs up Sia's spine and she spares a glance over her shoulder. The blue-green mass is long and chunky. It has a pale-yellow line running along the middle of its body, and there are green spots on either side of its head. *Is that a caterpillar?* She gasps as she sees the caterpillar rapidly move.

The winged beetle bites at the caterpillar. The caterpillar won't allow it without a fight. It's little "legs" grip down on the ground and then it springs its lower body up and flings the beetle off its back. The beetle goes back for more.

It bites at it again, but this time the caterpillar moves faster and catches the beetle in its mandibles. It clutches the beetle for only a moment before throwing it into position and swinging its body around to smash the beetle into the ground. It slams down like a hammer. The beetle recovers and surges up again. It's a battle of wills.

Sia stops fleeing and backs into a wall as she watches the battle with awe. The beetle tires first. It flees to acquire weaker prey. Victory is a silent affair for the caterpillar. It uncurls and continues waddling along the canyon as before. Sia's mouth gapes as she goes over the fight in her head. An idea comes to mind.

She decides to use the caterpillar as a shield between her and the unknown threats around them. When she sees a large dark opening in the canyon walls, she retreats until the caterpillar is in front of her. After it survives passing by the area, she scurries back around the perimeter of the creature to get a look at where they're headed. She doesn't want to spook the thing, so she doesn't approach it. One hit from it would probably split her skull open.

Immersive Mode

THE MANDUCA SEXTA IS VICTORIOUS
I did not expect that. That creature is very fierce. I wonder, do they eat flesh? Dernel watches Sia's actions through the device's triangular prism screen within immersive mode.
NEGATIVE
MANDUCA SEXTA CONSUME PLANTS AND LEAVES
Great. Continue monitoring her. She will need your help eventually. Be ready to step in. We will not get a second chance with this.

The sun beats down on Sia as she watches her guardian. Something is wrong. It kept a steady pace for several hours and then suddenly stopped moving. She was tempted to call out to it and ask what was going on, but…she doesn't have a death wish. They left the canyon an hour ago, and Sia continued following because every other space large enough to hide her was also large enough to fit a large insect.

Traps all around me. Where is my salvation? She crouches and glances over at her savior. *Maybe it's hungry? There isn't anything to eat out here. Isn't that what caterpillars do? Eat till they drop?* She looks over at her silent guardian. It doesn't appear to be breathing. *Wait! Maybe it's going to turn into a butterfly or moth?! But there's no cocoon…No, that can't be it.*

She grabs a rock the size of her hand and tests the weight. The caterpillar's color doesn't camouflage it from sight. It's the only colorful spot in the entire desert. It's incredibly vulnerable just lying there in the open. She moves herself far away from the caterpillar, almost double the space needed to be out of striking distance. She gathers three stones.

Immersive Mode

Do not overdo it or she will be suspicious.
PINPOINTING TARGET
CALCULATING TRAJECTORY

The first stone hits the ground right in front of the caterpillar. At least one or almost two meters from the target. She bites her lower lip and focuses on the caterpillar. She alters her stance for the second throw. It hits closer this time.

"Okay…here we go. Wake up!" She throws the last stone. This one hits the caterpillar on target with a light thud. It bounces off the rubbery skin. No reaction.

Sia's mood sinks. The sun is slowly progressing toward the horizon. She needs to find shelter…now. "Okay…okay…okay…" she mutters. She turns in a circle to see what's closest. There's a huge hill to her left and endless flat desert to her right. The hill is more sand than rock, so she doesn't fear falling. She jogs over to it.

It takes some time for her to struggle uphill, but when she gets to the top she sees: plant life, destroyed buildings, and…large dark structures that rise up into the air. They're towering over the surrounding buildings. Several of the rippling structures connect buildings together with weird tunnels made from an odd substance. The nearest one is dark brown, but others look charred and black.

She feels tempted to ask the device if aliens have landed and developed structures in the Wastelands, but the device would be as clueless as she is. All the documents they ***need*** were labeled classified the last time she had urged it to check for information.

Useless machine. Sia pauses at that thought. *It could have been lying all along. It probably knows exactly why all of this has happened. Exactly why everything went so wrong.* She frowns at that. *What was the truth and what were lies made to get me to follow their narrative?* She shakes those thoughts from her mind and focuses on the matter at hand.

Those buildings down there are the only viable shelters nearby. But the odd structures around them don't look inviting. Some of the structures resemble mounds of dirt, but others are something entirely different. Sia grits her teeth and climbs down the hill.

It's a bit steep, but Sia makes it to the bottom without any more injuries. She limps toward the closest building.

The door is ripped off the hinges and laying on the floor of the entrance. The building is weirdly altered. The stairs look like something took several large bites out of them. Sia walks over to where the stairs should all be and checks the second floor…where the second floor should be.

Sia sighs and exits the partially demolished building. *On to the next one.* This one is still intact. It's an apartment building. She goes through the lobby and steps over old fallen light fixtures and overturned furniture to find the stairwell. Sia frowns. *The last time I was walking around in darkness I had help from Puter…*

She stops to retrieve the lighter from her backpack. It's not much, but it's all she has. When she opens the door, she sees that the roof over the staircase is gone. *Well, that's less of a bummer.*

She puts the lighter in her pocket and tries the stairs. In case she needs a quick escape, she only goes to the second floor. The second-floor stairwell door opens easily, and she slides inside the dim hallway. Most of the hallway is dark, but one apartment door is open and sheds some light into the hall. She enters the well-lit apartment. The floor has collapsed in what she presumes was the living room area. The kitchen remains, as does a dark hallway into the rest of the small flat. She walks over to the high cabinets and opens them.

Nothing.

Sia cringes at the awful smell that erupts from the refrigerator. She holds her mouth to her inner elbow and quickly skims the contents. The fridge has several items left inside from who knows when the last occupants of the apartment had been there. An old milk jug lay on its side with a dark substance trapped within it. A hairy, dark mold climbs the lids of several old Tupperware containers and the side of the refrigerator. Many condiment bottles fill the side door compartment. Nothing. There's nothing she could use.

She bends to open a lower cabinet. A thick plastic bucket is revealed under the pipes of the sink. She retrieves the bucket and searches the counters. Broken glass and wood chips are scattered on the countertops, along with dirty oven mitts and dish rags. All piled next to the sink.

With a moment's thought, she turns and pulls off her backpack. She rifles through it for a few seconds before taking out her rubber gloves. After putting on the gloves, she turns to a low, wooden cabinet, holds the corner tightly in her gloved hand, and she kicks at it. The cabinet cracks with one kick but it slips out of her grip when she tries to kick it a second time.

She lets go of it and then goes to town. She kicks and stomps the cabinet until she can pull pieces of wood off and drop them into the bucket. Afterward, she grabs the dirty rags and puts them in as well. She takes one rubber glove off, puts it in her pocket, and uses her free hand to light the dirty rags on fire. When they light, she shakes the bucket a bit and waits for the rest of the stuff inside to begin burning.

She slips her rubber glove back on and holds onto the rim on each side before exiting the apartment. The bucket of fire keeps her way lit, so she isn't traveling in complete darkness, but already she can smell the melting plastic. She needs to find a hiding spot before she has to toss the entire thing aside. When she gets to a turn, she notices something weird about the walls. Material similar to the charred black cocoon structures are lining them.

Not going down that hallway. She doubles back and tests the doorknobs. *Why wasn't I doing that in the first place? Stupid. Dumb. Dumb. Dumb.*

She jiggles the handles until she finds an unlocked apartment. She slips inside and locks the door. The entranceway is simple like the last apartment. There's a jacket and hat still on the coat hangers, but no shoes or other accessories left behind. There's a long sofa sitting across from a damaged plasma screen TV that is hanging sideways off its holder. Large glass screen doors open up to a balcony.

Not preferable, but… Sia puts down her blazing bucket and grabs any flammable material she sees to drop inside and keep the flame going. Then she picks up the bucket and goes looking for a nice closet to hide in.

The rest of the home is very minimal. The hallway has a bathroom and a closet, but the closet has a sliding shutter door. *Next.* The bedroom has a thick layer of dust resting over everything, but overall, it's neat.

There in the bedroom is a closet with a doorknob. Sia almost smiles, but she's so tired. She sets down her bucket with the door open and backtracks into the living room. She drags the couch into the hallway and turns it on its side to obstruct the way. When she returns to the bedroom, she closes the door and moves the dresser and bed to block it. If something breaks in, she'll notice right away. The bedroom has a bathroom with a window. That's her only escape, but it's better than nothing.

Finally, Sia snuffs out the flames in the bucket and pushes it inside the closet. She drops her backpack and crawls inside as well. It's a tight fit, but she feels safe with walls around her and a door. No matter how illusionary it is. She sets her hand on the doorknob and rests back against the wall.

Her mind is blank. She stares into the darkness. She can't even see her own hands. If things were like before, she would use this time before sundown to research things within

immersive mode. But it's not like before. Nothing, no one, is like before, especially her.

D.Rednal

42%

Immersive Mode

The white walls of immersive mode are almost blinding. Unlike Sia's, Dernel has combined all the rooms to occupy one space. He sits on a white platform in the middle of his large room. The walls come up and meet to form a dome. The ceiling is black and accented with small red and blue dots.

Behind the platform, a spout sticks out of the ground and constantly sprays water out into the room. The ground is wet with several inches of water. Dernel's legs hang off the side of the platform as it pools around his ankles. The lukewarm water calms his spirit.

The room resembles his old classroom setup. During his imprisonment, rooms like these were what kept him sane for so long. During times of great hardship, the device handpicked the most cherished of Dernel's memories to simulate.

Taste, touch, sight…all of these things are simulated here. Senses that were cut off by the ExplorerTech scientists quite some time ago. Now that his energy levels have recovered, S.I.D can remain online for longer periods of time within Dernel's mind, but their current standard of life can't be sustained forever.

Dernel is looking at a virtual screen. The top of the screen reads: Chen, Sia, and below that it reads: Age 6. He goes over Sia's memories. He watches her as a small child. He watches how she interacts with other humans and her family. How she acts when totally alone. She's a fairly innocent individual. *Why is this distance acceptable for her people? Their mental handicap must make alienating each other unavoidable.* "Apex to S.I.D."

S.I.D TO APEX

"I think I figured out a way to improve our relations." Dernel pauses the projection of memories at a scene in Sia's past where she experienced a betrayal. "This…" The screen shows a fifteen-year-old Sia crying in a bathroom, flushing jewelry down a toilet.

S.I.D IS UNAWARE OF THE SIGNIFICANCE OF SUBJECT 001'S MEMORIES

TO ASSESS THE RELEVANCE OF THE INFORMATION VIEWED FACTS THAT ARE—
"I'll explain."

…

"Her progenitors abandoned her for outsiders they were fond of. Such actions that would be viewed as dishonorable before the council." An image of Sia's home in Washington City is projected in the air in front of Dernel. "The betrayals continued…" The image of a middle-aged couple appears. A man of Chinese descent, with short black hair and almond shaped eyes, stood unsmiling next to a woman of European descent. She has long, curly auburn hair and a bright smile on her face. "Her male progenitor grew infatuated with a deceitful outsider who accused Sia of unscrupulous behavior. Stealing, malicious gossip, lying, and other unsavory things. All things that Sia herself was not partaking in, but her progenitor did not take her word for it. In the end, she allowed her emotions to rule her." The projector shifts to the memory of Sia as a fifteen-year-old. "She discarded items that the individual used to frame her as a criminal. It's off-putting how easily it all could have been solved with a pod's connection. He could have read into her mind and seen the truth of the matter. Our blessing puts aside many hardships." Dernel solemnly nods and waves a tentacle in a circular motion. The projections vanish. "She was attached to 'Puter' in much of the same way I am attached to you. Except I have always had my pod alongside me. That new connection quenched a need she has always had. Now she is abandoned and betrayed all over again. We have to make her see that we are all on the same side."

...

"I think our best plan is to meld with her. It is the only way for her to see why things became the way they are. Why she was put in this vulnerable position. If we do not take the chances we have now, she may seek to cut ties completely and run straight into our enemies' hands."

DEEP AND EXPLORERTECH PERSONNEL WOULD EXPEND NUMEROUS RESOURCES TO MONITOR THE POPULATION FOR ANY ANOMALOUS BEHAVIOR

"Exactly, and if she looks for a doctor to cut us out of her head, we will never get out of here."

AFFIRMATIVE

PREPARE FOR MELDING AT WHAT JUNCTURE

"Soon. While she is resting…then she can meditate on it while out of danger."

ASSEMBLING POTENTIAL MELDING SEQUENCES

"Let us go over what memory would be most efficient. I do not want to overwhelm her."

2017

Beneath the Sea

A brown megalodon streamed past a cargo ship and dipped back underwater. Its passenger held tightly to its dorsal fin. He noted the numbers on the side of the boat.

The megalodon dove deep into the ocean until it approached a green force field. The barrier encompassed a

large underwater civilization. Each building was carved into the rock, coral, or ground. None were alike any other, several facades were decorated with colorful organisms that made the structures their homes. Some of their tendrils swayed in the current while others curled up as traffic rushed by. Inhabitants swam or skittered across the ground, passing through seaweed and schools of fish.

Nature and technology coexisted there. As technology continuously increased, the council were kept busy evaluating what advanced their society and what disrupted it. Usually, the proposals brought forth were for the betterment or entertainment of their own people, but nothing that would be shared with the outside world.

The megalodon accelerated forward into the barrier and was welcomed easily into the Treading Port. Its rider released his grip on the megalodon and rubbed a hand underneath the creature's eyes and along its snout. It raised its head and opened its jaw in enjoyment. Its rider placed his head beside the creature's massive jaws and smiled while hugging as much of the brown spotted behemoth as he could reach.

"Essic, I will see you later. Go rest in the depot until I put out a ping," Dernel told his Escort.

The megalodon sent a series of images into Dernel's mind: the cargo ship, humans, and trash floating on the surface of ocean water.

"I will report the location of that cargo ship we saw as well. I know you worry about the taint. They would not dare drop waste in this region. Additionally, they saw you. I am sure they will know better than to break any maritime laws while monitored."

An image of an anchovy popped into Dernel's mind.

"Yeah, they might be dumb. I **will** report it. I will not forget."

The megalodon rumbled for a moment and pulled away to swim to the large cavern that leads to the Escort Depot. It has reserved space for large aquatic Escorts.

The Treading Port is a series of floating platforms over the city. The platforms were made from black volcanic stones. Only Escorts stopped in those areas to drop off their pod mates. There are several ways to exit the port platforms.

Many Underling have pectoral fins or propulsion abilities. Those with such talents usually only use Escorts for long distance travel and have no real need for the platforms. They could "fly" off to their destination from anywhere. Or, an Underling could drop off the corner of a platform that is positioned over a tube that would slide the occupant to their destination.

Lastly, an Underling could hop off and follow the long ribbons of braided kelp that were positioned near the platforms. The ribbons helped someone find their destination while walking along the sea floor. Not all Underling could swim, so these varied exits were appreciated by the 30% that were limited in their travel. Each kelp had a different color along their tops, middle, and base to aid an Underling in finding each sector.

Dernel untwined his dark arms to become separate appendages and dived off his platform. A flexible limb shot out and grasped an orange-tipped brown rope of kelp. All four of his tentacles rapidly worked together and lowered Dernel to the reef below. The coral poked at his scaled feet and signaled the end of the descent. Dernel then spun away from the rope of kelp and swam toward his destination. A cloud of bubbles was left behind after his speedy departure.

He passed by natural bridges and swam through rocky passages to reach a subterranean cavern used for social activities. Many others are scattered around it, but in order to be admitted into that particular cave, Dernel had to first pass through a thick halocline[2] and navigate to the correct passage without the help of his eyes.

---

[2] When seawater meets freshwater the difference in salinity forms an opaque zone where the less salty water remains above the heavier, saltier water. It can appear foggy until you reach the topside which is incredibly clear and high in oxygen.

The halocline was dyed orange to notify the citizen of the zone they were traveling in. The orange color denoted that this specific cave system had fresh water compartments. Some Underling had adverse reactions to such things. Dernel, his pod mates, and his friends did not have any issues with the change in salinity, thus the current meeting was booked for this area.

It was a joyous occasion. When Dernel broke free of the thick orange fog of the halocline, he could see several individuals waiting for him. The freshwater area was so clear it was as if they were sitting topside. His pod mates, his brother and sister, were chatting together beside two large stalactites protruding from the roof of the compartment. They leaned back against the rocky structures like vertical lawn chairs. Their limbs were comfortably tucked around themselves.

He was meeting with his friends as well. Five Underling he communicated with regularly and worked with in the research halls. There was one unfamiliar Underling—Carmel's pod mate—but they were invited to come along as well.

Carmel worked with Dernel in the research halls and had many white spines around his head and arms similar to a puffer fish. His pod mate, Tyre, had red spines that resembled a lionfish. Such similarities happened in a pod-family unit. Within Dernel's pod, his sister resembled him the most. She too had tentacles that could be compressed into two humanoid limbs, and her scales were a dark blue, almost black. Their brother had a transparent, iridescent baby blue fin on his head and attributes similar to a remora, such as the sucker-like organ along his back that allowed him to remain attached to Dernel's Escort for long periods of time. He was an oddity. The rest of the Underling were red and green with scaly appearances, excluding Dernel's old lab partner who clearly had blobfish qualities.

When everyone saw Dernel exit the orange fog, they gathered in the middle of the cavern to settle on the smoothest portions of the floor. Dernel swam over to them in excitement and gushed the details of his latest plans. "I am bringing a proposal to the council. It will be a complete change from the usual way things have been done. I have planned a system for all levels."

"All levels?" Carmel leaned an arm on a smooth shelf of rock. His thin, white mane of spines stood at attention even when he cocked his head to the side, puzzled by the announcement.

"Well, my first device is for mankind," Dernel revealed.

Surprise was etched on everyone's face.

"The council won't allow you to breach the confidentiality clause in our Neutrality contract," Waller commented.

"This could remove so many conflicts that we have had between our people and within their own societies. The device can temporarily attach to a subject during a tribunal and record memories straight from the subject's mind. It can read their physical signals and can ascertain mental health. It would be invaluable to mankind. With less time focused on their judicial strifes, imagine the breakthroughs they could help us engineer," Dernel argued.

"Ascertain mental health? We have connections for that, so it would definitely be of no help here," Tyre remarked. "Unless you think it could be of use for those Deep rejects." The bright red spines along his back wiggled and radiated amusement.

Waller laughed at that.

"Do you really think the council would reconvene with the United Human Initiative for that? How well has it performed in your sessions?" his sister, Lenn, questioned. She hovered closer to his side and settled down on her dark tentacles while she listened intently to his reply.

"It was the easiest part of my plan. It has passed all the checks without fail. Once I have a human subject to test it on I can recalibrate it to their specific biology. All the tests have been practiced on orphaned ones in the Health Sector who have no bonds. It imitates our natural telepathic conditioning. They responded wonderfully. This could help all removed ones with orphaned pod bonds from passing on. But…there is

more. I have a secret weapon…" Dernel said with a twinkle in his eyes.

His compassion for all forms of life had always made him tear up when thinking of the ways he planned to fix the world. No more helpless Underling. No more helpless humans. They shared the same planet, the different qualities of life shouldn't be so drastic.

Underling had a limited amount of hardships in their lives, mostly centered around the death or two that would occur in pods. A terrible occurrence that could even result in entire families withering away while mourning. The famine, pestilence, and torment that occur in human societies were unheard of in their world. He couldn't pull his mind from that as a child. Why do they allow that cycle to continue? Why doesn't anyone fix it? What purpose is their suffering fulfilling?

"Secret weapon?" his brother, Zara, muttered as he leaned against Lenn. His webbed hands clutched at her shoulder as he clung to a tentacle. He radiated excitement.

Jenga raised a green, webbed hand to gain attention. "What do you mean secret weapon? Are you making destructive materials? I thought you were focused on earthly peace?" she asked.

"Yes, it is a human term. I have an unknown project that will definitely pique the elders' interest and push forward talk to reconvene the UHI summits," Dernel said.

"So…what is it? Is it to be withheld from us as well?!" Stace asked. His long-scaled body joined the crowd of interested ones. They all huddled around Dernel's form.

"Yeah, this is…what is it?" Mackie asked as her round bulbous nose nudged at his head. She leaned on Dernel's arm and squeezed his shoulder. "Did you bring it along with you?"

Everyone pulled back a bit and examined Dernel's bare form. His lean, toned body was free of fabric that was prone to snag on coral and be torn. His dark tentacles floated around him while he idled. The pale underside of his tentacles could be seen, and nothing was held on his miniature suction cups. Zara swam around his brother and returned to Lenn's side with a shake of his head. Dernel didn't seem to have a new device with him. Dernel's thin lips pressed firmly together, suppressing a smile. After the significant pause, he finally announced his grand news. "I have made a successful time jumper."

"What?!" everyone shouted. His friends yelled question after question. He couldn't suppress his grin any longer and sharp teeth were revealed. His pod smiled right back at him.

Zara and Lenn eased back from the excited group and projected feelings of awe and joy. Zara grasped several of Lenn's tentacles in his hands. "What sort of time jumper? How far can you travel with it?" Zara asked while brimming with excitement. Lenn wrapped her other tentacles around her younger podmate and flashed Dernel a row of serrated teeth.

Dernel returned the smile as he continued. "It can go several weeks into the future or the past if enough hydrone is processed into the device," Dernel replied.

"Hydrone? Isn't that a volatile substance? Highly corrosive, and in some instances, it can poison the organism handling it," Mackie commented warily. She nudged at Dernel until he made eye contact with her.

"Yes, which is why I use it along with a dimensional space converter to utilize a subspace that the subject's physical and spiritual being inhabits while living on this plane," Dernel reassured her. "I nor the subject have any physical contact with it after activation."

"Is that a play off of Velia's subspace theory?" Jenga's scaly tail swished excitedly behind her.

Tyre huffed and a bundle of bubbles clouded his face. He swept them away with a webbed hand. "Didn't Cornel dispute that anything packed into subspace with a converter would be obsolete because the loss of consciousness would result in the loss of product?"

"Not the loss of consciousness, death you dweeb," Carmel corrected. Mackie and Dernel nodded.

"Actually, I have fixed that problem by including a system that funnels the energy directly into the individual and incorporated several failsafes into the design in order to keep consciousness present before and after the hydrone is processed. A synthetic mind meld is one such failsafe. Also—" Dernel explained the basic structure of his hydrone processor and its dimensional converter. After discussing the technical side of things, Dernel explained his interest with the land dwellers.

"Always, the amount of false convictions is blamed on the technology of the time, lack of resources, and urgings for the defendant to plead guilty on both sides. With my invention, their alibi could be shown before a judge or jury and verified. False witness statements can be thrown away. Of course, there might be some exceptions, but overall, I really think this could resolve a lot of cases and free up a lot of time in many of their civilizations," Dernel said in his lecturing voice. Mackie listened with her eyes closed. Her head leaned on Dernel's shoulder as she contemplated what he had said.

"Judge, defendants…witness statements…haha, you've really gone all out with researching their judicial system," Jenga said with a helpless look on her face.

"Well, if it helps, I did not know even a quarter of what I know now before I researched it," Dernel reassured the confused female.

"When did you find time to do both projects? 'Ling, a converter for hydrone processing takes intense engineering sessions, and the research for the rest of that." Carmel waved his pale arms around his head.

"When you're passionate about something, you find the time," Mackie muttered. Her head nuzzled the side of Dernel's neck.

"You're a husk." Carmel pointed at Dernel and rolled his eyes. Dernel laughed and shook his head. His chin nudged at Mackie's head and he raised a tentacle to rub at her soft, smooth skin.

The conversation shifted to everyone else's news and progress on their own endeavors until they were interrupted by a Depths Depot employee. "Thaya and Essic are quarreling again," a male Underling with two long black pectoral fins shouted into the compartment. The employee was wearing an orange ribbon around his neck, half submerged in the thick halocline. He circled within the orange haze, waiting for Dernel to follow him.

Dernel sighed. "Thaya should not even be allowed in there," Dernel grumbled and turned back to his companions. "I will let you all know the outcome of the meeting. The date should be announced soon." He rose from his seat on the rocky ground and prepared to dive and follow his guide.

"It'll be a breakthrough for Underling and Mankind! You'll be famous outside the tide, brother!" Dernel's brother exclaimed as Dernel swam toward the exit.

"Connect us when it's over!" Dernel's sister shouted.

"No sneak peeks!" Dernel shouted over his shoulder then disappeared.

"This one will suffice. Show this to her while she sleeps. Do not force the meld if she rejects our connection. I do not want to further damage relations while making amends."

AFFIRMATIVE
CONFIGURING MELD PARAMETERS

43%

Immersive Mode

She's in immersive mode. That much is clear. The stark white walls, the absence of pressure, the doors, and the general atmosphere all coincide with elements from immersive mode, but this is different.

Firstly, it's wet. Sia walks down the hallway and enjoys the pleasant sensation of room temperature water soaking her feet. It's surreal. Something she'd imagine wanting as a child, to live in a home submerged in water and bubbles. The lack of bubbles doesn't disappoint her, which is probably a sign of maturity.

The second difference, there is an end to the hallway. Usually, the halls are endless and ebony doors are scattered throughout with the promise of endless entertainment. At one end of the hall is the continuous path of knowledge, but along the other end of the hall she sees a dark shape.

She's hesitant to identify what it is. Memory of her last revelation still aches her heart. Surprises have always been unpleasant. This one is bound to be as well.

She wants to ignore it. Truly. And she would if it...wasn't inside her own mind. She can't hide from this, and so it's best to get it over with. With all that has happened, everything she's seen, she wouldn't be shocked to meet the boogeyman at the end of this hall.

She should ignore it, but until she gets a surgeon this is her life now. There's no rest in her dreams or the reality of the waking world, leaving her a bitter mess. Seeing her own original nightmares pale in comparison to the otherworldly memories that have been forced into her mind. Most are mundane, but one brutal scene still brings chills up her spine. She doesn't want to see anymore. She doesn't understand what they mean. Her own memories would be the breath of fresh air she needs right now.

Her feet lead her to the other end of the hall while her arm drags along the wall. When she passes a door, she tests it to make sure a temporary escape is available to her. None of the doors she tests are locked.

The end of the hallway opens into a large dome shaped room. The ceiling is no longer white, red and blue constellations are strewn across a pitch-black sky. It's beautiful, but there's something familiar about it. An eerie feeling envelopes her. At the center of the room is a fountain, the source of the water. That was the dark shape she'd been walking toward.

Elegant script is etched into the fountain, she falls to her knees and rubs a hand along the carved characters. She's knee deep in the water when he makes his presence known.

"Hello."

Sia freezes for a moment before huffing, a scowl is fixed on her face. Of course, she doesn't turn around just yet. She braces herself, and when her resolve is at an all time high, she jumps to her feet. Nothing prepares her for seeing the Underling face to face for the first time.

For that's who this must be. He's almost two and a half meters tall. She feels dwarfed for the first time and retreats to the fountain's stone rim. Sia is speechless. She rounds the fountain. The distance doesn't lower her fear, but she does release a breath she hadn't known she was holding.

"Hello, Sia." His words aren't coming from his mouth, which stays shut. The words travel from his mind into her own, clear as day. It's a soft voice, calm, and only a level above proper whispering.

"It's you! You!" She points at him with an accusatory look upon her face.

"Yes." He hasn't moved from in front of the fountain.

Sia pants and drops her finger.

"Yes?" He repeats himself, but now Sia can hear the inquisitive tone.

"You're Dernel."

The tall, navy blue creature nods. His scales glisten under the unusual light that illuminates immersive mode. "Yes, that is my true name." Her eyes trace the intricate pattern of his skin. The little marks that make him appear so real.

He's not here, but...

His own thoughts interrupt hers. "You saw my memories."

Sia takes a step forward. "Yes! That…that giant shark and those …not people, but so real…I—" She swallows and tries to calm herself, align her thoughts to make coherent sentences. "It…it looked so real. Felt so real."

"Yes, our consciousness' were meld together…twice now. It is the usual form of communication where I am from. My people can easily communicate with our…family with melds. Usually it takes skin contact to use a meld with a stranger, but we have the next best thing." He touches the back of his head.

"We do?" Sia frowns and mimics his gesture. Her fingers touch the thin metal plate at the back of her head. "Oh."

"With a meld, you can see all of my memories when given access."

Sia nods at first, but freezes at a thought. "Wait, have you seen all of my memories?"

Dernel is motionless for a moment before giving her a stiff nod. Sia backs away from the Underling.

"I wanted to understand you. I wanted to know you were an ally."

Sia furiously shakes her head. "You can't do that! You could have asked. You could have spoken to me."

It's Dernel's turn to shake his own head. "Organizing this is not an easy task. I cannot flick a tentacle and appear before you at your beck and call. Energy and time were needed and now we have that. I could not do this before."

"Time and energy?" She doesn't know if she believes that, but he does sound sincere.

"Yes."

"You left a message for me in Coldstone. You contacted me then and I was weak. Why not ask me like that?"

"I had already seen your memories by then."

Sia scowls at the Underling. "Just forget it. Of course the Underling doesn't understand the meaning of common courtesy, a right to privacy, human rights!"

Dernel flinches at that. "I...I respect your rights." He sighs. "Please, understand …privacy is not a word used beneath the sea. At sea, we are of one mind. Information is shared, and I was in utmost need of information. Sia, please forgive me."

Sia is silent.

"You saw my memories…you must have seen my attack. I am not a voluntary participant in this …" He gestures to the world around them. The pristine walls, fountain, and the myriad of doors. "I understand you did not join this precarious situation willingly, but neither did I. Your help is paramount to my own survival and so I would like to apologize and ask for another chance."

"A chance to steal my body? A chance to belittle me inside my own head?"

Dernel opens his mouth and the sharp edges of his teeth make Sia recoil. A shutter goes through his body, but no sound is brought forth from his lips. A yawn?

"S.I.D is not well adapted to communicating with humans."

"Puter was never like that. Puter was kind."

"S.I.D was created to cater to Underling. The Synthetic Intelligence Developer 2.0 was created to adapt to human

speech patterns and react accordingly to build trust and harmony between the subject and itself."

"No, Puter was really kind. That's not something you can calculate and...and...react accordingly to."

"That is how it was programmed."

"Puter was my friend!" Dernel tilts his head, it's very lizard like and further highlights how alien he is to her. Sia seethes. "He was my friend and you destroyed him and replaced him with your cold imitation." Dernel shakes his head in the negative, but Sia doesn't allow him to continue. "You still haven't explained why you stole my body."

"I thought that was self-evident."

"Explain!" Sia takes another step toward Dernel. Then another.

"When I first learned about you, I thought I could communicate my presence with a simple sign, but none that I could think of would make sense to you. Then I thought maybe to be passive while you slept would be better, but that was not as easy as I thought it would be." He recalls that beautiful sunrise he'd seen. How precious that memory is to him after years of darkness and pain. "Finally, I believed that I could borrow your body for a short time and solve my own...problem, but it became clear to me that would not be fair to you. We all deserve a choice."

Sia glares at the Underling, but nods at his last statement. "Yes. I do deserve a choice."

"I do not have much time." He steps forward so that his clawed feet are less than a meter from her own, but Sia doesn't squirm. She looks up from the monstrous webbed toes and cocks her head back to meet deep, dark brown eyes.

"Existence has become a hell for me and for you. I believe, if we work together, we can depart from this country, from this terrible place, but only if we work together." He raises a hand to show her his dark palm. "I promise I mean you no harm. You shall be my ally, and we shall work to move forward as one. My information shall become yours." He lowers his hand, but Sia's gaze is locked on the long appendages attached to his fingers. They are light blue and sharp. "You will awaken where you last were. Be safe, my friend."

Sia looks up from his hands and blinks. The walls tilt and her stomach drops, forcing a grimace across her face. The walls tilt the opposite direction and she's forced out of immersive mode.

IMMERSIVE MODE DEACTIVATED

2034

Wastelands, New Cinalia

Darkness is the first to greet her. The ache in her legs reminds her where she has stuffed herself. Her backpack is held to her chest, and there's a bucket between her bent legs. She sighs and knocks her noggin on the wall before stiffening. This isn't a game of hide-and-seek. Someone, something finding her won't be a matter of being out of the game.

She listens for several seconds before moving around to place her ear to the closet door. Nothing. She grasps the doorknob and turns it bit by bit. She eases the door open. The door isn't wrenched open. Nothing makes a sound. With a sigh, Sia opens the door fully.

Gasp!

Her heart jumps into her throat and she chokes on her scream. She slams the door closed. It shut on the strap of her backpack. Her back hit the wall of the closet. White. White forms the size of a dog are crawling around the room. She waits for the creatures to come at her like the roaches. For them to…

She doesn't have to wait very long. The doorknob jiggles. The creatures nudge against it. Sia's breath hiccups. The creatures attack the wood of the door. Sia can hear it cracking under the strain. Sia shivers. *Mom, Aaliyah, I'm trying. I'm really trying…Let me make it through this. Please,* she pleads. She trembles as she thinks about what to do.

There isn't much time. She has to act soon. Sia tears off her rubber gloves. They're her only pair and she doesn't want to ruin them. She shoves the gloves into her empty pocket and bends over. She lifts the bucket and pulls out her lighter.

A few garments have been shoved to the side, away from the empty hangers gathered at the middle of the closet. It's all she has. She grabs a garment from off a hanger. She can't see what it is, but it's thin. It lights quickly and she drops it into the bucket. Then she grabs another garment—a long sleeve shirt—and lights a sleeve on fire.

She coughs as the fumes from the burning fabric fill the closet. She grabs the bucket and balances it on her knees. Ready to toss the flaming contents at the creatures and run.

The creatures make little grunts as they destroy the door. The cracking becomes louder. Small holes widen, and Sia blinks rapidly in the dark. Abruptly, she's able to see tiny details on the creatures' faces. *Are these albino ants?!* Sia steadies herself and grabs the shaking doorknob.

The insects are focused on the door when she grabs the edge of the hot bucket with one hand, turns the knob, and shoves the door open. The pale creatures go flying. Sia ignores her burning fingertips and chucks the fiery contents.

High pitched squeals fill the air. Several of the translucent-skinned beings screech and scramble to the other side of the room. One remains; none of the flaming material hit it. It crawls toward Sia, and she swings the bucket as hard as she can at its head.

The backpack strap is tangled around her ankle, and she doesn't have the time to fix it. She darts for the bathroom door dragging the pack across the ground and throws her leg back to reel it in before slamming the door shut. She steps out of the strap and tugs it off the floor. Her fingers ache.

She rushes over to the window. Her heart is pounding incessantly in her chest. She yanks the window up and curses under her breath. It's locked. The fingers on her right hand are red and abused. Jerking on the closed window smears blood onto the gray paint.

"God!" she shouts before unlocking the window and jamming her palm at the top of the window frame to open it. It doesn't budge.

The scuffling outside the bathroom door stops, but she can hear furniture moving. Something bigger has arrived. Her knees almost buckle at the loud crash she hears outside the door. "Dammit! No…no…no, please!" Sia's eye drips tears of frustration as she pushes up against the window frame. It remains still for a moment, but the next moment it is opening with a soft creak.

Sia's heart skips a beat as she takes off her backpack and shoves it through the opened space. The window screen rips and crashes below. It isn't night, but it isn't fully morning. The light of the sun hasn't yet crossed over into the termite-infested town. When Sia gazes down at the dark ground, she hesitates. *Is it safe?*

The bathroom door splinters under a heavy crash against it. That scares Sia right out of her skin and through the window. She slides through feet first, turns over, and scrapes her belly along the bottom sill. Her hands hold tight to the edge while she hangs. She lets go.

When her feet touch the ground, she bends her knees and falls over. A wave of pain goes up her ankles and knees. She fears that she may have broken something. Maybe she should stay down, but panic forces her to rise to her feet. After snatching her backpack up, she drags herself away from the building and back toward the hill.

The sun's rays shine right past the dark hill that she presumes is where she came from. By the time she limps halfway, morning has fully dawned. She doesn't hear anything pursuing her but hearing anything is hard with the roaring of blood in her ears and her heavy panting. When she gets to the hill, she scrambles up it with the last of her adrenaline-fueled strength.

She lies still. Her eye is wide with panic. She itches. Her panting doesn't stop as she nervously looks around for the

white, transparent critters. "They must avoid the light. I'm fine in the light. Just stay in the light." Sia tries to stand, but her wobbling knees don't allow it. She crawls up the rest of the hill and peers over the other side.

There lay the caterpillar from yesterday. Sia's heart sinks. Her breath hiccups and she holds back a sob. It's as if electricity travels through her entire form. The hairs on her arms stand up and her knees lock, forcing her to kneel.

The caterpillar's body lies in the same spot as yesterday, but its skin is vastly different than before. Hundreds of holes riddle its skin, and within each hole is an egg sac. Ovular white eggs sacs have burst from within the caterpillar, and the larvae have feasted on its remains.

Sia crawls toward the canyon she exited. She clenches her teeth and tries to focus on something else as she drags herself away from the repulsive sight. Anything.

"That's a bad omen," young Sia remarked as she walked to school with her dad.

That made him stop in his tracks. "What did you say?" her father asked while he searched for what prompted that statement. There's a broken mirror left on the curb in front of a neighbors' home. "There's no such thing as bad omens," he said before he continued to walk.

"Mommy said—"

"Mommy is mistaken. She was probably joking with you."

"Mommy said bad omens foreturn bad days!!" Sia shouted over her father.

They crossed the street. Sia stayed close to her father as large vehicles drove past them. The wind picked up and blew his dark hair across his face, he threw up a hand and held it to his forehead to keep his sight clear.

He squeezed Sia's hand as they stepped off the curb. Their contrasting skin tones were more obvious with the bright spring sun beating down on them. Sia's skin glowed golden brown while he remained beige. When they reached the other side, her father spoke again.

"Don't blame other things for why your decisions go wrong, LinLin. Look at the facts and decide what is logical. Things that make sense," he tightened his grip on her hand. "Not omens, not propaganda, rumors, not even me. Letting fears and superstitions dictate how you act is a clear sign of ignorance and childishness." He stared down the street as he spoke.

Sia cocked her head to the side and listened to her father intently. She nodded at his words, though she didn't understand what he was referring to.

"No more omen talk. Did you practice your spelling words with Mommy yesterday?" her father asked.

"I did! I did best! But Aaliyah kept interrupting and spelling with me, and I told Mommy that she didn't win because she was cheating. She was copying me, Daddy. I spell the best!"

He dropped a hand onto her little head. "You do. But stay on your toes, or Aaliyah will surprise you. She won't be a baby forever."

Sia huffed and moved her head away from his hand. "I'm the best, Daddy. I'll always be the best!"

She doesn't make it to the canyon. Sia whimpers softly and then falls forward with her head on her hands. Her knees pang, but she can't pick herself up. "Tell me what to do," she moans into her hands. "I don't think I can make it…I don't think I can do it."

Dernel's memories come back to her, as do the words he spoke to her after the meld. He was right. The fact was she couldn't escape this hell alone and neither could he. That caterpillar had fought valiantly for its life and the life of those parasites. What if she was aiding a…monster? "Who do I trust?"

The morning has only begun, but it takes less than a second for something to go wrong. She coughs wetly into her hands and lifts herself up to look around…at the Wastelands. Her final resting place? Her grave? If she died here, could she truthfully say she had done everything she could to get back to Aaliyah? Everything?

"Okay," she croaks. "Heal me and I'll fight them. I'll gather your men. We'll fight them and get you out. But—" Sia swallows thickly. "—if I'm not in danger…my body is mine. If—" She licks her cracked lips, "—if not, I'll end us both. I'm not like you. My family is probably dead. I'll meet them on the other side, but your family is still alive, and you'll probably never see them again."

Sia coughs. Gradually, the aches in her legs disappear. The cuts on her hands seal up, and the swelling around her left eye decreases. A sharp pain runs down the entire left side of her face. *"Mmmnnnnnn…"*

TEMPORARY BLINDNESS WILL OCCUR AS CORRECTIVE MEASURES ARE TAKEN TO HEAL THE –

I don't want to speak with you! Sia shouts within her mind. Her eyes are closed. The effort brings up another bout of panting. Though she doesn't say it out loud, the response is instantaneous. The machine goes silent.

The left socket is incredibly damaged. She knows that. She's the one who's half blinded. It will take time, and she can wait. She doesn't prod at the eye. She gets up and jogs toward the van she deserted. Her body feels numb, and she's light on her feet.

10 minutes later…

The mercenaries had been prepared for a long drive and left two gas canisters in the back of the van. Sia fills the tank and is left with half a canister. Sia settles down in the van and grabs a strip of fabric off the center console. She places it over her left eye and loosely ties it behind her head. The ExplorerTech jumpsuit she acquired at the Coldstone labs is discarded into the back. Underneath, she wore two gray moth-bitten shirts and a pair of black jeans that she found in the locker rooms back at Coldstone.

She turns the key in the ignition and pulls off. It's a rocky ride. She sternly gazes at the terrain in front of her. She recalls her mother's response to what her father had said.

[illegible]

The wooden door opened and the figure that could be vaguely seen through the door's opaque glass entered. It was her mother. She wore a blue business suit and black heels. "Hey, baby. How was school? Did you have a good day?" Her mother slipped off her heels and tossed them beside the shoes neatly set off to the side.

Sia walked up to her mother while she licked a popsicle. Her chin and lips were stained blue. "Daddy said your omens are a mess and cheedish. And I should be loogicum when making decisions," Sia informed her mother.

Sia watched, cross eyed, as a dark brown hand came down to caress the side of her face. Her mother's manicured nails' traced her chin before the hand pulled away to toss a few stray braids over her shoulder. Her mother unbuttoned her suit jacket one-handed and nodded while she mulled over Sia's words. She turned and set her tan purse up on the hallway table as she slipped on some house slippers.

"Well, omens are just a way to translate feelings without wasting time explaining yourself to other people. It's like a secret language for the perceptive. Aunt Yoni would know what I mean." She unzipped her purse and pulled out her keys to hang them on a wall hook. "It's not the sign itself. It's the feelings the sign incites in you. Usually, it's a clear warning that **something** is not right in your current direction. If you feel that gut instinct, **never** ignore it, baby, okay?"

Sia didn't agree, but she didn't disagree. Neither of them made sense to her. She focused on consuming her delicious blue popsicle. Sometimes the stick had a funny joke on it, but she had to eat it all before the words were revealed. That was always the best part, the big reveal.

"Mmmm…"

Part 3

44%

2034

East of W.A.R.T.S, New Cinalia

3 days later…

A forest green truck drives along the bumpy road behind a black armored vehicle. The front bumper of the armored truck has a large snow plow attached to it. The vehicles drive through the wastelands toward the grasslands.

Right before a brutal sandstorm hit, a messenger arrived at the communications center, but they couldn't head out until after the powerful storm subsided. An ally requested a meetup.

Meetups are never held at the same location these days. None of their allies wanted to be the first to invite the other to their headquarters. Their alliances weren't born of trust, but of necessity.

Unlike their allies, the Mercenaries were fine with people knowing their headquarters, but they still had rules. The most important rule: any group larger than a solo messenger will be shot down immediately, no questions asked. All incoming traffic is monitored and without an escort, entrance into the merchant hub is prohibited.

Ika sits up in his seat chewing on a piece of jerky. His rifle is propped up between his legs. The rubber straps of his goggles have tangled with the blue scarf hanging loosely around his dirty, pale neck. The uneven terrain of the road causes the goggles to shift, gently bouncing against his collarbone.

His gray eyes are attentive to the road in front of them. Periodically, he checks in with the truck behind them with his radio. He barely registers the salty meat as he works it around in his mouth. A hill comes within sight.

"Stop there. Wait for the heads up," Ika says into his radio. The green truck stops driving within sight, but outside the range of any firearms. Less to do with the occupant's safety and more to do with the current price of business with this particular ally. They'd found they can get them to agree to pretty much any mission if the reward is explosives. Ika finds that annoying. There's only so far he can travel with explosives before he needs to use them.

The armored vehicle pulls up near a hill. On the right are identical trees for miles. The bark of the trees are charred black. The branches are naked of leaves. To the left is a vibrant green field. Of course, some of it is yellow and short, but the abundance of green grass is a sight unseen in the Wastes. As the years pass, more and more of the land is becoming viable once again.

Ika remains in the vehicle as the driver gets out. He tosses his bag of jerky on the center console, without looking away from the mercenary approaching the grass mound.

The mercenary stops walking halfway between the hillside and the armored vehicle. "Kraaaaa!" the mercenary sloppily calls. A figure pops up from the other side of the hill. Then two, three, six. Six figures stand atop the hill.

Ika opens the glove compartment and pulls out a pair of binoculars one-handed. He holds the binoculars over his eyes and sees two familiar forms. The man, or rather the Savage, that had summoned them to this rendezvous point.

The group leader, Raco, and his partner, Nils, stood atop the hill among four unknown people. When they identify the mercenaries, the two Savages walk toward the driver.

That's odd…where's the other creep? Ika tosses his binoculars onto the dashboard.

He opens his side door and hops out of the truck. The door blocks his sight for a moment while he retrieves his weapon. Then he strolls up to his driver and nudges him at the waist. The driver goes back to the armored vehicle to let out their three other men from the back of the truck.

Four hooded unknowns stand tall intently watching their interaction. A moment later, a figure comes barreling down the hill behind the two Savages. Ika can recognize the lanky figure right away. Slim the Savage.

Raco, Nils, and Slim are inseparable. Where Raco goes he always takes his two partners. At first, Ika had thought the two were his bodyguards, but later learned Raco didn't need a bodyguard.

As Ika waits, he scans the area for any more unknowns. Grass, trees, dirt road. The mercenary's trucks are the only vehicles around. When Raco gets just out of arm reach of Ika he stops.

Raco is coated from head to toe with mud and is wielding a short spear at his side. It's unusually crafted with a sharp blade welded onto the end of a piece of metal. There are spikes along the shaft for blocking and tearing away weapons. It's tucked under his armpit and extends out three feet past his hand.

While Raco eyes the shorter male, wind passes by and stirs the unusually thick hair atop the Savage leader's head. It's curly and white. On Raco's left, a buff male with a bald head and patchy skin glares at Ika. On his right stands a slim woman. She's completely bald as well. She looks over the perimeter and bares her teeth at Ika. She's missing some teeth, but the ones that still remain have been sharpened.

Ika grimaces at the Savages. "We agreed to meet with you and your…buddies. Who are those people up there? They don't look like your usual sort." Ika gestures over Raco's shoulder with his chin.

Raco glances over his shoulder and a bit of the mud coating his neck crumbles to reveal his albino complexion. Raco's pink eyes return to Ika and he grins sharply at the mercenary "Those guys? Friendly bunch. We met them quite a while ago." Ika raises an eyebrow at that. "Their leader's a spider enthusiast."

"Arachnologist," Slim corrects while adjusting the strap of the bag digging into her shoulder. The dirty messenger bag is plump and makes wielding a weapon impossible with its bulky, bulging frame swinging across her torso.

"Invaluable information about those targets you gave us has come from him. Bit of a freak though," Raco laughs. "But I don't mind. Freaks get the job done."

Ika refrains from rolling his eyes and waits. They all sit in silence before Raco turns to Slim.

"Here." Slim can't wait to get rid of the bag. She throws the strap over her head and hands the bag over. The contents inside clink together as the bag transfers hands. Ika almost flinches at the disgusting smell of the bag but holds it close.

It's quite heavy. Every pocket is filled with something. Raco lazily looks over the armored vehicle. Four men are hanging back with their weapons drawn. Nils remains focused on every movement Ika makes.

Ika doesn't hold the bag for long. He gives it a quick once over, gathers the strap in his hand and holds it out to the side. A subordinate lowers his weapon and comes jogging up to get it.

"Look about right?" Raco questions the silent guard. The man sets the bag onto the ground and runs his hands around the outer pockets. He unzips the main compartment and digs a hand through the contents.

"Hmmm." Ika gives a noncommittal grunt. Raco fidgets and sets a hand to his hip while the guard finishes checking the bag for explosives. No wires, no odd smelling items inserted into a side pocket. The guard stands and nods down at Ika.

Ika is about to raise a hand and signal the other vehicle when Raco takes several steps backward. "Why don't you come meet them?"

Ika pretends to pause and give it a thought. "Your spider friends? No thanks." He signals the other truck. When it pulls up, the mercenary's temperamental doctor hops out of the back of the truck and runs over to retrieve the messenger bag that contains the goods. The doctor scowls at the poor condition of the bag and tsks at the fact that all the glass and plastic bottles are stuffed inside without much care. One good drop would shatter all the precious insulin inside. After a quick count of the insulin containers and pill bottles, he yells confirmation to Ika. "Is all here!!"

Ika nods but keeps a firm grip on his weapon. "So close to your territory, but you haven't yet come across them. Don't you find that interesting?" Raco comments. Nils and Slim fall back to the hill where the unfamiliar hooded figures still stand. Raco stays behind, scratching his flaky hair. "I figured, why kill em when we can join em. They have some interesting ways of securing their location and access to…"

Ika turns his back on Raco. Raco's face stills as he is ignored. He licks his lips and spits onto the ground. He head tilts back as he watches Ika stroll away from him. The corner of his mouth twitches before he can clamp down on the nervous habit. When Ika passes his armed guards, the mercenary checks back over his shoulder and Raco raises a hand to wave. Ika doesn't wave back.

Ika averts his eyes and bypasses the armored truck to get to the second vehicle. He knocks twice on the side of the green truck and continues to the back.

"The keys." Ika is thrown a single key from Priya. "Change of plans. We might need to cancel out this subscription. Priya, you're in charge. Stay back after the exchange. Pace yourself. Nard and Turner, you're with me. Pheno and Kid, into the back." Ika doesn't wait for a reply before walking back over to the Savage leader.

Everyone moves into position. As he approaches the Savage leader, he eyes the man's form from top to bottom. Unlike his companions, Raco looks to have been completely submerged in dark mud and he smells awful. Even more than usual.

Feces? the thought crosses Ika's mind, but he doesn't want to imagine what possessed the other man to bathe in waste. "Here." Ika is about to toss the keys to the Savage, but the other man backs away and points farther up the dirt road, the other side of the hill.

"Pull it up there. You'll regret it…if you leave without an introduction." After speaking, Raco lopes away without checking to see if Ika will acquiesce.

"…" Ika grinds his teeth and debates dropping the keys and leaving. He inspects the man's uneven stride. Raco limps up the hill and disappears over the other side. The four unknowns retreat to the other side as well.

Turner and Nard are waiting beside the truck when Ika opens the passenger door. They all get in and he tosses the keys to Turner.

"Pull it up there," Ika mutters before he checks his weapon and pats the sides of his legs. *Check. Check. Check.*

Turner pulls the car up the road and leaves the keys in the ignition. When they get out, they're on the other side of the hill and can see several figures standing together facing away from them. Ika sighs and walks over to the group. Turner and Nard stick close with their weapons drawn. The area around the pit has been tread over by feet and vehicles so many times that grass ceases to grow there. It's all rocks and dirt.

There are seven hooded figures and three Savages standing over a pit. When they get closer to the small crowd, muffled screams and groaning are easily heard. Ika keeps his distance from them and remains on the other side of the pit. The three mercenaries look down into the pit. Ika pales. Nard and Turner freeze, their weapons waver and point toward the ground.

The pit is a deeply dug hole that connects to a tunnel. The tunnel is dark and wide enough to admit a sixteen-wheeler truck with room to spare. They can't see how far it actually goes.

"Interesting, isn't it? They have tunnels like those that go on for miles…right across this field even!" Raco calls over to them from the other side of the pit.

Ika warily side eyes his men and suppresses a sneer. "What is this?" Ika asks loud enough to be heard from across the pit.

All of the hooded figures look over to Ika. They seem as nonchalant as his facade. They keep their hoods up, and their heads bent forward, so their faces are concealed in shadows. Some of them are wearing dark shorts and some are wearing torn pants. Their skin complexions vary from pink to dark brown.

A hooded figure answers. "A transaction." It's the voice of a woman.

Ika tilts his head back and looks to Nard in his peripheral. Nard's hands tremble. Gradually, his pistol raises to aim for one of the figures.

"These nice fellows have decided to exchange some snacks that their pet hasn't deigned to consume yet. Useful workers indebted to their saviors…" Raco snorts. "Or back to the deli." Raco doesn't disguise the wink he sends over to Ika, grinning widely.

He knows…of course he knows. Ika blindly reaches out and grasps Nard's elbow. "Those people are already dead, you hear me?" Ika whispers to him before glancing at Turner. Turner's eyes are wide in horror. He's frowning down at the pit and the people below…at the two men below. Ika releases his grip on Nard's arm to examine the pit once more.

There are around twenty people bound and gagged within the pit. It smells and Ika is sure that human waste makes up much of the mud down there. Among the mass of people, there are two familiar men. Their legs are tied up and connected to the rope binding the person beside them. Their hands are forced to clasp together at the wrist with a bit of rope then pinned against their chest with another. Even with the damage and grit, Ika can recognize the oriental tattoo on the man's neck, and the decorative patches on his leather jacket. One of the patches is a symbol all mercenaries would recognize, a black star. *It's Ralph.*

Ralph looks severely beaten. Half his face is swollen, and the side of his skull looks deformed. Mud and waste are smeared all over both men.

Ika's eyebrow twitches as he goes over the situation. "You wanted to meet us." Ika sweeps his hand into the air in a tense wave and faux salutes the hooded figures. "We've met. Anything else?"

A different hooded figure speaks. "The future will be quite different from what it is now. From what it was. The culling has not been completed." Their voice sounds male.

Raco nods. "They agree that our new beginning only truly begins after we've cleared the weak, so the mighty don't suffer under their parasitic hold."

"If we get rid of the weak, who do we profit from? The mighty don't have a habit of sharing well," Ika responds.

Raco laughs. Nils and Slim retreat from the crowd. The hooded figure stares at Raco, he coughs and quiets down. Ika squints at the pair. "I hope this isn't the start of a lecture…We have places to be." Ika gestures to the sky with his weapon.

The hooded man continues. "Your man has informed us of the deal you have." Raco takes a few steps back behind the hooded figures. The hooded man steps closer to the pit's ledge and gestures down at the people within the pit with the sweep of his long sleeve. The sun bounces off a glint of metal in the man's hand.

My man? "Oh, really? What of it?"

"Pick any that you want. There are more to come. We even catch valuable insects that your man said you process for their most useful parts," the hooded man replies.

Ika wants to scowl at Raco, but the man is hidden behind the other figures. Instead, he keeps his form loose while

flicking the safety off his weapon. As Ika opens his mouth to reply, the screams below get wilder. Turner and Nard step closer to the pit and raise their guns.

A gigantic wolf spider crawls out of the tunnel and grabs the legs of the nearest human. While it consumes the person, the ropes that are eaten pull on those connected to the other end of the rope.

"Aaaaaaah!!" A woman pulls her gag over her chin with her forearm and screams. "Help me! Please…Help me!!"

"You should hurry. The best ones might get gobbled up first." The hooded man lifts his hand and Ika tenses and prepares to shoot at a glint of silver, but the hooded man doesn't pull out a weapon. He pulls out a whistle.

Nard and Turner are still frozen in shock. The wolf spider drops the twisted, dry corpse of its latest prey and tugs another person toward its mouth. The woman at the other end of the rope is kicking and wriggling against the earth, but her efforts are to no avail; the wolf spider uses its legs to press on the ropes and drag her toward its waiting maw. The other captives are in a daze, beaten so badly they're no longer coherent of their surroundings. The woman's situation is dire.

"Do it." Ika lifts his rifle and takes aim. Swiftly, Turner reaches into the back of his pants and grasps his flare gun. It fires into the sky. Raco drops down to his belly. Nard shoots at the wolf spider. The hooded figures scatter at the sound of gunfire. Three of them rush toward the mercenaries. Ika shoots down all three of the hooded men. Gunfire fills the field northeast of their position. The whole situation becomes unmanageable from there.

"*Help me!!* Noooo!!" The woman writhes against her bindings. A layer of thick hair protects the spider's skin like an umbrella repelling rain; the bullets are an annoyance but do no real damage. It retreats into the tunnel with its prey to eat in peace. The wolf spider clan leader along with his remaining three followers jump into the pit. The leader blows his whistle.

The whistle prompts the wolf spider to be bolder, it drops the woman and rushes out of the tunnel. It leaps onto the bound people, crushing them beneath its large abdomen. Its legs press down on heads and limbs as it rears back to swing at the firing men.

Turner and Nard reload. They aren't intimidated by the party trick. Before the spider can swipe at their positions, they fire simultaneously at a joint in its raised limbs and retreat to a safe distance before repeating the assault.

The leader and his followers are escaping into the spider's tunnel. Ika grunts and shoots both followers in the back of their heads. Their bodies collapse and reveal the whistler's fleeing backside. He's taking aim to finish the man off when the ground trembles.

Directly behind them, the truck of explosives drives towards the pit. Turner and Nard run off to the right. Ika runs around the edge of the pit toward the other side and spots Raco, who has remained on his stomach and out of danger. The Savage leader is crawling away on his belly at an impressive speed.

The wolf spider's leader blows his whistle once more, and the spider jumps out of the pit. It lands on top of the truck. The vehicle swerves. The driver, Slim, bails out of the car. The wolf spider jumps off to stand beside the pit as the truck careens into the hole.

Most of the people were crushed under the immense weight of the spider, but one individual continued to crawl toward the tunnel. When the truck comes barreling down above them, she scrambles up and into the tunnel.

"What the hell is this?!" Ika storms over to Raco.

Spotting impending doom, Raco rolls onto his back and crab walks backward. Ika reloads his weapon and Raco collapses onto his bottom and sticks out a hand to block his face from harm. "Wait…wait! Aren't you glad? I found your men!"

"Don't pretend you care. You used these people and planned to double cross them, but they double crossed you

first." Ika brings the rifle up to his shoulder and cradles it. The snug fit of his sling around the back of his wrist centers him while he adjusts his stance.

"No!" Raco tries to stand and stumbles backward as Ika aims for his head. "Yes! Yes! I was captured, but I saw your men and knew you would be happy…" Ika takes a step toward the Savage. "Full of joy! Cheery even! Isn't there a finder's fee or something?" The Savage attempts to negotiate. Raco holds out his hands in surrender and bows his head in submission. His eyes remain on the ground while he explains the situation. "We failed in killing them. They had too many people and the spider. It's some kind of circus freak! It's fast. It travels through those tunnels to anywhere within five to ten miles of this place. It's a menace. Look at it." The Savage points at the gigantic predator not too far from them on the other side of the pit.

Ika's focus on Raco's bowed head keeps a siren going off in the Savage's head. Raco itches to throw up his spear, stab the man through the calf and make a run for it, but he knows better. The merc would rather be stabbed through the leg than let an enemy slip through his grasp. The earth would have to quake beneath them to skew Ika's aim from any of Raco's vital areas. The man doesn't seem to blink when he has a shot already lined up. Raco knows when he's beat, but all isn't lost. It's unusual for men of his stature, but the blond is a reasonable man. When Ika's stance shifts slightly, Raco releases a soft sigh, Ika glances over his shoulder.

The large front-facing eyes of the wolf spider are focused on its attackers. Nard and Turner release a barrage of bullets at the enormous mass of dark brown hair and legs while Slim and Nils attack its legs with their machetes. Ika spies something unusual crossing the road toward their skirmish.

A mob is running toward them, exiting the trees. Ika curses and begins firing at the hooded people running toward them. Raco picks up his spear and runs over to defend his men. The Wolf spider followers are wielding all sorts of weapons. Metal poles, knives, spears, and even large rocks.

Ika keeps moving as he shoots down one person after another. He aims for the head—the usual showstopper these days—but he never knows what sort of freaks they'll come across. If the person seems a bit more feral than the others, he spares a bullet for their chest as well. Best to be sure they're dead.

Ika clears a few before running out of bullets. A maniac stalks up behind Nard; the black man is unawares, dodging an attack from the Wolf Spider's many legs. Ika runs to intercept their metal pole. The rage that has boiled just beneath the surface of his calm facade fuels him with strength. He grabs the barrel of his rifle like a bat and swings with all his might.

The body of the rifle whacks the follower in the face and knocks him unconscious. Another follower comes forth. Ika swings again, but the woman catches the rifle and yanks it. Ika releases his hold on the weapon. She stumbles back a step and tosses the gun aside to rush the unarmed man. She rushes straight into the knife he tugs from his thigh holster. The full tang five-inch blade is sheathed to the hilt in-between two ribs and her sternum. The pressure in her chest forces out a stilted cry.

Ika rams his shoulder into her chest, sweeps the blade to the right, and wrenches it from her body. She collapses, pressing her hands to the large wound in a futile attempt to stop the bleeding, to stop the pain, but she's already drowning. Her weak attempts at survival are ignored. Ika picks up his rifle and knocks her unconscious. He steps over the two bodies and scans the area. The Savages work through the rest of the followers at an impressive speed.

The end of Raco's spear pierces a man's shoulder—with a kick to the chest the man drops, breathless. The moment after the Savage yanks his spear from the man's shoulder, it's swung backward and the spikes on the shaft pierce the neck of a follower creeping up behind him. The spider follower falls to their knees trying to hold their flesh together.

"Ika!" Nard yells before shoving his leader to the ground. Ika gasps at the sudden impact. Nard raises his pistol to fire, but the wolf spider swipes down and bats away his weapon. With another swipe, it's long hairy leg impales Nard's forearm.

"Aaaaaaaaah!" he screams and falls to the side with his arm pinned to the earth. Ika scrambles to his knees and adjusts his grip on the knife. He slices at the leg of the spider pinning Nard.

"Boss!" Ika hears Kid cry out. She cuts through the green field's high grass, pumping her arms at her side. When she sees Nard's legs kicking up against the earth, his voice screaming in pain, she grabs a grenade from her tactical vest and sprints over to their position. Her ginger hair falls into her face as she rushes to get within range of them.

Ika saws at the appendage, pressing his weight into the wound, but can't pierce the spider's thick skin. It pulls away its leg, but drags Nard along. Ika grabs hold of the man with his arms wrapped around his waist, and attempts to hold him down, to keep him away from the spider's maw…but he isn't strong enough.

"Aaaah!"

"Get away!! Stand clear!" Kid screams at them.

"No! Get back!" Ika yells with his cheek pressed to Nard's stomach.

The spider flicks its encumbered leg. Nard flies. He hits the ground with a thud and doesn't rise. Ika spins through the air, and when he hits the ground, he rolls and rolls. After a split second he rises, but the impact tore the air out of his lungs. His arms falter and his chest barely rises off the earth. He coughs and tries to get up again.

But it's over. Turner succeeds in shooting out a main eye and the Wolf Spider screeches. Its head dives for the ground at hyper speed. Turner jumps back, to get out of range, but falls over a body. Kid throws her grenade. His leg is grasped by the spider. Sharp, black fangs bite into his lower leg and tear through flesh and bone.

If there's one thing Ika knows he'll never forget, it's the gut-wrenching screams that are ripped from Turner. Ika crawls toward his position, fighting to breathe, and is frantically searching for a weapon when Kid's grenade explodes at the back of the spider's head. The explosion interrupts its plan to inject Turner with its venom; instead it drops the mangled leg from its maw and whirls around. Severely wounded and out for blood, it charges Kid.

She backs up two steps and freezes. There's no time for her to pull her weapon from its holster. The creature is there in the blink of an eye.

It grabs her head in its fangs while a barrage of gunfire attacks its sides. It spins around to escape the armor-piercing rounds. Kid's body swings in its mouth, her legs kick out and her slim arms flail for a grip on the spider. Something to take the strain off her neck. Her muffled screams are deafening inside the mouth of the arachnid.

Another grenade is thrown, and it destroys three of the legs at once. The wolf spider tightens its maw, screeching in pain, crushing Kid's head. Her limbs go still. For a second, the body dangles before it plummets to the ground, a sack of lifeless flesh. It remains lying along the side of the pit as the gigantic spider tips backward into the hole. It falls alongside the damaged truck.

Priya and the other mercenaries arrive. Ika's eyes water as he fully stands and tries to straighten to…

"I've got you!" Pheno yells as he injects Turner with a strong painkiller. The medic pulls out a tourniquet to stop the blood from flowing out of the injured leg. Turner's cries of pain dwindle as the painkiller takes effect.

"We had to clear out the field. It was going to be an ambush," Priya reports in. She's unharmed. Several men continue to fire at the spider's remains. Better safe than sorry. Two mercenaries drag forward a hooded man in torn jeans, the leader of the Wolf Spider Clan. "He says you'll want to speak to him." The mercenaries toss the hooded man to his knees.

Ika catches his breath. His adrenaline levels are dropping, and he can already feel a migraine coming on. "Strong, huh?"

The hooded man spits blood on the ground, his lower jaw is already forming a bruise. There are scratches on his face, and he's lost his whistle.

"The strong know when they are beaten," the hooded man stoically replies.

"Hmm…" Ika looks over the destruction and dead bodies. His hands begin to tremble. He squeezes them into fists and conceals his hands within his pockets.

"We're losing light here, Boss!" a female mercenary calls out from atop the hill. She's watching their vehicle, the road, and carnelian stripes spread across the sky.

"This place'll be crawling with critters soon. What do you want me to do with them?" Priya asks.

Ika catches a figure shift in his peripheral and turns around to face the retreating Savage pair. "Hey!" Nils is nowhere in sight. Raco is holding Slim up with her arm over his shoulder. They're walking toward the road and the charred forest. "We had an attack in the Wastes, a week or so ago. Do you know who's active out there?" Ika asks.

"Week or so ago? No idea, Bossman. Me and mine were leaving Coldstone around that time before we finished your job," Raco reveals. "Breeding. Children don't raise well in the wild."

"You don't consider Coldstone the wild?" Priya finds that thought too ludicrous to laugh at. Most of the region of Coldstone is surrounded by uninhabited land, but the parts of the city and wilderness actually settled is full of feral locals.

"It's definitely tame compared to the rest of this world." Slim's head nods against his shoulder. "It seemed a good idea at the time. Maybe I'll test out the bay area next!" Raco yells the last sentence over his shoulder before continuing toward the charred forest. Ika rolls his eyes and turns away from the Savage pair. Priya watches them limp away.

"We aren't going to escort them closer to their camp?" a new guard asks from behind the hooded prisoner. Ika and Priya ignore the question.

"You lived in those tunnels?" Ika asks the prisoner.

"Yes," the prisoner replies through bared teeth.

"All these years?"

"With the help of my partner, we were able to sustain ourselves with slaughtered insects and the supplies from travelers," the prisoner answers with his gaze fix on the burning pit. A long, hairy limb sticks out from the smoking hole.

"Your partner?" Priya asks. She raises her weapon and scans the area.

"The spider," Ika motions toward the arachnid with his chin and the prisoner averts his gaze. "You won't survive very long without that thing to mooch off of. Dependence. That's a trait of the weak isn't it?" The prisoner shakes his head and lowers his gaze even further. Ika's eyes wander to the pit and the dark tunnel that's filling with flames. "You live in darkness, you die in darkness…" Ika mutters before telling Priya. "Let's do these guys a favor. Light it all up."

Priya nods and orders the rest of the men forward to help her complete Ika's orders. "Remove all the explosives from the truck and destroy those tunnels. Leave their bodies where they are. The critters won't be long. If you see anyone suspicious running away. Leave em. They won't survive out here without their monster to cull people. Julie, help the wounded," Priya commands.

Ika watches the prisoner wallow in his circumstances. The man isn't bound, but it's clear that attempting to escape would be pointless. A pathetic whimper travels from the prisoner's mouth, and that's when Ika is fed up with the sight of him. He decides to retrieve his lost blade and rifle from the field of bodies.

After retrieving his items, he limps over to the armored vehicle. The back is open. Pheno is treating Nard's arm. The

black man seems to be alright. When Ika passes by, they make eye contact. Nard grimaces and turns his eyes away, leaving Ika to settle his gaze on the bundle of cloth lying on the ground outside the truck.

Kid's body is wrapped in a large off-white cloth. A patch of blood stains one end of the bundle where her head should be. She's gone. They'll never see her scarlet locks bounce atop her head again. Turner's unconscious. The tourniquet is still tight around his thigh. Below his knee is a mess. He's stopped bleeding out, but he needs to be taken back to the medical ward at W.A.R.T.S. as soon as possible. They'll probably have to amputate it.

He walks around to the driver compartment. His trembling hand opens the passenger door. He sets his rifle inside and climbs in. He gingerly sits and sets his head back. His eyes flutter shut. "Let it go…" he mutters. "Let it all go."

Multiple explosions sound off in the distance and dark clouds of smoke rise to further blacken the darkening sky. His eyes open to see the progress the sun has made toward the horizon. A horizon Ralph's crew will never see again. That lump of flesh lying on the soil, the result of a young woman's sacrifice, won't appreciate the view. Will the heavens matter to Turner when the earth has wrought his body into the state it is today? Will he care to look up?

Ika tries to breathe slowly out of his nose and catch his breath, but it's too much for him. He taps a fist to his forehead and huffs out a long, angry groan. He can't let it go. Ika struggles with the door before slamming it open.

He stalks back over to the pit area with swift, decisive steps.

The prisoner's form is lit up by the blaze rising from the pit. The dark hood has fallen back. Greasy brown hair sticks to his sweaty face. His hands lay open on his lap as he watches his domain crumble.

When the prisoner hears footsteps approaching, he doesn't rise or turn to investigate. He trembles. Muffled explosions and gunshots pervade the area. Ika stops behind the prisoners' form. Ika's breathing has calmed down.

Finally, there's a lull in activity.

Flames heat the air, but Ika finds the temperature to be refreshing. It's cleansing. The stress lines on Ika's face evaporate. His feet scuff at the dirt. He idles closer to the animated cadaver. A bead of sweat rolls off the prisoner's face onto his shaking hands. Both men hang onto their convictions until one of them can no longer endure the hush that has descended over them.

"It's only—" The prisoner straightens to peer over his shoulder, but Ika grabs the back of the man's head and his bicep and pitches him into the raging flames. The lanky man is tossed over the edge and smashes into the melting hood of the truck. He's ablaze in seconds. His body slides down the wreck into the mass grave below, his screams drowned out by the static hum in Ika's mind.

Ika's hands no longer tremble. His wide eyes slowly blink at the turn of events. He forces out a shuddering breath and shakes himself from the moment. He returns to the armored vehicle, slips into the open door, and sets his head back against the seat. It's about time to return to W.A.R.T.S.

The armored vehicle speeds across the wastelands, but it's too late. They won't make it to their headquarters before the sun sets. When darkness falls, they're nowhere near a structure to hide within. Their only choice is to drive with their headlights off. The driver puts on night vision goggles. They stick to their usual route.

An hour passes with no incidents, but an hour and forty-five minutes into the drive, they sideswipe a large structure. The tires screech and they swerve off course. Ika's head collides with the window and his knees hit the underside of the dashboard. He groans.

The driver regains control of the vehicle and curses as he holds his head.

"Go check," Ika orders. Quickly, the driver grabs his pistol from the center console, and goes to check the damage on the

truck. He slams the door shut. Ika locks it. They don't have time to waste. The night hides unspeakable things. "Christ…damn it." Ika mutters while prodding at the bruise on his forehead.

"What the hell did we hit?!"

45%

2034
Wastelands
Southeast of W.A.R.T.S., New Cinalia

The back cargo area of the armored vehicle is silent. Two benches have been installed to each wall, but it isn't a very comfortable area. The walls are white and a small LED light on the ceiling has been activated, so the passengers don't have to sit in complete darkness.

Priya sits near the door to the back of the truck. Her brown lips are pursed as she observes the injured men. Nard is sitting up, holding his arm. His eyes are closed, but Priya knows he's awake. Whenever the truck drives over a bump, she hears him suck in a shallow breath.

Turner is lying on the ground between the two benches with his thighs bound together. The doctor and a mercenary sit on either side of him to keep his body still. He is unconscious. Whatever the doctor gave him has made him unresponsive.

The other mercenaries have bowed heads as they rest or tinker with their weapons. Priya keeps a bundle between her feet so it doesn't get jostled and unravel. A bloody white cloth wraps around the stiff bundle. It's best not to focus on what

or who it is. She clasps her slender fingers together and meditates on the past few hours.

We've been through much worse, Priya reminds herself while keeping her leg rigid.

Brutal images of people smashed under rubble, screaming children, and charred corpses flash across her mind. They all have been condemned to this lifestyle since 2018.

Suddenly, everyone is thrown around. The truck spins out of control. Priya puts out her hands to grab hold of the corpse as it slides down the floor. She collides with another mercenary with the body held down by both her hands. Pheno throws his body across Turner's leg to protect his damaged limb. Nard is thrown to his side and grasps the bench to keep from squashing the doctor.

The truck stops. Priya releases her grip on the corpse and pulls her radio from her waist clip. "What the hell did we hit?!" Priya shouts over the radio.

"He's looking. Everyone good?"

Priya's gaze sweeps over everyone. They're alert now, except for Turner, and they seem fine.

"We're good. Turner can't take any more of that. What's our ETA?" Priya asks.

"If we haven't damaged anything? Fifteen minutes," Ika replies.

Priya sighs. "Sounds good."

The driver makes his way around the truck with his night vision goggles secured on his head. He checks each tire. No damage. The plow attached to the front of the vehicle bypassed the structure completely, but the passenger door is damaged. It's superficial, nothing that'll keep them there any longer.

What have they hit? It's large and sandy. *A rock?* He reaches out to touch it. It's a vehicle. He clears away the sand with his gloved hands. It's the back of a van. Quickly, he follows the side wall to the passenger side. It's tipped into a ditch on the side of the road.

If they hadn't been driving so far on the right, they would have overlooked this crash entirely. He clears sand off the window and leans forward to press his goggles to the glass. When he squints, he can see…the driver's side door is open.

"Who are you?" an unfamiliar voice says.

"Wuuh?!" he exclaims and backs away from the vehicle. He raises his gun. He can't see where the person is. He searches for the owner of the voice.

"Where did you come from?" The voice is coming from the figure standing in front of the wrecked van. They stand outside the ditch on the other side of the hood.

Tall man wearing unusual headgear. Not armed. Merchant? The mercenary warily watches the stranger. "What happened here?" the mercenary asks. He's sure not to speak too loud. Who knows what could be listening.

"The sandstorm took me off course and made me crash into this hole," the man answers. He takes a step toward the mercenary.

"Stay right there, sir. I have a weapon aimed at you. Let's take this slow," the mercenary says.

The figure raises a hand and motions to the van. "I…I have supplies. If you take me with you, I'll give you a portion."

The mercenary grasps the radio at his waist and presses the transmission button. "I've found a merchant out here. Stranded by the storm. What do you want to do about it?" the mercenary reports in. There's silence for a moment.

"Only one person?" his boss asks.

"Yeah. Unarmed. His merchandise is stuck inside a ditch. That's what we hit, his van."

"We'll gather it up tomorrow. Confirm he's unarmed." Ika orders.

The mercenary nods and puts the radio back on his waist clip. "Stay where you are. I'm coming toward you," the mercenary calls out.

The man remains still with a hand spread out in front of himself to stay steady. The mercenary comes closer and puts out a hand to touch the unknown man's shoulder.

The man trembles and grasps his hand before letting go. "Sorry, been out here alone for too long," the man apologizes.

"Are you unarmed?"

The man lifts up a crowbar from behind his back. "Just this," the man answers. "Thought maybe you were a critter trying to eat up my stuff. Thank god you aren't."

"Do you want to join us?"

The man nods his head. "Yes, yes. Please. Do you have a camp nearby?"

The mercenary ignores the question and begins patting the man down. Swiftly, he touches along the man's arms, stomach, spine, and his legs.

"Woah, there. I don't have anything else with me!" the man exclaims but doesn't struggle away.

No weapons. The mercenary steps back and calls it in. "No weapons confirmed."

"Let's go. We've been held up too long. Tie him up and put him in the back." Ika orders.

The mercenary nods and grabs the man's shoulder. "Drop the crowbar there." The mercenary orders. A soft thud is heard.

"Tie? Is that necessary?" the man says.

"It's safer if you just follow our orders. We aren't very far from our camp. Then we'll release you." The man is silent as he is manhandled through the darkness. His shoulder crashes into the side of a truck he can't see. The mercenary is reaching into a pocket for paracord when he hears the sound of large wings.

He knocks twice on the back doors of the truck. It opens. He shoves the unbound stranger into the truck and rushes to the driver's side. The back doors slam shut. When he gets inside, he starts up the vehicle and begins speeding down the dirt road. There is no time to waste.

W.A.R.T.S. has artillery for large winged beasts, but without being directly outside the facility they are open to all sorts of attacks. Just one winged beetle could ram them off their course and strand them in the Wastelands. Turner doesn't have time for that. The driver focuses on the road and pays attention to both sides of the roadway. There's no more time for mistakes.

"Hi?" The dirty man waves to the armed mercenaries.

The man has a cloth wrapped around one eye, short black hair, and a thick dirty jacket on. His skin seems to be dark brown, but the skin on his neck is a few shades lighter than his dirty face. With a shower, he'd probably be around her complexion. There are traces of blood on his clothing, but Priya sees no bleeding wounds. He's wearing jeans that could have been blue at one point, and black boots.

He's a tall man. Priya guesses he's around six feet tall. He sounds young. Probably in his early twenties. She can see crusted blood along his square jaw and on his chin. Probably from crashing into the ditch during the storm.

Everyone, except for Turner, has a weapon drawn and aimed at the young man's head. Nard awkwardly holds his pistol with his left hand.

"Where are we headed?" the young man asks.

No one answers. He sighs and looks around at each of the mercenaries faces before his eyes widen a bit. Priya supposes he notices the body at her feet and Turner's injured form. He shuts up after that and turns toward the doors with his back to them.

Foolish. Priya squints at the back of the young man's head. *We could kill you and take your keys, idiot boy.*

A loud thud hits the roof of the truck. The vehicle jerks to the right and then swerves to the left. The passengers hold out their empty hands and steady themselves as the vehicle moves. Everyone looks at the ceiling.

There is a stinger embedded in the roof.

"Fu—" Priya mutters a curse under her breath while shifting her weapon to the ceiling.

Nard lowers his gun to his thigh and sighs. "It's one of those days," Nard comments.

"Yeah," the other men agree.

"Yup," the stranger chimes in.

"That's life. Stay alert. We've got fifteen minutes until we're home free. The guards won't fire until we're within range. Whatever this is better fly off if it knows what's good for it," Priya retorts. Another thud hits the ceiling of the truck. Then another and another.

"A…a swarm?" a female mercenary whispers.

"***Don't think!*** Wait for ***my*** orders!" Priya fights the urge to growl. A swarm of hornets is hunting them.

46%

2034
Wastelands
Southeast of W.A.R.T.S., New Cinalia

Everyone gets into position to defend themselves while stuck in the rapidly accelerating death trap. Priya gently moves the bundle toward the doors. The new passenger tries to get out of their way. Without a weapon, he'll be no help at all.

"Slide back beside him," Priya orders the stranger while pointing at Turner.

"Uuuh." The young man can't think of a reason to object, so he sidles his way to the back of the truck. Turner is still unconscious. Nard adjusts his awkward grip on his gun and fixes his back in a corner. He aims toward the punctured ceiling.

Bam!
Bam!
Bam!

Three more hornets slam into the truck and jam their stingers straight through the metal roof. The truck swerves once again and everyone holds out a limb to stay upright.

"Woah!" the stranger exclaims as he loses his balance.

Nard catches his shoulder, so the young man doesn't crush his injured comrade.

"Careful there. He's been through a lot," Nard comments before reaching back and pulling out a large blade. "If any of them get in here you stick them with this."

Nard holds it out to the stranger by the blade. The young man grimaces and hesitantly grasps the thick handle. Priya allows the exchange. The man is an unknown, but what choice do they have? An extra man to guard Turner could be the difference between his life or death.

The hornets pull away from the roof one after another. Everyone is confused.

"Did they leave?" a male mercenary asks.

The entire vehicle shudders as a large hornet lands on the roof. Skinny appendages stick through two of the holes. At that moment, Priya figures out what they've been doing all along.

"They made punctures to open the...Fire! Fire!!" Priya orders.

They all aim for the skinny appendages that are pulling on the roof. The metal tears. Bullet holes riddle the roof. Amber ooze drips down through the holes. It's a successful kill, but the frame of the roof is weakened even more by the bullet holes.

The stranger bats a line of amber hornet blood away from the sleeping injured man. It's sticky. When he shakes his palm, it doesn't come off. Regretfully, he smears the goop on his pant leg.

Not even five seconds later another thud sounds from the roof. The ceiling groans under the weight. There are no sudden movements.

"What's it looking like back there?" Ika asks through the radio. "I'm seeing large forms hovering above the roof."

Priya is pulling the radio up from her hip when the hornet grabs hold of two of the holes and pulls back while flying against the wind. The roof screeches as it bends. Priya drops her radio to better grip her weapon.

"Wait!" Priya yells to her men.

The stranger tries to make himself small. He covers his ears with the palms of his hands, the knife in his lap.

The ceiling peels back like a sardine can. Night hornets hover over the opening and prepare to zoom in and enjoy the fruits of their labor.

"Shoot!!" Priya orders.

The hornets are riddled with bullets. They're too close to dodge the shots. Their punctured wings crumble under their weight, dropping them from the sky. Not even a second later, two more hornets replace them.

"Again!" Priya orders.

The truck shakes as they're rammed at the side by the other giant hornets. As they're jarred once more, each shot narrowly missing the tops of their comrades' heads. A hornet dives in and stabs the nearest mercenary.

"Gaaaaah!" The man tries to halt the stinger's progress through his chest, but it's futile. He claws at the stinger for a moment before his heart stutters and stops within his chest.

A moment after the stinger injects him with fluid, the hornet rises out of the truck. The body slows its ascent and gives the mercenaries time to shoot the escaping yellow-striped hornet. It drops dead on the roof. The truck swerves once more. The dead hornet slides off the truck along with the body still attached to its stinger.

With the hole unobstructed, another attacker has a chance to dive in. The truck is rammed on the side and everyone moves around to be clear of the hole. Their weapons shake in their hands as the world trembles. The attacking hornet slips inside and aims its stinger for the stranger in the corner.

"Woah!" The stranger ducks under the stinger and dives to the empty ground.

The hornet is shot in the back, but it isn't enough. It's persistent. It needs to give the swarm a better chance at overtaking their prey. It needs to kill one.

The stranger grabs the closest thing—a bundle of cloth—and chucks it at the hornet. Its stinger rips through the middle

of the bundle and it prepares to fly up through the hole with the last of its strength.

"*No!!*" Priya rapidly fires at the large beast. She steps on the stranger's abdomen to get closer and shoot its red and yellow head. The head explodes and the black arms of the hornet slacken as its body drops to the truck floor.

"Uhh…Could you maybe—" the stranger calls up to the woman.

"Don't touch her! Her sacrifice deserves honor. Not to be left out there to rot and be eaten…" Priya steps off the man's stomach.

What is she talking about? The cloth wrapped around the "heavy supplies" unravels. *Oh. Oh god.*

Priya reaches down and tugs the pierced body off of the night hornet's stinger. The decapitated body isn't very large. He can see pale, childlike fingers flop out at the sides of a tan leather jacket. On the shoulder of the jacket is a patch, a black star.

Priya wraps the body back up in the dirtied white cloth. Gently, she lowers the body to the floor and gropes at her hip for her radio. It's not there. She turns to her men at the doors. "Any of you seen my radio?"

Pheno checks Turner's vitals. Nard spots the knife he'd given the new guy on the ground. Nard sighs. "Not much of a fighter," Nard mutters as he bends down to reach the knife.

The stranger is quiet. He feels guilty about defiling someone's corpse, but also grateful to the corpse for saving his life. "What was his name?"

Priya accepts the radio from her subordinate, and her gaze softens as she thinks of Kid.

"We called her Kid." Priya answers.

"Kid? That's not much of a name."

The truck drives over a bump. Priya ducks her head so it doesn't collide with the ceiling. She takes a step back and holds a hand to the roof to steady herself. "She was from one of those wandering groups. Real tough," Priya's eyes cloud as she remembers meeting the young woman for the first time. "Her real name was Car—"

The truck is rammed on the side and Priya loses her balance. A bright yellow night hornet stinger drops into the hole, but it has no space to stab anyone. Instead, it grabs Priya's arm and clothing with four of its appendages and flies up into the dark night. Priya spins in the air, kicking and screaming in the hornets grasp. Nard drops his weapon and grabs the radio off his hip.

"Stop! Stop the truck!" Nard screams into the radio. "They got Priya!" The truck doesn't stop. The tires protest the wild turn the driver executes at hearing those words. Ika's night vision goggles tap against the door frame while he lowers his window. He slides his body through and balances his lower abdomen on the sill as the truck speeds back down the road. He lifts his rifle, holds his breath, and aligns himself with a target.

"They got Priya!" Nard repeats into the radio. The hornet holding Priya curls down to pull her body higher, into a better position to sting, as another hornet rushes over to sting her as well.

Bang!

A bullet cuts through the head of the hornet approaching Priya's body. He takes aim again, but the truck is rammed by a group of hornets and it forces him to fall back into his seat.

"Damn it!" Ika scrambles back into the window, but Priya is out of sight. It's all winged creatures and darkness. The hornets appear to be flying away now. The swarm is retreating from something. The stars can spare no light to illuminate Priya to his eyes. Ika tears off his goggles and blinks out into the dark night. Nothing. He lowers himself back inside. He kicks the dashboard and rips the goggles from around his neck to toss them at the windshield. The driver presses a button and raises Ika's window back up.

"Boss?" They're still driving in the opposite direction. Before Ika can give an order, they hear a siren go off. They're

within range of W.A.R.T.S. That siren is an alert for a coming sandstorm. It goes off once more and shuts off. "Turn around. Head to W.A.R.T.S." Ika commands. Ika changes the frequency on his radio and listens in.

"Warning! Anyone within range of HQ, enter the vehicle depot. Anyone within range of HQ, enter the vehicle depot. All wards will be shut down until the storm passes. All wards will be shut down in ten minutes. Warning! Anyone within range of HQ, enter—" Ika grunts and changes the frequency back to his team's.

"We can't go back! Priya is out there! We have to go get her!!" Nard screams into the radio.

"Sandstorm." Ika presses the radio to his chin, eyes transfixed on the darkness on the other side of his window.

"I don't give a damn about no damn storm!" Nard rages into the radio.

"..."

"Chief...Chief, come on. We lost Kid. We lost Ralph and em...We can't...we can't lose—" Nard begs into the radio. The radio slips from Nard's hand. Pheno frowns and retrieves it from the ground.

"We need to rush Turner into medical as soon as possible. He's already lost a lot of blood. I don't know how much more of this he can take," Pheno reports.

"Roger," Ika replies and changes the frequency again. "Incoming. Numero Dos, incoming. We have two injured. One critical. ETA 5 minutes," Ika calls in.

Someone from the radio room replies not a second later. "Roger that. Dos, we'll have a space open for you and your men. Hurry. The storm is fast approaching."

Ika sets the radio onto his thigh. He runs a hand through his dirty, blond bangs as he looks up at the night sky through his window. A few constellations are still visible to the naked eye. The only beauty that Cinalians can enjoy without fear that it may be destroyed before their very eyes. Ika grimaces as he spots Algol[3]. He turns away from the sky. A bright blue star winks down at the wrecked earth beneath it. The demon star winks once more down at the pitiful world. No one winks back.

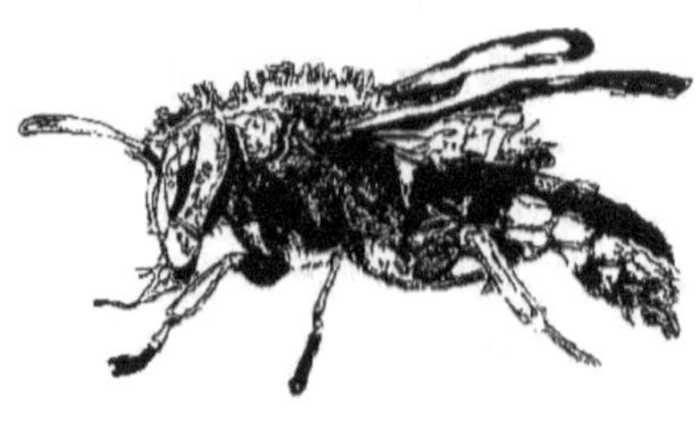

---

[3] Algol is a star that is easy to see with the naked eye. It is not alone. A companion star eclipses it and makes it appear as if it is blinking. Algol's nickname is the Demon Star.

47%

2034
Vehicle Depot, W.A.R.T.S.

They speed into W.A.R.T.S with a couple minutes to spare before the gates are locked down. The armored vehicle is a wreck. The roof has been peeled back, there are dents in several parts of the metal, and bullet holes have damaged every wall.

The people within the vehicle are worn in mind and body. The newcomer feels shell-shocked after the series of events that occurred not even ten minutes ago.

Two mercenaries burst the back door open and rush to grab something to carry their injured comrade on.

"Over here! We dragged over a medical cabinet and a bed for him," a male voice comments from outside the truck.

"Careful now!" Pheno shouts as he follows the group.

The stranger sits still on a bench inside the truck as everyone evacuates the filthy space. The remains of a red and yellow night hornet lying across the sticky floor. The newcomer sighs and slides along the bench trying to avoid the dead insect before hopping out of the truck.

The young man's uncovered brown eye observes the area. *So, this is the vehicle depot that was mentioned.*

A door slams shut from behind the newcomer. Ika stomps by and pauses to look back at the new guy. The young man tilts his head down guiltily and glances through his eyelashes at the stern fellow. When he sees the heated stare the guy is giving him, he flinches. *Dammit. Dammit. Does he think I'm to blame?*

Ika glares for several moments at the new guy before waving a hand and continuing in the direction he was primarily going.

"Uuuh." The young man turns around in search of where to go. His thick, soiled jacket is uncomfortable in the warm underground parking garage, but he's afraid to unzip it. *Was he waving at me?* He fiddles with the zipper of his jacket.

"Let's go!" He hears the man shout.

The young man runs to catch up to his quick-footed guide. They pass by vans, cars, and groups of people setting up tents. The area appears to be an underground parking lot. Some people have small grills set up to heat up food, and others are boiling water. There are not many children, but the young man can hear tiny voices conversing somewhere. His vision isn't as perfect as he'd prefer, but his hearing is flawless.

He hears several people speaking in different languages as well. A high pitched voice was loudly speaking Spanish before he heard a gasp and fast footsteps approach from behind.

"Hermano!!" a woman yells from behind the newcomer.

His guide stops walking and turns to the speaker.

"Hermano, did you just get in? ¿Que pasó?!" The woman marches toward his guide.

She's taller than the guide and wearing an open jean jacket. Her black crop top shows off her dark brown toned stomach, and her tan khaki shorts have additional pockets stitched into the fabric. The man stays silent until the woman is within arm's reach. "Anita," the man whispers while deeply frowning.

She ignores the dirt and blood and holds him close. He remains still in her embrace as she whispers things to him. Her black curly hair hides most of her face from sight. The young man steps away from them in order not to intrude, but before

he steps out of hearing range he hears her whisper. "No es tu culpa. It's not your fault. Esta bien, cariño. It's okay."

The young man blows air through his teeth to make it harder for him to hear anything else. He looks away from the couple and dodges out of the way of several people rushing by. Everyone is setting up for the sandstorm, and it doesn't look like a new arrangement. There isn't any confusion or panicked faces.

"Move out the way!" a man holding a heavy pot of water shouts.

The young man hops back and out of the way. "Sorry, man. My bad," the newcomer apologizes. He looks back to see the couple has pulled away from each other and his guide is looking his way.

"Let's go, new guy!" his guide yells.

I'm right here. No need to yell, the young man thinks before following along. As he passes by the woman, he glances at her face. Her hazel eyes make contact with his brown eye. He sucks in a breath and averts his gaze. He blushes. *Caught being nosy. Gosh.*

His hand runs through his black hair and bumps the knot that keeps the cloth over his eye tightly wound around his head. When they get to the other end of the main floor, they come upon a stairwell that goes even lower underground. The young man pauses at the top of the staircase. "Where are we going?"

The guide taps his palm on the peeling yellow paint of the staircase railing.

"This leads you down to where our boss usually is during these storms," his guide explains.

"Why do I need to meet him?" the young man asks.

"Look, ki—Hmm, what's your name?" his guide asks the taller man while lifting his chin and scanning his larger form.

"My…Marcus," the young man lies.

"Mymarcus?"

"Marcus. Just Marcus…"

"Well, Marcus…" his guide continues.

"What's your name?" Marcus interrupts to ask.

"Ika. Marcus. Look. We're low on men right now. Usually, we don't just take in merchants from the Wastes, but we'll be low on a lot of things without the manpower to protect our current routes. We already have to deal with one group of Savages…I can't even think about how irritating it'll be to deal with the others." Ika sighs. "Anyway, what do you have to offer us for your protection?"

"I…uh…well…I have bouillon cubes, rice, and some other things. I can probably get more if I got a chance."

"Got a chance?" Ika asks.

"I need help getting a new vehicle to transport my things back."

"Well, vehicles, we have a lot of. Rice and those cubes? Nada. Maybe this might be good for us. Us coming across you." They start down the stairs again, but Marcus hears Ika murmur words under his breath. "At least for now."

Marcus pauses. He waits for Ika to start down the next staircase before voicing his concern. "Excuse me?"

Ika stops walking down the steps. "What?"

"What do you mean 'At least for now'?"

Ika raises an eyebrow and huffs. "If you haven't noticed—people don't last very long out here. We're all bound to die before we're ready. Get used to it," Ika grumbles before rushing down the rest of the steps. Ika opens the door at the bottom of the stairwell and exits into the next area.

Marcus doesn't follow right away. He waits several moments to gather himself and meditate on the situation. The faster this storm passes the faster he…No, *she* can escape these people. This is the worst possible outcome she could think of. Who would have thought that Sia would run right into the same mercenaries she'd been with at the start? She's done her best to disguise her looks and voice, but how long can she fool these people? The only thing that could make this even more of a disaster is if she ran into the Wanderer pair as well. *God. I'm screwed.* Sia taps a fist on her forehead before

refocusing her thoughts. She needs a plan before walking down there. She needs an angle.

While Sia is communicating with the device, Ika exits the stairwell with a deep frown and leans against the wall beside the door. He forces air out of his nose and tries to collect his thoughts. *Calmate. Calmate.* He adjusts his black jacket and scans the area for his boss's wheelchair.

This area of the vehicle depot is reserved for managers and the head of W.A.R.T.S. A lot of the rations and inventory are moved here during storms. A group of guards sit off to the side of the stairwell entrance and at the elevator at the other end of the level.

There are several tables set up in a square formation. At one table, a group of people are sitting and checking ammunition. Across from that table, people are looking over large lights and a generator. The table nearest to the exit only has empty chairs. At the head table sits a man in a wheelchair who's speaking with a person with long, deep burgundy locks atop their head. The standing individual is holding a sheet of paper and motioning to details on it. Their voices combine and echo throughout the makeshift room.

Everyone's clothing looks worn, but no one is dirty or smelling of foul things like Ika. He shoves his trembling hands into his pockets and strolls over to his boss. By the time he gets over to the tables, most of the people that were conversing are leaving to go to the upper level.

Ika grunts and lifts a chin in acknowledgment of Dennis. Dennis lays a dark brown hand on his advisor's wrist and moves the paperwork away.

Ika walks deeper into the level away from the tables. Dennis wheels after him. When Ika feels they are far enough not to be overheard, he stops and turns to his older brother. Dennis pushes down on his brakes and focuses on his brother's tense face. "What's up?"

Ika slides the bottom of his shoes against the asphalt and lifts a trembling hand to rub an eyebrow. The frown of his lips gets deeper and deeper as time goes on. He sighs and turns away from Dennis.

"Lobito, I heard Turner is out and Nard was injured. Lo entiendo, it's tough with your team out for the count, but…Keep your chin up." Dennis unlocks his brakes and glides closer.

"Turner's lost his leg," Ika whispers.

"Aah." Dennis tugs on the lobe of his pierced ear.

"Nard's arm was impaled. Priya is gone. Ralph's squad isn't missing…They're all dead." Ika blurts out to finish the debriefing.

Dennis blows his breath and doesn't speak until he can figure out something to say. Something to lift the responsibility from Ika's shoulders and absolve him of the blame he can see burning his brother's insides. In his peripheral, he can see minute trembles that start at his brothers' fingers and ride up his arms.

Ika sucks in a breath and blinks away the tears welling up in his eyes. "A lo hecho, pecho. What's done is done." His voice wavers at the last word. He tsks at himself and rubs the sparse hair on his chin. He rips the blue scarf from his neck as if it's restricting his breathing. It falls to the floor.

"Well." Dennis struggles to address the awful situation. "Kelly's men are on their way here. It should be any day now."

Ika nods and the hand rubbing his chin idles toward his lower lip, he nibbles at the thumbnail. The salty mud underneath the nail dissolves in his mouth. He can taste a hint of blood as well. His own or…

Dennis swipes at the other man's arm to pop the thumbnail out of Ika's mouth. With an exhausted sigh, Ika shoves his dirty hand into his pocket. "Where are your snacks? You know Anita hates you doing that. Anyway," Dennis pushes forward with false cheer. "Good news. Sidney caught word of a humanitarian group that's coming through near Brook. West of Brook, if he caught the coordinates correctly."

Ika grunts and licks his chapped lips. It's nothing new. Humanitarian aid used to come by frequently at the start of all this and they always left before making contact with natives. Usually, dropping a crate in a vacant field. Some merchants have even transported entire crates directly to W.A.R.T.S because they have no tools to open the large containers.

"Have you eaten?"

Before Ika can answer the stairwell exit slams open and the stranger marches through. Ika almost forgot about him. He stands upright as he eyes the new guy from across the room. The stranger scans the room and spots Ika.

Ika can see determination that hadn't been on his face a couple minutes ago. When Marcus gets closer to the pair, Ika doesn't look away. There's something familiar about this man. He can't quite figure it out, but…

Black hair and dark skin aren't unusual. They're the usual case these days with not as many tourists as before. The young man, Marcus, is tall and has wide shoulders. His jacket hides much of his upper body. Ika can't tell if he has any muscle beneath the puffy jacket.

What is it about him? Ika examines Marcus's shoes. Black rubber boots. Ika blinks a few times. Ika looks back up at that brown eye as the young man speaks.

"I think we should get back to my supplies as soon as possible!" he shouts.

Ika opens his mouth, but Dennis speaks first. "Hermano, who is this?"

Ika shrugs. "We crashed into his van on our way here."

Dennis thinks on that for a moment before coming to a decision. "You can leave when the storm passes. Not a moment before and several hours after. We never know when nature decides to hit us again just to be a frigid bit—"

"No!" Marcus interrupts Dennis. "We don't have time for that. We have to go now! By the time the storm finishes everything will be destroyed. He said you need the supplies. Shouldn't this be your first priority?"

Dennis's brows furrow. "We aren't endangering any more lives for some of your stuff."

"It's food! Rations! Things you can't live without!" Marcus insists. "Who are you anyway? Didn't you say we were meeting your boss?" Marcus directs the latter question to Ika who is comically widening his eyes.

"He *is* the boss." He cocks his head to the side, challenging Marcus to continue. Marcus's shoulders droop.

"Rompiste tu camioneta, tal vez por tu bien, bobo.[4]" Dennis mutters to himself. "You'll wait, rest, and when the storm ends, we'll lead you back to your crash," Dennis tells Marcus.

Ika suppresses a laugh and walks away. Marcus huffs at Dennis's decision, but has lost momentum. His head swivels back and forth, eyes fixed to the ground, when he spots Ika's blue scarf. "Oh!" Marcus exclaims before reaching down and scooping up the baby blue cotton scarf.

Marcus trots over to Ika and grasps his shoulder. Dennis places a hand over his gaping mouth as he watches the disaster about to happen. *Tonto[5], what you doing?* Dennis waits for Ika to strike.

"You dropped your scarf!"

Ika adjusts his footing and brings a hand up to grasp Marcus's wrist.

CAUTION!
OVER THE SHOULDER THROW INITIATED
It happens in a split second. Ika pulls Marcus's arm to initiate an over the shoulder throw, but Marcus takes two steps to the side. Ika accounts for the change in Marcus's position and slides a leg behind Marcus. As he reaches down to scoop Marcus off his feet…something unusual happens.
SUKUI NAGE (SCOOP THROW) INITIATED

---

[4] You broke your truck, maybe for your own good, idiot.
[5] Fool.

Marcus steps forward two steps and spins out of Ika's grasp. The younger male blinks as he looks at Ika's tense form. The blue scarf is still dangling from his other hand. "Uuuh. Sorry?"

Ika steps forward and Marcus steps back. Ika glares at the other male. He'd thought the younger man would have easily succumbed to that throw, but he'd immediately reacted to his movements. Not many can do that.

Dennis's eyebrows are raised to their highest point. *The hell?!* Marcus tosses the scarf at the shorter male and cautiously retreats to the stairwell. He checks over his shoulder several times before jogging to the exit and vanishing behind the metal door. Dennis wheels himself over to Ika while the man rotates his wrist. Dennis chuckles. "No juzgues a un libro por su cubierta, Lobito[6]. I guess you found your match"

"Ha ha, vete para el carajo, pendejo[7]," Ika mutters under his breath and stalks to the stairwell as well.

Dennis pretends to be offended and gasps. "You kiss my mother with that mouth?!" he shouts at Ika's back.

Marcus is long gone by the time Ika opens the stairwell door.

---

[6] Don't judge a book by its cover, little wolf.
[7] Go to hell, motherfucker.

48%

2034
W.A.R.T.S., New Cinalia

Marcus rushes into the crowd on the main level. He finds a spot behind a tent to crouch and hide. Marcus glances over his shoulder before whispering. "I don't know what the hell just happened, but thanks for the save."

He, or rather, she clears her throat a few times. Pretending to be male is easier with the device keeping her vocals on the lower end. No one has looked twice at her. Her height and angular face have always been a disadvantage for her love life, but now it seems to be her saving grace. She stared right in Ika's face and he didn't recognize her. She rubs a hand along her square jaw and smirks. *Maybe I was built for espionage.*

WHY DIDN'T SUBJECT 001 MENTION THE GPS SCAN AND KNOWLEDGE OF THE COORDINATES TO ACQUIRE THEIR—

If I told them Priya is alive they'd want to have proof and know how I know. Then we're back to being interrogated.

APEX WOULD NOT HIDE THIS INFORMATION

"I'm not—" Sia bites her lip. *I'm not Apex, and he said my orders are the same as his. Revealing this information would put me in danger. Isn't that against priority one?*

AFFIRMATIVE

This is a good thing. A door slams open and heavy footsteps stomp toward the tents. She pretends to tie her shoelaces until they pass by. When the footsteps continue by without incident, Sia rises and mingles with the crowd. She's one of the tallest and her height is a clear advantage. It gives her a clear view atop their heads while she stalks through the throng of people like a snake in the grass. In the distance, white sheets are hung up over thick cords of rope. It screams 'medical area' as clearly as police caution tape signifies a crime has been committed.

She weaves through the crowd until she's nearby. *We have to do this alone. If we succeed, they'll be indebted to us. That's what you want. No one's going to trust us this early, and we don't have enough supplies. If you want men to storm those labs for Apex, we need people that won't just leave us behind when things get tough. We need to make them want to repay us and want our approval.*

She peeks into a gap in the white screen and sees Turner's unconscious body laid out on a makeshift stretcher. The sheets on the thin cot are stained red. Turner appears like a corpse for several moments, but the tiny tremors in his chest and shoulders verify that he's indeed still among the living.

He and Ika were the two most involved with us before. If we can fool those two into believing I'm a guy, we can fool them all. This could work.

A wooden table is sitting beside the cot with a few items on top. There are small glass bottles with clear liquid inside of them. The labels are small. Beside the glass bottles are packaged cylindrical items piled atop each other. There is a large strip of letters that reads 'Warning:' and minuscule letters with information about the item.

Can you identify those things from here?

SCANNING…

MORPHINE

UNUSED SYRINGES

All of those are morphine?

AFFIRMATIVE

Well…I think he can spare a few for his friend. Sia inches over to the other side of the bed. Everyone seems to be busy.

"What are you doing?" an accented voice pops up behind her.

Sia jumps and spins around. She doesn't see anyone. Sia tilts her head and looks to the left. *What the hell?* She frowns at the short man standing off to the side in her blind spot. Sia adjusts the blindfold on her left eye. *Damn it.*

"Worried?" Pheno moves the faded white sheet aside as he slides past Sia.

"Y…Yeah but…but I didn't want to disturb him." She shuffles over to the other side of the bed and faces away from the table. "He looked really bad off. I'm glad you were able to help him out." Sia's nervous tone causes Pheno to examine the quiet form on the bed.

Pheno steps over to the foot of the bed and gestures to the bulky bandaged knee joint that peeks out of the stained sheet. Pheno sighs. "We had to get rid of much below the knee, but it went well."

Sia nods to the doctor. Her polite smile thins as she imagines the surgery. "When will he wake up?"

"Not sure. The supplies here are scant. We put him under as soon as we could." Pheno gestures to the metal shelving unit against the wall. "I don't have what I want. I don't have what I need." Pheno shakes his head. "He will wake and we shall see what comes next. No need to worry."

Sia's mind blanks for a moment. The polite words she had been taught to say as a child would not fit this situation. After a long moment of silence, Sia remarks. "Then I won't…" Pheno nods and sits down in a chair near the bed. Sia slides past the sitting man and gives a small wave. "Well, I'm—" She points to the flimsy white sheet that blocks the bustling crowd outside from seeing what's been done here.

Pheno nods dismissively and pulls a wad of papers from his pocket. He looks down at the pages. Sia awkwardly nods and scurries off in a random direction. After a moment of following the flow of the crowd, Sia spots parked vehicles. She nudges her way to the edge of the stream of people and

stumbles out among old, modified automotives. When she's hidden among the cars and trucks, she pulls a bottle of morphine and a sealed syringe pack out of her jacket pocket. Sia gazes at the items with a triumphant smile. "Pretty cool, S.I.D. I didn't know you could do that."

...

"Now, you need to wow me with your automotive knowledge. You know how to hotwire a car?" Sia pockets the items again and waits for a response. It takes a moment but the device replies.

AFFIRMATIVE

"Good. Good. Well, let's go."

Ika pushes open the door to the stairwell and jogs into the crowd on the main level. The door crashes into the wall, swings on its hinges, and closes by itself. He keeps his eyes up high and marches through the gaggle of civilians. When he reaches a cement wall, he turns in a circle and returns back the way he came.

Faded white sheets stick out in his peripheral. Ika alters his plans and strides toward the makeshift emergency care corner. He slides a hand into a gap in the sheets and lifts the sheet to gain entrance into the cordoned area. As usual, he frowns at the lack of certain elements that were a comfort in the old world. The absence of EKG machines, IV poles, anesthesia devices, and sterilization equipment fills him with trepidation. He falters when he gains sight of the bulky stump hidden under the blanket. His jaw tightens.

"I'm surprised. You're my second visitor," Pheno comments while reading the messy scrawl on his papers. Ika steps forward and presses his palm against Turner's head. The injured man's forehead is damp with sweat, but he doesn't seem to be in immense pain.

Ika wipes his hand on his pant leg. "Did it go well?"

Pheno's shoulders raise slightly. "Time will tell."

Ika sighs and rubs his forehead with the back of his hand. He glances over at the top of the seated man's head. *Not very reassuring, are you?* Thinning brown hair dusts across a tanned scalp. The doctor's hunched shoulders almost meet his ears as he examines his notes. Pheno pulls a short pencil out of his pocket. Ika's eyes fixate on the medic's stained sleeve as his small hand scribbles on a crowded page.

Pheno seems to sense Ika's attention and lifts his head to make eye contact with the other man. Apathetic eyes of black meet Ika's stormy gray orbs. Ika's upper lip twitches at the indifference in the medical professional's gaze. Ika averts his eyes and turns back to Turner's unconscious form. A phrase from an old television show he used to watch pops into his mind. *Fire the receptionist.*

The doctor's brow creases and sets his paperwork onto his knees. "You think the guy we found has access to medical supplies?" Pheno asks.

Ika stares at Turner's ghostly complexion. "He didn't mention having any meds. Just food."

"Well, if you find the time…" Pheno mutters. "I shoulda asked when he was here." The doctor scribbles something out of his notes and taps the end of his pencil against his thin lips.

"What?"

"Too slow today…I told you. The new guy was here first."

Ika's brow raises. "Did he mention where he was going next?"

"No."

He strides over to a sheet to exit the area. "Which way did he go?" Pheno points him in the direction Marcus had exited the makeshift medical quarters. Ika vanishes on the other side of the sheets. He briskly marches toward the mass of flowing bodies. Ika grits his teeth as he elbows through the crowd. When he reaches the other side, he breaks away from the sea of dwellers. He's standing beside a cement beam when he pulls out his radio. "Anyone see a tall guy in a puffy brown jacket? Unknown face. Over."

He leans against the beam and taps the radio against his thigh as he waits. The cement is cool against the back of his

neck. He slides a thumbnail between his teeth and tugs on the edge of it as he waits. The nail is salty and firm under the scraping of his teeth.

Ika blinks up at the cracks as he digs his tooth beneath his thumbnail. Thin lines mark the ceiling of the underground parking garage. Scarring from the first major disaster this place withstood. He's debating tearing off the nail when a transmission comes through.

"Unknown face? There's a guy walking around the trucks right now. Over."

Ika's hand drops from his mouth when he hears that. "Copy."

49%

2034
Vehicle Depot, W.A.R.T.S.

Ika pockets his radio and makes his way around the edge of the crowd. When he gains sight of parked vehicles, he jogs toward the packed lot. He finds Marcus arguing with a guard. The guard is gripping the young man's forearm and holding it up to his chest. Marcus is forced to stand on the tips of his toes.

"No. I wasn't **ordered** here!" Marcus kicks at the aggressive guard's shin. "I'm looking for something! Let go!"

The behemoth is unfazed by the kick. "Then tell me what you're looking for. Odd, that you say you're not trespassing, but I got a message to look out for an unknown person wandering around." The guard pulls out his radio.

"I feel profiled. I'm being profiled!"

"What? What are you talking about?" The guard frowns and shakes Marcus's arm. "Answer the question. What are you looking for?"

Marcus winces at the tight grip. "You don't have to be so violent with me. I didn't do anything! There must be a real intruder and you're wasting your time with me!"

"How about you—"

"Good, you've found him." Ika strolls over to the pair.

The guard turns around and yanks Marcus along as he acknowledges Ika. "Brown jacket, unknown face, sir. Is this the guy you're looking for? The thief?"

"Thief? No, he's…I just needed help rounding up the lost merchant. Good work." Ika nods at the guard.

The guard nods back and releases his hold on Marcus. Marcus stumbles forward and rubs his forearm. He stands beside Ika and whirls around to glare at the large guard.

The guard hooks a thumb in his belt and sneers at Marcus. "I could escort him to the Merchant quarters, sir. This one can be a handful."

"I've got it," Ika waves the guard away.

"He's got it," Marcus repeats and copies Ika's hand movements out of sight, above his head. The guard glares at Marcus, his hand idles by his side, above his weapon holster. Marcus takes a step behind Ika and raises his eyebrows, challenging the man to continue.

"I said, I've got it from here." Ika repeats. The guard drops his hand away from his side, nods again at his superior and jogs back over to his post. His short ponytail is the last thing seen as he disappears past an armored black Hummer.

Ika turns to the younger man. "So, what were you looking for?"

"What?" Marcus's brows meet and he scratches at the top of his head. Ika frowns at him and waits for an answer. "Well, the thing is. I don't know where the beat-up truck we came here in…went. I thought it would be easy to spot and got lost."

"Follow me." Ika leads the way through the maze of vehicles.

Marcus is a step behind at all times. "I…uhh…I appreciate the help. I…I didn't lose anything. I just…It's just I left it behind and couldn't find the truck. It's not mine, per say, but that man gave it to me, and I didn't think he'd appreciate me leaving it with that—"

Ika abruptly stops and Marcus collides with his back. They stumble forward a step. Marcus grabs Ika's shoulders to straighten up and Ika elbows the other man away from him.

"Ouch." Marcus breaks away from the other. "Sorry! Sorry. Why'd you stop so quick?" Ika gives Marcus a blank stare and dusts off a shoulder. Before them is the hole-ridden armored truck they'd exited in a hurry. "Oh." Marcus clasps his hands together and tips his head toward Ika in gratitude. "Thanks."

Ika turns away from the truck and pulls out his radio to call in that the search is over. Marcus climbs into the truck. The hornet's body is just as they'd left it. The wings are crushed under the red and yellow body.

Marcus sits beside the remains on a metal bench and scans the floor. Ika turns to him after completing his radio message, and frowns at the mysterious merchant. "Can't find it?"

Marcus nervously smiles and rubs his sweaty palms on his knees, "Well, no, but I—" He gestures to the hornet remains.

"Hurry up. I need to drop you off at your quarters." Ika taps his empty wrist.

Marcus blinks down at Ika and visibly swallows. He steps over the hornet remains, and moves the winged corpse with his boot. Viscous, amber blood coats it. A squishing sound emits from the corpse's back as it's raised off the floor. Marcus grimaces and pulls his foot away. The corpse thuds back down on the floor. Marcus rubs his hands on his thighs and steps over to the other side of the body. He peers down at the floor for a long moment.

Ika ignores the other man and sits on the bumper of a car beside the damaged truck. He pulls out his radio and presses the scan button to search for any information broadcasts. A look of triumph crosses Marcus face before he frowns and concentrates on his new task. He kneels on the floor and reaches underneath the metal bench welded to the wall, retrieving a long bundle of white cloth. The stained sheet almost unravels again.

"Woah!" Marcus exclaims as he catches the bundle between his legs. He ties the loose ends with two knots and holds the bundle against his chest. Ika rises from the car bumper when he hears the loud exclamation and returns to check on the odd man.

Ika is holding his radio to his ear. He lowers his radio when he sees what Marcus is holding. "What are you doing?!"

"Your friend…I don't think I could sleep tonight knowing she was left here with this thing." He adjusts his grip on the bundle and hops out of the back. "It'd be a shame to leave her behind."

Ika turns off his radio and puts it back on his waist clip. "Follow me." Ika stomps off to exit the car lot area.

"Uuh…." Marcus follows while taking a good look at where they exit the car lot. They head toward the entrance of the vehicle depot. Ika is a few meters ahead of Marcus when the gated entrance to the underground garage comes within sight.

Stray bits of sand are flying around at the entrance. The four guards are wearing green scarves over their faces while they sit in lawn chairs several meters away out of range of the storm. Night vision goggles are slid over their eyes. They're armed with rifles, and even while relaxing, their hands remain holding their weapons.

They are talking amongst themselves and staring at the spiked, metal gate. Wires are twisted around its outer frame. They trail along the concrete floor to connect to the generators lined up off to the side.

"Stop there," Ika leaves Marcus and marches over to a guard. Marcus adjusts his grip on the bundle and holds his chin up to breath some cleaner, less death-smelling, air.

10 mins, you said?

AFFIRMATIVE

Ika strides back over from speaking with the guards and motions for Marcus to come forward. "We'll leave her with these guys. They know what to do." Ika reaches out and takes the bundle from Marcus.

"Oh…It's not heavy. I can carry—"

"I've got her." Ika glares up at Marcus before turning and carrying the body over to the guards. The guards ignore Ika as he walks over to the left of the entrance, in the range of the storm. The wind rustles his blond hair as he walks across to a shadowed corner. He crouches down and places the body gently to the floor. He splays his fingers out on the stained sheet and bows his head.

Marcus joins the guards. He stops behind a wide man with some gray hair peeking out the neck of his scarf. "How long do you think this'll last?"

At first, the man doesn't answer, and Marcus thinks he spoke too softly. He opens his mouth to repeat the question when the guard replies. "No one can say. One day or five."

Marcus frowns and nods. "Oh. Okay, I get it. Unpredictable."

"Yeah," another guard joins in. "And even if this were to last a day it might be a short lull before it picks up again. I hate this weather. I'll never get used to it."

"Used to be a fair here about this time of the year," another guard turns away from the storm and looks at Marcus.

"A fair? Here?"

"Oh man," the three other guards groan.

"Just a few blocks from here, and you know that's what this place is named after," The standing guard motions to the storm outside with his rifle. "Wallace Allen Rode The Sy-clone."

"We keep telling you cyclone starts with a "C" not an "S"," one guard says. "Don't take him seriously, kid. He makes up a new story every time."

"Why the hell would it be named Wallace Allen Rode a…Why would the boss name the place after you?"

"Hey! I'm a great guy. I've been here since the beginning unlike you. At first, there was no name. Then after all the jobs were assigned, the name was announced…that's not a coincidence," Wallace settles back down onto his lawn chair. His green scarf stretches across his cheeks as he smiles.

"That's a crap name if ever there was one," a guard mutters. Marcus chuckles at the conversation.

"Ask the boss! We're buds. I know how precious I am to him," Wallace declares with his chin up. He crosses his leg over his knee.

"Lower your voice, you idiot. He's praying!" a guard shouts at Wallace. Marcus's smirk fades as he looks over to Ika, but the man is already walking over to them. His blue scarf is pulled up over his nose.

"Let's go," Ika's muffled voice calls out before he swiftly departs.

"Uhh." Marcus waves to the seated guards and catches up to his guide. "To the Merchant quarters?" Marcus matches his speed with his guide.

Ika grunts and continues facing forward with his scarf still placed over his nose. Marcus slows down and follows from behind. He turns his head and notes every turn.

The "Merchants Quarters" within the underground garage is just a few cots in a far corner away from the other dwellers. There is a black sheet hung between two cement beams that marks off the section. Twelve slim cots are settled closely together with a wool blanket dropped on each cot. Six of the twelve beds are occupied. Ika stops under the black sheet and waves toward the cots. "Here you go."

"Uh, where do I—" Marcus starts, but Ika has already stomped off somewhere else. "Never mind."

Alone at last. She walks over to a cot near the entrance and picks up the rough wool blanket. When she stretches it out before herself, it only covers up to her knees. "Sigh, of course." Sia rolls the blanket into a pillow and puts it at the head of the bed.

She lies down on the cot and ignores the creaking of the springs. She has to bend her legs at the knee and turn on her side to make sure her entire body is supported by the bed. It's been a while since she's had to sleep in a bed made for someone a foot shorter than her. Dirt from the bottom of her boots rubs off, onto the faded sheets. She closes her eyes, but her mind continues to work overtime about the current

situation. Their current problem. *How's it look out there? Can you still see her?*
     NEGATIVE

50%

2034
W.A.R.T.S., New Cinalia

Ika ambles away from the "Merchant Quarters" with a deep frown on his face. *Why does a complete stranger care?* He nods at a guard as he walks into the green zone. *Did someone tell him about Kid? Who? Why the hell does he care?* He mulls over those thoughts while strolling toward a section of the underground garage where his team usually settles down: the pink section. A pink cloth hangs over a piece of rope high above the entrance. Metal tables and wide tents decorate this area. Some of the tables have loaded weapons waiting for use or maintenance, while folded chairs are closed and stored atop the other tables.

Ika pauses behind a tent. He takes a deep breath and smooths out the furrow on his brow before turning the corner and meeting what's left of his team. He turns into an overall empty area with three tables. Tents surround the recreational space. This is where his team spends their time before bed.

Only one table is occupied. It has two folding chairs pulled in underneath it. A deck of cards is open and a few are scattered on the table top. An ace, a card with the number two on it, and a joker lie across the metal surface of the table. The only one occupying the space along with those cards is a despairing form hunched over in their chair. Nard's head hangs low, tucked into the shelter of his forearm fortress. His braids are spilled across the table. The table's metal frame trembles from the constant bounce of the injured man's leg.

Ika scuffs the bottom of his shoes against the concrete floor as he approaches his subordinate. Nard's knee falters in its bounce for a moment before continuing back to its manic quivering. Ika collapses into a folding chair at the other end of the table. He glares at the table top as he thinks of something to say. The bandaged brown forearm in his peripheral reminds him of the loyalty and courage all of his companions have shown, yet few have been rewarded. Were they destined to die, or is it the fault of his command?

His jaw clenches and each breath reminds him of the bruising on his stomach and back. Pains that remind him of life and its daily struggles. Struggles Carla and Priya have left behind in their journeys to the afterlife.

Life is loss. Cheap sayings fill his mind, but they don't quell the tremors he feels in his aching heart. Convincing himself that his grief is a waste of time fails. The expectations for their day were vastly different from this current outcome. Priya and Carla are gone, and Turner is disabled. His breath shudders. *Damn it.* Ika places a hand over his eyes and tilts his head back.

His nose burns as tears outpour from his eyes. He seals his mouth shut by biting his lower lip. His face is damp with anguish as the flow of tears spills down the sides of his tilted head into the folds of his ears and down his neck.

The chatter and traffic of people slink into the background as they disappear to their designated areas to catch some shut-eye. Neither man hears the call of sleep. They ruminate on what they did wrong, how they could have fixed the situation, and who they could have saved. The night is long.

Sia wakes up bright and early. "Noooooo. What the heck is wrong with these people?" she groans into the cot's stiff mattress. The clashing of metal cookware and loud chatter of

people passing by forces "Marcus" to give up on sleeping and finally start the day.

She stretches her legs off the thin cot and groans at the chalky taste in her mouth and the slick feel of sweat. Her shirts are damp beneath the uncomfortably warm jacket. She unzips the jacket and uses a thumb to pull at the collar of her two shirts to air out her chest. The minute change in temperature makes her feel less like a baked potato. She sniffs at her armpits and cringes. *Ugh, I smell like someone collected the sweat of a football team and sprayed a feral dog with it.* When she sits up, the cloth wrapped around her head slides down her nose. "Tsk!"

She unties the knot and her fingers graze the metal plating around the back of her head. She leans forward against her knees and cards fingers through her hair to cover the thin metal plate. Then she tightens the knot over the back of her head. She pats the knot to make sure it's secure then raises her head up to sit straight. Her eye looks up from the floor and is greeted by the sight of a small child staring into her face. Their green sunken eyes seem to peer right into her soul.

Her heart skips a beat. "Uuh." The metal legs of the cot screech as Sia abruptly stands up. *Did he see?!* She zips her puffy brown jacket back up and glances around the merchant quarters. There are a few cots occupied by sleeping adults, but no one that appears to have had a child resting with them. Sia doesn't remember seeing a child last night. *Oh god…oh god…where did he come from? Why didn't I hear him? Why didn't—*

"Did you lose an eye?" The young boy is chewing on the collar of his shirt.

"What?" Sia gapes at the child with wide eyes.

The boy pulls the shirt collar from his mouth to repeat his question. "You lose an eye or something?"

Sia nervously smiles down at the kid. "Uuh…sort of?" She sits back down and observes the child. The boy has a light complexion, but Sia is sure that it's a sign of illness to be that particular shade of white. He looks about eight or nine years old. He's barefoot and wearing shorts with a faded collared shirt. The fabric at the edge of the shirt is torn and threadbare.

The shorts appear to have been a pair of pants that were cut at the thighs. As the boy chews his collar, the bottom of the garment rides up to reveal his gaunt stomach.

"Sort of? You either lost ya eye or not." The child cocks his head to the side and raises an eyebrow.

"Well…uuh…the eyeball is there. But it…well…it's a useless eye. It's not working." Sia peers over her shoulder for a moment. *Why didn't you tell me the kid was there?*

THE YOUNG HUMAN APPEARS TO LACK SUFFICIENT NUTRIENTS AND AWARENESS OF ITS ENVIRONMENT

ELIMINATING THE JUVENILE WOULD NOT BE DIFFICULT

I'm not "eliminating" a child! That's never an option, okay?

THE YOUNG HUMAN IS A THREAT TO SUBJECT 001'S PHYISICAL WELL BEING

VITAL INFORMATION HAS BEEN SEEN

Children are off limits, okay?!

…

Okay?

AFFIRMATIVE

The stream of people nearby is constant. The sandstorm has altered everyone's plans for outdoor work, but hasn't affected their overall plans for the day. Survival depends on unceasing work and preparations. Sia can't pick out any guards from the crowd. No one looks like they are in a panic looking for their child either. *What do they expect me to do with myself until the storm ends?* When she looks back over at the child, he's settling down on the cot across from her. "Should you even be over here? Where are your parents?" The child shrugs and lies down on his side. The skinny body is dwarfed by the thin cot. "Are you alright?"

There's a light sheen of sweat on the child's forehead. The young boy huffs before lying on his back and turning his head to gaze at Marcus. "How'd it get poked out?"

Sia blinks. "What?" *Really? Back to the eye? Kid, you look like crap.*

"They said if you mess with the guns they poke out ya eyes. Did a gun do that?"

"No. Nooo. It'd be much worse if a gun did this." Sia rests a hand on the cloth covering her left eye. "I wouldn't be talking to you right now. That's for sure."

The boy nods his head a few times before grimacing and closing his eyes. He doesn't ask any more questions. Which is unusual…the children Sia is used to always need to be bribed to quiet down. This child barely started a conversation before shutting up.

Sia rises from the cot and slides over to the other cot. She kneels down beside the bed and touches the child's head. It's hot. "Hey, kid. Seriously, should you even be over here? Did you walk off from the medical area thing? Who's watching you?" The boy doesn't answer. "Hey!" Sia jostles the boy's shoulder a little. The boy whines and rolls off his back to curl up onto his side. "Tsk." Sia stands up and shuffles in place. She looks around the area again. "I'll get you some help."

She stands outside the merchant quarters next to a concrete column. "Excuse me…" She hesitantly lifts a hand to catch someone's attention. *Okay…okay…make eye contact with someone and they'll feel obligated not to ignore me.* Sia takes a step away from the column and lifts a hand to wave someone down. *Mean…mean…busy-looking…mean…there!* "Excuse me…Sorry, ma'am!" Sia makes eye contact with a dark woman advancing towards her.

The woman's pale blue eyes avert from the people in front of her to Sia's dark brown orbs. Her gaze brings a chill up Sia's spine. The contrast between her sky-blue eyes and dark brown skin shocks Sia speechless for a moment. Her hair is cut low, as if growing out from a close shave, and she's wearing a thin bulletproof vest over a pale orange dress. Her tattered sandals scuff across the ground as she leisurely walks among the crowd. Her long fingers loosely grip the handle of the large empty pot balanced on her hip. The woman frowns and breaks off from the crowd to stand beside Sia. "Yeah?"

"Um…uuh…There's…there's a sick kid over here." Sia gestures with both her hands back at the cots in the merchant quarters.

The woman eyes Sia from head to toe and hums for a moment. "Show me."

Sia nods dumbly. "Over here…I think he's got a fever." When they get to Sia's cot, the woman sets down her pot on the empty mattress and turns to the curled-up child. She presses her palm to the child's forehead.

"How long has he been like this?" The woman glares at Sia before kneeling beside the child. She pulls up his shirt and places a hand onto his stomach.

"He just laid down there…I don't…I asked where he came from! I don't know?" Sia sputters and stands over the woman and child.

The woman huffs and snaps her fingers a few times next to the child's ear. The boy is unresponsive. The woman slips an arm beneath the child's head and under his legs.

"Is it bad?" Sia lifts a hand to touch the child, hesitates, and lowers her hand back to her side.

"It's bad. He's burning up. Why did you let him sleep?!" The woman exits the merchant quarters and merges into the crowd. Sia stops at the column marking the edge of the merchant quarters and watches the woman march away with the child. She bites her lip.

FOLLOW HER

"Gaaaah…no!" She turns in a circle and faces the cots. *Don't we need to search for a way out of here to find Priya?*

FOLLOW HER

"Okay…okay!" Sia turns back around to chase after the woman.

51%

2034
W.AR.T.S., New Cinalia

"Sorry. Excuse me…ouch…Sorry!" Sia pushes against the flow of people until she can see the woman's orange dress. The woman stops walking to adjust her hold on the slender child and Sia succeeds in reaching her side.

"Where are you going with him?" Sia looks over her shoulder. The noisy crowd hasn't woken the unconscious boy.

"The doctor and his apprentices should be somewhere around here." The woman continues walking with the child snuggly pressed against her chest.

Sia matches her speed to walk alongside her. "*The* doctor? Is there only one?"

"He's the only one that stayed behind. The others are god knows where."

"You said they should be around…they have a medical wing, right?"

"Not really. All of our real spaces are out there—" The woman gestures to the ceiling with her head. "—in here's just temporary."

Sia's brow furrows in confusion. "The group I came in with had an injured guy and they had a whole setup for him." A man wielding a semi-automatic rifle nudges through the crowd in front with an entourage following behind him. The woman shoves past the group, but Sia is hesitant to elbow by the intimidating squad and is stuck waiting a few moments for the last of the five-person group to pass by. When she catches back up to the woman and child, she can see the area with the faded white sheets hung up. "See there?" Sia raises her arm and points at the white sheets.

"That's just a spot they cut off for an emergency. The doctor is probably where the sick are. Never expect him inside his actual quarters." The woman pauses and looks around the crowd. "Follow me."

They pass by the area cordoned off by white sheets and start walking toward where Sia remembers the car lot was. *Last night revealed one important detail. We can't sneak out of here with a car. The guards would never let us by.*

AFFIRMATIVE

What else have you figured out?

INSUFFICIENT MAPPING

THE SANDSTORM OBSTRUCTS CURRENT VISUALS FROM AERIAL VIEW

The woman takes her past the car lot and into a mass of tents where some people are gathered. They walk along the edge of the group. *But you have snapshots of the area, right?*

AFFIRMATIVE

So, what's the issue?

RESULTS OF INSUFFICIENT MAPPING EFFECT THE LIKELIHOOD OF ABSCONDING

WITHOUT REAL-TIME MAPPING TO MONITOR SUBJECT 001 THE EFFICIENCY OF PLAN DECREASES BY 42%

Sia's eyes scan over the people sitting down and chatting amongst themselves. They pass by a short table that holds a large pot of food that everyone is served from. *So, no more eagle eye vision? I think we can make it out of here without it, but I need to find a way to…ugh…I don't know.* Sia stops walking to sweep her

gaze over the area. *I didn't know how frustrating making mastermind plans were until I was stuck with you. Inspector Wrench-it always had a plan ready in a split second. Is this why bad guys go crazy? All the mental kung fu that goes on before a master plan? Maybe that's why they're dying to tell the hero everything they went through to pull everything off.*

...

STUDY OF THOROUGH PLANNING NEGATIVELY AFFECTING THE HUMAN MIND IS INCONCLUSIVE

Sia grins into a hand. *I'm joking.* She eyes her surroundings, dropping her hand back to her side. Everyone is happily chowing down on what seems to be tasteless oatmeal, and Sia can't find even one disgruntled face. They exit the tents and join a new stream of people.

It's another minute of walking before the woman turns to Sia with a deep frown. She adjusts her hold on the child and bites her inner cheek, sweeping her eyes around for a familiar face.

"What's wrong?" The woman's distressed eyes scare Sia.

"He's shivering…that's not a good sign. Come here. Take him." Sia steps closer and outstretches her arms. Slowly, the woman places the boy into her arms. When the child is firmly grasped by Sia's long arms, the woman fixes the position of the boy's head on Sia's shoulder. "Now, don't drop him." She pats the sick boy's shoulder. "Let's bring him to that area you pointed out before, and I'll keep searching for the doctor. I don't want to lug him all around this place. It's not safe. He needs to be cooled down."

"We need water for that, right?"

They both survey the tents and the people milling about. There isn't a drop of water in sight.

"I'll get the water and then we'll go back." The woman speeds up her pace, taking several long strides away from Sia. It feels like a clock is ticking. If the boy continues to overheat, will he make it?

"Ashanti! What are you doing with that fassy?" Sia hears a deep voice exclaim from behind them.

The woman that has been guiding her turns to the voice and her accent completely changes when replying to the man. "Nar! We need some wata to help the likkle boy! Where you see the fountain hose at?"

Sia watches the woman greet the stranger. She's surprised to see Ika walking beside the man approaching them, and realizes she's seen that man before. *Oh. He's from last night.* Sia's arms are wrapped around the shivering child, so she tilts up her chin in greeting.

Ika returns the gesture and furrows his brow. "Whose kid?"

"No idea, man. I…We think he's really sick. He's burning up, see." Sia stands closer to Ika to give him a better view of the unconscious child.

Ika moves several steps in the opposite direction. "I'll take your word for it."

Sia chuckles and adjusts her hold on the kid. Ika shoves his hands into his pockets. *First, Carla and now this kid. I guess this guy just…cares? What's his deal? What does he want?*

The woman and Nard are conversing about where to get water. After a few sentences are exchanged, the woman returns to Sia's side. "They'll help you get a bed for the kid and some water. Just sit tight until I return with the doctor." Sia nods and the woman, Ashanti, gives the boy one last concerned look and leaves, vanishing into the stream of people.

Nard tucks his arm to his side and jogs off in a different direction. "I'll get that wata. Meet you there in five."

Ika nods and takes off in another direction, leading Sia to their new destination.

"Where are we going to take him?" Sia adjusts her hold on the little boy and suppresses the urge to speak softly to his unconscious form. The child's shivering makes something inside her feel helpless and pained. She wishes she could openly comfort him, but Ika is the most observant man she's ever met. He'd notice something…he always notices.

"Back to where Turner was operated on."

"I don't remember seeing more than one bed back there." Sia stays a step behind Ika at all times.

Ika shrugs. "We moved Turner to his tent."

"Oh…How's he supposed to get the water to us? Wasn't he injured last night?" Sia remembers seeing a thick bandage wrapped around the man's forearm.

Ika shrugs. "He'll ask someone." He gestures to thick crowd they'd left behind. "We're not short on people."

Sia stifles a chuckle and nods. "Oh, okay. Yeah."

Ika leads them a different route than the woman had. They're walking along the other side of the car lot giving Sia a view of some wrecked vehicles that have been cannibalized for parts. There are men sitting in hollowed out cars, cooking food over a flaming metal barrel.

She and Ika are walking right up against the plain concrete walls and Sia can't help but feel a tinge of claustrophobia. *If the ceiling drops, there's only one way out.* Sia hugs the child closer and speeds up her pace. A shiver runs up her spine when she imagines large chunks of concrete cascading down to crush the people rushing from task to task.

Ants crushed within the walls of their own colony. No amount of screaming would result in a call to emergency services, but what else could these people do in those circumstances? Heavy-duty construction vehicles wouldn't come to their rescue. Hollering and tossing aside small rocks with their bare hands would be the best they'd have in that situation. Sia shakes her head and focuses on reality. *God forbid something like that ever happens.*

They enter the medical area from behind the bed. Ika strips the soiled, bloody sheets off the bed and tosses them onto the ground before Sia lowers the limp form of the child onto the stained mattress. The child is no longer shivering, but hasn't awoken. Ika idles near the bed. The chair that was beside the bed yesterday seems to have been moved somewhere else. Sia sits down beside the child's leg and pats his bare foot. *We're here, kid. We won't leave you.*

"Is this normal?" Sia gestures toward the boy.

"This?" Ika steps closer to examine the boy for a blemish of some kind.

"I mean…do people get sick a lot around here?"

Ika sighs and steps back away from the bed. "If you're worried, you're welcome to leave. No one's stopping you."

"But—" Sia makes the mistake of turning around and making eye contact with Ika. "Well…I…you know, dropping dead…uh…Maybe I *should*—" Trapped by his total focus, she can't decide what would make the most sense to say. She can't leave, she needs them. She bites her lower lip and tries to compose herself.

Ika glares back when she averts her gaze. "I don't know what this is, but it's something new. I haven't heard of anything spreading around the camp."

"So, this is patient zero?"

The child coughs a few times and rolls over onto his side. Sia flinches at the sudden sound and slinks down the mattress to sit at the edge of the cot. Ika steps even further away from the bed, the makeshift screen, pressing up against his back.

I don't have to worry about contracting…whatever this is, do I?

NEGATIVE

Thankfully, the child's interruption brings them to silence. Sia bounces her left leg. Ika steps out of her peripheral and holds an arm up to lift the white sheet out of his way. His shadow on the other side of the sheet moves off out of sight.

Any visuals on Priya?

NEGATIVE

You said I can hold my breath for ten minutes at a time, right?

AFFIRMATIVE

Maybe I can grab some night vision goggles and supplies then make a run for it. Most of the danger of a sandstorm is breathing, right?

STRONG WIND CURRENTS COULD RESULT IN DEBRIS HARMING SUBJECT 001

SPECIFICATIONS OF THE NIGHT VISION EQUIPMENT UTILIZED BY THE ARMED HUMANS ARE UNKNOWN

So, I need to let you examine the tech before you can know how useful it'll be for us? If this is their temporary space do they move inventory here as well? When we met their boss did you see anything down there?

AFFIRMATIVE

AMMUNITION

VESTS

LOCKED SUPPLY SHELVING ALONG A WALL 12 METERS WEST OF THE STAIRWELL DOOR

"Tsk…that'll give me some trouble." Sia rubs a hand down her face and sighs. *Truthfully, how likely do you think it is that Priya will be alive after 48 hours out there?*

WITHOUT MORE VARIABLES KNOWN ABOUT THE HUMAN SUBJECT DESIGNATED PRIYA THE PROBABILITY OF SURVIVAL IS SKEWED

Well, she'll be injured. Possibly bleeding out…in a sandstorm. Take a guess.

THE LIKELIHOOD OF SURVIVAL WHILE INJURED WITHOUT COVER IN A SANDSTORM IS 0%

But we saw her out there…she was moving. If she was able to hide, how good are her odds then?

47%

*That seems like good odds. I'm sure you're just pessimistic. She's survived all of this…*Sia drops her gaze to the child. *She best be alive…for our sake.*

SOLELY DEPENDING ON ONE PLAN OF ACTION THAT IS UNLIKELY TO BE ACHIEVED IS ILLOGICAL

You think I need a plan b?

AFFIRMATIVE

Well. Sia recalls that day on the river bank when Puter assumed command. *What do you think I should do?*

52%

2034
MedWing, W.A.R.T.S.

The sound of metal chair legs dragging across the concrete jerk Sia from her conversation. A couple seconds later, Ika backs into the medical area with a metal chair in hand. He sets down the chair and continues to hold up the white sheet for Nard. Nard comes in and stands aside. A lean man holding a pot by its metal handles enters, muscles flexing as he lugs the heavy pot onto the short table beside the cot.

"Now here we gooo!" The large pot is set down on the table beside the bed.

Nard slaps a thankful hand on the younger man's shoulder. It's a bit awkward, but with the injured arm tucked at his side he can't do much more. "Thanks, brotha"

"No problem." The young man clasps Nard's shoulder and glances over at the unconscious child. "Feel better, little man," he whispers before exiting the area.

Nard walks over to the pot, peels the damp rag from the rim, and tosses it at Sia. The rag drops into Sia's lap before she can snatch it from the air.

"Uuuh…Thanks. I'll just…" Sia shakes the rag out, dips it into the lukewarm water then squeezes it out. Droplets drip off

the tattered material onto the dirty cot. She wipes at the child's forehead and neck, then turns to wet the cloth again. She does this once more, then wipes under the boy's arms and legs. *It's going to be okay, little one.*

She continues to wipe the child down while the two men converse behind her. She lifts the child's shirt and the emaciated condition of his body is more apparent. Sia can count each rib with her eyes. She scrunches up her face against the tingling sensation that runs up her nose. *Poor baby.*

The wet cloth carefully glides across the boy's chest and stomach. With a hand behind the boy's head, she rubs the cloth down his back. The thin spine that pokes out his pale skin disquiets her. Finally, she douses the rag again and squeezes some of the water out before folding it and laying the cloth across the child's forehead. After making sure the boy's limbs are placed comfortably, Sia settles down on the edge of the cot to wait for the medical professionals to arrive.

"You're real at home in here." Nard laughs contemptuously. There's an edge to Nard's voice. Ika glances away from the child to Nard's stiff form beside his chair. "You don't seem half as much of a pussy as before."

Sia suppresses a nervous laugh and raises a hand to smooth down the hair along the nape of her neck. *This feels like high school all over again.*

"Hmm." Ika eyes Marcus's tense form. "Well, coward or not. He went back to clear Kid's body from the truck. I'm sure he's grateful."

Sia shifts in her seat to face the two men. "I…I am…I…I don't know what I would have done if those things had broken into my truck…I don't think I—"

Nard scoffs. "That's simple. You would have died."

Sia lowers her gaze to her knees and nods faintly. She licks her lips and appears to ponder deeply on the statement.

Ika squints at the bobbing head. *I'm not so sure about that. Not with those moves from last night. Why is he playing dumb?*

Sia stops nodding and straightens up in her seat to meet the steely gaze of the other man. Nard's dark gaze hasn't raised from Sia's form since she finished assisting the child. His sneer strengthens and Sia's scalp tingles at the intensity of it. Sia gulps and squeezes her sweaty hands into fists in her lap. *I can't let him push me around. I can't show fear.*

"You know what?" Nard steps over to Sia.

Sia focuses on Nard's forehead as he steps closer to her. "What?"

DOES SUBJECT 001 CONSIDER THE HUMAN TO BE A THREAT

No.

Nard slaps his hand down on Sia's shoulder. Sia flinches at the sudden action. "I never believed that saying until yesterday." Nard smirks at the flinch and squeezes down on the younger man's shoulder. "No good deed goes unpunished. It's right isn't it. You're a prime example of that."

EXORBITANT PRESSURE DETECTED ALONG THE CORACOCLAVICULAR LIGAMENT
REQUESTING TO ELIMINATE THE IRRITANT

No! We need these people!

Sia opens and closes her mouth to say something, but all that comes out is a weak: "Oh." The weight of her guilt bears down on her, her head lowers and she blinks multiple times. "I'm sorry…I…"

Ika doesn't need to see the younger man's face to know he's frightened of Nard. Ika shakes his head minutely at the Jamaican. Nard laughs again. "Don't apologize…I'm sure you'll find some more things to screw up." Nard squeezes Marcus's shoulder once more before walking over to stand beside Ika.

Ika gestures with his head for Nard to follow him out. They exit the makeshift infirmary together walking side by side. The pair cross the short distance from the medical area to the stairwell in silence. Ika opens the heavy door and motions for Nard to enter first.

"Are you gonna tell me I was too harsh on the guy?" Nard steps into the stairwell and leans back on the rough, plastered wall.

The wall is cold against his warm skin. Ika waits for the door to slide closed before speaking. "You're saying he was freaking out last night and didn't help fight the hornets?"

"Didn't ya hear me before? He's a pussy! He scrambled along the ground like a dumbass. He was going to chuck Kid's body at em! Even after Priya helped him, he let em pull her right out from in front of him. No muss, no fuss." Nard spits on the ground beside him.

Ika scowls. He runs a hand across the peach fuzz that's grown on his chin. "What was he looking for back at the truck…if it wasn't Kid's body. What reason did he have to…" Ika turns away from Nard to walk down the stairs.

Nard can't hear what Ika is muttering to himself. "What?"

Nard pushes off the wall with his foot and follows after his introspective leader. When Ika reaches the lower level, he marches through the door right into a wondrous sight for sore eyes.

"Kelly!" Nard exclaims at the back of a dirty blond head.

I bet this would really hurt…if I could actually feel it. What an ass. Sia rolls her shoulder and watches as the two men leave. It's not long before a middle-aged man with burgundy dreads rushes in. Sia remembers seeing him down below when she'd spoken with their leader.

"Is the doctor on his way?" Sia hops off the cot and out of the man's way.

The man leans over the child and touches the kid's head with the back of his hand. "Yeah, yeah. I don't know how this kid got over here. We have a whole mess being handled over by the resident tents. These back-to-back storms are killing us. Being cooped up so close together without fresh air." The man sets a tan hand onto his head and pantomimes tugging out a dread. "It's crazy, you know?"

Pheno comes in a moment later. Sia scratches the back of her head before waving at the man. "Nice to see you again, Doctor."

"Pheno."

"Excuse me?"

"My name is Pheno. Don't bother with the 'Doctor'."

Sia hums in understanding. "Okay."

"What happened with him?" Pheno doesn't walk over to the boy, but to the large pot.

"Umm…I woke up and found him lying on a cot across from me. He seemed really sick, and I noticed he had a fever. He's…" Sia frowns at the unconscious boy. "He's starving."

The man with dreads shakes his head while sitting down beside the child. "Everyone is. We can get at more of our rations when this storm ends." The doctor exits the medical area without even examining the child. Sia's eyes follow the doctor's retreating form, but trails back to the man speaking to her. "We've been trapped down here since the last storm. Didn't even get any time to move more inventory…"

"Well…that sucks," Sia sympathetically chimes in.

The nurse's lips tip into a sad smile. "Ha…yeah, sucks."

"Umm…so…Should I wait here or—" Sia inches toward the exit one step at a time while backing away from the medical assistant.

"This isn't your kid, right?"

"No!"

"Then you can go."

HEAD BACK TO THE CAR LOT

The meeting tables are still positioned in a large square, but the materials from the night before have all been cleared away. The head table at the far end of the square, farthest from the stairwell, is empty. Dennis is out of sight.

Kelly turns away from the table he's leaning on to give Nard a hug. He wraps an arm around the other man and gives two pats between his shoulder blades. When Nard steps back, Kelly

continues to loosely grasp Nard's shoulder. He gives him a once-over. "Damn, you look like crap, man." Kelly's eyes are drawn to the thick bandage on his arm. "What happened to you?" Kelly backs off and lifts himself to sit on the edge of the table.

Ika leans back on his heels and examines the scout. There are deep shadows under Kelly's eyes. His clothing is as tattered as usual, but his boots are heavily coated with mud and plant life. There's sand in his hair. The scouts' goggles are around his neck overlapping a black bandana.

"Did you guys get stuck in the storm? I'm surprised they let you in at all. We could have finally got rid of you." Ika settles down at a table adjacent to Kelly.

Kelly rolls his eyes. "My condolences. You can't be the last blond standing, yet." Kelly runs a hand through his wild locks and shakes his head. Flakes of sand fly everywhere. Ika leans back in his chair with a frown. Nard chuckles at the pair. A man wearing a black hoody walks over from a supply closet with a protein bar in hand.

"Uzu!" Nard goes over to slap a hand on the young man's back.

Uzu flinches under the powerful slap on his back. "Good to see you too, man." He takes another bite of his protein bar and sits down at a table across from Ika's.

The three other members of the scouting team exit the stairwell behind Nard. Things are looking up. Everyone seems a bit windswept, but overall, they're in good health. After a quick reunion, the other scouts sit beside Uzu at his table. Nard goes to sit beside Ika.

Elijah and Dennis appear from around a corner. Their forms are momentarily concealed by a concrete column before they converge with the chatting men. Dennis wheels over to the head table. "Okay…okay, let's get this over with. Kelly, what happened out there? The girl got one over on you, too?"

Kelly clears his throat. "Got one over? Well, that's…"

Uzu rolls his eyes and nudges Manu. Manu leans forward on his elbows. "Exactly what friggin happened! The dimwitted broad pretended to be sick and was foaming at the goddamn mouth."

Kelly's leans back in his chair while listening to Manu's description of things. He swipes a hand over his mouth to cover a grin then coughs. "She's definitely resourceful."

"She stole my ride. We had to walk for hours to gain cover." Uzu cuts in.

"Winston and Tony hung back at our rendezvous point near the Wastelands when we headed in toward the abandoned labs. The place wasn't as damaged as we first thought. I'd like to petition to go back for any supplies they might have left behind. Pheno might find some uses for some of the stuff there, but I'm not sure if they were a pharmaceutical company or not." Kelly reports to Dennis. "We parked out front and went straight in. The first thing we noticed was a few dozen roach corpses."

"They were huge asses! I'm talking—" The large man struggles for a way to properly describe them with words and settles for holding out his arms at each end of his torso. "About this wide and this tall. Damn ugly too."

Kelly ignores the interruption and continues. "She started her broadcast early. Which should have been a sign that she'd noticed us enter the building."

"Didn't she even say she knew we were out there?" Uzu chimes in.

Ika furrows his brow and watches Dennis in his peripheral. The leader is gently tugging on the lower lobe of his pierced ear while attentively focusing on Kelly and his crew.

Kelly sets his elbow to the table top and runs the fingers of that arm across his forehead. "We thought it was a coincidence, but she was playing us. She continued to talk until I stumbled upon her on the fourth floor. She was standing in front of a window ready to jump out. When I caught up to her, she was surprised and ran into the window sill before falling a couple feet onto an overhang. I thought we'd lost her there but colliding into the window seemed to have injured her. We

encountered her again when we were leaving. She fell unconscious and we loaded her up into the van."

"Which seemed to be her plan all along, so she could steal my van." Uzu knocks on the table. "Come to think of it the weather was getting worse at that point anyway."

"After we'd gotten away from the labs, she started acting strange. I thought it was the head injury, but the moment we stopped the car and got out to regroup…" Uzu runs his tongue over his front teeth as he tries to suppress a smile. Manu taps the fingertips of his right hand on the table and glowers at the table top. Winston and Tony smirk at each other. "She jumped up and stole the van right from under our noses." Kelly chuckles at the memory.

Dennis's brows furrow. "You don't seem too bothered."

"I'm impressed actually. She fooled us into thinking she was dying. I've never seen anything like it. She really seemed to be going through some sort of seizure or something. How'd she manage that? No idea." Kelly shrugs. "We were able to rendezvous with Winston and Tony after acquiring our packs and getting shelter."

"You got your van back?"

"Oh no, actually…I'm surprised to say, she drove off and threw our packs out a mile or so down the road."

Dennis frowns at the information. "So, she didn't want you dead?"

"Seemed to be an 'it's not personal' gesture in my opinion. Have you confirmed where she's from yet?"

Dennis shakes his head. "Washington City is still the only place she mentioned in anyone's presence…and any other place has either been confirmed to be uninhabited or is an untraveled territory."

"Let's say she was telling the truth. Wasn't Washington City one of the first places bombed? I can't imagine how they'd survive a direct hit."

Dennis makes eye contact with Elijah. Elijah nods. "From what we've gathered, they probably would have lived underground this entire time. She said they have generators, enough resources to feed their people, enough materials to cloth them, and clean conditions. But there's one thing we can confirm: She didn't have any branding marks."

"So, they're a free people?" Kelly asks.

"As far as we know, or her master is so influential they don't need to brand their women. She didn't appear to be that troubled with the separation either. In my opinion, she wasn't in much of a rush to meet back up with them. She barely spoke about them," Elijah continues. Ika nods along with his assessment.

"A lot of us are thinking this is a scout from Richards' Bay." Dennis runs his fingers through his tightly braided rows of hair. "But besides our suspicions, there isn't a lot to go on."

"Have there been any broadcasts?" Kelly asks.

"No." Dennis slowly shakes his head and lowers a hand off the table to grasp the left armrest of his wheelchair.

"But that's not very unusual for them. I find it unusual that they'd only send one woman out to the edge of the Wastes. What's their game plan?" Elijah ponders aloud.

Dennis sighs and moves on in the agenda. "I'm glad we've got you guys back. Unfortunately, we've got some bad news." Kelly leans forward on his elbows. His men adopt solemn looks. Dennis waits a moment before announcing. "Ralph's team is confirmed dead and we've lost a few people from Ika's crew as well."

Kelly dips his head forward. "I'm sorry to hear that."

Everyone takes a moment to let the news settle in. Uzu lowers his hood to reveal short brown hair. He bows his head and mutters a few words under his breath. Manu tips back in his chair and focuses on the ceiling with a grimace. Winston and Tony sit silently with mournful eyes.

"We've lost a lot of good people recently, and these storms have been beating our asses. Anita will be handling the mourning services after the current storm lets out." Dennis continues. Everyone nods in agreement. "Some good news,

depending on how you look at it, we've got a new addition to W.A.R.T.S."

Ika rolls his eyes at the name. Elijah chimes in here. "We've got another merchant source that is willing to trade for protection, but we still aren't sure if he has a point of refuel or if he's only stumbled across the supplies recently."

"Or, he could have killed and looted the real merchant," Winston comments.

Nard snorts. "Doesn't seem the type."

Dennis raises a brow and tilts his head. "From what I've seen he's quick on his feet."

"Cowards usually are," Nard fires back.

Ika places a hand on Nard's elbow. The Jamaican relaxes back in his seat and awkwardly crosses his arms over his chest.

"We've got an outbreak of some kind," Ika announces.

Elijah turns to Ika with surprise. "What do you mean? Has Pheno told you something?"

"The new guy came across a sick kid. The kid was definitely out of it. He looked like one of the orphans. Has Melissa come forward about anything?"

Dennis squints over at the other man and scowls. "An orphan? If something spreads while we're cooped up in this bunker…" He runs a hand over his face then settles the hand over his eyes.

"This will be a disaster," Elijah adds.

Dennis sighs once again while shaking his head. "So, we've got funeral rites to handle, a new guy that may be a big help or a new hindrance, and a possible contagion loose. Great."

"Maybe whatever that kid's got will take care of the new guy before we have to?" Nard mutters.

Elijah's eyebrows shoot up into his auburn hair. "Is it contagious?"

"Too soon to tell," Ika replies before standing from his seat.

"I'll need Pheno down here, ASAP. We'll need to reconvene this to talk about if we'll be continuing trade with the Savages of group R. Meeting adjourned." Dennis raps his fist on the table three times before unlocking the brakes of his wheelchair and gliding over to his younger brother.

Kelly tries to meet Ika's eyes, but Ika's gaze is glued to the table top as he grasps the top of his chair. The tall blond drags his fingertips across the table dividing the parallel tables and strolls over to Ika. His shadow comes up over Ika's shoulder. "You good?" Kelly gazes down at the other man with an eyebrow raised.

Ika scrutinizes the metal surface of the table for a moment before raising a shoulder momentarily. Kelly lifts a hand to sympathetically pat Ika's back. Ika pushes in his chair and rotates around to stand face to face with Kelly. Kelly's hand sinks back to his side.

"It's a damn shame, man, really. I figure it has to do with the Savages? Did Raco finally flip the script on you?"

Ika averts his gaze to stoically watch the other men exit the room. "Something like that."

Kelly opens his mouth, but thinks better of what he's about to say, and closes it once again. He shuffles in place.

"Let's go, man! I'm starving!" Tony calls to his scout leader while holding the door to the stairwell open.

"Go serve yourself! I'm not your mother!" Kelly calls over his shoulder.

"Tisha hides all the good stuff for you! Give her a smooch or two and get me some of those salted meat cans. Don't be a selfish bastard!" Tony yells back. The flesh at the back of Kelly's neck and along the sides of his face reddens. Kelly turns on his heel and glares at his comrade while pulling a face. He marches over to the exit and shoves Tony through it.

"What?! Everyone knows—" Tony's voice cuts off when the door slams shut behind the two men.

Dennis wheels over to the end of Ika's table. He locks his brakes. Ika stands silently beside his wooden chair. "How are you doing?" Dennis focuses on the deep circles under Ika's eyes.

Ika watches the last of the men exit the lower level. The door slams shut and he meets his older brother's gaze. "I'm fine."

"You don't look fine."

Ika snorts. "I'm just tired." His gray eyes mist over as he stares off into the distance. Dennis tilts his head and waits for more to come. "I'm tired of all of this. I…I wish I didn't have to wake up anymore and deal with it. Everything. If it's not one thing, it's another. It never stops." His voice fades into nothing.

"What happened to that excited muchacho that found this job exciting?"

"He grew up," the strain in Ika's voice increases.

"Tsk." Dennis runs his hand over his head. *¿Anita, dónde estás cuando te necesito?*[8]

Ika raises a hand toward his face, but thinks better of it and shoves his hands into his pockets.

"You aren't thinking of doing anything…um." Dennis grips the armrests of his chair before attempting to speak his next question. "You're not having any…dark thoughts, are you?"

Ika sighs and shuffles a few steps away from the table. "Of course not."

Dennis raises an eyebrow. "Of course not?"

Ika closes his eyes and debates talking further. Dennis won't understand the decisions he's had to make, the people he deals with day in and day out…the hours of unrest. Because of the accident, Dennis has been confined to their base. Safe. Ika and Anita handle all of the outside arrangements and deal with all the degenerates that come with a disaster of this size. And it'll never end. Unless he finally meets his inevitable end. Every form of help on this God's green earth has forsaken them. They are the damned.

The radio on Ika's hip, as well as the one hooked onto the side of Dennis's wheelchair, comes to life. A message blares from the small transceivers. "I don't know who else is seeing

---

[8] Anita, where are you when I need you?

this, but I need backup along the back end of the wreck yard. Louis is being held up by…Damn it! Louis is down!" The message cuts out for a few seconds before blaring back to life again. "I've never seen anything like this! This guy is fu—" The audio cuts out for a moment. "—ryone up! I don't see a weapon! He might have a knife! He's attacking so fast…I'm going for Louis! I repeat, back end of the wreck yard!"

53%

2034
Wreck Yard, W.A.R.T.S.

**SUBJECT 001 HAS STATED THAT THEFT IS
ABHORRENT YET SUBJECT 001'S CURRENT
ACTIVITIES ARE CONTRADICTORY TO THAT
VIEWPOINT**

"Priority number one…right?" Sia shoves a backpack into the trunk of an abandoned car from the back seat. Her legs are hanging out of the junker. The door has been removed from the rusty frame, while the remaining doors have grimy windows that are smeared with dirt. She checks the rear-view window and over her shoulder out the windshield, through the smudged glass she's cleaned with her jacket sleeve. The coast is clear.

It's complicated. Lying and stealing is bad, but this is life and death. It's normal to lie and steal if death is the likely consequence, okay? If it wasn't…I wouldn't be doing this. Sia shoves one last time and the backpack slips through the small opening between the collapsible seat and the trunk. She shifts around to grab the other backpack from off the ground and rams it into the trunk as well.

PROCESSING NEW REASONING
INDEXING…

Okay, so we should get back to the Merchant quarters now. Sia leans her forearm on the headrest of the backseat and gives the area outside the rearview mirror a cursory inspection. Her eyes sweep across the damaged cars at the edge of the car lot, and the torn-apart wrecks in her field of vision. Not that anyone would be following her. *I'm pretty inconspicuous.* Sia smirks and sits back on her heels, breathing a sigh of relief.

EQUIPMENT ACQUIRED
EXIT STRATEGY PENDING

Yeah…Priya will have to hang on until the morning. There are less crazy insects out and more—

A large calloused hand grips the back of Sia's collar and yanks her out of the car. "Ugggggh!" Sia chokes as she hurtles backward out of the car.

DANGER

Sia's arms wrap around her head to cushion her skull from making contact with the concrete. She lands heavily on her side. Sia cringes as the small bottles of morphine within her jacket break into pieces. Liquid seeps into the shirts beneath her jacket and down the top of her jeans. The assailant kicks Sia. She gasps. The glass that has shattered in her pocket is driven into her side. She presses her hands down to her side and curls up around the injury.

LEFT LATERAL ABDOMINAL INJURY DETECTED
SILICA HAS PENETRATED THE SUPERFICIAL FASCIA
ALONG THE EXTERNAL ABDOMINAL OBLIQUE
NANO INFIRMARY PROTOCOL INITIATED

The assailant doesn't continue their attack. "So, you really are a thief?"

Sia's eyes widen when she hears that familiar deep voice. *Oh no. Ponytail guy.* The pain recedes as nanotechnology repairs her body, but she feigns injury.

"What do we have here?" The guard kicks away Sia's legs and leans into the old junker to peer into the gap between the seats. He reaches in and tugs out a heavy backpack. "Jackpot. Did you think you were going to get away with it?"

Sia crawls backward out of range of the guard's boot, and scrambles up to stand. The guard roughly unzips the backpack and snorts. He drops it, causing the contents of the tattered backpack to spill out onto the ground. "Food, night vision goggles, bandages…you planning a trip or something?" The guard glares down at her.

Sia presses a hand to her wound and points a bloody finger at the sneering guard. "You can't just attack someone for no reason! What the hell is wrong with you?!"

"Sure I can! Especially when they steal equipment and food!" The guard dips forward and grabs Sia's index finger in his large hand. Sia grimaces as her finger is twisted and her arm is awkwardly held above her head. She raises her other hand to grab the man's bicep.

"You really thought no one would notice you steal all this gear?" The man takes a step backward and Sia is dragged forward. "How dumb are you? Only mercs are allowed to handle night vision gear. Limited supply." The angry guard kicks at the opened backpack. "And these snacks? No one gets these from inventory with the rationing going on. How did you score those?"

"Aaah…Aah…it was in a truck. I got it from some armored trucks! Please!" Marcus whines against the guard's tight grip. *Dammit. What do we do?! He's going to get us in trouble…if they take the supplies back, we'll never get to Priya in the morning. I'll probably be kicked out into the storm. She needs those bandages. Dammit! The morphine is gone. Damn it!*

"I know your type! You scout out groups for their women and children there are and plan an attack while they're vulnerable!" The guard pulls Sia in to shout in her face, to terrify the youth, but receives a glazed-over look.

S.I.D. REQUESTS TO ELIMINATE THE THREAT

No! That'll ruin their trust of us even more! We can't kill any of these people.

Sia's head rattles from left to right when the guard shakes her back to attention. "Oh, this getting too boring for you?" The guard pulls his sidearm from his holster.

S.I.D. REQUESTS TO SUBDUE THE THREAT

You promise not to kill him?

The guard clicks the safety off his weapon and holds it to Sia's head. "I'll give you till the count of five to tell me why you're really here. Five…" The touch of the cold metal to her temple tenses her up. She stops struggling against the guard's tight grip. Her mouth goes dry. Surprisingly, her knees remain still and continue to bear her weight.

THE HUMAN WILL NOT EXPIRE

"Four."

Okay. Help me. Help…this guy is a psycho.

"Three." Sia's body is taken over by the Synthetic Intelligence Developer and fakes a loud whimper while dragging the hand clutching the guard's bicep down the arm to caress the male's shoulder.

INCREASING STRENGTH IN LOWER
EXTREMITIES AND LEFT HAND FOR 50 SECONDS
BY 20%

"Tw—" Sia's fingers dig into the flesh of the shoulder. "Ack!" The guard's hand spasms. He cringes and brings his arm back toward his body. His releases Sia's finger and S.I.D wrenches the gun away to strike him across the face with the backend. The guard stumbles back and collides into the rusted car, but he doesn't collapse. "Oh!" The guard prods at the cut on his jaw.

OPPONENT OFFENSIVE RESPONSE
MISCALCULATED
INCREASE STRENGTH BY 30%

Sia whirls in a circle and absorbs the feeling of being in immersive mode once more. She runs her hand along an unblemished wall and sadly smiles at the solid feel of a smooth wooden door under her palm. The deafening silence of this space is comforting after being stuck underground with all the noisy W.A.R.T.S. dwellers.

"Plea...se, Apex...me! Help! I need...I need...you bad!" Sia remembers the last time she was here and shudders at the difference flashing red and green lights can have on an atmosphere. Sia lifts her chin and concentrates on what she wants. She focuses on the blinding white ceiling. Two triangular visual prisms pop into existence and lower to come within reach.

"Uuuh...Why are there two?" Sia hesitates to reach for the objects. They stop lowering and hover at eye level. The left device is emitting a flashing light every second, while the right device displays the underground garage and moving figures. Teeth bite into her lower lip for a moment. Then she reaches up to grasp the device with the peculiar flickering light. *Apex? Is this...a new edition?*

She leans against a wall a few steps from the other floating device and holds the prism up to her face. When she peers into the device, she notices a shape writhing in the darkness, but the lights give her a headache. She lowers the device and blinks her eyes a few times. After a moment, she lifts the device once again and tries to see what's occurring. The lack of sound definitely makes it more difficult to comprehend.

"This would be easier with sound." Sia lowers the device and lets it dangle at her side, against her outer thigh. Screaming erupts from the ceiling and almost terrifies Sia off her feet. The device slips from her curling fingers, pain resonates throughout her head. She covers her ears with her hands, but it's no help. It's worse than nails on a chalkboard, climbing up her spine, vexing her nerves until they're a shriveling mess. She wants to curl into a ball and escape it. "Down! Turn it down!"

There's no reaction to her command. *What is it doing?* "Turn it down!" The screaming stops momentarily then a rush of water blasts across the room. Sia drops to her knees. She's weak from the full body cringing session.

When she reaches for the device, the light is no longer flashing on the screen. The screen seems to be playing a recording from a surveillance camera positioned high up in a corner of the room. Fluorescent lights illuminate a black medical recliner with metal armrests. Across the reclined examination chair are multiple restraints that prevent the dark form from escaping. The tiles around the base of the chair are split and cracked. Light green sludge is smeared across the floor.

The creature is being sprayed with jets of water from two different angles. It trembles violently as it's being hosed down. When the water collides with its form the impact shifts it to the side. A dark green substance drips from the seat. "Why are they doing this?"

A medical cabinet and an examination table are in the background, but Sia can't see any other items or people standing in the camera's field of view. She presses her fingers to the screen and mimics the movements she would make on her smartphone to zoom into an image. The image adjusts and a long appendage can be seen wriggling in the light green sludge. "Oh man." Sia shudders and taps the screen twice, nothing happens.

"Zoom out," Sia orders, but the device doesn't comply. The dark form glistens under the bright lights except for the deep holes in its flesh that are seeping green fluid. Along the creature's side, scaly skin has been peeled away to reveal white muscle and bone. Its back arches off the leather and a deep, terrified wail erupts from the tortured being.

She circles her finger around the screen and taps a few times before shaking the object. Amid her frustrated attempts was the correct gesture, the device zooms out. She slides her fingers over the top of the reclined medical chair and uses her fingers to zoom in like before. The image adjusts.

EEEEEEERR

Sia closes her eyes and grinds her teeth as a loud siren noise erupts from the ceiling, but it ceases after a moment. Sia blinks away tears. She returns her gaze to the visual prisms screen. The first thing she notices is that the water is no longer spraying, but the next moment she gasps. Glaring up into the camera are dark brown eyes.

54%

2034
Wreck Yard, W.A.R.T.S.

"Oh…" The guard leans on the junker and rotates his injured shoulder. "So, you're finally done pretending?"

The gun doesn't waver from the guard's head. "Stand down."

The guard clenches his jaw and rubs his hand along the injured skin. "Go ahead, shoot me."

BLUFF IDENTIFIED
GUNFIRE WILL CALL FORTH MORE
DISTURBANCES

"Get down on your knees and put your hands behind your head."

The guard drops to his knees. He sneers at the blank face staring down at him. S.I.D walks around the man with the gun aimed at his chest, but the moment the gun is within reach the guard springs forward. S.I.D's body stiffens, the barrel of the gun is grabbed. S.I.D releases the gun, raises its knee, and rams it into the guard's temple. The guard's large body collapses to the cold cement floor. S.I.D kneels beside the body and checks his pulse.

ASSAILANT SUBDUED
THE HUMAN REMAINS ALIVE

It retrieves the gun from the ground.

THIS MODEL APPEARS TO BE A GLOCK 35 GEN4 .40 CALIBER

After a short pause, to acquire information on the disassembling techniques for the weapon, S.I.D's hands move with precision. It drops the disassembled weapon and steps over the body to grab the items that spilt all over the ground. It crouches and uses a hand to sweep the equipment back into the ragged pack. It slides its arms through the straps and bends down into the junker to retrieve the other backpack.

THE DESCENT PLAN B INITIATED

"What the hell?!" Another guard rushes over with his weapon drawn.

The other backpack is placed over its shoulder to keep its hands free.

"Hey, what the fu—"

"The male has succumb…" S.I.D grasps the shard of glass left in Sia's pocket.

"Suck? What?" The guard's gun lowers momentarily as he checks on his friend. "What did you do to him?!"

S.I.D jumps over the body and rushes forward. The newcomer stumbles backward at the abrupt movement and fires. The shot echoes throughout the garage. Screams of fright erupt from nearby, and the element of secrecy is lost. The bullet pierces S.I.D's bicep, but the wound doesn't stop S.I.D's approach. It grasps the hot barrel and forces the gun down toward the guard's feet.

The guard fires again, but this time the bullet pierces his own foot. S.I.D stabs the shard of glass into his forearm. When he keels forward in pain, S.I.D wrenches the gun from his hands and put him unconscious.

Footsteps rush its way from the car lot. S.I.D drops the extra backpack, turns on its heel, and bolts for the entrance of the underground garage. It sprints along the edge of the concrete wall toward a sea of tents when it hears a motorcycle driving up. Up ahead, two men are heating their meal over a lit

barrel, and a plan develops. It slows and shoves the two men away from the barrel.

The men back up with their arms raised to defend themselves. "Back off!"

"Who the hell are you?!"

Their slurred speech notifies the device that they're not a threat. S.I.D turns its back on them. The motorcyclist's black helmet comes within sight when it rounds a wrecked car, and heads right for S.I.D with a spiked bat in hand. It stands there, motionless, while the drunks berate it from behind.

The motorcyclist swings the bat over their head. The drunks back away, seeing the approaching motorcycle, but S.I.D aligns itself with the barrel and kicks it. The barrel flies through the air, coals and broken pieces of burnt wood flying from its center. It collides with the front wheel of the motorbike, and the driver goes flying across the cement floor, face first. Their half helmet doesn't help lessen such a rough frontal collision. The body remains still.

S.I.D doesn't check their vitals. It picks up the bat and enters the tent area with it dangling from his already healed arm. The crowd has thinned. S.I.D crouches and hides behind each tent.

Finally, it makes it to the tunnel that leads to the exit above ground and sprints to cover the rest of the distance quickly. It hides behind a cement pillar and waits.

"Eyes open, everyone! He knows what Dennis looks like and might be heading for the lower levels! Civilians back to your tents. Stay low to the ground!" Nard is shouting through the sparse crowd of men and women that are warily watching their surroundings. He stops at the base of the tunnel and scans each pillar. *We've got four men watching the main exit. Six guards watching the lower level…and Kelly's men walking this entire place. He's not going anywhere.*

Ika marches toward Nard with his rifle in hand. "What's going on?"

"I don't know. There was a gunshot. I heard the same broadcast as you, but by the time we got over there the men were dropped. Found a drunk that said someone in a puffy brown jacket attacked Joseph. Pheno's already been called over there." Nard turns his back on the tunnel as he addresses Ika.

"Marcus?"

"That's what I'm thinking, too. I didn't think he had it in him." Nard pulls his knife from its leather sheath on his hip.

"Why would he blow his cover now, and not when he was face to face with Dennis?"

S.I.D jogs up the tunnel within the shadows. When it can hear the winds of the sandstorm raging outside, it pauses, crouching behind a column, and takes a moment to assess the newest obstacle.

The four men from the night before are on guard duty. Instead of facing away from the tunnel and viewing the electric fence, the men are aiming their weapons toward the center of the tunnel. They haven't caught sight of S.I.D's crouching form.

INITIATING PREEMPTIVE CONDITIONING NANO INFIRMARY SHIELDING ACTIVATED ENHANCING LOWER EXTREMITIES AND LEFT ARM BY 50%

S.I.D rises and speeds up the rest of the tunnel into the open.

"Stop! Or we'll shoot!" The guard on the far left calls out a warning.

S.I.D throws the bat at the guard in the middle of the lineup. The guard jerks to the side to move out of the bat's path of destruction, and bumps into the man beside him, disrupting the defensive line. The device rushes for the gap that opens up.

The guard on the far left hesitates to shoot, but the man beside him doesn't. A spray of bullets fires at S.I.D's legs. It leaps at the off-balance guards with arms outstretched, and they all fall to the floor in a mess of bodies. The guard stops firing. "Raise him up! I think I shot him! I got him!"

S.I.D steals the knife on the hip of the guard beside it. The guard behind S.I.D wraps an arm around its neck. S.I.D thrusts

the knife into the guard beneath it twice before it slashes across the arm wrapped around its throat.

"Aaah!"

S.I.D grasps the bleeding arm and presses its fingers into the wound while bending the arm back. It uses the injured man as a shield.

"Drop your weapons." S.I.D holds the knife to the guard's jugular. The whimpering man cringes as the sharp edge presses against his Adam's apple. The other two guards lower their weapons to the floor as their third man groans against the ground, clutching his abdomen. "Throw them over there." S.I.D motions to a dark corner off near the electric fence. The guards hesitate until S.I.D presses the blade into the hostage's neck. The cut bleeds even after the blade is lifted.

"Aah! Pleaa—" the hostage pleads as the guards throw their weapons into the corner.

"Retreat down the tunnel. Disobey and the response will result in death." The monotone voice frightens the guards. This isn't the man they met last night; it can't be. They grab an arm of their injured comrade and hurry down the tunnel. S.I.D retreats backward until it can gain cover behind the toll booth near the exit. S.I.D and the injured guard disappear behind the wide booth.

"Wait…please, let me—" S.I.D rams the guard's forehead into the edge of the booth and releases its grip as the body crumples to the floor. Behind them is, just what it was looking for, the generators that are hooked up to the electric fence. Strong gusts of wind rattle the rolling gate. With its eyes, S.I.D traces each wire that is twisted around the gaps in the gate. It stands over the two generators and examines the parts to identify what models they are.

RETRIEVING INSTRUCTIONS ON SHUTTING OFF PORTABLE GENERATORS

S.I.D's hands reach for the side of the nearest generator to carefully—

Bang!

A bullet pierces its spine.

Bang! Bang!

Two bullets pierce the back of its knees. S.I.D keels forward onto the generators and is shocked. Its body is thrown back by the surge of electricity, and the sleeve of Sia's jacket smokes as it convulses on the ground. The awkward load of the backpack cushions its fall and forces it to lay on its side.

SYNTHETIC INTELLIGENCE DEVELOPER HAS BEEN SHUT DOWN TO PREVENT DAMAGE DURING THE SURGE EVENT

ERROR

COLLECTING ERROR INFORMATION REBOOTING SYSTEM IN 60 SECONDS

ERROR

A PROBLEM HAS BEEN DETECTED RESOLVING ISSUE REBOOTING SYSTEM IN

...

3600 SECONDS
3599 SECONDS
3598 SECONDS

"Bastard."

"I think we finally got him."

Incomplete

2035
New York, New York

A middle-aged woman wearing a black suit jacket with a tan wool trench coat hung over one arm strolls into a quiet coffee shop. Her thick heels clack on the wooden floors as she approaches the counter. She digs into her coat pocket to retrieve her wallet.

There are no lines. She always exits her job fifteen minutes before the usual lunch crowd arrives. When she straightens up to order, spiked wallet clutched in her manicured grasp, the barista smiles at her.

"Hey, Ms. Jackson. Same as usual?" The young man sports a handlebar mustache and is wearing a black employee uniform with the name tag pinned to the front.

"No, actually I'm thinking of just a large hot chocolate with a lot…a lot of whipped cream." Ms. Jackson lifts her hands to demonstrate how high she wants her mountain of cream to be.

"Sure thing. It'll be ready in a jiffy." The young man spins on his heel and grabs a large cup out of the dispenser. The woman adjusts her coat in her arms while she waits. "Got good news today?" the young man, Adam, shouts over his shoulder as he makes her beverage.

"Just successfully finished a big presentation and wanted to celebrate." She blows a braid out of her face and searches the cafe for available seats. There are a few students on computers occupying the round wooden tables near the counter, but farther back in the room is an empty corner.

"Here you go!" Adam hands the hot chocolate over with a napkin.

The woman turns back to the counter and grasps the delicious smelling drink. The generous helping of whipped cream quivers as she struggles to hold it while digging out her debit card. She settles the drink down and pulls out her card to pay. Adam swipes the card and hands it over. "Thanks, Adam."

"My pleasure, Ms. Jackson. It's nice to see you in a good mood." He tugs out her receipt from the register and drops it into the trash can beneath the counter.

She smiles at her wallet as she zips it up and puts it back in her coat pocket. She folds the coat back over her arm and grabs her drink by the protective cover to sit at the vacant table in the corner. She sets her coat across the lap of her black suit pants and digs in.

Her head dips down into the whipped cream and she moans in appreciation at the sugary flavor. She takes a sip of the hot chocolate. The heat scolds her tongue a bit, but then the refreshing taste flows down her throat. It forces an even wider smile upon her face. Self-consciously, she dabs at her brown skin to remove the whipped cream mustache from her upper lip. While she sets the napkin on the table, her eyes wander to the other customers.

One table sticks out the most. Near the shaded windows along the side of the cafe, a father is sitting at a table with a baby blue stroller. He's breaking apart a muffin and slipping small pieces to the child. He's a lean man with high cheekbones and is wearing relaxed exercise wear. His sleepy eyes are bright and joyful as he makes faces at his small child.

What a lovely man, she thinks while raising the hot chocolate once again to her full lips. The moment vaguely reminds her

of her own father, but she ignores the sadness that clings to that thought and pushes her seat back. *I should get back before everyone is rushing out the main doors for lunch. I can start on my emails...* She puts on her coat and marches out of the cafe without looking back.

When she enters her job's glass facade, she waves at the guard before he buzzes her in. She strides through the security barrier and metal detector.

"That was quick," the guard comments.

She dumps her empty container into a trash can beside the reception desk. Her heels clack against the polished, black speckled granite flooring as she makes her way to the elevators. "Time is money!" she yells over her shoulder before pressing the elevator button with her pale blue nail.

When she exits the elevator, a group of people hop on to start their lunch break. The carpet floor under her heels silences her shoes. Her corner office is straight ahead, past several rows of cubicles, but she changes course when she's halfway there. She sticks her hand in her pocket to fiddle with her wallet's round metal spikes and observes the cubicles around her.

What is that? Besides the usual drone of the A/C unit and keyboard typing, she can pick out the sound of whimpering. She strolls down the aisle nearest to her and peeks over the partition walls to search for the source of the noise. She's halfway across the room when the soft sound of a woman weeping in a cubicle at the opposite end of the room can be clearly overheard. She squeezes her wallet, slips her hand out of her coat, then strides over to the distraught woman.

She recognizes the employee, an older woman with short, brown hair. Her signature polka dotted headband, which is usually worn overtop her curled brown locks, is missing.

Cheryl again? She suppresses the urge to roll her eyes. "Cheryl, is everything alright?" She stands beside the cubicle with a frown. *Stressing over stuff that isn't work related is a misuse of company time.*

Cheryl's cubicle is cluttered. She has stacks of papers scattered across one side of her work area and multicolor sticky notes decorating the walls along with a tattered animal calendar.

"What happened?" Ms. Jackson waits for Cheryl's reply, but the crying woman hiccups and continues weeping with a tissue pressed up against her nose.

Another coworker pops their head up. "She was reading an article about the latest findings in New Cinalia by the Purple Diamond Humanitarian group."

Ms. Jackson's frown deepens and she swallows the comment she was going to make.

Cheryl sniffles. "They've stopped searching the islands that were evacuated when River City was bombed, but they've resumed contact with the mainland…and…and…" Ms. Jackson walks around to the other side of the partition to set a comforting hand on Cheryl's back. She rubs little circles on the blue, cotton sweater. Cheryl tosses a soiled tissue into her small trash bin and pulls another out of the box beside her keyboard. She takes a few calmly breathes and blows her nose.

Ms. Jackson cringes and steps back around the other side of the cubicle. The other coworker continues watching from their cubicle.

Cheryl takes a few more breaths before continuing her explanation. "These relief workers have finally gotten access after a lot of the groups have stopped looking. It's been years and—" Her voice cracks. She takes another breath and starts again. "They've found a missing person. A man named Chen Sia was found at one of the campsites they brought supplies to. God bless his family. They will be so…I was just thinking of the relatives we still haven't…we have no idea."

"Has his family come forward? They know?" Ms. Jackson's eyes widen and she rushes around the cubicle wall to view Cheryl's computer screen. "Are there photos?" She uses Cheryl's mouse to scroll up the page. The screen displays a photograph of a group of people standing next to a crate

smiling widely. Their hazmat suits look dirty around the knees and one volunteer isn't wearing his. His shirt has some stains on it that resemble blood.

"No, no. The author said they're trying to make contact with the family now. It's so exciting. Oh, I want to see a reunion," Cheryl hiccups, and tears begin streaming down her face once more. "It'll be so heartwarming. Even now...while these..." She angrily groans. "They told us we weren't turning our backs on Cinalia because no one is left, but this is proof. They made contact with around 50 people so far. There might be hundreds! Thousands out there needing help!"

"Life always finds a way." Ms. Jackson pats the woman's shoulder and gives her a little squeeze." I understand what you're going through. If—"

Cheryl shakes the hand off her shoulder and turns in her chair. "No, it's okay. You don't have to pretend...I just...it's been almost seventeen years and we still can't return home. The place I was born and raised is still a part of the radiated zone."

Ms. Jackson straightens up and looks down at the sobbing woman with pity. "I think you should clock out early today, Cheryl. You can email me your finished assignments and I'll forward them to your supervisor."

"No, no I can—"

"Take your time, Cheryl. I know how hard this can be. Truly."

Ms. Jackson walks away from the cubicles as composed as always. Cheryl calms down. When her coworkers return from their lunch and see her ruined makeup, a couple pause at her cubicle.

"Got railed for a late assignment?" a middle-aged woman with glasses guesses.

"No. I'm...I'm not having a great time right now. Actually, I'm on my way out." Cheryl puts some paperwork into a folder and slips it into her pink purse. Her coworkers leave to continue working, but the woman wearing glasses remains leaning on the cubicle wall.

"Ms. Jackson know about this?"

"She's the one who granted it to me."

"Oh, hope you feel better soon, Cheryl." The woman taps the cubicle wall and strolls away.

Cheryl waves, adjusts the strap on her shoulder, and heads toward the elevator. After pressing the button to call the elevator, she turns toward her manager's office and raises her hand to wave farewell. Unfortunately, the privacy shutters are down. She lowers her hand and departs.

Within Ms. Jackson's office, the phone is in use. "Have you gotten any calls today?" Ms. Jackson is leaning forward in her large leather chair with a finger rubbing circles on her temple. The landline telephone is held to her ear. "No. I'm okay, Ma, it's just…" She bites her lip before sighing and blurting out her next statement. "I think maybe they've found Sia. They said it's a man but they've been wrong before, right? I remember…I remember she was tall. It could be a misunderstanding. I think we should call these people." There's a pause before she shakes her head. "No, I don't know who, Ma, but…"

Her mother interrupts her. She blows air out her nose and swivels around in her chair to blankly stare out the window at the reinforced glass. She sighs when a cloud drifts by and makes it hard to view the world outside. Instead, her own face is reflected. The unhappiness in her dark eyes is matched by her clenched jaw and slouched shoulders. Finally, her mom allows her to reply. "I'm at work, but when I get off, I want to call. Could you try to find out more information on this? Please?"

Her mother's reply is curt.

"Ma. This won't be like last time. I feel it."

Her mother doesn't agree, but she won't let this go.

"And they stopped looking! It was never confirmed what areas were destroyed! We don't know anything! I've heard that they didn't even let any of the workers go beyond the coasts.

They only flew around before calling off most of the rescue teams!"

Her mother finally responds, but not to the part she wants her to respond to.

"It's not a conspiracy, Ma. I...alright. I have to finish this and then I'm coming by your place." Ms. Jackson hangs up and sits back in her chair. She wipes her eyes with her sleeve and picks up a photo from her desk. It's a picture of her older sister and her at five years old. Sia's face is frozen in laughter while Aaliyah's face has a bit of fear on it.

They were in the front yard of their grandmother's house, standing on a stone walkway. Sia had placed Aaliyah upon her wide shoulders and interlocked their fingers. Sia's usual straight locks were sticking up in random directions. Aaliyah's own hair texture was similar to their mother's and was in two "afro puffs". She remembers gripping the sides of Sia's head as she spun them in a circle. Round and round and round.

At first, she was delighted, but Sia lost her balance when she stepped off the stone walkway into the grass. Sia threw out an arm to steady herself and released the hold she had on Aaliyah's slim ankle dangling across her chest. Aaliyah slid backward off her shoulders. That's when their father had snapped the photo.

She'd been afraid she was going to hit the ground, but being caught and swung around into a hug released a giggle from her instead of a scream. "Whoops, sorry. I got you." Sia shuffled from side to side to regain her balance and nuzzled the side of her younger sister's head. Aaliyah giggled and fought to get free.

"Aaliyah! Sia! We're going to eat out with Grandma! Head to the car!" their mother shouted from the screen door.

Her heart clenches as she relives the memory frozen in the photograph. Her lower lip quivers and she takes a deep breath to compose herself. She swallows and swipes a hand down her face. She misses her sister more than ever now.

D.Rednal

Cleaning Up The Future Setup

Download Incomplete. Try again?

Yes   No

About the Author

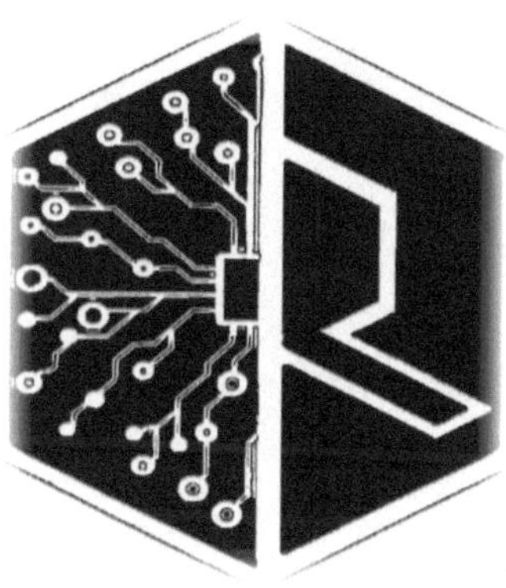

D. Rednal is a South Jersey based author. Rednal has been employed in many different fields such as a factory worker, bookkeeper, retail worker, childcare professional, and even a house sitter, but none of those jobs have tested Rednal's patience like writing a book.

To learn more information and download your free map of New Cinalia, visit:
www.drednal.com

Be sure to review as soon as possible. Thank you. Cleaning Up The Future Book 2: Exiles coming soon!

www.ingramcontent.com/pod-product-compliance
Lightning Source LLC
Chambersburg PA
CBHW031044110726
47900CB00003B/809